"Kramer's unique take on the TV series *The Brady Bunch* is a delight: funny, sweet, sexy, smart, and more charming than the show. With Kramer's enchanting sense of humor, the blonde, lovely Brady girls and their irascible brothers, loving parents, and housekeeper Alice are off on a romp that rivals Shakespeare for a comedy of errors. Readers will be up all night before drifting off to dream of a love story like this." —*RT Book Reviews*

"Kramer scores with the inaugural House of Brady imbroglio . . . Though [she] includes her characteristic lighthearted touches, she's smart and confident enough to take her characters and their situations seriously, turning what could have been a one-line joke into a deep and appealing story." —*Publishers Weekly*

"The Impossible Bachelors feature[s] delightfully witty and vibrant prose to match the books' unforgettable titles . . . Kramer's clever and engaging style is now employed in the service of finding the perfect mate for each of the six Brady siblings. Libraries should buy a bunch."
—*Library Journal*

"An emotional story that will leave readers loving Lady Marcia." —*Romance Reviews Today*

"[An] entertaining homage to [the] television series."
—*Night Owl Reviews*

"Fans of the TV sitcom *The Brady Bunch* will be amazed at how cleverly and unexpectedly Kramer improvises on the show in her latest incandescently witty, completely captivating Regency historical." —*Booklist*

The Earl is Mine

KIERAN KRAMER

St. Martin's Paperbacks

This is a work of fiction. All of the characters, organizations, and events portrayed in this novel are either products of the author's imagination or are used fictitiously.

THE EARL IS MINE

Copyright © 2013 by Kieran Kramer.
Excerpt from *Say Yes to the Duke* copyright © 2013 by Kieran Kramer.

For information address St. Martin's Press, 175 Fifth Avenue, New York, NY 10010.

ISBN: 978-1-250-00989-0

Printed in the United States of America

St. Martin's Paperbacks edition / March 2013

St. Martin's Paperbacks are published by St. Martin's Press, 175 Fifth Avenue, New York, NY 10010.

10 9 8 7 6 5 4 3 2 1

For Kristin Reynolds Wray Wilda,
an extraordinary woman and beloved sister

Acknowledgments

As always, I'd like to acknowledge the remarkable team at St. Martin's Press for bestowing such love and attention on my House of Brady series, especially Jennifer Enderlin, my dream editor. And big hugs to Jenny Bent, my agent, whose steadfast support and great humor lift me always.

I'd also like to thank Kati Rodriguez, my incredibly kind, able assistant who loves romance novels and has her own blog with Jamie Murawski at http://romancingrakes4the luvofromance.blogspot.com. And I have to celebrate the fabulous group of readers who make up the Regency Rockstars, a street team I share with Vicky Dreiling. All of you are remarkably generous women with huge hearts! Many thanks to Vicky, too, for her friendship, which has meant the world to me.

Finally, I'd like to thank Chuck, Steven, Margaret, and Jack for being the family that has given me my own happily-ever-after.

The Main Players in the House of Brady

Michael Sherwood, Lord Brady	The Marquess of Brady; "Daddy" to his three step-daughters; "Father" to his three sons
Caroline Sherwood, Lady Brady	Michael's second wife and the Marchioness of Brady; "Mama" to her three daughters and three stepsons
Gregory Sherwood, Lord Westdale	Heir to the Marquess of Brady; Caroline's stepson
Lady Marcia Sherwood, now Lady Chadwick	Eldest daughter of Caroline; Michael's stepdaughter; married to Duncan Lattimore, Lord Chadwick; stepmother to Joe Lattimore
Lord Peter Sherwood	Second in line to the marquessate; Caroline's stepson

Lady Janice Sherwood	Second daughter of Caroline; Michael's stepdaughter
Lord Robert Sherwood	Third in line to the marquessate; Caroline's stepson
Lady Cynthia Sherwood	Third daughter of Caroline Sherwood; Michael's stepdaughter
Alice O'Grady	Family housekeeper at Ballybrook in Ireland

Prologue

The figure who slid into the Earl of Westdale's coat every morning wasn't happy. His name was Gregory Sherwood, and he had everything a man could want. But like a prisoner who can't bask in a beautiful day outside his barred window, Gregory couldn't enjoy his family, his wealth, or his title.

He was the legitimate heir to the Marquess of Brady.

But he wasn't his son.

And he was doomed to a lifetime of lies.

"You know Mother meant for us to save those pieces for the women we're to marry," his brother Peter said in the light Irish accent all three Sherwood boys shared. He peered over Gregory's shoulder as he sorted through a small chest on his dresser and pulled out a silk box. In it was a ruby ring their late mother, Nora, had left him in her will. "Are you going to propose?"

Gregory stopped his search and glared at his younger brother. "What do you think?"

"Really?" Peter gave a short laugh. "You're jesting, aren't you? Marriage is a long time."

A *very* long time.

But then Gregory remembered sweet, shy Eliza last

night, how he'd known exactly what he was doing when he laid her down on a sofa in an out-of-the-way sitting room at a Mayfair mansion during the height of a masquerade ball and slipped up her gown. Her parents had been throwing her at him for years, so it wasn't as if the seduction would take her by surprise. She'd given a virginal cry when he'd first entered her, and there was the moment right before she'd peaked, her slender legs wrapped around his back, her hips arching upward while she sighed softly against his neck.

He'd felt more than his usual pleasure when he released his seed into her. There would be no turning back. Eliza was a lady. The knowledge that he'd do right by her had focused him, had cast away the shadows for just a moment. She'd be the beginning of a life he created on his own, not one that had been thrust upon him—as blessed as it had been, as grateful as he was for what he clearly didn't deserve.

"But why tie yourself down now?" Peter asked him. "You're much too young."

"Mind your own business." Gregory strode past his brother and brushed shoulders with him, just hard enough to drive the message home. He tucked the small box in an inner pocket of his jacket, adjusted his cravat, and left the bedchamber, a cavernous oblong space almost like a hunting-box bunk room. Father had designed it when the boys were small, and Gregory still shared it with his two brothers when he was home.

"I'm coming with you," said Peter, and followed him out the front door.

"Go away," Gregory told him.

"No. I'm not going to let you do this without a fight.

This is serious, Gregory. You can't give away Mother's ring so easily."

On the pavement, Gregory whirled around. "So easily? Do you think that little of me? Or the woman to whom I'll present this symbol of my devotion?"

"Devotion? Is that the same thing as love?"

"Go away, Peter. You know nothing of love." Not that Gregory truly knew anything of the romantic kind, either. He couldn't begin to guess whether his mother and the marquess, the only father he'd ever known, had been in love. And if they had, did it count—when one of them was keeping a secret from the other?

But Father and Caroline, his second wife, whom Gregory called Mama the way his three stepsisters did, were most certainly in love, even after a decade of being together. And while he was glad of it, they were awfully in each other's pockets.

The thought of such intimacy at the soul level made Gregory's cravat feel tight. He'd be faithful to Eliza, and they'd no doubt meet regularly between the sheets—she had a sweet, welcoming nature and wouldn't deny him his conjugal rights, he was sure—but as for staring into each other's eyes and sharing dreams, hopes, and all that balderdash . . .

Well, no. A monolithic no, actually.

It was his duty to take a wife to secure the Brady line. But a part of him would never, ever belong to the House of Brady. That part that would remain undutiful. Would seek illicit pleasure. Would work desperately hard to forget his impossible position—that he belonged nowhere.

That part would take a mistress and leave his gentle, dutiful wife at home.

His brother huffed. "You're not ready."

"I *am* ready," Gregory uttered low. "I don't take this step lightly. I've put a great deal of thought into the matter."

And he had, for a man whose attention was drawn more to other things: his interest in design; his sporting life; politics and gaming; and his more mundane duties as heir, which Father and Mama were anxious for him to take up. And then there was his constant need to play a role—to hide the ugliness that was his secret. Some nights, he went to bed exhausted from its weight.

Peter's pupils were wide and black, his mouth thin. "You haven't considered this enough. Not nearly."

"Wait a minute." Gregory moved closer, his chest up to his brother's. "Are you implying that Eliza isn't worthy of my regard?"

Peter didn't back away. "I'm not implying anything. I'm coming right out and saying you're too besotted to see straight."

"I will *never* be besotted, Peter, by any woman."

"Then explain why you looked so feverish searching for that ring? I could have shot a pistol next to your ear, and you wouldn't have turned to look. If that's not besotted—"

"You don't trust me," Gregory said, feeling the irony of his words.

"Not about this, no." Peter's tone was firm. "You don't value that ring the way you should, and I'm glad Mother's not here to see what you're doing with it."

"I've had it with you and your insults." Gregory pushed him hard on the shoulder. Peter flinched but didn't lose his footing. "Come on, little brother." *Little* half *brother.* "Show me what you've got besides words."

"Forget it." Peter stared at him, his eyes flat and hard.

"Go ahead with your stupidity. See if I care. You'll regret it later."

He spun on his heels and stalked off.

Gregory stared after him, annoyed that he'd succumbed to his childish temper. Here he was, feeling man enough to marry Eliza. And yet Peter had managed to put a damper on the day.

If someone could so easily do that, how strong was his commitment, really?

He pushed the thought aside as ridiculous. Even apart from the fact that marriage was now a real necessity, he could easily see himself marrying Eliza. Her pedigree was impeccable. She was a good conversationalist and a pleasure to look at. And she accepted him at face value, which was imperative in a bride.

If he was on the young side, then so be it. His friends would get over their pique—and they'd damn well better get over any amusement—if they wanted to continue calling themselves his friends.

He walked the several blocks to his intended's house with a purposeful stride. Every step he got closer, the muscles in his thighs, his calves, and his belly grew more tense. So proposing marriage was hell on even the most self-assured man, he was discovering. What would she say when he gave her the ring?

What would *he* say?

Dear God, he hadn't even thought of practicing a speech. Being cast adrift without a map at a young age had given him practice navigating an uncertain world. He raced his best races when he handled the reins loosely, when he didn't analyze every curve in the road. And his finest work as a new architect had all been done when he'd acted upon inspiration, the kind that grabbed him mid-sentence while conversing in a London coffeehouse. Or came to him in a dream. Or seemed to unfold as he was sketching, not knowing exactly in which direction he was pointed.

One benefit of losing his mother, his father, and his entire identity in a day: Life couldn't throw anything at Gregory he couldn't handle.

He rang the bell, sure at least of his welcome. The family appeared to approve of him—even the butler—as well they should. He was heir to a marquess. Of what could they disapprove?

He intended to ask Eliza to marry him first—a secret, intimate proposal that would take her by surprise, as all properly romantic gestures should; he owed her that—and *then* he'd play the usual societal game and request an audience with her father, which would be a matter of course. After her father's approval was won, Gregory would pretend to ask her to marry him for the first time in Lord Baird's library—but he and Eliza would know otherwise.

"Lord and Lady Baird are out. Lady Eliza's in the back garden," the butler informed him before Gregory could even ask. "She's showing Lord Morgan and Lady Pippa Harrington her mother's roses." An invisible mantle came down at the mention of Pippa. *Not* her. "May I take your cane and hat?"

"Thank you." Gregory concealed his annoyance at being thrown off kilter and handed the cane and hat over.

The silk box burned a hole in his pocket, but he'd have to delay the big moment. Dougal could be gotten rid of easily, but Pippa was another story. Gregory saw her once a year at a birthday dinner for her great-uncle Bertie, his godfather, in Devon, and had done so since he was eight—

old enough to travel alone without crying—and she was three. She was rarely in Town, so he couldn't simply fob her off. And prying her loose from her old friend Eliza might be difficult, as well.

Nevertheless, he'd get rid of the two interlopers—and they wouldn't even know they'd been dismissed. He'd use the effortless charm that came straight from his mother—and not Father, as everyone assumed—to convince them they were leaving of their own accord.

"The quickest way is through the billiard room," the butler said, indicating the route with a sure hand.

Gregory strode through the house and out one of the French doors onto a small pebbled path.

There came Pippa, striding toward him, her face slightly flushed. She'd never be able to sneak into a room with that fiery Titian hair. And she always wore at least one thing that was unusual. Today, it was a dramatic yellow-gold velvet spencer with tight sleeves that ended in large cuffs with outrageously large emerald paste buttons. Beneath it was a simple ivory muslin frock. There was no bonnet in evidence, but that wasn't a surprise.

She was like Mother, who'd never shown the smallest regard for whether anyone approved of her. Of course, Gregory knew now that his mother's insouciant manner had been an act. She *had* cared what people thought. Very much so.

"Swear you won't tell our secret, Gregory." Mother *cradled his head on her frail chest and stroked his curls.* *"It would only hurt your father's feelings and embarrass the family. But I had to tell you, darling, else I can't fly. I can't fly straight to heaven as I know you want me to do."*

"I swear, Mother. I'll never tell. Never.*"*

Lucky him, helping his mother to heaven. Thirteen,

he'd been, and he'd lived in his own sort of hell ever
since.

"Gregory?" Pippa glowed as usual. She wore the same
broad smile he'd seen the day she'd come into her great-
uncle's house from the moor with her two front teeth missing, a smudge of dirt decorating her nose, and a field mouse
cupped in her hands, a birthday gift for Bertie. "You're
looking straight through me—as if I were a ghost."

"You're the furthest thing from one," he said smoothly.

And he meant what he said. She was more alive than
anyone he knew, which was why he couldn't help being
suspicious of her.

Did people like Pippa and his mother ever consider
what their private joys did to other people? What price
the rest of the world paid for their adventures?

Since Mother's death, Gregory had ceased joining
Pippa in their annual childish high jinks—he was always
called Captain, and she was Lieutenant; their crab-apple
wars were legendary—and he'd refused to spend time
with her exploring the dramatic fells of Dartmoor, claiming to prefer his godfather's library.

But that was a lie.

He simply didn't want to be around *her*—a girl with
bright eyes and a ready laugh and an earnest readiness to
conquer the world.

"What's wrong, Gregory?" she'd asked him in Bertie's
library once. Out of the blue, when he'd been quietly pe-
rusing the shelves. She'd stood at the door, her head cocked
to the side like a robin's.

"Nothing," he'd told her. He'd been sixteen. She'd been
eleven.

She did the same thing several other years as well, the
last time occurring when he'd just graduated from Oxford.

"What *is* it?" she'd said over dinner, when Bertie's attention had been diverted by Pippa's mother and obnoxious second husband.

"None of your business," he'd said quietly. It was the first time he'd ever admitted to anyone that anything was wrong. "Don't ask again."

Small tears had formed in her eyes, and she'd looked away, at a candle flame wavering on its wick on the mantel.

Since that night, nothing else had been said.

Thank God.

Everywhere else, he was Gregory, the successful, sociable eldest son of the Marquess and Marchioness of Brady. But there was no hiding from Pippa, who seemed to read him as well as she did the sky and the moor she so loved. She sensed his misery. His darkness. It pressed against his polite smiles, made it difficult for him to maintain his façade as the London wit, the ambitious young architect, and the substantial heir.

Now he lifted her gloved hand to his mouth and brushed a polite kiss across her knuckles. "It's a rare thing to see you in Town, my lady. And a distinct pleasure to see you so soon after Bertie's birthday. How is he? Aside from the fact that he's—"

"Older?" There was a twinkle in her eyes.

"Yes, older." She had a clever way of handling awkward moments.

Of handling *him*.

"My uncle's very well, thank you." Her grin was demure. Knowing. She was well aware that he avoided her. "Mother and I wanted him to come to the Danvers-Tremont wedding, too, but you know Uncle Bertie. He's determined that the next wedding he attends must be my own."

To Gregory, was the unspoken conclusion to that sentence, they both knew.

"So you are here for the wedding," he said.

"Yes."

"With Lady Eliza?"

"Yes, actually."

"Old schoolmates always have much to talk about."

"And weddings only add to the conversation," she said, the merest flash of discomfiture crossing her face.

Or was it heartbreak? Gregory somehow doubted it. The groom was a bland, boring aristocrat, not Pippa's type at all, he should think.

And then he realized. Perhaps she wanted rid of him, too. "I'm sorry," he said immediately, feeling foolish. "I'm preventing you from leaving. Perhaps you plan to stop by the new exhibit at the British Museum?"

She wasn't a ribbons or baubles sort of girl, he knew. But surely the exotic animal exhibit would tempt her.

"I've already been," she said, "and it was fascinating. No, my lord, I'm in no rush to leave Eliza's. I'm enjoying my chat with you." Although when she smiled this time, it seemed to take her some effort. "I was just going to retrieve my reticule in the drawing room. I brought a bit of charcoal and a small pad of paper—I wanted to sketch the back of the house."

"That's interesting." He fought to suppress any impatience in his tone.

"I'm exploring a new hobby." She looked to the right and left—as if they had company—and leaned toward him. "Making sugar sculptures."

"Oh?"

Dimples peeked out, and she nodded vigorously. "I'm mad for them. Garden scenes with tiny temples and shepherdesses, gilded horses, fanciful flowers, woven baskets. So when I visit a place I like"—she lifted a hand to encompass the garden and the house—"I sketch it. In case someday I'll want to reproduce it as part of a pastoral scene for a dessert table."

He looked all around him. Eliza's house was the most boring edifice he'd ever seen. An imposing structure with stark and unimaginative lines, it sat like a fat salt box on the kitchen counter. The gardens weren't much more interesting, either, with nary a fanciful thought put into their design.

"It *is* lovely back here," he lied. "Shall I fetch your reticule for you?"

She stole another glance around the garden and blushed. "Oh, no, thank you, although—" She hesitated, and that awkwardness came between them once more. "Would you like to accompany me? I could catch you up on all Uncle Bertie's theaters. The newest one recently opened in Bristol."

"Of course." He opened the door to the billiards room again. And as he listened to her, something began to niggle at him. It wasn't anything particularly important. But it was a matter of slight curiosity: What was Dougal doing here? He'd had the occasional dance with Eliza at various balls, spoken with her at soirees, and said hello to her if they met up in the park when she was in Gregory's curricle. But other than that, they were mere acquaintances.

In the drawing room, Gregory was distracted when Pippa removed her gloves, placed them by a modest straw bonnet lying carelessly on top of the pianoforte, and retrieved the charcoal and pad of paper from her reticule. Her movements were sure and capable.

Eliza had delicate, tapered fingers. Last night, they'd felt like butterflies on his back.

Pippa's hands were entirely different, and seeing how ordinary they looked gave him a slight sympathy toward her. She might know her way around a moor, but in more polished company, she didn't have the élan of his future bride.

Then again, who did? Eliza, demure as she was, ruled the ranks of young ladies out in society. But she did it with an understated elegance that charmed all those who came in contact with her.

"So are you staying with Lady Eliza?" he asked.

They began to make their way through the house back to the gardens.

"No." Pippa paused by the billiard table. "Mother, Mr. Trickle, and I are at the Grillon Hotel. I escaped to see Eliza this morning. She told me it was her only opportunity. She's very popular. I don't know how she manages her schedule."

Gregory could swear he saw her fingers clutch the charcoal stick and pad tighter.

Something wasn't right. She swallowed oddly.

"All you all right?" Gregory leaned toward her, and smelled lavender in her hair. "Shall I get you some water?"

"Oh, no, indeed, but thank you," she said in a tone that was overly polite, and somewhat distant at that. She sounded as though he were a stranger.

He knew they only saw each other once a year, but he was certainly no stranger. And it was he who usually acted cool—not her. It was a peculiar feeling.

Pippa didn't dislike any person.

He suddenly didn't want to be the first.

He threw open the billiards room door again, and they

walked back outside. "Forgive me for prying, but I wonder what brought Dougal here today?"

She glided smoothly ahead of him on the narrow path. "I've no idea," she said over her shoulder. "He and Eliza must know each other."

"They must," he agreed.

Where were they?

Pippa paused to take in the view of a lush hydrangea. "Those colors are so beautiful, aren't they?"

"They are." Although to Gregory the hydrangea was no more worthy of a compliment than any other hydrangea he'd ever seen.

Impatience to see Eliza gripped him, and he had to strive to remember to loosen his fingers, let them hang at his sides, and relax his jaw.

Pippa looked up at him with bright eyes, hazel turned green against the backdrop of garden shrubbery. "It's odd seeing you away from Uncle Bertie's."

She was nothing if not frank.

"It is," he said, and it was. It felt wrong somehow. Perhaps that was what accounted for his unease. Seeing Pippa in the wrong place. And sensing her nervousness.

That was it.

She seemed hesitant to move.

He'd be glad to take the lead. With one deft move, he sidestepped her on the path. "If you'd like to sketch, there's a bench right there you might have missed, three hydrangeas over." He pointed to the east. "I'll find Dougal and Lady Eliza."

"Very well." Her voice was a little thin.

He sensed that she didn't dislike him, after all, which brought a feeling of relief followed swiftly by guilt: He was too hard on her. Much too hard. It wasn't her fault that she was free, more free than anyone he'd ever known, even as society—and Uncle Bertie, in particular— shackled her to the usual expectations.

How had she done that, anyway? Learned to live within her bonds so well?

"I'll see you in a moment, my lady."

She looked up, a flash of trepidation in her eyes. "Yes," she whispered.

Good God, she wasn't even trying anymore to hide it—she was worried about something, something that must be going on in amid the flora and fauna.

But what?

He took long strides over the grass, abandoning the pebble path, and headed to the back of the garden, where a line of rosebushes stood like sweet sentinels surrounding a statue of Mars.

Where the deuce were Dougal and Eliza, anyhow? They didn't really know each other well. They couldn't—

And there they were.

Past Mars, on the right, behind a tree. Dougal had her up against the trunk, and he was kissing her deeply, his hand roving her waist and caressing her breast.

Eliza was like a different woman. Her hands clung to Dougal's shoulders in a fierce grip. Her back was arched into him, as if she couldn't get enough of his mouth.

She hadn't been nearly as fervent in her response to Gregory. She hadn't been passionate with him at all, truth be told.

For the second time in his life, he felt as though he'd been shot three times through the heart in rapid succession: The woman he'd come to claim as his bride had betrayed him. His best friend had, too. And so had Lady

Pippa Harrington, who despite their differences shared a rare bond with him: They were both mutual survivors of Uncle Bertie's annual birthday dinner.

He left the entangled lovers to their own devices and strode to the bench where Pippa was making lame sketch marks and snatched the pad from her hands. All that was there was a doodle of a heart with an arrow through it, and then of a face, a man with curly hair and distinctive brows—

Him.

Gregory tossed it on the bench beside her. "So much for you and your sugar sculptures."

She stood, her face white, stricken. "I'm so sorry. But don't despair. You can do anything you want. Go anywhere you want. Whereas I—"

He pulled her close. Her face was an inch from his, her breasts pressed against his jacket.

"Stop talking," he told her in a low, dark voice.

She gulped and refused to take her eyes off his. He could feel her heart beating hard in her chest. Her eyes were so very green, and her lashes—those thick lashes . . .

And then he kissed her as if she'd had practice, but he knew she hadn't. Not Pippa. She was as fresh as that morning air on the moor, as untried as a closed rosebud.

He was unrelenting, demanding more of her with every passing second.

More.

And when he found her responding, moaning low in her throat when he pinned her in his embrace between his muscular thighs, he didn't care that the hardness of his arousal butted into her belly, that after this kiss was over, he was done with her.

He took what he wanted, caressing her derriere and her waist with a possessive hand, plundering her mouth with the desperation of a man who was angry and alone.

A host of images paraded through his head: the ruby ring in his pocket; his dying mother's whisper that his natural father, whom she wouldn't name, had died long ago; the smiling faces of his family on Christmas morning, a holiday which had felt vaguely sad to him ever since he'd learned the truth; his friends at Oxford, laughing and drinking without a care in the world—

Eliza.

"No," Pippa managed to gasp against his mouth, and slid out from under his arm. She stood there trembling. "You won't use me like this. I'm sorry what's happened, but it's not my fault."

The careless sound of a jaunty bird whistling on a branch nearby sounded oddly chilling. But fitting. There was no sunshine. Nor songs. Not really. They were a cover—like Pippa—for deceit. For wrong.

Gregory turned on his heels and strode toward the house.

"Gregory!" she called after him.

But he ignored her.

"Gregory!" she called again, this time from right behind him on the pebble path.

He shut the door to the billiards room in her face.

Then he strode through the house and took his cane and hat from the hall tree before the astonished butler could hand them over himself. He walked directly home, seeing nothing along the way.

Peter came in as he was packing a bag in the quiet of their bedchamber. "Where are you going?"

"The United States," Gregory said, then reached into

his pocket, removed the silk box containing their mother's ring, and tossed it to him. "Keep it. I don't want to see it again."

Peter said nothing, just held the box in his hand.

Gregory went back to tossing cravats and shirts into his bag. "You knew, didn't you?"

Peter still said nothing.

"You *knew*." Gregory stood tall and stared down his brother. He was the fourth person to dupe him today.

"I suspected she was in love with Dougal. But I had no proof. I tried to warn you—"

"Out of my way." Gregory grabbed his suitcase and stormed out of the room.

He didn't belong here.

He didn't belong anywhere.

Pippa was right. He could do anything he wanted, be anyplace he wanted. He was a novice architect, and while Father and Bertie had been the ones to turn him in that direction, it was up to him how far he wanted to go with it.

His first stop in America would be Federalist New England. He'd go next to the District of Columbia, followed by Jefferson's Monticello in Virginia, and then perhaps farther south to Charleston and Savannah and St. Augustine. After that, nothing was stopping him from going out West to see how Americans housed themselves and built their institutions—churches, schools, banks, mercantile shops—on the frontier.

Other than Peter, the only family member home at the moment was Mama. He'd already sent word to her that he was leaving imminently. At the front door with the carriage waiting, the marchioness embraced him as hard as she could. "I wish you could wait for your father—"

His father. Gregory never got used to the pain of hearing

those words. It pressed on him now. He had to fight—
fight—to hold it back.

"I can't." His voice was hoarse. It was so unlike him to
reveal his true self to Mama or anyone in the family. He
had to leave. For their sakes, too.

"Something terrible has happened." Mother held tight
to his arm. "What's wrong?"

"Nothing." He ignored the hurt and confusion he saw
in her eyes and put on his hat.

"Oh, Gregory. Don't leave like this. Please. We love
you, dearest."

However high the wall of hurt between him and the
world, the tenderness he saw on Mama's face reminded
him of his duty. He paused long enough to kiss her cheek.
"I'll write when I get there." He schooled his tone to
sound reassuring. "Don't worry about me."

Then, without waiting for a reply, he jogged down the
front steps of the house, onto the pavement, and into the
carriage—without a backward glance at the House of
Brady.

Chapter One

One Year Later

For Lady Pippa Harrington, it wasn't going to be the usual Sunday family dinner at Uncle Bertie's. Those were full of ridiculous speeches by her stepfather, Mr. Wilfred Trickle, followed by taut silences and the occasional *grrr* from one of Uncle Bertie's eight corgis under the table. No, tonight, Pippa's great-uncle was celebrating his birthday, and as a guest he'd have his godson Gregory Sherwood, Lord Westdale, son of the Marquess and Marchioness of Brady—one of the most eligible bachelors in London and an up-and-coming architect.

And the last man on earth I want to see, thought Pippa.

But he was back in England—back from an extended stay in America.

"Pippa?" Mother stood at the door to the small, private studio near the kitchen, her soft brown hair in a tidy chignon held back with painted Spanish combs, her delicate shoulders draped in a spectacular spangled gold shawl.

Her exotic accessories had come from Uncle Bertie's trunks. He owned five modest theaters in southwest England, including his pride and joy, the Roger, in the big city of Bristol. Every once in a while, costume inventory in transit from one theater to another between shows made its way to his country house, where Mother, Pippa, and two maids repaired or retired them, depending on their general state.

"Oh, Mother!" Pippa looked up from attaching the final miniature crown to a tiny window on a pale silver sugar sculpture she'd made for Uncle Bertie's birthday celebration. "The red gown is beautiful on you. Are you Desdemona?"

"I'm not sure," Mother said shyly, but she had the proud look of a young girl at her debut. "I think the entire ensemble might be a combination of Lady Macbeth and Kate, from *The Taming of the Shrew*."

Pippa laughed. "You're not the least bit like either of those ladies. But you look lovely, and you should dress like that always. Not only on Uncle Bertie's birthday."

"I wouldn't dare," said Mother. "This is for Bertie. You know how he is."

"Yes, I do, and you need to be like that, too." Pippa was kitted out in a severe ivory satin frock with seed pearls sewn in a square pattern across the bodice—an altered Ophelia from *Hamlet,* actually—protected, for the most part, by a sunny blue floral apron. "You were well on your way to becoming the toast of the London stage at one time, and no matter what your situation in life, you should never forget it."

Mother ignored her, but she knew very well Pippa was implying that Mr. Trickle, whom Pippa had secretly nicknamed the Toad—with his protruding eyes, ample jowls, and bald head covered in a perpetual sheen of perspiration—had stolen nearly all the light from his wife's eyes. Some of the blame also had to go to Pippa's own late father,

Uncle Bertie's nephew, who'd fallen in love with Mother when he saw her on the stage, married her, and cast her off when he'd tired of her.

Now Mother's limpid blue gaze took in the pretty disarray of molds, marzipan, and cutting tools surrounding Pippa's sparkling creation on the table.

"What do you think?" Pippa spread her arms wide so her mother could experience the full effect of viewing the miniature castle unimpeded.

"Very nice, as always, darling." Mother pulled distractedly at her shawl. "But shouldn't you be preparing yourself for this evening?" With a harried eye, she scanned her daughter for imperfections. "Now that Gregory is back, you must at least *try* to entice him to marry you. Your gown is perfection, but your hair needs taming."

"After you leave, I'll braid it." Pippa strode across the room to a drawer and pulled out a comb.

"Here?" Mother sounded aghast.

"Why not? I even have a spare tiara in this drawer." She pulled one out and blew on it. "See? It's only missing one false emerald. I'll fix it with some green marzipan. Gregory will never notice." She set it back down and returned to the table.

Mother sighed. "It's all that walking across the moors that makes you so uncivilized. It's unseemly."

"But the fells are far too pretty at every turn of the season to stop my daily hikes." Deftly forming a marzipan turret for the castle, Pippa looked up with an arched brow. "I wish you'd join me. It would do you good to get away from—" She nearly said the Toad, but caught herself just in time. "Nothing's ever the same on the moor."

The way it is here, she wanted to add. Day after day of

tension between the Toad and Mother, Uncle Bertie steadily ignoring them, lost in his own theater dreams. And Pippa wishing for . . .

Wishing for something else.

"Pish," her parent replied. "Every day, the moor's the same. Sky, meadow, tor. Over and over again."

"But it's *never* the same." Pippa was hurt on behalf of every living creature she'd encountered on the moor, and on behalf of the dramatic landscape itself, a giant, breathing presence—with moods from light to dark—cradling them all.

Ah, but what did she expect? The Toad was a nasty influence on Mother. A dozen years ago, she'd often gladly traipsed hand in hand with Pippa over rough pastures filled with gorse and heather or stood on a rocky outcrop and shouted into the wind.

But those days were no more. Pippa vowed she would never let a man steal her happiness. She would marry for love only, and that didn't seem a bit likely, not when she lived outside the tiny village of Plumtree, which was well off the beaten path.

"Mother, please," she said now. "You know from Uncle Bertie's past birthday dinners that I'm not interested in marrying Gregory, and he doesn't want to marry me, either. We're going to have a perfectly ordinary meal this time, and life will go on as usual—at least until Madame DuPont calls me to Paris."

Madame DuPont was Uncle Bertie's old amour. Her spinster daughter would soon be traveling to Italy for six months, and while she was gone, Madame required a companion, preferably an excellent reader. She'd written Bertie to ask for a recommendation.

"I don't approve of your going to France." Mother's

tone was agitated. "You're much better off staying in Devon and finding a husband. Gregory is the perfect one."

An image of him kissing her hard beneath the trees in Eliza's garden—punishing her, taunting her—flooded Pippa's mind, and she felt a moment's shame and anger.

Why had she responded? A year later, and she still regretted it!

She tried for patience. "But this is such a golden opportunity. I'll have a place to live—a safe place with a respectable widow. And on my days off, I'll improve my sugar-sculpting skills under the great Monsieur Perot's tutelage."

"He won't have you in his kitchen," Mother insisted. "You're a woman, and a lady, at that. Only men make fine pastry chefs. You'll find yourself pining away for England, and when you return, you'll be even more firmly on the shelf."

Pippa sighed. "It's a chance I'll have to take. And I have Uncle Bertie's blessing."

"But how can he support your going to Paris when he wants you to marry Gregory?"

"He won't go back on his promise to me just because Gregory chose to come back to England unannounced." Pippa gave a short laugh. "I suspect tonight, because Uncle Bertie loves us both and adores drama, he'll be tempted to interfere, but whatever he says or does won't make any difference to me. As for Gregory, he'll have his pick of dozens of debutantes in London to marry. Bertie's machinations will no doubt fall flat with him, too." She threw her mother a tender look. "Don't forget that I'm like you." *The former you,* she wanted to add. "I have dreams I want to pursue. And it's not as if six months is a very long time."

Mother let out a sharp sigh. "Well, make haste here. Gregory awaits." She sent Pippa one last warning look then departed.

Slowly, Pippa circled the table and looked at her little castle. Everything felt different now that Gregory was here. The studio seemed bigger and brighter, but she felt smaller, her little castle a feeble testament to the fact that she'd done nothing grand with *her* life.

At least not yet.

But if she could embrace the unpredictable, brooding nature of Dartmoor—which she did, with every ounce of her being—and if she could endure the despicable Toad and his cruel, conniving ways for ten years, she could certainly withstand Mother's disapproval over her spending half a year in Paris.

She swallowed hard. She could even face seeing Gregory again.

With one brisk movement, she swept up some crumbs of sugary dough into her hand and flung them into the fire. "There," she said to the tiny room which had housed her dreams for the past year, a room Uncle Bertie had used to sketch designs long ago. "I've spoken my wildest aspirations to the world."

Well, almost all of them.

One dream she'd never said aloud, even though Gregory alone already knew what it was. He'd seen it on that sketch pad, but he'd also tasted it on her lips, read it in the way she'd hungrily kissed him back in Eliza's garden.

Quietly, she hung the apron on its hook and began to braid her hair. She wasn't daunted by mere mortal men. A year may have passed since she'd seen Lord Westdale, but she'd known him forever.

Despite the awkwardness between them, he was nothing to fear.

The small mirror next to the door assured her that her braided hair was neat and proper. She placed the tiara on her head, put her chin up, and took a deep breath as she left the studio.

Several nervous moments later, Pippa rounded a shadowy corner and peeked into the drawing room to spy on Uncle Bertie's birthday dinner guest, and her whole body reacted with a suffusion of heat.

She was sure—positively sure—that the effect no longer came from girlish fantasies of love. She'd told herself she was well over that. The heat in her palms and on her face now came instead from a combination of embarrassment, chagrin, and humiliation. He'd given her no chance to explain the part she'd played in that horribly awkward situation with Eliza.

She was tempted to be angry, but it always dissolved when she thought about the heartbreak that afternoon, hard and harsh as his expression had been when he'd slammed the billiard room door in her face.

Oh, that expression. She'd seen a whole world in it. What he believed, and what he didn't. And he hadn't believed in love anymore—if he ever did. That much was clear.

In the soft glow of early evening candlelight, he was deep in polite conversation with her uncle and Mother, while the Toad glowered in the corner, alone.

Gregory's profile, Pippa thought, moved her for far more than the usual reasons. He was classically handsome, yes, but she saw the sensitivity in his mouth, the intelligence in his forehead, the unplumbed depths . . . of *him,* in his eyes.

Her stomach tightened. One long year she'd pined for him.

The oddest sensation—half dizziness, half wonder—seized her and left her breathless. It was the same heavy feeling she got at night when she looked out her window and remembered their kiss and was so overcome that she had to turn her head into her pillow and breathe goose feathers for a few seconds.

But then the visitor saw her and stood to greet her.

Pippa pretended she hadn't stopped to stare at him and walked in with all the sangfroid she could muster. Good God, she thought, he was completely, utterly different. Gone was even the remotest sign of hurt. Of vulnerability. His eyes were hooded, dark. Inscrutable.

"Lady Pippa." His tone was perfectly cordial, but apart from that, Pippa couldn't distinguish anything else in the greeting.

"Lord Westdale," she said in a throaty voice, genuinely moved by the changes in him. "How are you?"

And she meant it. How was he?

He'd grown even more into his splendid good looks since she'd last seen him. She had to gather her wits when he bent that head of glossy black hair over her hand.

"So good to see you again," he murmured smoothly.

Liar.

She refused to let the warm, bold pressure of his fingers on her own disconcert her. "It's been rather a long while," she returned, striving for cool but failing miserably. There was that catch in her voice, after all. The truth was, she relished his touch.

He stood tall again. "No more than our usual year. But

while I was away, I recalled Plumtree and its inhabitants fondly."

"As we did you," she said, "and wished for your safe return."

To me, she thought.

They eyed each other, measure for measure. It was a whole new world between them now. Gone was her childhood playmate—long gone—but also absent was the artificial friendship that had sprung up between them over the years. In its place was . . . what was it, exactly?

She couldn't say she hated it. A layer had been peeled away. Now there was only a man. And a woman. A woman rejected, yes. And a man betrayed by two clandestine lovers and Pippa, at least in his mind. Yet it was a more honest place than they'd ever been together before.

"We're very glad you're back," she said gamely, and took a chair near Mother's. "How was your American tour?"

"Productive. Pleasant." Gregory sat on a sofa across from Uncle Bertie and threw his arm across the back. He was at his most casual and charming, but the deep undercurrent between them belied his words and his pose. "I met up with several good friends, made new ones, too, and managed to see a great deal of the country's best architecture, as well."

"Did you receive my letter?" Pippa dared to ask him. "I sent it to the address in Savannah your mother provided. Hopefully, you caught up with it. But I suspect you didn't."

"I did receive it, yes."

"And you read it?" she boldly inquired.

"Of course." He arched a brow. "I'm sorry I wasn't able to write back. Time got away with me."

And pigs flew.

"Heavens, I never expected to hear *back*." Pippa swept open her fan and waved it in front of her breasts. "You're an important man, my lord."

Who can jump into a lake of those wretched American alligators, for all I care, she said with her eyes.

"We could debate my importance," Gregory said matter-of-factly.

Which was why she was blindsided when for the first time in their long acquaintance, he looked at her as if he saw her without a stitch of clothing on her body.

How had he managed to sneak that look in?

And why?

She guessed he was using the garden sketch against her in every way he could—and it was working, damn him. It was working very well.

"So your parents are in the area, too?" Mother asked Gregory in timid fashion.

"Yes, Lady Graham, they're in Dawlish. My stepmother loves the place, so Father took her there for a few days' holiday and some good sea air. They were anxious to see you, but he's got very little time to spare away from Whitehall. They asked me to convey to you their deepest wish that you come to London as soon as possible as their guests."

"How kind," barked Bertie.

"You've such a lovely family," said Mother.

"Your stunning stepmother puts every other woman her age to shame," rasped the Toad, which was rude of him as his own wife was Lady Brady's age.

There was a few seconds' painful lull in the conversation, and just when Pippa thought she might actually jump out of her own skin, Uncle Bertie said in a leading fashion, "Speaking of family . . ."

In a great scarlet chair facing a modest fire, he sat with his stocky legs apart, his back straight, his stomach protruding like a pillow, all because he refused to remove the corgi sleeping behind him. His mouth drew down, and he lowered his brows at Gregory.

It was his recitation mode.

Pippa braced herself. Surely he wouldn't do what he usually did—which was matchmaking—not when he knew she was going to Paris. If so, who would he dangle in front of Gregory this time as a rival for her affections? And how did Uncle Bertie manage to get anyone interested in the first place? Her dowry was nothing, in tonnish terms: his theaters upon his death.

"My great-niece's latest admirer—" he began in a ponderous tone to his godson.

"A handsome lad with fine manners and an abundance of funds—" interrupted the Toad in his croaking voice.

"Is Mr. Broderick Hawthorne, heir to Lord Dalrymple," Uncle Bertie finished just as a corgi squeezed out from behind him and climbed onto his lap.

Pippa's throat constricted. She'd no idea who the man was.

"He's coming sometime next week"—Uncle Bertie wriggled his great girth back into the chair—"and wants my great-niece as his future viscountess. He seeks my blessing. I'm curious to know your thoughts on the matter, godson, as I've never met the man."

Uncle Bertie! Pippa almost sank through the floor. He winked at her, which meant he had high hopes Gregory would be jealous. Knowing there was even further humiliation in store, she burrowed deeper into her chair, toes curling in her slippers, stomach taut with tension, head dizzy with apprehension. Mother touched her false pearl choker, her face ashen white.

Gregory deigned to speak. "I met Hawthorne once. I seem to remember he had a voice like a loud gong and a head that kept splitting into three and back again to one, like a magical mythological creature. Of course, I was in my cups at the time. But I'm still not sure that accounts for the impression."

He sent Pippa a bold, lazy stare. She narrowed her eyes back at him.

"Don't tell me he's an ass." Uncle Bertie leaned forward, his fists on his chubby thighs. "I want to hear more. Shut your ears, Helen and Pippa."

It was a little late for that. Pippa gripped the arms of her chair and stared at their guest.

"He was a sore loser at cards," Gregory replied indifferently. "And despite his lack of chin and his protruding teeth, he declared himself God's gift to women until I challenged him on that point. Of course, the only available judge in the competition was a stooped crone nicknamed the Duchess, who brought us all rum punch and beef sandwiches. But she counts, doesn't she?"

He had the nerve to turn to Mother.

"Of course," she said loyally.

"Thank you, Lady Graham." Gregory gazed at her as if she were a duchess herself—or maybe a queen.

Pippa wanted to be angry, but it was good to see Mother glow the way she was meant to in that splendiferous costume.

"Is that the extent of it?" Uncle Bertie persisted. "He might not be as handsome as you, but he's still Dalrymple's heir. And I don't lose well at cards myself."

Everyone in the room knew that. He'd sulk until someone brought him a fresh glass of whiskey or Pippa hugged
his shoulders and kissed his head.

Gregory shrugged. "The Duchess loudly proclaimed
that she preferred my devil-eyes to Mr. Hawthorne's puppy
ones. She hadn't a word to say about my friends Sir Hugh
and Lord Bromley. They were too happily leg shackled to
command feminine attention."

"Poor sods," said Mr. Trickle.

"Their hard luck," Gregory replied, his face perfectly
serious, the scoundrel.

"Demme, godson." Uncle Bertie gave a chuckle. "You
do resemble the spawn of Satan."

"Lord Westdale could have sported horns and pointed
ears," Pippa said with exasperation, "and still have won
this dubious contest. The Duchess saw that Mr. Hawthorne was obviously the ruder of the two"—*only just
barely,* was the look she sent Gregory—"which is why you
can write him and tell him not to bother coming to woo
me, Uncle Bertie."

He gave a wry shake of his head. "Hawthorne might
be a tad vain, but that's nothing a dose of marriage can't
cure."

Gregory's eyes glinted with amusement. "Anyone who's
able to procure the hand of the elusive Lady Pippa will, I'm
sure, be subject to a heartfelt remedy of all his ills."

Oh, he was incorrigible!

Although he *had* called her the elusive Lady Pippa,
which sounded rather grand. But how could she care
when a bucktoothed, chinless loser at cards was coming
to offer for her the next week—and Gregory didn't even
mind? Not only did he not object, he seemed to relish the
idea.

He wasn't jealous at all.

"We're here to celebrate your birthday," she reminded her uncle with a bright smile to mask her fury and—she must admit—her disappointment. "Tell us about your favorite one."

"Not now, Pippa." Uncle Bertie leaned forward and pushed at Gregory's knee with his hammy fist.

Oh, dear. The push. Pippa bit the inside of her lip. The push meant the excruciating moment had finally arrived.

"I'm not entirely sure Hawthorne's suitable to marry Pippa," Uncle Bertie said in the understatement of the year. "But I'll see her settled before I die—and with the right man. *You're* the husband for her, and you'll never do better than my Pippa."

Dear God!

Pippa wished she could be grateful—a tiny part of her heart was always touched at this speech of Uncle Bertie's—but instead, she felt a great affinity with the corgi by the hearth scratching his fat, bald hindquarters and whining.

Gregory looked calmly into his godfather's eyes. "Bertie—" he began.

Uncle Bertie's face took on a stubborn look. "It's my birthday wish, young man."

"Bertie," Gregory said again in an unruffled manner, although he didn't look at her. "I agree Lady Pippa's not getting any younger."

She sat up straighter. Of all the nerve!

"That fact alone would make her an ideal candidate for marriage," Gregory went on, "but—" He paused a long second. A long, *rude* second. "But I'm afraid Lady Pippa is far too *whimsical* at the moment to become a wife and mistress of a well-run household, much less a ramshackle one, which is the sort I prefer. I don't plan to marry for years, you see. However, consider it a promise that I'll ensure she marries well, to someone who cherishes her as much as you do."

Pippa's heart reluctantly warmed. He'd find someone to cherish her!

"It might take years," Gregory continued—years? She wasn't *that* difficult to cherish!—"but I swear it on my mother's grave."

Pippa wondered what his mother had been like. He'd never talked of her. But wait—she couldn't be diverted from what was going on, which was the spoiling of all her plans.

"I don't want to marry," she reminded everyone, but not a single person acknowledged that she'd spoken. Not even a dog looked her way.

Uncle Bertie rubbed his chin. "That's an extraordinary promise, godson."

"It's my gift to you." Gregory's mouth and eyes were serious.

Pippa nearly sputtered. Gift to Uncle Bertie? Did her wishes not count for anything?

Bertie stared at Gregory a moment. "I accept it," he finally said. "I'm an old man. It's time to pass the baton to the younger, better man."

Pippa stared back and forth between them, her face agog. This conversation simply couldn't be happening.

"You're hardly old," Gregory replied. "And I'm *not* the better man." He spoke low, and Pippa detected strong emotion in his reply.

She was horrified to find that she felt vaguely jealous. Gregory was genuinely affectionate to her uncle and her mother, but not to her anymore.

Never to her.

"I'm her stepfather," Trickle croaked. "*I'm* in charge of whom the girl marries."

"Shut up, Wilfred." Bertie patted Gregory's knee.

"Yes, do be quiet, Wilfred," Mother added, and stared adoringly at Gregory.

"I want it to be *you,* godson," Bertie reminded him one last time, and linked his pinky fingers together to drive the point home.

"I know you do," Gregory replied softly, "but we've gone over this already. Remember what I said." Swarthy and tempting, like a handsome satyr sent to torment her, he looked directly at Pippa.

"Right." Bertie nodded with great vigor. "She needs challenges."

Pippa couldn't help her chest heaving with entirely appropriate indignation. "I'm not interested in marrying you or anyone else, Lord Westdale." Her voice shook with fury. "I'm going to Paris, and I'm going to become an extraordinary sugar sculptor."

"You've proved my point." Gregory's tone was neutral but firm. "You're far too whimsical for your own good. London is where you belong. And London is where you'll find a husband. I leave tomorrow for a house party near Ashburton. On my way back to Town, I'll stop by to fetch you. You'll stay with my mother and sisters. That should be in about two weeks' time."

"Fine idea!" crowed Bertie. "I don't know what I was thinking letting her hare off to Paris."

Pippa pointed a trembling finger at Lord Westdale and looked at Mother and Uncle Bertie. "But he ran away from England for one long year," she insisted, her voice trembling. "Why should you listen to him?"

No one said a word. The tension in the room was thick.

"Doesn't anyone care that I want to make sugar sculptures for a living?" she whispered. "That I have a dream that will make me happy? Mother? Remember you were an actress?"

Silence.

"Uncle Bertie? You gave up architecture to build your theaters. Because they make you happy. Remember?"

He glowered at the fire, refusing to meet her gaze.

What had happened?

This was all Gregory's fault. Again.

Pippa looked at him. His eyes burned with something that made her wonder if she should check to see if her neckline hadn't slipped down any further. Not that she would. She refused to look down. He wanted her to, no doubt. He was hoping she'd blush and stammer, too.

But instead she raked him with a scornful glance. He'd slung one leg over the other in careless man fashion, an act which stretched the fabric over his thighs to a serious degree, showcasing pleasantly obvious muscles that had no right to be as attractive as they were.

He appeared completely unperturbed by her flagrant perusal of his person. "Duty is its own reward," he said quietly. "You must marry, Lady Pippa."

"Please stop talking about this," she choked out. "Could we—could we have dinner?"

"Let's do," Mother said in a thready voice.

Pippa stood, feeling as vulnerable as a young lady with a precarious hold on her dreams could, especially when faced with a patronizing earl across the carpet who'd decided to be the arbiter of her future.

Gregory crossed the floor before Uncle Bertie—still

wedged into his chair—to take her arm. It was a lovely show of "Let's put this behind us, shall we?"

Together, they walked to the dining room.

"Ignore Bertie's disappointment about us," the earl said. "He'll forget it on the morrow."

"No he won't." Pippa's tone was wooden. "He never does."

Gregory pulled out her chair, his nearness causing her to stop breathing long enough that when she did breathe, it would have been an audible gasp for air had not the heavy panting from the crowd of corgis under the table served as a distraction.

She was mortified that after all she'd been through tonight, part of her was still attracted to their glamorous visitor. The entire time he'd kissed her in Eliza's garden, Pippa had known he was using her. Punishing her. So what did this infatuation with him make her? Some kind of empty-headed fool?

Which was why when he asked for the open saltcellar with the darling matching duck spoon at dinner a few minutes later, she reached for the set with alacrity but then wouldn't let go of it right away.

He didn't deserve to use the duck spoon. And for that matter, he hadn't deserved to kiss her. But finally, she relented and handed him the cellar.

When Gregory's mouth twitched with something like amusement, Pippa supposed he had good reason. Here he was, an important man deigning to leave the social whirl in London to come to Dartmoor for an old man's birthday and being forced to sit next to a girl who was pleased by very small things, like duck spoons, fake tiaras, and sugar sculptures—a girl he'd just promised to see to the marriage altar with another, as-yet-unnamed man.

For a moment, it was as if time froze and she were observing the scene from the outside looking in. As the clock on the mantel had done since she was a child, it sounded slightly ill, going *tock*-tick, *tock*-tick rather than the more regular ticktock. The same oil painting with the same ship battering through the same choppy seas hung on the wall above the sideboard. The carved roses on the elaborate plaster molding that marched down the seams of the ceiling and framed the cupids painted there were elegant, but she'd seen them a thousand times, and now the fulsome border made the room feel less an airy chamber than a suffocating box.

Dear God, this is my life.

Pippa cast a sideways glance at Gregory and he gave her a secret, knowing smile. He must have taken particular pleasure in rebuffing her today. Oh, he was a heartless, wretched, *monster* of a man! And try as she might not to, she leaned half an inch closer to him.

Chapter Two

At the table Pippa eyed Gregory as if he were the devil incarnate. And that was a good thing. He had only a few more hours to go pretending that nothing had gone terribly awry between them, and then tomorrow morning, he'd be on his way.

But then she leaned closer to say something, and everything in him clamored to lean toward her, too. He had no idea why. Despite his new grasp of her as a woman—brought on by her betrayal and that kiss they'd shared in Eliza's garden—and not as a mere placeholder in the annual tradition with Bertie, she wasn't his type.

Eliza was his type. She'd been undemanding and serene—at least with him. Not with Dougal. He couldn't forget that with Dougal, she'd been assertive and excited, and now the two were married.

Was that love?

Not that it mattered to Gregory. In fact, to hell with love. He believed in lust. It didn't last, but while it did, it was marvelous.

"Your hair looks beautiful in the candlelight," he told Pippa.

Why not? He was leaving, and she didn't like him anymore, at least not the way she must have liked him before he'd snatched her drawing pad and kissed her a year ago.

It had been the most memorable kiss of his life—

But he'd like to forget it.

All his angst, his sorrow, his anger, his pain, and his guilt had come out in that kiss.

He hated that Pippa knew him. She might not be aware, but she knew him better than anyone else.

She'd tasted something of the wretchedness of his soul in Eliza's garden that day.

Not surprisingly, tonight she'd made clear that she wasn't the least bit in love with him. Pity, that. His bitterness had had focus when he'd held her heart in his hands.

So now, in a sense, amid the rubble of her betrayal and the remnants of his resentment, they were back to the old days, the old ways. He could tell Lady Pippa Harrington the truth and not worry about the implications, the same way he could compliment a fellow at White's: "Nice horse, nice cravat."

She *did* have lovely hair.

Her brow puckered. "Are you flirting with me? After all those nasty things you said earlier? And after you kissed me so rudely last year? I remember, you know, for all the wrong reasons."

Perhaps going backward wouldn't be as easy as he'd thought.

So be it.

"Wrong reasons are often associated with great pleasure," he murmured. "Shall I show you later what I mean? I'll ensure you won't forget this time, either."

She sucked in a breath, then whispered, "You're wicked," just as a footman wearing his best important face came striding through the doors.

All eyes turned to watch as he carried a diminutive castle on a silver tray and carefully placed it on the center of the table.

"Happy birthday, Uncle Bertie," Pippa said with a proud smile.

The castle gleamed in the candlelight. It was Gothic and rococo and all sorts of oddness. There were even two gargoyles perched on its roof. It shouted *fairy tale*—the intriguing kind with both hunchbacked witches and shining princesses—and was the exact opposite of the clean, simple, rational architecture Gregory preferred. But there was something about it . . . something that made his breath catch in his throat when he saw it.

You could marry her, were the first highly illogical words that came to his mind.

But of course, he couldn't.

You could marry her, the thought came back, more strident now. He thought of a miniature witch inside that castle sitting at her crystal ball and casting a spell over him. *Save her from a boring life. She's too good—too damned whimsical—to waste away.*

But of course, he wouldn't.

It would be madness.

He would marry for duty many years from now, and Pippa would never suit as his wife. She was nosy. Demanding. She would stir him up. He couldn't afford to reveal anything more to her—or to anyone else.

And he couldn't forget that he couldn't enjoy his life of wealth, and status. It must be void of happiness. Of pleasure. It must be entirely dutiful. He owed the Brady family that. And if he married Pippa—who was made for pleasure and didn't even know it—he'd be happy.

So Pippa was entirely *wrong.*

A few more hours, he reminded himself. A few more hours, and he'd be on a horse heading to Thurston Manor.

Uncle Bertie leaned forward and held his quizzing glass up to his eye just as the largest and most elaborate of the round castle turrets fell off the sugar sculpture. It landed on top of a candle and put it out, but not before there was a sizzle, a snap of flame, and a wisp of smoke.

Mother gave a little cry.

A snort came from Mr. Trickle.

"My, my," said Uncle Bertie kindly. "I like it, Pippa. Even if it *is* a bit of a mess."

The acrid smell of burned sugar filled the air.

"Oh, dear." Pippa bit her plump lower lip.

"Cheer up, my girl," Bertie said with spirit. "Love changes everything, you know. In my mind, this castle's perfect just the way it is because *you* made it."

"You're a dear to say so, Uncle Bertie, but that's not good enough," Pippa fretted. "See why I must go to Paris?"

Gregory did his best to ignore the feeling he had inside, that Pippa's pitiful, desperate plea made him mad to save her, to tuck her under his arm and ride off with her on the piebald stallion of his boyhood dreams (the one he never got and would never grant himself) and hide her in a castle somewhere with gargoyles on every corner, peak, and turret.

But then the dining room doors swung open again with a loud bang against the wall. Brick, the decrepit butler who fifty years ago once played Puck from *A Midsummer Night's Dream* at Uncle Bertie's very first theater, entered and gave a little leap. "Strike me pink! If it isn't Mr. Hawthorne, Lady Pippa's suitor, at the door."

Gad, no. Gregory felt a sharp stab of surprise and annoyance.

"I told him ye weren't home to visitors at this hour, Lord Carson," said Brick to Bertie, "but that didn't stop *this* gentleman."

No, it wouldn't, thought Gregory, stewing.

Brick stuck his thumb over his shoulder. "He's got a room at the Blue Doubloon in Plumtree, and has come to propose to Lady Pippa." He leaned toward the company and whispered loudly, "He looks like a stoat and smells like one, too."

"Brick," said Lady Graham reprovingly. "He can hear you, I'm sure."

"There are to be no proposals this evening or in the near future." Uncle Bertie's tone was ominous enough to send the corgis from under the table to their second favorite lounging spot, directly on top of the overlarge feet of the footman against the wall, whose shoes must have carried delicious smells from the kitchen. "Send him away, Brick, and tell him next time to come when he's been summoned."

"But he claims that Mr. Trickle invited him for tonight's festivities and has agreed to let him marry Lady Pippa," squeaked the butler.

"Marry me?" Pippa was outraged. "I won't marry a vain, bucktoothed stoat. I don't care how rich he is or how many titles he has!"

"Heavens," Mama cried. "Does this mean Pippa won't get to go to London with Gregory?"

"What the devil?" Bertie swung his head to Trickle, who sat with an affected innocent expression. "You've overstepped your bounds, Wilfred."

"But I told you already tonight," Trickle reminded Bertie, "I'm her stepfather. And I want her to marry *now*. There's no turning back. If you're peeved, direct your displeasure to Lord Westdale. None of this finagling would have been necessary if he'd finally have come up to scratch this evening." He looked around the table with a sickly smile. "We all knew the chances of *that*, and I gambled on them."

Gregory's cravat felt tighter than usual, and he'd gladly have thrown Pippa's atrocious little stepfather out the window at that moment had it not been Bertie's birthday. But it was, and he would behave as the future Marquess of Brady should. He wouldn't speak unless it was absolutely necessary.

Of course, in this case . . .

Speaking was absolutely necessary.

"Lady Pippa is going to London," Gregory said firmly to the entire table. "If Hawthorne wants to marry her, he can woo her properly during the Season along with myriad other fellows. If you or Hawthorne have a problem with this, Mr. Trickle, we can discuss it over dueling pistols."

There was an ominous silence. Trickle sank an inch lower in his chair, but his eyes glowed with fury.

"Right," said Brick cheerily. "I'll tell Mr. Hawthorne what you said, Lord Westdale."

"No, Brick." Pippa raised a hand. "Tell the visitor I'm off to Paris soon, and I'll be away six months. Oh, and please let him know I'm not interested in marrying anyone at all."

Brick's face crinkled up. "Are—are you sure?"

"Tell the man to *leave*." Uncle Bertie pounded his fist on the table. His face was near puce. "But thank him for coming," he added more gently, "and give him a bottle of my best mead. It's my birthday, after all."

"Right," said Brick, and scurried from the room.

"Speaking of birthdays," said Pippa before another

awkward silence could settle over the room, "we can eat parts of the castle. The gargoyles are delicious. And the doors are edible, too."

She broke one off and took a nibble, and Gregory's trousers grew unexpectedly tight at the sight of the sugar on her lips.

"Break me off a gargoyle, then, Pippa," his godfather said in indulgent tones. "I want the ugliest one you've got."

"Nothing would give me greater pleasure." Pippa leaned forward, her ivory beaded bodice strained so that her bosom was lifted high, and broke off the tiny monstrosity. With a smile of triumph, she stood up, her rounded backside so close to Gregory he could caress it if he wanted to, and strode proudly to the head of the table.

Gregory could think of something that would give her a far more selfish pleasure than watching Bertie sample his birthday treat. But he suppressed his lascivious thoughts and took a discreet breath.

Tonight's crisis had been averted. Bertie was happy, and Gregory was still a free man. Only a few more hours and then he'd leave at dawn. He was aware, however, that in the short time he'd visited, his priorities had made a momentous shift. Pippa was the apple of her great-uncle's eye, so nothing could go wrong there. As Gregory wasn't going to marry her, he had to make sure she was settled properly. When he returned from the house party to fetch her, there could be no stuff and nonsense.

He thought of the yellow spencer with the enormous paste emerald buttons she'd worn in Eliza's garden, her laugh, the extravagance of her lips, her pert breasts, and that damnably adorable sugar castle—and a frisson of foreboding passed through him.

Pippa was *made* for stuff and nonsense.

* * *

And so another birthday for Bertie was over, and Pippa had survived Gregory's visit. She was fairly content when she went to bed, although in the morning, she would remind Uncle Bertie that she wasn't going to London with Gregory. She was going to Paris without Gregory. After that, she'd spend her life ignoring Gregory and making sugar sculptures. Nothing would ever be about Gregory again.

But every thought she had when she retired to bed contained Gregory's name, and it was driving her mad. She wanted to *forget* Gregory!

"I can do it," she said, and slipped into a soft muslin gown—her favorite, with lace at the cuffs and neck. But the feeling of the fabric sliding over her breasts reminded her of the one time Gregory had slid his hands over her breasts. And when she lay down, she remembered all the nights she'd imagined kissing him by pressing her face into her pillow in silly but pleasurable fashion.

Well after midnight, which was the last time she'd looked at her bedside clock, Pippa was dreaming of feeding Gregory a sugary gargoyle and then kissing his mouth when she heard an unfamiliar whisper, "Lady Pippa!", in her ear. "Lady Pippa, wake up!"

It was more impatient than threatening, this voice.

And it was male.

Male.

There shouldn't be a man in her room!

Her eyes flew open to see a man with no chin and large teeth anxiously biting his lower lip and leaning over her. He was dressed in traveling coat, trousers, and boots. She gave a little cry and sat up, the bedclothes clutched to her chest. "I'll kill you if you try to hurt me. I've got a pistol under my pillow, and I know how to use it." She reached behind her back, pretended to retrieve the weapon, and pointed her finger at him beneath the sheets.

"That's your finger," he said matter-of-factly. "You can put it away. I won't hurt you. I'm Broderick Hawthorne, here to marry you."

"What?" she choked out. "How did you get in? Is there a fire?"

"Of course not." He chuckled. "I used a key." He held up a small brass one, the spare one.

"Mr. Trickle must have given you that!"

"Indeed, he did." He sat next to her, and Pippa scrambled to the far side of the bed and stood. "Think of me as a dream come true, my lady, the best dream you've ever had."

She narrowed her eyes at him. "Not only are you extremely vain, you're the furthest thing I can imagine from a dream come true. This is entirely inappropriate, sir." She felt anger in every limb, making them tremble. "How dare you enter my room uninvited? Please leave immediately." She threw a glance at the door only to see that her key was not in the lock.

Hawthorne raised a second key and waved it lazily over the coverlet. "You'll have to kiss me to get this, sweet damsel."

"I said *leave*." Her stomach lurched, and she couldn't help but think that Gregory and Uncle Bertie would be furious if they knew what was happening. She should scream right now—Uncle Bertie's hearing was excellent— and she would if she had to. But if she could resolve this dilemma without involving anyone else, she'd prefer that. Uncle Bertie wasn't getting any younger, and his heart didn't need the jolt it would surely get if she cried for help.

Mr. Hawthorne stood. "Hurry, now. I've got a coach waiting for us at the end of the drive. I've already got a special license. We can marry anywhere, not be forced to journey all the way to Gretna."

She pointed a shaky left index finger to her door. "Get out of here. I'm not going to marry you. I'm going to Paris. And neither you nor any male shall interfere with that plan."

"Don't be unreasonable, my lady. What's done is done. Your stepfather and I—"

"I'll scream if you come any closer," she interrupted him. And she would. She'd scream bloody murder, and she'd have to hope Uncle Bertie's constitution could endure the ensuing mayhem that was sure to result.

Mr. Hawthorne looked down at her gown and then back at her face, his expression distinctly admiring. "The only plan you need, dear lady," he said, "is to wed the right man. And I am he. You'll forget all about going to Paris once you share my bed."

"Don't you dare mention the word *bed* again." Anger and fear made her voice shrill. "I'm losing patience with you. Go now. Or I *will* scream. I promise you that."

"Go ahead and call the guards, or whomever it is you want to come rescue you." He pulled off a boot and let it fall to the floor with a thunk.

"What are you doing?"

"Getting undressed." He pulled off another boot. "What does it look like?" That boot dropped to the floor, too.

"Be quiet, you vile man, or you'll wake the house."

He tittered and shrugged off his coat, throwing it on the bed. "If you won't come with me, I'll stay here. You're already in your nightgown. You'll *have* to marry me."

"No I won't. I'll tell Uncle Bertie you entrapped me."

He emitted another obnoxious laugh. "Trickle warned me you might not be cooperative." He'd unraveled his cravat and was fumbling with the ties of his shirt.

She'd have to convince this awful man to see reason. "Why do you want to marry me? I have only a modest dowry to offer you. This is going a bit far, don't you think?"

"You're a lady, and a beautiful one. I don't need your money. I only want you in my bed. I have a difficult time meeting women, you see. I seem to intimidate them. Trickle understands." When he pulled off his shirt, his torso was so thin and white she was reminded of a flounder skeleton left on a platter for a cat to lick clean.

He flexed his scrawny arms over his head. She grimaced and looked away, not in the least interested in seeing any more of him.

"Why question your good fortune?" he said. "You've landed a virile and wealthy husband. You'll never get a better offer."

She gave a little cry of frustration and spun around to face him. "Is there any way I can bribe you to give me that key and let me go?"

"No." His hand was on the placket of his trousers.

"Don't touch those trousers," she said, "and put your shirt back on. I'm warning you." She picked the linen garment up off the bedcover and tossed it at him.

He pursed his lips and gave her what he obviously thought was a come-hither look. "You might as well give in. There's no escape. Trickle and I saw to that before I got here."

"What are you talking about?"

He put his hands on his hips and thrust his scrawny

chest out. "There's someone in the village who's seen us together and has all the lovely details." His yellowed smile was complacent.

"I don't believe you." Her heart thumped in her ears. "No one in the village would ever speak against me, no matter how much money Mr. Trickle offered them. They've known me since I was a child!"

"You *are* a naïve girl, aren't you?" Once again his hands reached for the placket of his trousers.

"You won't get away with this," she said. "Uncle Bertie trusts me implicitly. And Lord Westdale will call you out. He'll see you and Mr. Trickle for the liars you are. If I were you, I'd ride away as soon as possible before trouble really hits."

She strode to her clothes press and picked up her ivory satin evening gown from the night before, crushing it to her chest. "Stay here if you must. I'm leaving."

She walked purposefully to the window, unlatched it, and threw it open. There was a trellis there. It was old and she'd not tested it—at least not in the last few years. Without another thought, she tossed her gown out and quickly straddled the sill.

She was almost over it when he quashed her plan, grabbing her wrist. "Oh, no you don't."

She tried to pull away, but he tugged her closer. Despite his skin-and-bones appearance, he was surprisingly strong.

"No!" She tried to pull away again, but he cupped his hand around the back of her head and tried to kiss her.

Ugh! He was awful and rude, and his foul breath was unbearable.

She hit him in the ear with the side of her fist. She'd no idea how she'd learned to be so savage, and he yowled and let go of her. She immediately ran for the candlestick by her bed, and when she turned around, he was already upon her. She'd time for only one blow, so she struck him as hard as she could on the crown of his head.

His eyes rolled up to the ceiling, and he fell to the rug. Thank God.

Pippa took in a deep breath and let it out just as the first cock crowed. In the faint beam of dawn light that came through the side window and burnished away some of the darkness, she saw that he was still breathing.

She wrapped her arms around herself to stop the trembling. She must go. She couldn't stay. She could explain what happened to Uncle Bertie, but there was the Toad. He was too dangerous now. She didn't believe for a second that he'd succeeded in bribing villagers to speak against her. But perhaps he'd tried, which was bad enough.

A pang at the thought of leaving Uncle Bertie and Mother assailed her, but surely Uncle Bertie would look after Mother.

She crept over to her bed and opened Mr. Hawthorne's coat while she prayed he wouldn't awaken. Then she palmed the key to her room and opened the bedchamber door.

Without looking back, she pulled it shut behind her, and headed downstairs. She could comply with what the world expected of her, or she could fight. It was time to seek out her happiness. When would she ever get another chance?

She'd little time. Any second Hawthorne could wake.

Downstairs she entered the sewing room and spied the trunk in the corner. When she was finished there, she wrote a hasty note in Uncle Bertie's library and left it in the dining room, next to the remainder of her castle standing in its glittery but imperfect glory on the center of the table. It was still splendid, despite both the accidental and intentional assaults upon it last night.

A sense of rightness filled her—big enough to swallow her fear of the unknown—and she left the room with purpose in her step. Sensual daydreams about swarthy, infuriating earls—and marriage to any man—were for women who had nothing better to do.

Pippa was going to Paris.

Chapter Three

Something wasn't right. Gregory had stayed up far too late in his bedchamber staring at the faded royal-blue velvet drapes of the canopy bed and wishing for sleep. But he couldn't stop thinking about the fact that Pippa was three doors down on the other side of the corridor and that all he had to do was go to her—

And he'd be happy. He knew he would be. Maybe for an hour, which was about the time it would take him to gird himself to return to common sense again. But it would be a good hour. A memorable one.

That was the thing, he realized in the middle of the night. Why had he even bothered to go to America? It hadn't changed anything. He still felt trapped in a dark, locked room. But he spent one night at Bertie's—*one night*—and he was reminded that Pippa, of all people, could make him feel light again.

He was shocked and aghast. It made no sense. She was a lady. And she was Pippa, a real nuisance. But something about her made him question his plan to marry for duty and play with a mistress.

I'd love to play with Pippa. The thought came to him when he was naked and spread-eagled beneath soft, clean sheets. That ivory dress and the winking locket at the cleft of her breasts had driven him mad all evening. And she didn't want to marry him, either, so it wasn't as if he'd be breaking her heart if they *did* have a dalliance.

But there was Bertie. And duty. Gregory had promised to marry Pippa off properly. Only a selfish bastard would do anything else.

"Then I want to be a selfish bastard," he whispered aloud before he blew out the candle.

At about four in the morning, he finally fell into a deep sleep, and in his dreams he heard thumps and even a shouted, "No!" But he never woke until someone pushed at his door. Even then he opened only one eye. Someone was in the room. He could hear him snuffling about. A servant with a cold? Bending over the grate to add coal?

But then there were more snorts and snuffles and clickety-clacks all about the floor. He forced himself to roll over and face the door.

It was an invasion of corgis, and he remembered he was at Bertie's and that he mustn't have shut the door hard enough last night. The corgis had nudged their way in.

What did Pippa look like while she slept? He wished he could peek in her bedchamber to see—and to say good-bye one last time.

"Good thing you woke me," he said to the furry mass of bodies on the floor, and then stole a glance at the window. The day was overcast. With a sigh—because tonight he'd be late, damned late, to the house party—he reached for Uncle Bertie's timepiece on the bedside table. He'd given it to him last night, as a gift for taking care of Pippa.

"What do I need to look at the time for anyway?" Bertie had said. "Wear it on grand occasions. It's my lucky watch. I wore it when I first met your mother as a baby, and then years later, you and Pippa."

"Thank you." Gregory had clutched the orb of burnished gold in his fist.

Bertie got a wicked gleam in his eye. "I also suggest wearing it when Pippa gives you trouble."

"Then I suspect I shall don it frequently when she comes to Town," Gregory said dryly, and left to the sound of Bertie's laughter behind him.

Now he saw that it was ten-thirty. He cursed loudly enough to send the herd of corgis leaping in a frenzy of longing to climb the vast mountain that was his bed and become masters of it—and him.

But there were no bed steps, thank God.

He sat up, threw his legs over the side, and stretched his bare arms above his head, which reminded him of how Pippa had put her arms around his back and neck in Eliza's garden a year before and held on to him as if he were a runaway horse she wouldn't let go. He'd only remembered that later, when he was in his cabin of the ship sailing to America. Every night he was away from England, he'd thought about that kiss.

He'd have to stop thinking about it now—and of Pippa in her bed. Otherwise, he'd not be able to don his trousers.

But wet noses on his calves and his feet brought him back to perfectly sober thoughts. "I'm late," he told the gathered company, who were all ears and wagging tails.

He readied himself in a few minutes. His driver, Oscar, would be waiting impatiently, no doubt, Gregory's trunk strapped behind the carriage.

Nobody was in the breakfast room, and he stole out of the house quickly.

Once on the road, rain began to fall lightly—and then

harder—and he was glad for his dry seat. He wasn't worried about Oscar, either. They'd been on enough trips together that Gregory knew the man welcomed harsh weather as a challenge to his driving skills. He made sure Oscar's flask was always filled with the Marquess of Brady's finest Irish whiskey and that his driver's coat was of the best material available, with the large, flat gold buttons featuring the crest of Brady that Oscar loved to flaunt in every inn yard they entered. He couldn't boast any other way—the Sherwood family all traveled in unmarked coaches.

Gregory closed his eyes and hoped the horses were feeling spritely, that the road was smooth, and that the rain didn't uncover many rocks and form lakes instead of small puddles.

He rested in a gentle haze of napping—he'd lost sleep, after all, thinking of Pippa—until the rain beat so fiercely on the coach roof that he opened his eyes to look out the window. In the distance, trudging along the edge of a field, he saw a solitary figure, a boy or a young man with a large sack held over his shoulder, his top hat squashed flat by his hand as he held it on to his head, and shockingly without a greatcoat to protect him. He was bent, gusts of wind and rain pummeling him, and a more miserable creature Gregory had never seen.

He lowered the window and was promptly hit with slashing needles of rain.

"Oscar!" he bellowed. "Pick up that fellow, will you?"

"Right, my lord!" Oscar called back to him. "I'll sit 'im up here with me. I got a spare blanket under the seat!"

"Very well," Gregory yelled back. "But if he's too far gone, he can come in with me." He shut the window, glad to return to his cozy shelter.

The coach came to a halt, and Gregory knew that Oscar was standing up and waving his arms at the traveler.

The fellow lifted his head, pulled out a pair of spectacles, and shoved them on his nose. They appeared too large on his face and were surely useless, as he couldn't possibly see through them in the torrent.

"Get over here," Oscar cried. "Ride up here with me! We'll take you to the nearest town!"

The figure hesitated, then slowly began to plod in their direction. His shoulders drooped. He was exhausted, Gregory could see. His spectacles fell off, and he bent to pick them up. This time, he didn't bother to put them back on but held them in his fist.

"Hurry up—we don't have all day!" Oscar yelled to him. "I've got good, strong drink to warm you!"

The traveler tried his best to speed up, the bag on his back bouncing against his shoulders. *Nothing like the promise of a drink to warm you,* thought Gregory. *He's glad for the ride—and perhaps the company.*

How long had he been walking? And where was he headed?

Oscar jumped down from his seat onto the road and waited for the man to crawl over a stone wall. He limped the rest of the way to the coach, his face pale, his lips a bit blue. The lad couldn't have been more than eighteen or nineteen, and he had delicate features: an upturned nose, large eyes, and an expressive mouth. Gregory had no doubt he'd been teased about his looks by other boys. But his expression, especially about his eyes, was fierce enough.

"I'll help you," Oscar shouted to him through the deluge, and took his elbow.

The stranger stumbled.

Gregory slid over on the seat so he'd have a better view

of the side of the coach. Oscar gave the fellow a boost to the box—or tried to. The stranger fell right back down, obviously too weak to pull himself up.

That was enough to convince Gregory to open the window. "Come in here!" he cried. "In the coach with me!"

The fellow pushed his hat lower and shook his head no.

Oscar gave him a little shove. "Do what the earl tells you!" he yelled.

The man stupidly put his spectacles back on in the pouring rain.

"For the love of God, don't stand on ceremony!" Gregory threw open the door and waved with his hand. "Get in!"

With a strong push and a "Harrumph!" from Oscar, the young man half fell into the coach, streams of water running down his tailcoat, boots, hat, and even off his ears and onto the floor. Gregory was more than somewhat wet now himself, but it was still better to be inside than out in the elements. Oscar shoved his flask at him and Gregory pushed it back. "Save that for yourself, thanks. He can drink from mine." And then he pulled the door shut.

The traveler slumped into his seat, and his eyes rolled up in his head.

"Wait!" Gregory blindly reached under his seat for his flask.

But the stranger fell into a dead faint, his body slumping sideways on the tufted leather seat cushion. His hat and something brown and grotesque—resembling a flattened dead squirrel—fell off his head and onto the floor, revealing a crown of tightly pinned Titian-colored curls.

Chapter Four

Dear God, it was Pippa! Pippa in man's clothes! A surge of shock traveled the length of Gregory's body, and he cursed like the veriest sailor. What was she doing dressed as a man and walking through a rainstorm so far away from home? How had she gotten this far? What in the world had happened to her?

Her slender legs, encased in buff breeches and Hessian boots, and slanted across the edge of the seat, were completely immobile, but she was breathing evenly, thank God.

He tried not to notice whether her breasts were evident, but he couldn't help seeing that she'd managed to disguise her feminine figure completely.

The flask. He needed it *now*. For both of them.

With a sweep of his hand, he located it in the folds of a lap blanket and pulled the cork out with his teeth and took a quick swig.

Soaked as her clothes were, they gave the impression she was a successful secretary or accountant—or even an upper servant with the day off. Her brown-and-tan-striped cravat was a bit uncommon, but Gregory wasn't surprised she'd gone that route. She always wore at least one thing on her person that was eye-catching. The brown tailcoat and tan waistcoat, on the other hand, were perfectly un-exceptional.

Gently, he touched her temple and brushed a tendril of hair back. "Pippa, wake up."

Her eyes fluttered and opened. "Gregory," she said softly.

His name had never sounded so sweet. But a black fury rose in him, choking out the gratitude he felt that she was safe. *"What kind of foolish game are you playing?"*

She merely stared at him, water pooling under her cheek.

"Answer me, Pippa." Threat laced his words, but in-side, his heart knocked against his ribs. She looked so forlorn. A waif of a girl. And there she'd been, battling the elements on her own. Who knew what kind of stranger would have stopped to pick her up if he hadn't?

"Don't make me go back." Her voice cracked. "I beg of you."

Any man with three sisters and a loving mother knew the power of soothing words to a woman in distress. But he'd not reward her folly. He'd keep her alive—that was enough.

"How the hell did you get this far from home?"

"A farmer's wagon. But he dropped me off when he got where he needed to go."

"Here." Gregory's voice was gruff. "Let me help you sit up."

She made a move herself, but he took the burden off her by lifting her under her arms. She was like a rag doll, and his wrath increased.

"I suppose you're angry—" Her voice was thin.

"You guessed right."

They were close. And private. Like two lovers running away. But they weren't. Not by a long shot.

"Here." He handed her the flask. "Drink this. It will prevent another faint, and it will warm your bones."

Without hesitation, she took the vessel from him, lifted it high, and poured some in her mouth. Instantly, her cheeks grew round and she waved a hand in front of her face.

"Swallow it," he urged her.

Her eyes, already made large by the elfin hairstyle, widened further.

"Pippa."

She stared at him as if she were ingesting poison, swallowed loudly, and sputtered, her fingers clenching her throat.

Ah, she was such a girl! But he'd not pity her. No, indeed. "Dress like a man—expect to act like one." His brogue came out along with his temper.

"Good heavens." She inhaled a great breath through her nose and wiped her hand across her mouth. "I pity the brute creatures who enjoy such vile stuff."

She reached for the door, and he caught her by the wrist.

"Oh, no you won't." He pivoted her unyielding arm onto her lap. The straight line of her back and her narrowed eyes spoke volumes, but that was her problem, not his. "You'll have more." His tone brooked no argument. "You're shivering."

She leaned forward, her mouth a straight line, her eyes snapping with her own fury. "I'd rather *die* than have more."

He got nose to nose with her. "You just might—if you don't."

They stared steely-eyed at each other, and he was glad to see her angry. It would get the blood moving through her veins almost as well as the whiskey would.

"Very well," she muttered, "if it will mean you leave me alone and I may be on my way."

He tried not to show his obvious triumph when she drank from the flask again with an unsteady hand and let out a long breath. "Are you happy now?" She winced and handed it back to him.

"You're welcome." If she was looking for more comfort, he wasn't going to offer it. Of course, he was fall-on-his-knees happy that she was coming back to life with a vengeance, but she didn't deserve to know this, not when she was wrecking all his plans. "I'll be sure to tell the marquess you send him your highest compliments. He says it's an old Brady recipe handed down by the leprechauns."

"In that case." She beckoned with her index finger for another taste—and then another. "I feel better now. I *think*." She thrust the silver vessel back at him. "Thanks to your father. And the leprechauns."

Not you, was the unspoken sentiment.

He corked the flask and left it on his seat. "You need to change clothes."

"I can't," she said immediately. "I'm off again."

"Over my dead body."

She made a moue of impatience. "Dammit all, Gregory! I've already felled one man today. Don't make me do the same to you."

"Hah. As if—" And then her words hit him *"What did you say?"* She couldn't be serious.

Her eyes became shuttered. "It's a long story."

"And you'll tell it." He was already burning to exact vengeance on whoever had forced her to defend herself and then run away. "If you're hurt—"

He'd kill the man. Plain and simple.

"Of course I'm not hurt," she said scornfully.

In the midst of his stone-cold anger, he admired—and was touched by—her show of bravado. "Was it someone you met on the road? Or—it wasn't that damned Hawthorne, was it? Give me the name. *Now*."

"Hawthorne," she said, "but—"

It was as if she'd thrown a match onto dry straw. "That sorry—"

"And the Toad—Mr. Trickle—helped him. They wanted him to carry me off."

Gregory saw red. Those conniving bastards! He'd enjoy every moment of thrashing Hawthorne until he ran from Plumtree with his tail between his legs. Unfortunately, Trickle had to stay in the equation for Lady Helen's sake, but Gregory would be sure to make life miserable for him.

"You must change clothes," he said. "I promise I won't look. And no one will ever know. When you're situated comfortably again, we'll discuss what we're going to do."

He wrenched open her sturdy canvas sack. Thankfully, the items folded loosely inside—two shirts, two white cravats, a tailcoat, a waistcoat, a pair of pantaloons, a pair of men's shoes, and three pairs of stockings—were dry.

"I can't change clothes," she said. "Not with you here."

"Surely you don't expect me to wait outside in that deluge."

"But it's not proper."

He sighed. "There's a time for proper, and a time for common sense."

She looked fretfully out the window. "It *is* pouring cats and dogs."

"Yes, it is."

She still said nothing.

"I told you I won't look," he reminded her.

"Well—"

"I dare you," he said. "Take off all your clothes, and if you do, I'll—"

"You'll what?"

"I'll buy you a hot beef pie at the next inn."

"You will?" Her face brightened like the sun.

"Of course. And then we'll change horses and turn around so I can scare Mr. Trickle near to death and beat the daylights out of Hawthorne."

"I've already taken care of Hawthorne. And we can't turn around." She folded her arms over her chest. "I'll only take off my clothes if you'll let me stay."

"No." He couldn't help feeling a stirring of lust when she so blithely referenced taking off her clothes.

They stared at each other again, at an impasse.

He leaned forward, his elbows on his thighs. "Listen to me, you stubborn girl," he whispered fiercely. "You'll take off your clothes, or I'll take them off for you."

Her face blanched, but her chin came up. "I'll do it myself," she uttered like the scrapper he knew she was. "And fie on the man who thinks he can take a peek and live to tell the tale."

The whiskey was having its effect. He wanted to laugh, but he daren't. He pretended her threat carried weight. She deserved that bit of dignity. After all, they were about to flout society's rules in the worst possible way.

"Here." He held up the blanket in front of his face,

relieved he could relax his smoldering expression. "Do it now. I can't see a thing."

"Hmmm . . . everything?" From the other side of the woolly barrier, she suddenly sounded more like the old friend she'd always been before that day in the garden. Perhaps she couldn't maintain the tension, either, when there were practical matters to be sorted out. "My breeches aren't too bad."

"They're soaked straight through," he said. "Why didn't you take a greatcoat?"

"I'd little time, and I'd no idea it would rain. It swoops in sometimes, off the sea, without warning. Are you going to ask me if I brought a snuffbox next?"

"No."

"Well, I did." She sounded distinctly triumphant. "Quite a masculine one, too, with horses prancing on the front—one has his foot on a serpent."

"I'll hold the blanket up all day if I have to until you get dressed, so no more delays. We'll discuss your escape when you're dry again."

"It wasn't an *escape*," she insisted, making a few breathy noises. He assumed she was working on removing her coat, which he'd noticed was particularly tight. "I had nothing to fear back home other than the Toad and his wily ways, but I could have taken him on and won. No, what happened this morning merely inspired me to go forward with my plan to go to Paris much sooner than I'd anticipated."

"Right," he said dryly. "You'll tell me the details of this plan. I insist."

"Perhaps I will—but only when I feel like it. Don't condescend to me, Gregory. Do you know anything about fate?"

"I know it's fickle. Like women." He heard more signs of a struggle. "Trouble with your coat?"

"Yes, blast it. And women are only fickle with you because you're fickle, too. Haven't you figured that out yet? There was a cartoon of you in the London papers recently. Did you see it?"

"No. I avoid the gossip rags."

"Well, you were striding down the gangplank of a ship—shirtless, mildly drunk, a lovesick young lady of the *ton* on either side of you, a lustful look in your eye, a scrap of paper with a draftsman's sketch of a fragmented heart upon it in your hand, and a banner above your head proclaiming, 'The Ignoble Architect of Disappointed Hopes Returns.' The message was clear: Respectable young ladies are not to lose their hearts to you."

"You're awfully nosy about my affairs." He tossed the blanket aside. "Let me."

She held out an arm. "*Just* the sleeves, my lord. And I'm not nosy. Can I help it that everywhere I turn, there's a new, scandalous story about you?"

He gave the outstretched cuff a good tug. "So now I'm back to being the rakehell, eh? The one you must warn off."

"Where there's smoke, there's fire," she said airily, "as you proved in Eliza's garden—"

"And you were there, too, kissing me back, right under your friend's nose." The sharp, back-and-forth movement of her body toward and away from him as he tugged was doing nothing to help him detach from his recognition that she was all woman beneath her manly garb.

"I might have," she said, "but I wasn't myself. I regret that now—a great deal, I assure you."

"*I* don't." He enjoyed hearing her phony gasp. She

knew damned well he didn't regret it. "But I did think the whole deliciously wicked episode behind me."

"It wasn't delicious!" she insisted.

"Are you sure about that?" He stared her down a few heated seconds until she looked away. "As I was saying . . . I thought it was behind me, yet here you are, dressed as a man in my carriage when I'm on my way to a house party to which *you're* not invited."

"If I'd known it was you—"

"Don't tell me you wouldn't have gotten in. We both know your survival instincts outweigh your pride."

"Yes, they do—which is why I'd have run in the opposite direction had I known this was the Brady carriage. A haystack would have served me just as well till the storm died down."

"I'd like to throw you in a haystack right now and leave you there with your beloved field mice. It would serve you right."

She didn't seem to hear him. "Damn my fragile sensibilities. They're to blame. Seeing you made my heart lurch. In terror, of course. And just like in a bad dream, my knees turned to jelly—and I couldn't run. Or I would have."

Imp. "Am I like Frankenstein, then?"

"Nearly," she said with enthusiasm tempered by agitation.

Both were good to see. They meant the blood was flowing down to the tips of her toes. He yanked sharply on her sleeve—which seemed to get tighter and more slippery the more he worked on it—and refused to remark on her answer to the Frankenstein question.

See what she made of that.

"Well, you're a man without a heart, at the very least,"

she said into the silence. Was it guilt making her tone uncertain?

"I am, aren't I?" He gave a long pull, and the sleeve moved forward a good four inches. "Would that you never forget." He stopped pulling and did his best to look as if he were the most menacing man on earth, one who'd crush her heart under his feet were she sorry enough to ever fall in love with him again.

It was all true. So it wasn't difficult.

Her pupils widened, but he went straight back to work on her sleeves, pretending he hadn't noticed the frisson of worry etched into her brow.

"There," he said when she was finally free.

"Thank you." She gave a little shiver. And no wonder. Beneath leather braces holding up her pantaloons, she was sheathed in a voluminous shirt that was also soaked through and clinging to her skin. Underneath that was a swath of white fabric binding her breasts.

Too well, he couldn't help thinking in the rakehellish recesses of his brain.

She wrapped her arms around herself. "Please get behind the blanket again."

"Yes, madam." He held the makeshift curtain back up. "Let's finish this off promptly."

"Uncle Bertie's trunks are filled with costumes," she said, and then her voice came to him muffled: "I've played with them for years." Her hands grappled with bunches of the shirt over her head, and then her head must have popped out because her next words were clear. "I'm rather expert," she added proudly, and dangled the sodden garment over the top edge of the blanket, where it landed on the floor.

As both his hands were occupied, he'd have to wait to shove the blasted thing under the seat. No use opening the door to wring it out, either—the sheets of rain came steadily on.

"Unwind the band of cloth," he said. "We'll need to dry it out."

She paused. "I shouldn't."

"You'll be wearing a shirt and a coat, remember."

"True," she said hopefully. "And it's not as if I'm . . ." She trailed off.

"Go on and take it off," he said, ignoring her implication. She might not be bursting out of her bodice as so many fashionable women were, but she was proportioned like a Greek goddess and exceedingly tempting, exactly the way she was. In fact, her modest gowns drove him mad with wanting to see more, to feel more, as he'd done once before—but only barely before the kiss had abruptly ended. "You're uncomfortable, surely."

"I am." She blew out a sigh and began the process of rendering her upper half naked.

The sound of the cloth unwrapping was subtle but audible, and Gregory felt an overwhelming urge to sneak a peek. Just one little glance over the edge. If she were looking down, she wouldn't even notice, would she?

But of course, he wouldn't succumb to temptation. *You're a gentleman,* his conscience chided him.

He hated his bloody conscience.

A few tortured seconds later, Pippa held a straggly bundle of cloth stripping over the blanket.

"Drop it," he said.

It landed on his boot with a squishy sound.

"I need a new dry shirt." Panic laced her words. "And coat. Please hurry."

Oh, how a man's mind could turn to mush in the presence of a near naked woman! But she was a naked, *cold* woman, and he had an obligation to help her. "You'll need to hold this side of the blanket then." He jiggled the left corner.

When she took it, he reached behind him and passed the dry shirt to her free hand over the barrier. They switched ownership of the blanket corner, and seconds later, she'd donned the new shirt.

The same maneuver took place with the coat. It was a bloody circus act they had going. He was the lion—she was the vulnerable maiden.

"Better?" he asked after a moment of hearing her struggle—the blanket was rippling with her efforts.

"Better." Finally, she pushed the woolen barrier down.

Anxiety hovered about her eyes and mouth, but in her dry jacket and shirt, she already looked vastly improved: alert, robust, even alluring—as if she'd taken a cold shower under a waterfall and had been rubbed down with a towel and put before a fire. It was entirely charming of her to appear so well, considering she was in a damp carriage and still wearing drenched pantaloons.

"It feels good to have the top half of me warm again," she said, but her teeth knocked against her words, like tiny hammers.

He hid his concern with a steady gaze. "Let's get the bottom half the same way. I'm going to remove your boots."

"I can do it myself."

"Allow me," he said. "While I remove them, why don't you wrap up in the blanket?"

"All right," she said, sounding a bit nervous.

He lifted one slender calf—he refused to think of it as

sweet—and the boot came off with a tremendous sucking sound, followed by a long trickle of water.

"It's like the Flood in here," she muttered.

When their eyes met, he was glad to see a small twinkle in hers. It sent warmth rushing to the vicinity of his heart—a very unwelcome rush.

"The other," he reminded her as if she were a wayward soldier, and her expression dimmed.

Good. They didn't need to be friendly. Not when he was in possession of her leg. If he followed its trail, it would lead him to a forbidden place he had no business thinking of at all. In fact, he was so thoroughly disgusted with himself, when he lifted her calf, he was a little too quick and her toes snagged the underside of his thigh.

"Sorry," she whispered.

He sent her a silent glance replete with disapproval and tried to be satisfied that no water came out of the second boot.

"I'll do the rest," she offered.

"Let me get your stockings," he said. "Sit back"—*far, far back*—"and stay warm."

She didn't question him this time, and her cheeks flushed when he began the task of peeling her sopping wet hose off. He had to work very hard not to attribute any suggestion of intimacy to the action. Her ankle was splendid, her flesh a healthy pale pink, but her feet when they appeared were faintly blue.

He rubbed them hard with his hands, and she giggled outright.

He paused. "Ticklish?"

She put the tip of a thumbnail up to her mouth. "Yes."

Her toes still weren't the color they should be, so he

lifted both her feet and laid them flat against his shirt, then wrapped his coat around them.

"You can't do that!" she squeaked.

He shrugged a shoulder. "Just warming them up." He looked at the roof of the carriage. Gave a little whistle, then gazed out a window for some thirty seconds.

"This must be uncomfortable for you," she said, still sounding anxious.

"Yes, it's like having two blocks of ice against my chest, but they're warming up, little by little, aren't they?"

"Yes," she whispered. "But really, you shouldn't. You really, *really* shouldn't."

With every passing second, the encounter was getting cozier and cozier, especially when she burrowed her toes deeper into the linen fabric, inadvertently massaging his nipples. The minx. She had no idea how those two blocks of ice were turning into instruments of torture of a different kind.

"I'll endure," he said, his eyes on a lonely outcrop of rocks on a distant portion of the moor.

"I should be sorry for you, I know, but this is *heaven,*" she exclaimed. "Much better than a warm brick."

He turned to see that she wore a blissful look on her face. If she thought this was heaven, she knew little of men and women and the things that happened between them.

Low on her seat, utterly relaxed, her wet hair curling about her face, she might have spoken with all the pure sincerity of an angel, but she was beginning to look too much like a hoyden for her own good.

"Right, then. They're warm now." He opened his coat for entirely selfish reasons. He had to get rid of her—the sooner, the better. Lady Pippa Harrington was far more dangerous than he was, if only she knew.

As if to prove his point, she removed her feet from his chest only with a great deal of reluctance and a long, feminine sigh.

"And now"—he reached beneath the seat again and took a long swig of Father's whiskey to numb the fire building in his groin—"you'll change out of your pantaloons."

Chapter Five

"No," Pippa told Gregory firmly. She drew the line at pantaloons.

"You must."

He'd never looked quite like this before. Was he feverish? In pain? Surely he wasn't sleepy. He looked as though someone had given him a witch's potion that was either going to make him very sleepy or very *naughty*.

"Don't even think of it," she warned him, even as her heart beat faster remembering their kiss in the garden.

"Of what?" He suddenly looked perfectly sane again.

"We're done with changing clothes." She enunciated clearly to remind herself that she was strong-willed and no one could stop her from going to Paris, especially not Gregory.

He shook his head. "You need to be dry."

"I can't. I—I really can't take off these pantaloons. So please. Don't ask."

He stared at her a moment, and then a knowing look passed over his face, disappearing so swiftly, she could have imagined it. "I understand," he murmured. "If we wrap the blanket around your legs, that should help warm you."

And then it dawned on her. He thought—he thought she had her courses! How would he know about those? She supposed unmarried men did, but where did they find out? No one had told her anything about hers, not even Mother. She'd told Pippa she'd be visited by a special fairy each month when she got older, and it had been terribly disappointing to find out what that fairy was.

"It's not what you think," she blurted out.

"I don't think anything." His face was placid. The perfect gentleman's face.

"Yes you do! But you're wrong. The truth is"—she was avid to confess; anything was better than the embarrassing assumption he'd made now—"I'm not wearing drawers. We don't do that in the country. You city people might—I hear they're quite fashionable, but why make more laundry?"

"*That's* why you won't change your pantaloons?"

She nodded miserably. "I thought you'd be aghast."

"But *I* don't wear drawers, either," he said, the edge of a smile gracing his lips—a very attractive smile—"so don't be embarrassed."

"Y-you don't?"

"Of course not." He gave a chuckle low in his throat. "Only the high sticklers do."

Oh, dear. This was a most intimate conversation. "I thought you were one." She looked at one of his coat buttons.

"Only when I'm at Court. You seem to be forgetting—I did much of my growing up at Ballybrook in Ireland, out in the country." He leaned forward again. "So no excuses. Off with the pantaloons." He reached into the bag, pulled out another pair, and placed them on the back of her seat.

This time when he put the blanket between them, her

head buzzed with outrageous images. She shouldn't be thinking of Gregory with no drawers, but she was. She thought of him sliding into his own pantaloons that very morning at Uncle Bertie's. Had he simply rolled out of bed naked? Or did he wear a nightshirt?

Slowly, her knees butting the blanket, she unfastened her braces and shimmied out of her pantaloons, nudging them with her bare toes to Gregory's side of the floor.

Good God, she felt exposed, even with the blanket, the long shirt, and the tailcoat.

"Your hair," he said gamely, still holding up the blanket. "How did you manage that?"

She couldn't help a little smile. He was doing his best to distract her. Half sitting, half standing, she donned the new pantaloons and attached them to her braces—they did feel wonderful, and he'd been right. She'd needed dry clothes.

She peered over the edge of her little fortress. "I've several wigs, thank goodness. The one I used today will have to dry out." She gave a little laugh. "We've no more need of the blanket, by the way."

His eyes lit up. "Very good." He tossed it aside. "It is officially retired after having spent several minutes in worthy service to an excellent cause."

"Will it get a pension?" She resumed her seat.

"No. I'm afraid it's not covered." He arched one brow.

"That was an awful joke. But thank you for your help and the beef pie you're soon to purchase for me. Are we almost there?"

"Soon." He handed her dry stockings and the spare shoes. "A half hour. You can stay in the carriage while we change horses."

"I told you, I'm not going back home." She donned the stockings and shoes then reached across the space between them and got her canvas bag from his seat. Rummaging through it, she pulled out another wig, along with a brush and a small jar of pomade. And then she began to pull the remaining loose pins out of her hair. She would repin her curls. She didn't need a looking glass, either.

Gregory smirked. "Surely you don't think you'll get away with this disguise for longer than a minute or two. Your face is too delicate to pass for a man's. I noticed instantly that you appeared effeminate."

"The spectacles help a little," she insisted. "And I'm wearing rather high collars. Plus, I'm a good actress. It's in my blood. I can walk and talk like a man, with just the right amount of confidence that people simply feel sorry for me that I'm not more hearty, like you. I already have a story concocted about how I spent several years of my childhood in bed with a wasting disease that was miraculously cured when I began to eat carrots, I think. Or maybe I drank goat's milk. I haven't decided."

"That's ridiculous."

"If I act as if I believe it, so will everyone else. Same with my being a man." She shivered as she laid pins on the seat beside her. Yes, she felt oodles better than she had when wet, but she was tired and hungry. She just wanted to curl up in bed with an enormous quilt over her and fall asleep.

"Leave your damned hair alone." Gregory patted the seat beside him. "Come here and rest against my shoulder a moment. I can't give you any more whiskey, but we have the blanket."

She hesitated, a rolled-up curl between her fingers.

"It's your chance to get warm all the way through," he said.

Which was exactly what she needed. So she switched

over without a word, and he tucked the blanket around them both.

"Hold on to me," he said.

Dare she? At the moment, all she wanted was a warm place to burrow and think of nothing. Tentatively, she wrapped her arms around him, and he did the same for her, his chin on her head. There was instant, glorious heat between them—exactly what she required.

"I *am* angry, Pippa." His voice resonated somewhere near her temple, and her eyelids drooped. "You should have come to me when you found yourself in the position you did and not run off harum-scarum. As soon as you've recovered, we've got to return you home. I'll take care of the mess there, I promise."

Oh, but this feels like home, she thought, and before she could worry about the complications that presented, she fell fast asleep.

Chapter Six

Pippa was wrapped in a delicious cocoon of warmth. She didn't want to wake. She snuggled closer and sensed it was Gregory. She'd dreamed of being with him like this—safe, on their own. Together in the same place all the time rather than once a year.

This was better than making sugar sculptures. Better than Christmas morning. This was . . .

Wait—was she really with the last man on earth she needed to see?

Panic assailed her, and her eyes flew open. She was looking straight into his coat. And if she turned her head a tad, she saw a carriage seat. *His* carriage seat.

It all came back to her in a horrifying—if somewhat mesmerizing and occasionally pleasurable—rush.

He'd rescued her from the rainstorm. She'd not been worried about the brooding clouds, but when the cold, lacerating sweeps of rain pelted her without cease, it took more out of her than she'd imagined a rainstorm could.

And when she'd entered the coach and realized who he was—

Well, it was the shock of it that made her faint, even more than the chill and damp and her sheer exhaustion.

She disentangled herself by pushing against his chest, and then she sat up, blinking. It was awful being awake. She wanted to go back into that lovely dream world . . .

"We've arrived at the inn," he said in a no-nonsense voice. "I gave you a few more minutes to sleep while Oscar went ahead to get things ready for us."

"Thank you." She didn't want to look at him. She felt shy, knowing that they'd been wrapped like lovers in a tight embrace.

"You're going to put on a fresh cravat," he said, pulling one out of her bag. "Shall I tie it?"

"Absolutely not," she said with a sniff. "I'm quite adept at the Waterfall. I tie Uncle Bertie's all the time."

"Fine." He handed it to her. "Then you'll slap a dry wig on, put your unfortunately soggy hat on top of it, hold the blanket over your head to stave off the rain—at least it appears to be tapering off—and go right to a private parlor for a meal. It doesn't appear to be crowded, so you should be fine. We'll stay less than an hour and turn around."

"Gregory, I *told* you, I'm not going back. It will be the same old thing—Uncle Bertie wanting me to marry you. Nothing else seems to matter." Her mouth tipped up in a teasing smile. "You could put me out of my misery at any time, you know."

He shook his head. "You'd hate to be married to me."

"I'd hate to be married to *anyone*," she said.

"Well"—Gregory couldn't help leaning closer to her—"you'd especially hate being married to *me*."

He spoke with such great conviction, their gazes locked in mutual recognition of the solemnity of the moment. She could tell he was thinking of the same thing she was: the childish drawing she'd made of him that ill-fated day, the one with the heart. He'd no idea she'd been infatuated with him until that moment.

"Stay away from me, my lady," he said, leaning even closer to emphasize his point. "If you need a reminder, why, merely revisit that cartoon."

"Good advice," she replied. "According to Uncle Bertie's friends in London, no one's quite sure what you got up to in America and are having a rum time discussing it while you cut a swath through society. Rumors abound. Were you living with natives? Consorting with the criminal element? Leaving a trail of cuckolded husbands throughout the former colonies?"

"It doesn't matter," he said. "The point is, I'm not good for you. Someday I'll marry, of course. It's my duty to the House of Brady. But I'm not one for finer feelings. And if you think I speak lightly, you're wrong."

"No," she admitted, "I can see you're not the same man you were before Eliza threw you over."

"Good of you to remind me that I had no say in the matter."

"But there are other changes, too," she said excitedly, ignoring his bid for pity. "You're a year older, for one. You must have worked hard in America. Your shoulders are broader, and your face has filled out. You look more of a man."

"Do I?" He got that look in his eye again, the one that reminded her that she must be careful or she could wind up kissing him again.

"Yes."

"Those are rather superficial changes, aren't they?"

"Very well, I'll go deeper." She looked him straight in the eye. "The truth is, your gaze is bitter. Your mouth is hard, too—although I saw glimpses of darkness in you well before—"

"I was thrown over by Eliza," he finished for her.

"Exactly." She paused. "We haven't talked about it in years. You won't let me."

"For good reason. There's nothing to say. Pardon the observation, but you've always been fanciful, my lady. You see me only once a year. Your analysis of my person and character can't be very accurate."

"Seeing someone only rarely can heighten one's powers of observation," she said. "What I've remarked on is true. And it's a shame."

"If that's so, then you're only proving my point: I'm someone you should steer clear of on the marriage mart."

"With all due respect, my lord"—she arched a brow—"I wasn't suggesting you marry *me* when I suggested you put me out of my misery."

"And you wonder why your uncle calls you cheeky?"

She chuckled and began pinning her hair. "Marry someone—anyone else. I don't care." Her tone was matter-of-fact. "Then Uncle Bertie will be forced to stop this pitiful ritual."

She stuck a pin through a curl and looked at him with clear eyes while she formed another.

"I see," Gregory said into the silence.

Pippa smiled softly, apologetically. "Not every woman wants to be Lady Westdale, future Marchioness of Brady, you know."

"You're making *that* very clear."

"But I'm sure a good many of them do," she encouraged him. "Perhaps you could go wed one—the sooner, the better."

"Right," he said briskly. "While I appreciate your advice, I won't be taking it. Now let's go inside."

Pippa put on her spectacles and followed him out of the carriage. The sudden whoosh of a wind gust hit her as her feet touched the ground, but she quickly grabbed the brim of her hat and regained her footing. She heard a chuckle from Gregory.

Good thing he didn't offer to help me, she thought with a toss of her head. *I'm supposed to be a man, after all.*

Just as her surprise travel partner had promised, a beef pie was set before Pippa by a barman who also brought her a mug of hot milk—and for Gregory, a pint of ale.

She took off her spectacles and inhaled the steam curling up from the pie. "I'm famished," she said.

"Eat." Gregory had his own pie to consume.

They both dug in with equal gusto. Oh, it was good to get some warm food into her belly! She'd hardly had a morsel last night. She never could when Gregory was there. Just looking at him made her a bit sick to her stomach. Not that he was ugly. Or disgusting.

Quite the opposite.

She was unused to seeing such a splendid specimen of manhood up close. Yes, she'd counted four handsome, brawny young fishermen in the village closest to Uncle Bertie's, and they'd each leered at her every time she walked by their boats (much to her secret satisfaction), but not one of them held a candle to Gregory.

She tried not to notice the broad shoulders and muscular upper arms his coat couldn't disguise—but it was no use. "Have you ever lifted a fishing net?" she asked him.

"No, but I pulled up lobster pots in New England with no trouble."

She had no doubt of it.

"Why do you ask?" He cocked his head the way he always did when she puzzled him.

"No reason." She felt herself flush with that odd feeling again and was glad the barman brought them a plate of cheese and sliced apples to distract them both.

"Uncle Bertie and your mother must be extremely concerned about your absence." Gregory made a sandwich of two apple slices with a piece of cheese in the middle and ate it in one bite.

"I left them a note explaining that I'll be perfectly safe and taken care of—" She nibbled on her own apple slice.

"Do you have money?"

She swallowed. "Not yet. But I've a plan—"

"You and your plan. What is it, exactly?"

She sighed. "I'll tell you, but don't you dare make fun of it."

"I won't."

She did her best to skewer him with a warning look, but he didn't seem at all perturbed or frightened. He was his usual self, gazing at her with a closed expression that revealed occasional flickers of emotion—whether he was amused or bemused by her, she didn't know.

"I'm going," she began darkly—

"To Paris," he filled in impatiently. "I think you should wear a sign on your back to let the whole world know."

She thumped the handle end of her fork on the table. "I told you not to make fun. I'm not one of your sisters to tease or mock."

He leaned forward on folded arms. "You're definitely not my sister"—his blue eyes gazed deeply into her own—"to tease. Or mock."

She felt a flutter near her heart when his pupils dilated

and something else appeared in his expression, something that held them locked into place and made her forget everything but him and the funny way her heart was beating.

"Start over," he said. "This time you can be sure I won't say a disparaging word."

"Right, then," she said, and gathered her courage, because speaking her dream out loud required it. "I touched upon this last night. I'm going to serve as a companion to a friend of Uncle Bertie's. But on my days off, I want to learn sugar sculpture at the feet of the greatest confectioner of them all, Monsieur Perot."

She was so relieved to see that Gregory didn't laugh. In fact, his brow furrowed, as if he were taking her seriously. Really thinking about it. It warmed her heart. Made her want to kiss him. Out of gratitude, of course— nothing else. She'd have kissed a pig right then if it had oinked its approval of her plan.

"Pippa—"

"What?"

"This Monsieur Perot won't allow a woman in his kitchens." He didn't seem to mind telling her.

"I'm not stupid," she said, feeling her temper rise. "I'll be disguised."

Gregory leaned back in his chair. "He'll know. First squeak out of you when you bang your thumb with a rolling pin, and you'll be gone."

"I don't squeak, especially when I'm in my man costume," she concluded firmly, and ate a slice of apple with a great deal of determination.

"He may not take you," Gregory said, "even if he believes you're a man. I'm sure he acquires students from fine houses, hotels, and bakeries. In other words, via references."

"I'll use *you* as a reference," she said.

"You will, won't you? You're that brazen."

She nodded, and ate a piece of cheese. If only he knew *how* brazen.

He crossed his arms and looked sternly at her. "You can't think Bertie will read your note from this morning and just let you swan off to France."

She took a gulp of milk and wiped her hand across her mouth. "Of course, he doesn't know I'm going to *Paris*. That's too obvious a destination. Not that he could run after me, in any case. He's not a good traveler these days."

"Then what did you say in the note?"

She stared at him, dreading this moment.

"Pippa?" His eyes flashed with suspicion.

She clutched her fingers in her lap and prayed. "I told him I ran off with *you*."

Chapter Seven

Pippa's confession shouldn't have surprised Gregory, but it did. He was reeling from it, in fact. He pushed back his chair and stood. "You didn't."

Because if she did, life as he knew it was over.

It was bad enough that he was traveling alone with her by accident—some might even say he'd saved her life by picking her up alongside the road and would forgive him for ignoring the proprieties—but to be traveling with her alone *on purpose*? The two of them supposedly running away together?

Bertie, of course, would be ecstatic. He'd even think that their talk of the night before—where Gregory had agreed to take over responsibility for Pippa's marital prospects—had played a part.

He'd have to marry her, for certain. His carefully guarded secret would be in jeopardy. And his plan to do his duty whatever the cost would be in tatters because one didn't do one's duty around Pippa. One broke the rules. Or ran across meadows or sang silly songs—or laughed.

One lived. And loved.

"See?" Pippa said, her face stricken. "I told you my

getting in your carriage was a very bad idea. I tried to escape, but you wouldn't let me."

"Of course I wouldn't let you." He began to pace the floor. "No person in their right mind would have let you." He paused and remembered with whom he was dealing. "I know I deserve this." He felt calmer. In control again. "For ignoring your letter in Savannah. For kissing you last year. This is a massive joke, isn't it, to bring me down a notch?"

"No, Gregory." Pippa closed her eyes and massaged her temples. "I am *not* joking. I really did say I was running away with you."

Bloody hell. It was as if he were watching himself from afar, and he was flailing.

And *failing*.

Dammit, every time he went to Uncle Bertie's, the world as he knew it turned upside down. But it wasn't Bertie. Every time Gregory was around *Pippa* something happened—something beyond his control. And inevitably, at the end of the day, he felt as if his own life were missing a vital ingredient.

He was still that young man sitting on the sofa while Pippa came inside with a field mouse trapped inside her closed hands, only to let it loose on the carpet.

"I—I didn't have much time," she explained. "I supposed Mr. Trickle would make sure Hawthorne was able to sneak out, and they'd deny everything if I told Uncle Bertie what had happened. So I had to write something that would be a believable reason for my running away. And it couldn't inspire worry in Uncle Bertie or Mother. You were the perfect solution."

He raked a hand through his hair. "I couldn't let you out in that rain—"

"You should have. Because the worst thing in the world is for us to be caught together. We'll have to marry if anyone discovers us traveling alone."

"But you"—his temper was getting the better of him—"you already told Bertie we ran off!"

"I asked him not to mention it to anyone yet, that as we'd decided we were desperately in love, after all, we craved privacy. I specifically requested that he not write your family—at least not until we come home from our six-month honeymoon in Italy."

"Italy?"

"I insist on going to Italy on my honeymoon," she said airily. "I will sit on a stone wall in the sunshine and eat pears and drink wine."

He sent her the drollest look in his arsenal of expressions.

"I confessed to him that your parents believed you'd gone off on one of your usual bachelor jaunts abroad. But of course, we're actually together." She felt a bit dizzy with the knowledge. "So now the whole situation looks very damning."

"I should say so. What if Bertie reads about me in the gossip rags over the next six months—which I plan to spend in London—and puts two and two together, that this is an awful lie?"

"He doesn't read the papers anymore," she said. "They give him a headache. And you never write, so . . ." She looked away.

He felt a pang of guilt. "So your story had an excellent chance of ringing true."

"Exactly." She sent him a sideways look with those large hazel eyes of hers, an entirely feminine pose that should have looked ridiculous on her in her cravat and coat but served somehow to make him hot with lust for her instead.

"I'm taking you back home." He wouldn't think about removing that ugly hat, unpinning her curls, and kissing her senseless.

"You can't *do* that." She spun away from him on her chair and faced the fire.

"Yes I can." He picked up his mug and drained his ale. "Bertie will understand when he hears what happened. There will be no repercussions, other than those to be suffered by Mr. Hawthorne and Mr. Trickle at my hands, and things will be back as they should be. I'll go to my house party, and in two weeks, I'll be back to take you to London."

She looked over her shoulder, her eyes shining with stubborn determination. "If you take me back to Plum-tree, I'll merely slip away again. You needn't worry about my having enough money. I'm hocking my father's ruby earrings."

"Pippa."

"I don't care," she said. "He was infatuated with Mother when she was on stage, but it wore off quickly when he married her and the scandal got to be too much for him. He essentially washed his hands of her. And me."

"So I've heard." Guilt burned in his chest. All these years he'd done the same thing—washed his hands of Pippa.

And it was inexcusable.

He would watch over her well now. If one thing had changed in him in America, it was his willingness to ad-mit that he'd taken the people in his life back home for granted. They might not be able to care for him if they knew the truth—but there was nothing stopping him from caring for *them*.

"Luckily," she went on stoically, "Uncle Bertie was a better man than his nephew, and when my father left, he took us both in." She shrugged a shoulder. "So I don't feel I owe my father anything. He was as bad a husband as Mr. Trickle. I don't mind in the least selling his earrings to pay my way to Paris."

"As much satisfaction as pawning those earrings might bring you, you're a woman alone. It's absurd."

"A man," she reminded him.

"You're not a man," he said low. "And as soon as another man finds that out, you'll be in danger. This makes no sense—"

"Some of the best ideas don't." She pushed aside the plate of apples and cheese and stood.

He came round to her and gently grasped her upper arms. "I promised Bertie," he said in his most reasonable voice, although he felt far from reasonable around her. The scent of her—even the defiant way she threw back her shoulders and lowered her brows at him—brought out the illogic in him.

"You're not my keeper." Her eyes flashed with resentment.

"Actually, I am," he said, "and what you're proposing is preposterous."

"Easy for you to say." She wrenched herself away and straightened her coat. "You get to do anything you want. Do you know how difficult it is to be a woman?"

"Of course not," he said. "But that's your lot, and it's just as difficult to be a man. You'll find *that* out in Paris."

"Good." Her tone was arch. "You're already imagining me there."

"*Au contraire.* I'm not imagining you in the City of Love at all." He looked out the window at all the puddles left behind by the deluge. "You're swimming in dangerous waters, young lady, right here in England."

She made a face. "You can't make me stay."

"I can, and I will." He went over and bolted the door.

She crossed her arms over her man's coat. "So you got a private room to entrap me?"

"The last thing I want to do is be here—in this room—with you." The two of them alone in a room together had always spelled *trouble*. He folded his arms and tried to stare her down.

"Good." She glared right back. "Then we're agreed. Because I feel the same way about *you*."

"We'll stay ten more minutes," he said in an even tone, although his temper was getting the better of him. "Ten more. Until you accept your lot with a modicum of surrender. A *modicum*. That's all I ask. And then I'll unbolt the door."

"I'm not going to surrender, no matter what. So what are we going to do for ten minutes?"

Oh, he knew it was wrong. But she annoyed him mightily, the stubborn little spitfire, and he was cold and tired—and she looked outrageous in that cravat. So he yanked one end loose and pulled her toward him. "We're going to kiss each other," he murmured, "and you're going to like it."

Chapter Eight

Gregory leaned forward and kissed Pippa, a light yet lingering kiss that sent her thoughts swirling into all sorts of hazy, pleasurable directions, the same way they meandered when she crawled into a hot bath and the water embraced her and sent her head lolling backward against the rim.

When he pulled back, she felt the way she did when she had to stand up from the tub—and saw the towel halfway across the room. Her mind cleared in a rush. "Thank you for the carriage ride. And thank you for agreeing to keep up the ruse that we're running off together. If you don't mind, I'd also appreciate—"

He kissed her again, and this time, his tongue parted the seam of her lips with a bold assurance that should have offended her—he was a practiced lover, obviously—but captivated her instead. She liked a challenge. And Gregory was one. He always had been.

While he held her cravat, he kissed her thoroughly, teasing her lips with his own skilled ones, and she kissed him back, not letting him get the advantage for a moment. She wasn't sure how well she was doing, but their explorations grew more heated. He pulled her bottom closer with his right hand and deepened the kiss.

She decided then and there that it was the greatest pleasure, kissing and getting and giving caresses so hungrily. She only wished she could do it every day, several times a day—more than several times, actually.

The thought made her desperate—desperate for him, so she dared to put her fingers in the curls at his neck and lazily comb them. His hair was like silk.

"You're delicious," he said, "even in pantaloons."

She giggled against his mouth, and he reached his free hand into her coat and caressed her right breast.

"It's perfect," he whispered. He looked into her eyes and ran a lazy circle with his thumb over the linen shielding her nipple.

He had her hypnotized.

And this time when they kissed again, something happened, something raw and needy between them that each had been suppressing in the carriage and up until that moment. Except for the warm and cozy bit at the end, the encounter in Gregory's vehicle had been mostly uncomfortable, awkward, and tense, all at the same time. This kiss was a reward for their endurance.

She couldn't help wanting to feel him as intimately as he was exploring her, so she ran her hand over his belly, her lips never leaving his, and pushed her hips into the firmness that bulged in such enticing fashion in his trousers.

"I like this," she said. "I never want to stop."

"You shouldn't say things like that."

When he ended the kiss—slowly, reluctantly, it seemed—she couldn't help following his lips with her own until the two of them were well and truly parted. She opened her eyes and looked into the deep blue depths of his. They dazzled her brain and made it hard to think.

"I—I do appreciate your trying to stay out of the papers while I'm gone," she said, her voice feeling like taffy. "I know for you, in particular, with your Don Juan ways, it will be a difficult task."

"It will, indeed," said Gregory in a scratchy, low tone. "I often practice my seduction skills on women dressed as men, and I anticipate at least four or five will crop up in the next several months. It will be hell avoiding them."

She yanked her cravat out of his now loose fingers and watched him over her shoulder as she moved to the window.

He said nothing. Neither did he move.

Good.

"I'm going now," she said over her shoulder. "Goodbye."

But as she retied her cravat, part of her was disappointed he hadn't followed her. She'd rather be kissing him than standing alone at this window, which looked cold, square, and utilitarian. Outside was a side yard filled with rows and rows of lumber immersed in several large puddles that had ripples across their tops due to the rising winds.

She tried her best to budge the frame. Surely, all it would take was one mighty heave.

"It's painted shut," Gregory said. "Don't you remember I tried to open it when we got in here?"

"I forgot," she said to the panes. She'd forgotten because when they got in here, she'd been daydreaming they were married and were on a trip to Paris together and that night, they'd have to stay at the inn in a cozy bed made for two.

She'd envisioned what would happen. She wasn't exactly sure of all the details, but she had a very good idea. It was something she longed for at night when she thought of Gregory. It must be entirely embarrassing, but with him, it would be exciting—a grand adventure.

Stupid of her, she knew, to indulge in such a fantasy. Perhaps the rain had made her delirious. Or the whiskey had made her mad.

She turned around to face him. "Are the ten minutes up?"

"Six to go," he said, looking at his watch fob. "But I'm willing to open the door now if you can walk through it peaceably and get straight into my carriage."

"Why, that's Uncle Bertie's watch." Her heart gave a little lurch as she wondered what her dear elderly relative was doing at the moment.

"Yes, it is," Gregory said, popping it back into his waistcoat pocket. "He gave it to me last night when I promised to look after you." He threw himself into a chair and tilted it backward, a favorite activity of his since he was a boy. "I suppose changing the subject is your way of saying you're not ready to cooperate."

She traveled to his side, her man shoes scraping across the floor, then nudged his shoulder with her hip. "Kissing me is hardly looking after me. And you promised we'd leave after ten minutes, whether I cooperate or not."

"You've already been a very obliging prisoner." He kept his eyes on the fireplace, crossed his arms behind his head, and looked the epitome of relaxed man. Relaxed, *handsome* man. "We could go back to what we were doing."

She scratched the side of her nose and moved away a step. "I couldn't kiss you for six minutes even if I wanted to."

"Oh, yes you could."

"Hah." She gave a shallow laugh. "Kisses can't last that long. We'd run out of breath."

"It's like magic," he said to the fireplace. "Somehow you don't."

"You would know," she said. "A gentleman shouldn't be kissing so many women for so long. It leads—it leads to a dissolute life."

"And what's wrong with that?"

"Nothing—if you're stupid. But *you're* not stupid. You can't fool me for an instant. You don't want a dissolute life."

He shrugged. "You think too much, Lieutenant."

That old name! It warmed her heart to hear him say it, although she wouldn't tell him.

"And you don't think enough, *Captain*," she told the top of his head. She longed to run her hand through those shiny, dark curls.

He stood up, and the front chair legs hit the floor with a loud thump. "Listen to me." He hovered above her. "You can't go to Paris—what would be the point if you did? Monsieur will say no to tutoring you. Can't you learn the art from books?"

"It won't be the same. Can you learn how to design buildings only from books? Or didn't you need a mentor to help you reach your potential?"

"A mentor is preferable, but it's not realistic in your case. What would you want to do, once you learn the art of sugar sculpting from Monsieur?"

"I'll come back to all of them," she said, "Uncle Bertie, Mother, Brick and the other servants, and the moor, after I've learned everything I can. When I live in Dartmoor again, I'll be in great demand. By then, I'll have learned to pack and ship my wares, and people will pay extraordinary amounts for my creations."

"You're a lady, Pippa. You're supposed to get married, have children. Don't you have an obligation to your family to make a good match?"

She sighed. "You know the answer to that. Of course I do, in the eyes of the world. But the moor"—she grasped both his hands—"it speaks every day, and it's much louder in its silence than any gossips, the Toad, Mother, and all the expectations that have been thrust on me since I was a little girl. The moor says that I have only one chance"—she squeezed his hands hard—"*this* chance, to live my life. And I'm going to take it."

He pulled away, walked to the window, and peered out. "We're grown now." His voice was steady when he turned back to face her. "Today you were preyed upon by a scoundrel who'll deny everything if he's accused. I thought you were merely in the garden or downstairs when I walked by your room this morning and found you gone. Hawthorne and Trickle had already cleared evidence of him from your room."

"I'm not surprised."

"And then you put yourself in further danger by naïvely throwing yourself on the mercy of what is, in large part, a cruel world. Furthermore, I'm on my way to a dull house party where I intend to work on a modest commission that will get me no further ahead in the realm of architecture than running away will do for you. This is real life, Pippa. It's time to put childish fancy behind us."

Her throat was suddenly hot. "When we were children, you were the perfect companion. We saw wondrous things together, and we acted as if only the present moment mattered. I always knew"—she gulped—"I always knew we would be friends—that there was no limit to our understanding of each other. But that didn't last long, did it? A dozen years ago, you changed completely. I suppose you grew up, according to your definition of the term. And now we've nothing in common. Nothing beyond—"

She couldn't go on, but she was thinking of how well their bodies fit together when they kissed.

She strode to the door, but before she could unbolt it, he caught her hand from behind.

"So we've nothing in common, eh?" he said close to her ear.

She shook her head.

"And I know nothing of joy?"

She nodded vigorously.

He encircled her waist with his palms. "If that's so, how is it that I can make you feel"—he raised his hands and cupped her breasts—"like this?"

She froze and tried to ignore the incredibly erotic sensations his hands aroused in her.

"And why is it," he murmured, "that I know exactly how to make *you* happy?"

"No you don't."

"Oh, yes I do." A beat of simmering silence went past. "I dare you to let me try."

"Gregory Sherwood, when you dare me, something always goes wrong."

"It won't this time," he said. "I promise."

She twisted around to face him. "That's what you always used to say."

He chuckled. "The last time I dared you to anything I was barely thirteen."

"True," she said slowly.

"Let me try again. But you must trust me. Do you?"

She gave a quick nod. "But I'm only saying yes because it's time you got back to your old self. You became quite dull as you got older. Moping about Uncle Bertie's library. Refusing to hike on the moor. Not laughing at my jokes. I don't believe you have it in you to have a lark. In fact, this dare is about *you*. Not me."

"You're going to regret saying that." He pulled her coat off and lowered her leather braces.

"Excuse me?" she said, her heart beating faster. "I need those braces!"

She tried to pull them back up, but he stayed her hand. "I told you to trust me," he chided her softly.

Her pulse thudded in her temples, but she couldn't look away from the depths of those eyes she'd dreamed about every night he'd been away in America—and long before that.

"I'll try," she said airily, hoping he didn't know how pent up she was with nerves. Mixed in with those nerves was a desire to kiss him again, too. But she was afraid. He was big. And handsome. And he knew how to kiss too well. That honeymoon fantasy she'd had when she got here was supposed to remain that. A fantasy.

She needed to get out of this place.

"I won't let you." His mouth barely tipped up in a half-smile.

"What?"

"Leave." He shot her an implacable look. "So forget it."

She narrowed her eyes at him, which could very well be the reason he gently turned her around so that her back was to him.

He pulled her shirt out of her trousers with ease as they were far too big at the waist. Before she could protest, he stuck his palms down the back of them, and she practically jumped at the feeling of his hot hands on her bare bottom.

"Gregory!" she called out sharply, and gasped when he yanked those trousers down in one fell swoop and made her step out of them.

"I'm not sure about this," she said, feeling quivery and shy. She was glad her shirt was almost as long as a night rail.

"Trust me," he said softly from behind her shoulder and caressed her upper arms. "Now I'll need you to put your palms on the door."

"All right." She could *do* that.

"And now . . . spread your legs for me."

She hesitated. "Are you sure? We're in a taproom. And—what if someone looks in the window?"

"It's like an ocean on this side of the inn. No one's going to be walking through that puddle. And if they did attempt such a foolhardy thing and peer in the window, they'd only be very jealous of what they see."

"Jealous? I don't know why." Pippa lifted her chin. "So far this isn't much of a lark."

"You need to be more patient."

"I don't like being patient."

"Yes. I know that. I believe everyone knows that about you, Pippa. Now go ahead," he ordered. "Spread your legs. I promise nothing will go wrong."

"Very well." She gulped. "What if—what if someone knocks?"

"We'll ignore it. I assure you, it's so loud in that taproom, no one will guess what's going on in here."

"I'll take your word for it." Slowly, she spread her legs.

And then he caressed her derriere with one hand. It was a fleeting caress—*too* fleeting—sending curls of pleasure to her feminine core. She blinked about a thousand times, wondering what she was getting herself into.

"It's all right so far," she lied—because already that one touch was something she'd never forget—"but if this doesn't make me happy, Gregory—"

She ended her statement on what she hoped was a threatening tone.

"It will. Just you wait." He gave her a light slap on the bottom, and she flinched.

Her nerves had never been so taut—not with fear, as she'd supposed—but with anticipation.

A second later, she was jolted by the feel of his mouth and tongue on her buttocks. "Oh, heavens," she gasped. "This can't be right."

"It is," he said. "And there's more."

"More?"

He proved it by exploring the intimate folds of flesh between her legs with his finger while he laid kisses on her backside and her hips.

"Gregory," she couldn't help whispering. "This is getting out of control. You promised me nothing would go wrong."

"It won't," he said, with a soft laugh against the back of her thigh, which felt heated beyond reason as he tasted its length. "You like things out of control, remember? Castles that don't fit convention. A runaway journey to Paris. A moor that's unpredictable every day you cross it. Admit it, Pippa. Control isn't something that matches up well with you."

"I suppose it doesn't." She was aghast that her breath was coming shorter and shorter. "But this is so unexpected that I'm not sure I—"

He found the nubbin from which all the pleasure she'd

felt heretofore seemed to radiate, and she released a quiet, lengthy moan. How could he be doing this to her?

She sounded like an animal.

But she liked animals.

She *loved* them.

So she squeezed her eyes shut and gave in to the sensations Gregory was conjuring as if from a magic spell in a giant, great book of spells hidden away from ordinary view, to be taken out when one needed—

Relief.

She needed relief in the worst way. But where to find it?

Where?

Where?

Her panting grew stronger.

"Let go," he whispered, and with his other hand, found the portal to her sex and sheathed two fingers inside her.

Oh, God. It was too much!

"Gregory—"

"Let *go,* Pippa."

It was a command. Not a request, and somehow—even though she'd always balked at Gregory's commands—this one worked. It reached a primal place, and she let go with a cry from her very essence.

When the waves of pure pleasure finally subsided, she leaned her forehead against the door and sucked in a large breath. Her legs trembled, and so did her arms from pressing so very hard against the door.

Gregory stood up and rested a hand—musky from the scent of her—lightly on her shoulder.

"You were right about something," he said close to her ear. "The Gregory the world knows—the well-rounded, successful man about town—isn't happy, and you seem to be the only one who notices. But giving *you* pleasure reminds me that there's a part of me that yet knows joy. And I liked it. I liked it so much, I want to do it to you again. And again."

His confession broke her heart and thrilled her all at once. She longed to turn and throw her arms around his neck. But she didn't know what he'd say. She couldn't act like that girl in the garden, the one who'd sketched his face and a heart beside it. He'd despised that girl.

Not that it mattered, really. She was leaving.

"We can't do this anymore," she said in a thin voice, her eyes on the door. "I'm going to Paris." She'd said it so often in the last twenty-four hours, it was beginning to sound as familiar as a nursery rhyme—a singsongy wish that pleased her but that no one else believed.

"I'm afraid you're not," Gregory said.

"I knew you'd say that. I don't know why I even bothered talking to you."

"In a few minutes," he went on as if he hadn't heard her, "I'm taking you back to your uncle's. After things are settled there, you'll come up to London and stay with my family. Surely the city has its share of expert sugar sculptors. I'll wrangle you an audience with them."

She swiveled to face him, her legs still so weak, she leaned on the door. "In between all the balls I'm to attend to find a man to marry me? A man who'll extinguish all my little joys, one by one, the way the Toad has Mother's? No, thank you."

She slid around him, but he followed and got to her trousers before she did. He tossed them to her, and she turned away and pulled them on before tucking in her shirt. "Your words were very pretty. I was even *moved* by them. But now I have to wonder if you were trying to seduce me into submission."

"Think what you will." He appeared in front of her again and looped the leather braces over her shoulders. "But the fact is, you can't go to Paris. And not just because you'll be largely unprotected pursuing Monsieur Perot. But because you'll be disappointed. The first time you go to Paris has to be when you have a light heart. And you won't when you know you've misled Uncle Bertie. He'll be worried. And you're too kind not to let that bother you."

She gave a little cry of frustration. "I wish you'd just—go away." She threw her coat on without his help. "Please. Go to your house party. Don't change your plans for me."

At the door she gave a desperate twist to her shoulders to shake him off, but he held her fast and laid his hand over the bolt. "It's not that simple, and you know it, in your heart of hearts. If I have to, I'll pick you up and carry you and put you in my carriage myself."

"You're making a mistake," she whispered, a lump in her throat.

"It certainly feels like it at the moment," he replied, "but I'm preventing a bigger one, whether you believe it or not."

And with that, he unbolted the door.

Chapter Nine

Pippa put on her spectacles and stood blinking for a few seconds. Then she began to move, wending her way through the inn dining room to no fanfare, Gregory behind her. She was numb with exhaustion *and* pleasure by this point, furious at Gregory and at herself for giving in to temptation when he was thwarting all her plans, and keenly desperate to escape, to the point that when the inn door blew open and a well-to-do family fairly stumbled in with three rambunctious children, she considered volunteering on the spot to be their nanny—anything to avoid going back home.

It wasn't home, really, anymore. Not after today. Not as long as the Toad was there.

Then she remembered she was dressed as a man.

A portly young man with an extraordinarily high collar and carrying a beautiful cherrywood cane hurried in behind the family of five and made a studied assessment of the company in the taproom. As he shook the rain off his tight auburn curls, he saw Gregory, and his mouth became a thin line.

"Hello, *Marbury*," Gregory said.

"*Hello,* Westdale." The newcomer had a gritty, unpleasant voice. "Fancy meeting you here."

He had a large forehead, beady eyes, a disagreeable mouth, and he sported exceptionally spindly legs that appeared incapable of supporting his short, rotund torso. *Why, he looks like a bowling ball balanced on two pins,* thought Pippa. However, in his navy coat with gold buttons and starched, white cravat, he wore the understated look of a follower of Beau Brummel, the sort of London guise that announced wealth and prestige.

Gregory wore a coat and buckskin breeches better suited to the country, yet he was the more imposing—and by far the more winning—of the two. "It's been at least a year."

"I've hardly noticed," Marbury said, and Pippa nearly gasped at his blatant rudeness. But Gregory seemed to expect it. "I'm on my way to Thurston Manor. And you?"

"To Plumtree to visit friends."

"Oh. Friends." Marbury let the word hang in the air like a curse.

Pippa felt he was quite ridiculous. One obviously had to meet certain expectations with him, or be judged lacking. Whereas Gregory, as controlled and commanding as he often was, gave the impression that he was well aware that the cosmos didn't spin around his needs and wants.

Of course, all of London society was critical, Pippa knew—it was a sport among the beau monde. Perhaps Marbury was only tired or hungry. He wouldn't be the first traveler to be grumpy. Why, in that cold, wet space between the coziness of napping on Gregory's shoulder and the moment she took her first bite of hot beef pie, she'd been ready to bite off the head of anyone who came near her. And after the fiery encounter she'd just had with the man—in which she went from soaring heights to the lowest low when he told her he was taking her home—she felt that same cross way again.

Someone who looked the exact opposite of cantankerous—a sweet, older man—ventured into the taproom then. He had silver hair receding at the temples and intelligent eyes. His clothes were neat but unexceptional, though the expensive cut of his jacket and the fine supple leather of his boots revealed that he was a man of some means.

"Get Mr. Dawson anything he wants." Marbury spoke with unnecessary harshness to the barman. "And do you take good care of your dogs here? I don't approve of people who don't."

He stole a quick glance at Mr. Dawson, who apparently wasn't paying attention to the conversation. He was eyeing the inn yard, where the branches of an enormous tree swayed heavily in the wind. Pippa exchanged a bemused look with Gregory.

What an odd thing for Marbury to say, especially as three dogs lay in a heap, legs before the fire, contentedly snoozing.

The barman, who'd probably seen everything under the sun when it came to human nature, wiped his hands on his apron and looked only mildly askance at Marbury. "We take excellent care of our dogs here. Anything else, sir?"

"Just that we don't have all day." Marbury's tone was cold and aloof.

Many people seemed to treat their servants that way, Pippa noted, but Gregory, whenever he was at Uncle Bertie's, never made a request of the house and stables staff without being gracious at the same time.

She crossed her arms over her breasts, and remembered with a shock that they weren't bound and that Gregory had known that and explored her there as if she were an undiscovered treasure.

He's not for you, she reminded herself. *He might be kind to servants, and he does know how to make your body exquisitely happy, but he's bossy and difficult and not—I repeat—not for you.*

"We'll eat in the private dining room," Marbury said to Dawson, his confident tone implying tacit approval of the plan. "Nothing but the best for a cousin of Lady Thurston."

"Thank you, but I'm not hungry," the older man said. "The weather being as it is, I'm content to sit by the fire out here and have some tea." He looked at the barman. "If you don't mind."

"Not a bit, sir." The barman turned away to do his job.

"I'd prefer to be alone for a few minutes," Mr. Dawson said to Marbury. "I've reading to do."

"Of course you do." Marbury was the epitome of bored politeness. "So do I. The history of the Thurston line. I hear it's quite noble." But when Mr. Dawson walked past him, Marbury turned to Gregory and made a disgusted face.

What a rude man he was! Pippa felt immediately sorry for Mr. Dawson, who wended his way through the tables and chairs to the fire, oblivious to his traveling companion's slights. She could tell Mr. Dawson was a nice man, like Uncle Bertie—and Gregory, when he felt like it—although he didn't fill the room the way those two seemed to do.

Uncle Bertie was a proper baronet—and proud of his

place in society—but once a year from the time she'd turned thirteen, he'd taken her on a regional tour of all his theaters. He called it their "annual adventure," and it was always a special time, one that spawned many heart-to-heart talks as their carriage rumbled down the roads leading from one bustling town to the next. Pippa knew beyond a shadow of a doubt that Uncle Bertie wanted her to lead a life of freedom, a life he himself had prepared her for. If she managed his theaters properly, she'd always have an income and a certain level of independence—and with that a chance to indulge in her own dreams.

Which was why his insistence that she and Gregory marry made no sense.

The popping sound of a new keg of ale being opened by the barman brought her to the present, and she watched as he poured two pints and passed them to Marbury and Gregory.

"I leave after one pint," Gregory said.

"Oh, come now. What's happened to the London partygoer?" Marbury jeered in his grating nasal tone.

"I can drink you under the table, Marbury, as you well know." Gregory stated it as an inconsequential fact. "Would you like something . . . Harrow? Valets get thirsty, too."

Pippa realized he was looking at her. Oh. *She* must be Harrow! "Uh, no, thank you, my lord." He was her jailer, essentially, and she wanted to be as rude to him as Marbury was, but she couldn't—not in her role as his valet.

That was a clever identity to take on, but she'd never tell Gregory so.

Marbury leaned against the bar and met her eyes for a moment before going back to speaking with Gregory about the latest goings-on in Town. He'd looked through her as if she were invisible, which was typical of the upper classes—not to mention a good thing in her case.

"So," Gregory said to him, "you're attending the same house party I plan to get to—eventually." He tossed a quick glance at Pippa.

Why should she feel guilty? She nearly stuck her chin in the air but thought better of it. Valets wouldn't dare.

"*You're* attending?" Marbury winced, then he jerked his head away from Gregory to observe a comely barmaid washing glasses.

At least Pippa thought it rude. Perhaps gentlemen did things like that all the time in each other's company.

Marbury slurped his ale and took his time returning his narrowed gaze to Gregory. "You might want to extend your stay with your friends in Plum Valley."

"Plumtree," Gregory corrected him.

Marbury waved a hand. "I hear the goings-on at Thurston Manor will be terribly dull."

There was a slight arch to Gregory's brow. "That's not what I've heard."

Oh, really? What *had* he heard? Pippa bristled. Was he going to enter upon a seduction campaign at the house party, too, with some other unsuspecting young lady—or ladies?

"Lady Thurston is purported to be full of surprises," Gregory said. "One never knows whom to expect among the company."

Marbury gave a droll laugh. "It's no secret Lady Damara's coming. I hear she's anxious to see you. I'd give anything to—"

And then he began to describe what he'd do to Lady Damara if he could get her alone and naked. Pippa's eyes widened, and her stomach churned with disgust at the thought that any woman would be subject to Marbury's pawings.

"Enough." Gregory cut him off testily, and it was a good thing he did. She nearly had steam coming out of her ears. "You're speaking of a lady."

Marbury's own eyebrows shot up. "That hasn't stopped you before. I heard the rumors. The new Lady Morgan's firstborn looks a bit like you, so they say."

The new Lady Morgan was Eliza! A ringing started in Pippa's ears at those shocking words, and her heart—her heart began to beat so fast, she had to put her hand on the back of a chair.

But Gregory moved faster. He grabbed one of Marbury's jacket lapels and yanked him up and toward him. "I advise you," he said through gritted teeth, "not to repeat rumors." And then he shoved him away.

Marbury almost lost his footing but recovered it by grabbing onto the bar. "God, man! I never said it was *fact*."

"Let's go, Harrow," Gregory said, and began to move toward the inn door.

Good for him! Pippa couldn't help but feel a small surge of satisfaction as she watched him stride away with an assured gait, his broad shoulders imposing, his general air unassailable. There wasn't an ounce of guilt in that walk. None.

She couldn't believe it of him—that he'd gotten Eliza with child.

Absurd. There was no way that baby was Gregory's. Much as she knew he'd enjoyed his share of women, this accusation was beyond the pale.

Marbury had gotten what he deserved.

Pippa was relieved that no one seemed to notice the

feud between two gentlemen that had erupted in the tap-room. The noise level remained constant—and life went on. Thank goodness. The farther she was from conflict in any shape or form, the better. No one could notice the valet . . .

It was her new mission. That and escaping Gregory.

Marbury's lips twisted above his pointy chin, and he took a gulp of ale. "I've always called him a high-and-mighty jackass to his face," he muttered at Pippa, "just to annoy him, even though he's not. I wish it were utter hell, working for him, but I doubt it is."

"It is sometimes," she said. "But only when he insists on shooting pistols two-fisted. He's a crack shot. We've gone through at least a hundred wine glasses in the past month alone. Makes a devil of a cleanup for me."

Marbury scoffed, but she could tell he wasn't sure if she was jesting.

Let him wonder. Pippa had never seen Eliza's new baby—had only corresponded once with her schoolmate since she'd gotten married, and it was only in response to Eliza's letter. She'd sent a small gift—some baby socks she'd knitted—but she preferred to cool the friendship as much as possible without being overt about it. And it was only because Eliza had never apologized for what she'd done—which was use Pippa as a diversion for Gregory that day in the garden.

If she had, Pippa wouldn't be so willing to walk away.

Gregory paused, his hand on the inn's front doorknob. "Harrow? Are you coming?"

She felt a desperate urge to follow him and turn her nose up as she walked by Lord Marbury. But then she remembered such a pleasure—aligning herself with the better man, the *victorious* man—would be short-lived.

She had a greater purpose: to elude that same man and get out of England.

Paris awaited, as did Monsieur Perot, although he had no idea his perfect student was coming his way: the student he'd surely longed for, one who shared his vision and his passion, who wanted to become a master sugar sculptor—

By hook or by crook.

"I'll be there in a moment," she called to Gregory in her best and lowest man's voice, and then pointed a thumb over her shoulder. Surely at an inn of this caliber there was a room to refresh one's self somewhere on the premises. "I have to go—somewhere."

She hoped he understood her meaning.

"See you outside shortly," he said, his gaze direct and expectant—shorthand for *Be there, or else*—and strode through the door, not bothering to shut it behind him.

She looked behind her for an escape, but Lord Marbury stood, straightened his coat, and glowered at the front door, blocking her view of the rear of the room.

"Follow that annoying master of yours and get out," he told her.

"I—I can't. Not yet." Perhaps there were woods behind the inn in which to hide. It had been raining too hard earlier for her to notice, but she had to try something, didn't she?

"If you're looking for a place to piss, go find a tree." Marbury laughed at his own rudeness. "Leave now, or I'll accuse you of making lewd jokes about the barman's daughter. See her over there in the corner?"

"Yes, I see her." The unsuspecting girl was still washing glasses. "*That's* not very nice of you."

"Who cares about being nice?" He shot her a look of scorn. "Your coat is rumpled. You're a pitiful excuse for a valet."

Pippa looked down and smoothed the front of her coat. *Hmmph,* she thought, *and you're a pitiful excuse for a man.* She eyed him with contempt.

"Take off that smashed hat," he said, "you lout. Don't you realize you're only drawing attention to your bald spot? For that's surely the reason why you wear it inside."

"I was on my way out—that's why I'm wearing it." She curled her lip in distaste. "At least I don't have too much hair like you. In your ears, that is."

He tried to grab her arm, but she was too nimble and found herself separated from him by a table.

"I could beat you to a pulp," he said.

"You'd never catch me to do it." She turned swiftly on her heel and made for the door, pushing her hat down for good measure. No telling how windy it still was out there.

"You'd better watch your manners," he called after her, "*and* your back!"

She ignored him and slowed her steps, not just to rile him but because she felt as if she were marching off a gangplank with a pirate at her back into shark-infested waters. Even with Gregory's assurances that he would take care of things when they returned to Plumtree, she knew he would leave again.

And she'd be right back where she started.

Out in the inn yard, he was clearly waiting for her, his black curls blown around his forehead by a steady wind. "Please get into the carriage." His tone brooked no nonsense.

She glowered at him, but she did get into the carriage. There was a part of her—as much as she was angry at him—that understood his reasons for returning her home and couldn't fault him for it. Society would say it made perfect sense.

But dreams don't always make sense, she thought. Hot tears stung her lids, and she blinked them back, listening as Gregory told Oscar to return to Uncle Bertie's. She sniffled a bit, noticing that fortunately the carriage no longer smelled of damp as Oscar had removed all her wet things. But suddenly Marbury's strong cologne assailed her nostrils in the worst way.

He'd stuck his head in the carriage door. "Forget what I said before," he said without preamble in that scratchy, cold voice of his. "I need you."

"What for?" Pippa asked, and not at all politely.

He narrowed his eyes at her. "To shine Mr. Dawson's boots, and you *will* do it. There's not a soul here who's not either elderly, female, a bratty child, or drunk—and that includes the stable hands."

"I refuse," she said, crossing one ankle over the other knee in a decidedly masculine fashion that made her feel brave and reckless. "You didn't ask nicely. And I think that's terribly important."

He narrowed his eyes at her again. "Just what kind of servant *are* you?"

When Gregory appeared at the carriage door, his eyes were icy and his jaw, square and hard. "What do you want with my valet?"

"I refuse to help him, my lord." Pippa held her breath and looked straight ahead, her belly taut as a bowstring. "He said I have a bald spot. He accused me of having a rumpled coat. And he called you a high-and-mighty jack—" She turned to look at Gregory, then back at the wall. "I can't say it."

"What's going on, Marbury?" Gregory put his hands on his hips. "Did you get into it with my valet in the tap-room?"

"No," Marbury insisted. "Well, yes. I did." He scratched a temple. "Look, Westdale," he said in what Pippa thought should have been a sheepish tone but was more a pedantic one. "I came across as a boor in the taproom. To both of you. But I made a mistake. I shouldn't have repeated that rumor. Or threatened to beat your valet to a pulp."

"You did that?" Gregory's tone was deadly.

"Yes," said Marbury. "But if you only knew how provoking he was! Seldom in my life—in fact, *never*—have I ever been so provoked by a servant. He's downright disrespectful, completely cheeky—"

Gregory held up a palm. "Stop right there."

"I'm *not* cheeky," Pippa blurted out.

"See?" Marbury put up his hands and let them flop at his sides. "I'll admit I was in a terrible mood after being assaulted by you, Westdale. How dare you throw me like that, by the way: *I,* your old friend Marbury."

"Right," said Gregory. "My old friend."

"And it's not often that I'm expected to be *nice,* of all things, especially to a servant." Marbury put a hand over his heart. "What peer has to be nice? It's—"

"It's how we behave in the country," Pippa interjected.

"He's talking again." There was a threat in Marbury's tone.

"So he is." Gregory put an edge of menace to his own words, much to Pippa's gratification.

Marbury sighed in obvious surrender. "Good God, what I'm trying to say is, let's let bygones be bygones, shall we?"

Gregory merely stared at him, his lips thinned.

"You and I have a long, checkered history," Marbury went on doggedly. "But we're mates in the end, aren't we?

Someday, we'll sit in Parliament together. Surely you'll grant your dear old friend Marbury another chance."

Dear old friend. Hah!

But something in Pippa gave a little. The odd man was amusing in his own way, and he was certainly trying. He'd obviously grown up used to getting what he wanted and didn't know how to deal with strong wills other than his own. She wished she could lean forward in anticipation of what Gregory would say to that little speech, but she sat as far back as she could on her seat, her two feet now flat on the floor, and tried to act disinterested.

As for Gregory's response, Pippa suspected that as a gentleman, he really had no choice in the matter. She saw in his eyes that he realized it, too.

Crossing his arms, he said, "What do you want, then?" Which was as close to an acceptance of Marbury's apology as the repentant scoundrel would get.

"Not much." Marbury's reply was brisk. "My own valet fell ill as we left London. He'll follow in a few days. But he was to take care of both me and my friend. Now Mr. Dawson needs his boots polished before we resume our journey. Do me a favor and lend me your man, unimpressive as he looks. It will only take a half hour—if he's any good."

Gregory made a frustrated noise and leaped into the carriage, taking the seat opposite Pippa. He looked down at their unhappy visitor. "I'll allow bygones to be bygones. But I'm afraid you'll have to find another flunky to polish your friend's boots. We have a schedule to keep. Not to mention a little pride. When you ask to borrow a valet, you don't insult him and then assume his employer won't object."

"Dammit, man." Marbury braced his hands on the carriage doorway. "Didn't you hear me in the taproom? Roger Dawson is Lady Thurston's cousin."

"Good for him." Gregory kept his tone perfectly bland, Pippa was glad to see. "Is there a further point?"

Marbury gave a sputtering laugh. "Surely you can understand why I want to stay in his good graces."

"Enlighten me," Gregory said dryly. "You seem quite anxious to. Old friend."

A little chuckle burst from Pippa's throat.

"Your valet can't have just laughed." Marbury stared at her, his expression incredulous. "If so, he should be fired on the spot. And why is he riding with you? He should be on the box."

"He's got dyspepsia." Gregory shot Pippa a warning look. "And his behavior and where he sits is my business, not yours. Go on, tell me what you want to say about Dawson. But you'd better hurry. We have to bloody well be on our way."

Marbury looked quickly behind him—there was no one nearby, listening—then back at Gregory. "Were you by any chance asked to design a dog cottage for Lady Thurston?" he asked in low tones. When Gregory nodded, he continued. "And you and I are both at this house party. I wonder if other up-and-coming architects will be there, as well."

"And your point is?" Gregory sounded bored, of all things.

"Lord and Lady Thurston are close friends of John Nash—"

"England's premier architect," Pippa said, and nudged Gregory.

He flashed her a look of annoyance. "I know that. *Everyone* knows that."

Marbury came dangerously close to wiggling in his excitement. "It's said that he is a huge lover of dogs, and they'll be consulting with him on the plans for the cottage, with him choosing the best design."

Pippa had to fight not to squirm in her seat and maintain a cheerless expression—she supposedly had dyspepsia, after all. But Gregory shouldn't sound bored. A cottage for dogs was rather absurd, but if John Nash were involved, this was *important*. It could mean his future.

She coughed and looked right at him. But he ignored her, so she coughed again.

"Quit the coughing, Harrow."

"Sorry." She grunted, but her eyes said it all: *This is it—your* opportunity.

He merely scowled and looked back at Marbury. "So Nash will help choose a design. Why would he be interested in an architect who designs for dogs?"

A slow burn began in Pippa's middle. Fine. If he didn't want to take advantage of an opportunity, *she* would find a way.

"Sounds bizarre," said Marbury, "but evidently he and Lady Thurston know each other and have both bred dogs their entire lives. While a separate cottage may seem preposterous to you and me, we must remember that there are many whose behavior with their dogs can't be explained."

Pippa's and Gregory's eyes met. *Uncle Bertie.*

"So this competition, if you will," Marbury went on in a condescending tone, "is our opportunity to lay our talent at the feet of John Nash. And whether I have the opportunity to show him plans for a fortress or plans for a doghouse, I won't pass it up. Nash has private consultations with Prinny, you know. The opportunities abound. Whomever he and Lady Thurston choose will surely have a fantastic start on a stellar career."

"How do you know these rumors are true?" Try as Gregory might to hide it, his interest was piqued.

Silly of her, perhaps, but Pippa could tell by the way he grabbed the hand strap on the wall on her side of the carriage and hung from it. The pose was casual, and from behind, she was embarrassed to note she found it highly attractive—exposing the merest fraction of his shirt and top of his pantaloons on the left side—but his fingers as they gripped the hand loop were almost white.

"I've only heard rumblings," Marbury said. "But why else would *four* of us attending this house party be tasked with designing this cottage? And why would Lord Thurston's personal secretary drop me a note and request that I give Lady Thurston's cousin a ride in my carriage?"

"Perhaps his is out of service," Gregory suggested.

"Grasping at straws is poor comfort when the truth hurts." Marbury sent Gregory a pitying smile. "Lord and Lady Thurston obviously have a particular eye on me. And that's a long ride from London. Dawson and I have bonded. I'm sure I'll have my foot in the door ahead of anyone's."

"Yes, and that ride from London was also ample time for you to shoot yourself in the foot," said Gregory equably, and settled back in his seat—his knee splayed and almost touching Pippa's. "Cheers, Marbury. See you in a few days."

"Come now, Westdale." Lord Marbury actually slapped the door. "I just groveled before you, then shared some valuable information I didn't have to—"

"The groveling was appropriate. And as for the valuable information, I'd have discovered it myself at the house party"—Gregory sounded testy again—"especially as so-called rumors abound, according to you."

The tension was ratcheting up again. Pippa felt too hot in her coat.

"You know timing is everything." Marbury's eyes flashed with annoyance. "Now you'll be sure to get to Thurston Manor earlier than you'd planned, thanks to me. So have pity, and lend me your valet. How hard is that? And you'll only win favor with Dawson by doing so."

"I doubt that," Gregory said. "I suspect that somehow you'll work it so that *you* do. Besides, you've already bonded with him, remember? Why should I even try? Not to mention that mere minutes ago, you were doing your best to dissuade me from attending the house party, no doubt because you want one less rival there."

"Do you blame me?" Marbury hiked both his shoulders up and put his palms out. "This is a competitive world. But the truly ambitious know when to cooperate."

"And when to move on," Gregory said. "It's only a pair of boots, after all, and Dawson's only a man—not a god. For the last time, good-bye."

He pulled his door shut at the exact same moment Pippa leaped out her own door and landed—blast it all!—directly in a puddle. Without taking time to worry about the fact that she'd also gotten wet for the umpteenth time that day, she rounded the back of the carriage as swiftly as possible in her muddied shoes and tipped her hat at Marbury.

"I'll be glad to be of service to Mr. Dawson," she gasped in passing, and ran toward the inn's front door at full speed.

Behind her, Gregory's door slammed shut. "Harrow!" he called in murderous accents.

Inwardly, she cringed, but she burst through the inn door, calling, "Mr. Dawson? Mr. Dawson? I've grown up with corgis! And I've heard lovely things about Lady Thurston." She turned and heaved her shoulder against the mammoth front door to shut it behind her, but the wind made it impossible. With no time to spare, she gave a final shove only to have the door pushed open by Gregory. They locked eyes for only a split second before she slung a chair in his path and looked wildly around the room.

Where was Dawson?

"What is it with these strange city folk?" said one apple-cheeked lady to an old man sitting next to her, his pint of ale frozen in the air.

"There you are!" Pippa cried.

The object of her search was still by the fire, one booted foot crossed over the other, a sheaf of papers in his hand. She arrived at his side exactly one second before Gregory did.

"I'm Harrow, valet to Lord Westdale, and I'm here to shine your boots," she proclaimed breathlessly.

"But they don't need shining, dear fellow," Mr. Dawson said in the sweetest manner. He really was a lovely old gentleman.

"No, they don't." Gregory folded his arms over his chest. He looked like a dangerous bull about to charge, but who was he angry at—Pippa or Marbury?

Maybe both.

Marbury entered the taproom at a more leisurely pace, looking like the cat who'd just downed the canary.

"Your boots may not need shining now," Pippa told

Mr. Dawson, "but they will. In fact, I'll be happy to serve as your temporary valet at Thurston Manor." She shot Gregory a just-try-to-stop-me look.

"Pulling valets out of hats is only one skill in my repertoire of tricks," Marbury purred as he approached and grinned at Mr. Dawson, who pointedly ignored him.

"My valet's *not* going to the house party." Gregory looked directly at Pippa when he said that. "In fact, we're leaving now."

"Well, which is it?" Mr. Dawson peered up at Gregory and Pippa. "Are you coming or going?"

"Coming!" Pippa said.

"Going," Gregory announced at the same time.

And it was as if their opposing words cast an unfortunate spell. At that exact moment, a large, dark shadow passed before the window, followed by a massive, earth-shaking thud, the screech of splintering wood, and the whinnies of frightened horses.

Chapter Ten

Oscar.

Gregory ran straight out the inn door.

The gigantic oak tree that had shaded half the inn yard lay on the ground. One of its huge limbs rested on top of a stranger's carriage that sat upon splayed wheels, its roof crushed to smithereens. Two trunks lay on the ground, their contents spilling out of them.

There were no horses attached to the carriage yet—a good thing.

To the right, Gregory's own carriage was in perfect order, although his new pair were jumpy, their haunches rippling and their eyes still white. Oscar, thank God, had them well in order, although inside his dark coat with the gold Brady buttons, he was paler than usual.

"Everyone all right?" Gregory called to him, vastly relieved.

"Fine, sir," the coachman said. "No one was hurt. We're lucky. Not so the owner of that carriage. I do believe it was Lord Marbury's."

Upon closer inspection of the crest on the broken door, Gregory saw that it was, indeed.

A heavy weight settled on his chest. He couldn't leave

just yet. He'd have to see to it that Marbury and Dawson got on their way. It was the right thing to do. But it shouldn't be difficult. They were at a posting inn, after all, with horses and carriages readily for hire.

What was going to be difficult was getting Pippa back into the carriage to go home.

That upstart—volunteering her services to Mr. Dawson! He'd admire her gumption any other time—but not when she was under his care and she was doing the opposite of what he needed her to do.

By this time, everyone else had left the inn to view the gigantic tree's demise and to exclaim over the coach. The bespectacled Pippa had mashed her hat low on her head to prevent it from being blown off by a random gust of wind and was deep in conversation with Mr. Dawson while she went about the business of picking up garments from the ground around the coach. Two children joined her.

But where was Marbury?

Already out back, Gregory surmised, trying to find new transportation. At least the man should be. Gregory would go looking for him, see if he could help.

He caught another glimpse of Pippa and Mr. Dawson, and couldn't help thinking she was extremely fetching in her man's clothes. She seemed perfectly content to stay there with the older man by the crumpled carriage, folding garments and speaking avidly about something.

But then Gregory saw her visibly slow down and act more like a man. And like a servant.

Good.

The falling of the tree had brought out her nurturing side. For a moment, at least, she'd forgotten about the fact that Gregory was taking her home.

But no sooner had the relief come than it went away. A

sick feeling gripped him. They needed to leave, and it was getting harder and harder to do so.

He'd resist panic. They need stay only a few more minutes. And after he'd finished being polite assisting Marbury, he'd head back to Bertie's with Pippa in tow.

Marbury was in the side yard talking to two stable hands sitting upon a tree limb so large Gregory couldn't have spanned it with his arms. The two laborers were drinking ale, and according to them, Marbury's driver was asleep in the hayloft.

"Is he drunk?" asked Marbury.

"He won't be of any use to you for at least half a day," one said. "When you arrived here, he was near drunk already, not that we can blame him with this rough weather."

"Damn that useless bastard." Marbury groaned. He glanced up as Gregory came closer, then added in a surly tone, "I mean that useless, *handsome* bastard of a servant. Is that nice enough, Westdale?"

Gregory didn't dignify the question with an answer. "You can hire a driver," he said instead, then looked at the stable hands. "But what about the horses and a carriage?"

He noticed for the first time how close the stables had come to being wrecked.

"We're going to have to get the horses out the rear door," said one stable hand. "The front one's blocked."

"And the carriage you're going to provide me?" Marbury asked.

The other hand laughed, but it was almost a sob, really. "'Fraid that won't be happening. The two we have are blocked inside. We'd have to saw out a wall to remove them."

"Gawd, it's going to take weeks to get rid of this limb alone," said the other, patting the branch.

Marbury cursed. "You two are as helpful as rocks. Is there any place nearby we can hire a carriage?"

"Not for at least another eight—no, maybe nine—why, I think it must be eleven miles!" The first stable hand heartily scratched an armpit and grinned, pleased with his wealth of knowledge.

"What about the next coach?" Marbury's neck and ears were turning red.

"Not until tomorrow afternoon, and in these muddy roads, it could be two days," the second stable hand said smugly.

"You can always ride to Thurston Manor," Gregory suggested to Marbury.

"Not a chance." Marbury raked both hands through his frizzy hair. "Dawson's an old man; that's too rough a business, especially with all the mud on the roads. He needs cushy transport. If he had some flesh on his rear, of course, he'd be fine. He's got the appetite of a flea. You need to take us, Westdale."

"Oh, no," Gregory said, "I'm not going to the house party—yet." And he turned to make the short trip back inside the inn.

"You were going anyway," Marbury urged him from behind.

"Later."

"Just go *now*. Your friends can wait, can't they? Or will they cry?"

But Gregory didn't answer.

"What's wrong with you?" Marbury demanded to know. "This man could mean everything to your future. I never took you for being all looks and no brains, but maybe you're better off being a prissy future marquess who cares more about his dance slippers than using his

God-given talents." He sniffed disparagingly. "Not that you really have any. I just said that because you're one of those people who's easily flattered."

"Believe me, the last thing I want is a compliment from *you*."

"You're making no sense, Westdale. None at all."

"Maybe not to you," Gregory threw over his shoulder.

Marbury managed to catch up with him, and with a sigh of resignation, Gregory held the door because something in him liked Marbury almost as much as he wanted to throttle him.

The short, roly-poly earl crossed over the threshold and looked back and up at him. "This whole business stinks to high heaven. You. Me. Going to the same house party." He chuckled. "As if anyone would willingly put us together. It's a plot. I know it."

"Say it a tad louder, why don't you?" Gregory muttered.

Marbury rolled his eyes and moved into the room with his usual swagger. It appeared everyone had congregated again, this time for a round of ales on the house.

The barman was wiping tears away from his eyes. "We're ruined," he announced to the general company.

There were lots of sighs and commiserating murmurs all around.

"No you're not," Pippa assured him loudly, a tankard of ale in her hand. "You'll clean up the tree—someday—and until then, you're still the Old Oak Inn. No one ever said the tree had to be *standing*. And then when you're done cutting it up and hauling it away, you'll rename the place—."

"The New Stump Inn!" Marbury called out scornfully.

Pippa narrowed her eyes at him then smiled at the

barman. "Don't worry, you'll come up with just the right name. I'm sure of it." She raised her tankard.

He put the flats of his hands on the bar and frowned at Pippa. "We've been the Old Oak Inn for nearly four hundred years, young man."

She swallowed hard and glanced around. "It's time for a change, then. Think how excited everyone will be to see the new name above your door."

Marbury leaned toward Gregory. "I've never known a valet to be so forward. So ridiculous. And his coat fits dreadfully." He raked Gregory with a shrewd glance. "Yet *you* look all right."

Gregory was underwhelmed by the compliment. "That's all that matters in a valet, isn't it?"

"Mr. Dawson seems to like him," Marbury noted.

"They apparently bonded at the site of your broken carriage," Gregory said dryly, and joined Pippa at the bar where she sat next to Dawson, who was lifting his own tankard of ale.

"Right, Harrow," Gregory said, already dreading her response. "Let's go."

It was time. He hoped she realized that she'd reached the end of the line.

She looked up at him with her large hazel eyes still somewhat hidden behind those awful spectacles—and he felt the hairs on the back of his neck rise. She was up to something. He could tell.

"Really, my lord," she said, "we don't need to travel to Plumtree. Feel free to go directly to the house party at Thurston Manor."

Gregory threw her a brittle smile. "Thank you, Harrow, for telling me, *your employer,* where I may or may not go."

The flash in her eyes told him there was an especially *hot* place she'd like him to go. "Of course we must travel to Plumtree."

"But you're a man who refuses to think of himself." Her tone was earnest. "You're only going to Plumtree so that I may see my dying grandmother." She looked at Marbury. "The fact is, she's *always* almost dying. Last year, she was this close"—she put her index finger and her thumb together and turned slightly so Dawson could see—"to dying of a fever that was so hot, you could fry an egg on her forehead."

"Really," said Marbury. "Let me get out my violin."

"It's true," Pippa insisted, and turned to Mr. Dawson. "But within a week, she was dancing at my cousin's wedding."

"Fancy that." Mr. Dawson's brow wrinkled, but he was most polite.

Pippa's nod was extravagant. "I promise you, Lord Westdale, I don't mind a bit skipping the visit to Plumtree." She thought for a moment then tugged her forelock, a deferential move that she'd seen the stable boy make on occasion. Unfortunately it pulled her wig slightly askew, so with a panicked look she gave a dramatic bow, managing to adjust her cap and hair while flourishing her arms. "Though you're kind to be so thoughtful. And modest. You were going only for me." She turned to Mr. Dawson and gave him a humble yet knowing smile. "I know I'm a loyal servant. As well as the best valet in England. But this is too much."

Gregory watched the display with a measure of mild amusement completely outweighed by acute annoyance. "Yes, well, your grandmother might recover, but I have at least a dozen other reasons for visiting."

Pippa nudged Mr. Dawson in the ribs. "My twelve

cousins. My aunt and uncle had a passel of children, and still they took me on. My parents died young." She heaved a great sigh. "In fact, Lord Westdale only hired me because he felt sorry for me. Now he watches after those cousins as if they were his own."

"Yes, I do," he said, "which is why I refuse to stay away. *Let's go*."

"But Westdale," Marbury said, "you're taking us to Thurston Manor. To hell with those cousins. They're after your money, I have no doubt."

"I don't care what you think—*Marbury*," Gregory said in the intense way that he knew made the round little man livid. "Hopefully, by tomorrow afternoon you'll be ensconced in a comfortable hired coach."

"While you attend to those greedy brats in Plumtree." Marbury scoffed and waved a dismissive hand at him. "I thank you for absolutely nothing, *Westdale*."

Gregory did feel a momentary twinge of conscience when Pippa exchanged a glance with Mr. Dawson—it was obvious they were friends now.

"Good-bye, sir," she told him. "And good luck."

"To you, too, young man," Mr. Dawson said with a warm smile. "I'll be sure to employ that remedy for blisters. And I'll never wear that old bottle-green coat again."

"Good, sir," Pippa said. "I folded it and put it at the very bottom of your trunk so you'll forget all about it. It would be a hideous color on you." She bowed and turned away.

And Gregory saw her eyes.

They were shiny and wet.

But she walked quickly outside.

Gregory's heart lurched. He hated to see a woman cry, especially Pippa—not because he liked her better than other women but because she only cried when she meant it, deuce take it.

Guilt about her and guilt about a sweet old man stranded at an inn made him reconsider his plan. "I'll take you to Thurston Manor," he told Mr. Dawson, who was watching Pippa leave.

"You will?" His eyes shone with relief.

"Yes. I suppose the visit to Plumtree can wait."

"Damn right it can." Marbury clapped Gregory hard on the shoulder. "I knew you'd give in. No one can stand up to me for long."

"I don't know that I have room for you in the carriage, Marbury." Gregory's tone was cool.

Suddenly, Marbury's bravado evaporated. "I'll ride on the top," he squeaked. "With the coachman."

"Not a bad idea," said Gregory, "but I know for a fact Oscar can't stand you. He might throw you off. No, you'll be safer inside with me. But you must be on your best behavior."

Marbury pouted a brief second. "All right," he said next. "But don't make me sit next to that upstart valet— Farrow, Marrow, Wheelbarrow, whatever his name is."

"Harrow," said Mr. Dawson. "If you don't mind, Lord Westdale, I'd be most grateful to engage Harrow's services while we're ensconced at the manor. I'll be sure to tip him well."

"No tips required." Gregory grinned, feeling light-hearted in spite of the fact that he would have Pippa— *Pippa dressed as a valet*—with him for two more weeks. "I hope you don't mind that he'll be riding in the carriage with us. He's prone to chills."

"And he has dyspepsia," added Marbury with a disgusted leer. "Ugh."

Chapter Eleven

Hatless now as proper etiquette dictated and praying her wig wouldn't slip, Pippa thanked her lucky stars as she beamed at her traveling companions from behind her spectacles. Only one of them looked pleasantly at her, and that was Mr. Dawson, who sent her a sweet smile. He was incredibly modest and kind. Pippa wanted to keep him as a pet of sorts, to cluck over and make tea for. She was so glad she'd be able to help him dress at Thurston Manor.

Not that she'd be in his room when he was completely undressed, of course. Surely he could manage pulling on his own pantaloons or trousers. She'd helped Uncle Bertie often the past several years, and he'd only required assistance with his cravat and putting on his coat. Occasionally, she'd brush him down and suggest he choose another coat or waistcoat—she was extremely picky about colors and fabrics.

If Mr. Dawson needed a bath, Pippa would claim she had a bad back and make a male servant help out there. She looked forward, however, to shaving him. She loved the soap, the razor, and the efficiency with which she dispensed of unwanted beard. She'd shaved Uncle Bertie many a time.

"What time will we get there?" Marbury's petulant voice repeated the question for the umpteenth time.

"After dark." Gregory sighed patiently, and went back to his book on the architecture of Rome.

His Apollo-like profile did something to Pippa's middle—in fact, being around Gregory heightened all her senses. It was torture pretending not to care that his thigh rested flush against her own the entire trip, sending heat into her skin when she didn't need any extra warmth.

And that beef pie she'd eaten simply wasn't enough. She craved cake or another sweet, like marzipan. And she wished she could share it with Gregory. She'd loved looking across the table at him when they'd both dug into their crusty beef pies oozing brown gravy. There was something about watching his beautifully carved lips move when he chewed, something that made her think of the way those same lips had devoured her own in Eliza's garden. And the way his eyes looked into hers—it was as if they shared an amusing and very personal secret no one else knew.

They did share a secret now, she realized. A very naughty secret. The memory of what they did in the Old Oak Inn private dining room made her shift restlessly in her seat.

"Do you mind, Harrow?" Gregory looked up from his book.

He was outrageously handsome. It really wasn't fair to people like Marbury.

"Sorry, sir," she muttered.

Her craving for sugar—and his kisses—grew stronger, and she fell into a daydream about what had happened in the private dining room, but this time, the castle sculpture she'd made for Uncle Bertie's birthday was somehow involved. She mused about a sweet, sugary drawbridge and a fine, soaring turret . . .

Just thinking about turrets and Gregory at the same time, she was tempted to giggle a little hysterically, so she hid her face in her hands and coughed, the heat of her cheeks nearly scorching her palms. It was a scandalous, shameless comparison she made in her head, one that was beneath her dignity.

But she kept going back to it and remembering how brazenly Gregory had let her know he desired her— pinning her between his legs and yanking her closer by cupping her bottom and kneading it while he kissed her with hot, demanding kisses. It had been the most primitive, pleasurable moment of her whole life.

And the most fascinating part about it had been that it had been perfectly right, the way sitting in the sun on her haunches and watching a bumblebee dance over a flower was right—or when she lifted her head to luxuriate in the smell of the thunderclouds rolling off the sea and onto the moor.

She sighed and indulged in a long, languorous stretch that left her feeling distinctly lonely, especially when she looked down at her breasts, which had come so achingly close to being exposed when she'd stood on tiptoe to kiss Gregory's ear and his jacket button had snagged on her neckline, pulling it perilously low.

And then there was the drawbridge part of the daydream . . . she could barely muse on it without moaning out loud.

His turret.

Her drawbridge.

She was an idiot. She was supposed to be thinking about how she'd find a way to keep her turrets on her castles, or she'd never succeed as a sugar sculptor. Who cared about Gregory Sherwood?

You do, her body said, refusing to forget that he sat right next to her and that at Thurston Manor he'd be walking around on those muscular legs and speaking with that tender mouth and caressing a brandy glass with the same playful thumb that had toyed with the tip of her breast.

"I'm ravenous," she told him. Of course, she didn't tell him what she was ravenous for. "When we get there, I want dinner immediately."

Not really, but it was something to say. Daydreaming was doing her no favors.

"We don't *care* what you want," said Marbury. "You're a valet."

"I wasn't speaking to you," Pippa replied.

"Did you hear him?" Marbury looked at Gregory and pointed at her, which wasn't necessary, as she was mere feet from him. His index finger was practically at her nose.

"Yes," Gregory replied, and went back to his book.

"I knew it," Marbury said with relish. He looked at Dawson. "Did you hear Harebrained's rude retort?"

"I believe his name is Harrow." The old man spoke in his usual pleasant manner. "And I did hear him, yes."

"Then why isn't anyone doing something?" Marbury scowled at Pippa.

She merely yawned. Gregory turned a page of his book. Mr. Dawson looked out the window and quietly hummed a tuneless ditty.

"I hate you all," said Marbury, and folded his arms over his chest. "Except for Mr. Dawson, of course," he amended. "He can be forgiven for playing the diplomat. In fact, he should be rewarded." He tossed him an unctuous smile, then looked at Gregory. "It's you, *Westdale,* who's at fault. How dare you go to America and come back with all these ridiculous notions of equality?"

He narrowed his eyes and stared at Pippa. She stared right back, but then she averted her gaze.

Marbury chortled.

She didn't care. She was tired and ached to lean against Gregory's comfortable shoulder. But she couldn't, of course.

Fortunately, Lord Marbury and his boorish witticisms managed to keep her awake—that and the fact that his knees knocked against hers off and on the entire trip. When they did, he would emit a small growl, like a wounded dog. Eventually, however, with the help of some of Gregory's whiskey, he fell asleep, his hands clasped atop his immense orb of a stomach, nodding off occasionally onto Mr. Dawson, who would methodically push him away.

An hour after darkness had fallen, they turned up a lengthy winding drive illuminated by a bright moon.

"We're here," Gregory announced.

Mr. Dawson, who'd fallen asleep against the carriage wall, awoke, as did the snoring Marbury. The crunch of gravel beneath the carriage wheels and the flaming torches greeted them as they ascended the final incline to the house, proclaiming in dramatic fashion that they'd come to a large, wealthy estate.

"It's about time," Marbury said. "Mr. Dawson needs some refreshment." He stepped on Pippa's toe—on purpose, no doubt—and she jerked upright in her seat and glared at him. "Harrow, you'll see to it as soon as we get out. Make sure it includes some ale."

"I'm sure that Lord and Lady Thurston will have a cold supper waiting for us at this late hour," Gregory informed him. "Harrow will go straight to the kitchens for his own refreshment."

Pippa felt a frisson of fear. As a servant, she'd be relegated not only to the kitchen but to the attics. Would she be assigned her own room? Or would she have to share? She'd die if that happened.

Her heart began to race. How would she change her wig? What if she saw the male servants naked? What if they scratched their crotches and expected her to? What if they somehow guessed she was really a woman and got angry—or worse—about it?

You can do it, she told herself. *Just think of Monsieur Perot.*

Events became one big blur as the steps were brought out, liveried footmen in powdered wigs surrounded the carriage, and everyone but Pippa was treated like a welcome guest.

She ascended the stairs to the front entrance and paused to look at the beautiful stained-glass window above the door when a footman shoved her lightly in the back.

"Where are *you* going?" he said. "Turn around this instant and come around the side of the house."

And she wasn't even allowed to be upset. She had to act as a valet and say nothing about that window nor linger to admire it. She must turn around, descend the steps, already having made a disgrace of herself, and not even have the chance to say good-bye to Gregory.

"I need to get the trunks first," she told the footman. "Or someone else does, please. I'll oversee it. I have a bad back."

He laughed. "You think we'd wait for a valet's orders to pull down the trunks? They're already in the house. Come on, let's go."

Pippa looked over her shoulder at the light coming

from the entryway. Gregory was besieged with men in their fine coats and women in their silk gowns and well-coiffed hair, greeting him as if he were a hero returning from the wars instead of from a long, probably lavish sojourn in America. They hadn't even waited for him to join them in the drawing room. They'd rushed to the front door to see him.

Which one had been Damara? Pippa couldn't help wondering.

And above all the action at the door had come the high nasal tones of Lord Marbury, lost behind Gregory on the steps, his back arching and his nearly nonexistent neck stretching in the hopes that everyone inside could observe that he was there, too. "Make way!" he was yelling. "Make way!"

Two footmen ahead of her on the path started with rude comments about Marbury, and Pippa felt a strange burning in her throat.

Loneliness. That's what it was. She was really and truly alone now, and she couldn't even lay claim to her own identity. Instead here she was pretending to be a man—and a valet—and not even a plausible one at that. What had she been thinking?

She wished there were a familiar face, even Lord Marbury, nearby to speak to. She heaved a sigh, then gave herself a shake and pulled her chin up. It was time to strengthen her resolve, to "straighten her spine," as Uncle Bertie often advised.

"You shouldn't make fun of your betters," she admonished in her strictest valet tones.

One of the footmen, who had a square jaw, turned to look at her. "Lord Marbury? Our better? You're jesting."

And then he proceeded to laugh wickedly with his sidekick, parroting Marbury's shouting "Make way!" in a fairly accurate and nasal fashion.

"Why, with those skinny legs and big round belly, I'd say he looks like a stuffed American turkey, wouldn't you, mate?" the other footman said in a Cockney accent.

They both guffawed and hit one another on the back in merriment.

"That's better than looking like a doll in a china shop," Pippa declared.

Both servants stopped.

"Do you mean us?" Cockney asked, his fists bunched at his sides.

"We can't hurt 'im—we'll get in trouble," said the square-jawed one.

"We can yank down his trousers," the other answered.

Square-jaw laughed.

"I didn't mean you two," Pippa said hastily. "I meant the little man, Mr. Dawson. He's so small, he's like a china doll."

Both footmen eyed her as if she'd gone mad.

She smiled miserably at them. "I'm starved." She *was* hungry, after all.

Cockney winked at her. "Cook has saved some left-over cold livers for you. That and a pint of ale should do you good."

"That's right." She tried to sound enthusiastic. "Although I'll need a glass of milk, too, please. Doctor's orders. And I—I think I'll skip the livers." She'd always hated them. "A piece of bread will do."

Square-jaw made a face. "You're a picky little bugger, aren't you?"

"He'd better not be when he sleeps with us tonight," said Cockney.

Square-jaw nudged him. "On the floor, he'll be, between our two beds."

"You mean between the two chamber pots under the beds. We'll be pissing over his head."

Ugh.

They both guffawed again and brought Pippa along a path to the kitchen door. Another half hour passed rather in a blur. It seemed everyone wanted a snack, so the other servants sat around the table with her. She bolted some bread and milk—which revived her—and listened to a cacophony of voices gossiping about all the visitors. So far, Gregory was winning as the most admired man. He was viewed as handsome, wealthy, and charming.

"He's dangerous, too," she added.

Everyone stopped talking.

"No, he is," she said. "Although I don't think he's killed anyone," she added into the silence. "The good thing is, I know I need never fear being mistreated with him around. He doesn't tolerate bullying of his servants—not that any of you would ever do such a thing."

And went back to chewing.

Slowly and a bit awkwardly, the conversation resumed. The talk moved round to the most admired woman in the house party—Lady Damara Poindexter.

Pippa stopped eating so she could hear every word.

So far, she'd heard Lady Damara had a figure like a heavenly angel, a laugh like the queen of the fairies, lips as lush as a red, red rose, and other bits of nonsense gleaned mainly from old songs—nothing original and truly compelling, until Cook declared—

"That demmed lady has eyes that scorch a man's soul and drive him mad with the need to possess her, until nothing is left of him but a vacant shell."

Everybody stopped chewing at that.

"I read that in a book," said Cook. "But she fits the bill."

"I won't count on her being in her own bed tonight," said one maid with a snicker.

"Right," said a footman. "Lady Thurston made sure Lord Westdale's room is conveniently on the same corridor but at the other end. We can't make things too easy for them. It takes away all the passion."

"I'll shut me ears as I walk by," said another maid, giggling.

Pippa's stomach began to feel sick. She didn't know why. It couldn't be because of Lady Damara going to Gregory's room. No, it had to be because she would be sleeping on the floor between two footmen, neither of whom was particularly friendly to their guests' servants, and their chamber pots.

Good God, what if they expected her to use their chamber pots? A bit more terror struck her. What if they challenged her to a pissing contest?

If they caught on to her disguise, Gregory would send her packing.

"Will you be waiting up for his lordship?" the cook asked Pippa.

"Yes," she said, glad of the idea. "I'll wait in his room. He doesn't like to ring for me when we're out and about."

"You're a nice little man, aren't you?" The cook beamed at her. "Before you go, you'll head to the attic to see your pallet first, so you don't wake everyone up when you go up to bed later."

"All right." The idea of sleeping between those foot-men was unbearable. But Pippa stood. "Can someone show me the way?"

"We will," her Cockney and square-jawed escorts said in unison.

But she sensed something sly between them. One of the maids giggled. Pippa looked around the table. "I hope you know that a valet deserves respect."

Another maid giggled, too. "Your employer didn't ever kill anyone. You just said that because—because you're a skinny little fellow and those guys"—she angled her chin to the footmen—"they could beat you to a pulp."

"At least he's thinking," said another maid. "It was a clever notion."

"I wouldn't challenge Lord Westdale," said Pippa qui-etly. She meant it in earnest this time. "He's the last man on earth you want angry."

And the first man she'd want on her side. She was proud—*proud*—to be his valet. Inside, she was shocked to realize that she admired him.

This time, the girls' eyes widened. Pippa lifted her chin and followed the men. Dear God, her dream to be-come a sugar sculptor was trying her, wasn't it?

But going up the servants' stairs and into the main house, she grew excited at the beautiful surroundings. A house party! How amusing! She'd never been to one.

The black-and-white marble floor in the corridor lead-ing to the front door captured her fancy like nothing else. Uncle Bertie's home was comfortable—*this* home was regal. She looked to her right and caught a glimpse of a library, and then straight ahead, the front door with that beautiful stained-glass window above it. From the left of the front door, a great swath of light fell on the marble floor. It came from the drawing room, where all the guests were gathered.

"Will the latecomers eat off plates in there?" she asked Cockney.

"No, they'll eat off the floor," he said, and rolled his eyes.

"Of course," said Square-jaw. "They've got a fine meal, too. If they don't finish it, I intend to snitch a bit of it to feed my collection of pet rats."

The footmen exchanged glances.

Pippa swallowed hard, but she wouldn't ask. They wanted her to. She could tell.

They turned smartly to ascend the stairs—two of their brethren might be watching from their posts at the drawing room door—and Pippa followed behind.

And then she heard Gregory's voice. He was telling the company about a remarkable American he'd met on the frontier, a man who inspired him with his grit and resolve to clear his land and build his log cabin. Everyone asked him questions all at once, and he laughed and said, "One at a time, please."

They *adored* him. Pippa swallowed a lump in her throat. She hated being a valet. She wanted to be in that room sitting by Gregory and listening to every word he said about America. And then she wanted Lady Damara to see that he wasn't eligible to marry her or have an illicit liaison with her because . . .

He was Lady Pippa Harrington's love.

"My godfather owns a number of theaters," she heard him say when she reached the stair landing.

There was a smattering of comments she couldn't understand, and then she heard, "Lady Pippa Harrington."

She stopped on the landing.

"Hurry up," one of the footmen said.

"Wait," she said, "my stockings are drooping." She bent down slowly to pull one up—a useless endeavor, really—and heard Gregory say, "Yes, she is an old schoolmate of Lady Morgan's."

Eliza.

And then he said, "She'll be coming to London soon, although she's quite happy in Dartmoor, traipsing the moors and indulging in her hobbies."

"What kind of hobbies?" someone asked.

It was Lady Damara, Pippa was sure. Her voice was like velvet. Or was it like the laugh of that dashed queen of the fairies?

"She plays the pianoforte," Gregory said mildly. "And I know she likes to read."

Oh, Gregory.

Pippa's heart sank. She wasn't going to London, and he'd said nothing about her passion for sugar sculpture. Why? What difference did it make to anyone, least of all him, that she had a gift? For that's what it was, her whimsical sculpting of sugary confections.

A *gift*.

"Your stocking is fine," the Cockney footman said.

"You're just eavesdropping," Square-jaw accused her.

She looked up at him. "And what if I am? You're enjoying it, too."

"You gettin' cheeky with us?" Cockney snarled.

She was so tired of that word *cheeky*! And he'd said it much too loudly.

"Ssshh!" she whispered. "I'm not being cheeky. I'm tired, that's all. Please show me the attics so I can go wait in Lord Westdale's bedchamber until he arrives."

She took one step forward—one sore, tired step—when

a voice from the drawing room called up to them. "You! On the stairs. Harrow?"

She looked down and saw the most welcome sight in the world—Gregory, and he was holding a full glass of something red. He looked marvelously healthy, not at all sad and decrepit, which is what she felt like after this very long day.

"Wait there," he ordered her, then looked up at the footmen. "He won't be sleeping in the attics. Take him to my dressing room right away, and put him on a pallet, please. A comfortable one."

Pippa's heart expanded with a feeling so light, she almost lost her breath. Gregory had been looking out for her all day. She must admit it. Even though she hated that he'd been trying to get her back home, not once had he stopped thinking about her comfort.

And then a young woman came out of the drawing room. She wore a spectacular turquoise gown with a sparkling chiffon overlay and a matching ribbon woven through her ebony curls. She put her arm through Gregory's. "What have we here?" she asked, and sent him an alluring smile.

Lady Damara. Without a doubt.

"That's my valet," said Gregory, his gaze still on Pippa. "He needs looking after. He's got a bad back."

"Poor fellow," said Lady Damara, eyeing Pippa as if she were a lame horse. "He won't be any good to you if he's crippled, will he?"

Pippa stared back at Gregory.

"He's a man of many talents," said Gregory. "He'll always land on his feet. Good night, Harrow. Sleep well."

But Pippa wouldn't answer him. Man of many talents, indeed. He hadn't told anyone she liked to make sugar sculptures, had he? He didn't care. All he cared about was beautiful women, adventure, and playing with architecture as a hobby. Why do more? He was to be a future marquess!

She hid her pique, of course, in the servant's demeanor she showed him by bowing quickly. Then she sped off with the footmen, who brought her—without another rude word—to Lord Westdale's bedchamber.

Chapter Twelve

Pippa was angry. Gregory saw it in the fleeting look of scorn she cast him the moment before she bowed her good night. Then again, she was wearing spectacles, and the light from the candles in the entryway could have deceived him.

Oh, who was he fooling? She was clearly upset. When she strode off with the footmen, her back to him, he sensed her bristling.

"He's a cheeky thing, isn't he?" mused Lady Damara on his arm. "Not quite the usual valet."

"No, he's not," he murmured.

Lady Damara yanked on his arm. "Let's go back inside. They're starting a game of whist."

"Right," he said, feeling distracted. He was really in no mood to socialize. He longed to relax—to read, to unwind. And to talk to Pippa would be nice. But of course he couldn't go to bed this early—not before midnight, at the least.

He was surprised how much he liked knowing that Pippa would be in his dressing room, waiting—

Actually, sleeping. That was what he hoped she'd do. She needed it desperately.

And you need her *desperately.*

He had no idea where that thought originated, but the image of the sugar-sculpture castle came to him in a flash.

A silly little sculpture—to accompany a silly little thought.

He put both away and focused on the beautiful woman at hand.

"Shall we establish a bet between us, winner takes all?" Lady Damara looked up at him, the picture of innocence, but he saw the glint in her eye. He knew that neither one of them would lose were they to bet. The invitation was clear, and she was most appealing.

"No bets tonight," he said gently. "It's been a very long day."

"Of course." She looked away, but not before he caught the slightly pained expression on her beautiful face. He hated to embarrass her, but facts were facts: He wasn't interested in a liaison with any woman who might believe she stood a chance of becoming his future countess and, later, marchioness.

He wasn't ready.

Lady Damara was miffed, and if there was anything worse for Gregory than being the object of scorn of one lady, it was being resented by two. The company had been playing cards and indulging in some fine claret when they'd arrived. Lord and Lady Thurston, perhaps slightly the worse for wear, had escorted him right into the midst of the festivities and plied him with a cold plate and a goblet that never seemed to empty.

He'd not had a chance to sit back and breathe. Which was all well and good, as he'd had the entire afternoon and early evening in the carriage to sit—and breathe.

Which sometimes was difficult to do when the world's squirmiest woman sat next to one and insisted on casting burning looks at one because she was bored. He'd refused to stare back at her because he'd found Pippa incredibly appealing in those pantaloons. Not only that, he knew she still wasn't bound beneath her coat by that god-awful strip of cloth, which Oscar had removed from the carriage, no doubt wondering what in hell it was.

During the course of the evening, he'd spoken with Lord Rochelle and Mr. Brian Forrest, second son of Lord Hall, both of whom he'd worked with on design projects under the tutelage of several architects in London. They confirmed what he suspected: They, too, had been asked to design a dog cottage for Lady Thurston.

So the race was on. Mr. Dawson kept a low profile all night, just as he had at the inn. Everyone was aware of his connection to Lord and Lady Thurston—he was a cousin and as such didn't merit much attention. It was true he wasn't the most scintillating company, but his presence amid the gathering of sophisticated guests lent the atmosphere a refreshing charm rarely found in more rarefied London drawing rooms.

The little man spoke to every gentleman there who'd designed something for Lord and Lady Thurston, although he didn't ask them about those projects. He kept to safe subjects, such as the weather and gardening, one of his favorite hobbies, and shooting grouse, which was something he'd only just begun to do. With Gregory, he made a point to tell him that he was also the oldest son of a large family, and they spent fifteen minutes discussing the merits and detractions of being the sibling in charge.

"It's a huge responsibility," Gregory said, and realized he'd missed being the big brother while he'd been in

America. "You feel as if when you're away, the younger ones can't do without you. Their worlds will stop turning."

"They often do," said Mr. Dawson, a twinkle in his eye. "It's not our job to get them spinning again, however. Every member of a family needs to learn on his or her own. You may only lend them advice. Not get in the way."

Gregory thought of Peter, of how he'd known Eliza didn't love him—

And hadn't told him.

But he'd had a year now to think about it. Who'd betrayed whom, really?

He looked down into the scarlet depths of the claret in his glass and thought about that day. He'd never have believed Peter if he'd told him that Eliza was in love with Dougal. Not in a million years. And Peter knew Gregory would react that way, which was why he never confided the full extent of his worries to him.

The plain truth was that Gregory had let guilt and jealousy come between him and his younger brother. Peter was a true Sherwood of the House of Brady. He should be Lord Westdale if all were right with the world.

He was truly Father's son.

And he was an excellent brother. He'd reminded Gregory that Mother's ring was special. It was Gregory who'd been in the wrong. He'd been willing to give a treasured token away to a woman he didn't love—a woman who didn't love *him*. The ring was the only thing he had left of Mother besides that grin of hers that he saw on Robert's face . . . and her piercing eyes, which now belonged to Peter.

He shook his head, gave a short laugh, and looked away—anywhere but at the knowing gaze of the little man before him.

"You have to learn to love what you see in front of you, young man," said Mr. Dawson, "and not what you expect—or even demand—to see."

Gregory turned back to him and raised his glass of claret. "Good advice. From one big brother to another."

He would think on it.

"Cheers." Mr. Dawson grinned and clinked his glass with his.

An inviting scene greeted Gregory in his bedchamber a long three hours after he last saw his "valet" on the stair landing. A small fire crackled cheerily in the grate, and on the bureau was an elaborate candelabra with four lit tapers casting a lovely glow. Another single candle sat on his bedside table, next to some apples and purple grapes arranged prettily on a china plate. The luxurious scarlet covers of his bed were thrown back, exposing an abundance of plumped pillows while an open bottle of wine waited on the far side of the bed, with not one but two glasses.

Lady Thurston was the supreme hostess. A wicked hostess. He wondered if Lady Damara were one of her dear friends. He hoped not—he didn't need three women displeased with him.

On the left side of the room, a closed door obviously led to his dressing room. Just looking at that door put his senses on high alert. He felt an overwhelming lust invade his being—

He wanted Lady Pippa Harrington.

What was wrong with him?

This was *Pippa*. Plenty of women in London could turn a man's eye more often than she would.

Pippa, as lovely as she was, wasn't attuned to the whole

mating ritual . . . she didn't exude an aura of feminine mystery. She simply didn't care, he supposed. Her mind was on other things—the beautiful morning, the delicious quality of every dessert she'd ever tasted, the latest novels, the amusing antics of her favorites among the village children in Plumtree, the state of affairs in England and the world.

When she walked into a room, men felt at ease with her. They didn't sit on the edge of their seats. The blood in their heads didn't rush to their groins. She was the type of woman who reminded a man that he hadn't had tea in a while and was famished—or that he needed to go visit his grandmother more often and make her laugh at his inane stories the same way Pippa laughed at them—with abandon.

She was the type of woman who reminded a man that he was still a boy at heart—and that he was more than the bleached-white cravat, the well-polished boots, the speech he'd delivered at Parliament, and the mansion on Grosvenor Square.

But she was also the woman who'd braced herself on a taproom door, her legs spread, and let him tease her until she lost control and cried out her pleasure.

Yes, she was *that* Pippa, too, and the memory made his sex stiffen with desire to see her that way again.

He strode to the dressing room door and gave a gentle knock. When there was no answer, he turned the knob slowly and peeked in. He wanted a glimpse of his valet—

His Pippa.

She would be no other man's until he could find the perfect mate for her.

Her hair was unpinned and lay in glorious disarray on her pillow. She was on her back, her legs spread wide beneath her blanket, her arms thrown out and dangling over the edge of the pallet, and she was . . .

Was she snoring?

Yes, she most definitely was—a light snore, as befitted a lady—

A lady who was wearing a man's nightshirt to bed. A lady who was sprawled in her bed the way a man would be. A lady who liked the intimate things he'd done to her and with her.

He smiled. He couldn't help it. Around Pippa, he felt careless. Care*free*.

"Good God!" she suddenly exclaimed, and sat bolt upright, her chest heaving.

So much for carefree. Gregory schooled his expression to be neutral bordering on light, professional concern. "Sorry. I was checking on you, that's all. I'm not only your guardian—on an unofficial basis, of course—I'm your current employer, and it's my duty to ensure that you're safe and comfortable."

"Oh. I noticed that earlier. I meant to thank you. All day, in between being a terrific nuisance—and coaxing me into paroxysms of unadulterated, wild animal passion—you've looked after me." She ran a hand over her brow and the crown of her head to push her hair off her face.

"It was my pleasure," he said. And yes, the word *pleasure* was weighted with all sorts of meaning.

"I suppose you had an interesting night," she said carefully.

"Yes, you could call it that." Lady Damara was miffed with him, but the talk with Mr. Dawson had done him good. "I'm thankful to get to bed, however."

"I was, too."

"No doubt you had an interesting night, too. I hope it wasn't terrible."

She shook her head. "Nothing I couldn't bear with equanimity."

"Good." He was glad the firelight behind him made his face a shadow. He could study her for any signs of fear or worry—and bask in her simple beauty—without her really being aware. "I want you to know that even if I hadn't seen you on the stairs, I would have made sure you never would have had to sleep in the attics with the male servants."

"Thank you." Her voice sounded subdued. No wonder— he'd woken her from a deep sleep. And she was playing a role, a role that surely couldn't be easy, and doing so in a houseful of strangers.

"Did you really enjoy this evening?" she asked him.

He shrugged. "It was all right."

"You appeared to be having a lovely time with Lady Damara. Was that she? The one who came out and took your arm?"

"Yes."

"She looks divine in turquoise."

"I suppose she does."

Pippa looked down and away from him. "She obviously wants to marry you."

He laughed. "Not necessarily."

Now it was Pippa's turn to shrug. "It would be most convenient if she did."

"Right. I remember why. So Uncle Bertie will stop pestering us to get married ourselves."

"Exactly."

"Of course, he thinks we're heading to Gretna right now."

"There's no way we could have made it so quickly." She sighed. "So I suppose he thinks we're staying at an inn. Hopefully, he believes we'll be in separate rooms."

"That's not usually what happens when people elope. They give up on pretense, I believe, and indulge their passions where they may."

She emitted a little laugh.

"What's so amusing?" he asked.

"Just that I heard in the kitchens that the servants expect you and Lady Damara to be together tonight. I assume that's what the wine is for on your bedside table."

Gregory hid his chagrin. He was sure those were props for use in a midnight affair, too. "Just because servants talk doesn't mean the rumor is true."

"Right. Like the rumor Lord Marbury mentioned about you . . . and my old friend Eliza." She gave another laugh, but this one was a bit sad.

Gregory sighed. "Do you believe it?"

Pippa stared at him. "I don't know."

It hurt him that she did. But why should it? It was true. He'd slept with Eliza—once.

Just once.

But he couldn't stand the idea of Pippa knowing. He couldn't bear the idea that she would ever, *ever* truly think ill of him.

"Tell me the truth about you and Eliza," she said, and even in the dark, he could see how her eyes were lit with more than curiosity. There was something else . . . she had another reason for wanting to know.

"You tell me why you're asking first," he said. "And then—I swear—I'll tell you the truth."

She heaved a big sigh. The room was silent a moment.

"Never mind," she said.

He was relieved, of course. "Tomorrow we'll talk, shall we? About what to do with you when the house party is over."

She sat up higher. "What do you mean?"

"I mean that I don't intend to take you back to Uncle Bertie's."

She gave a great gasp. "Really?" And before he could blink, she'd left her pallet and had her arms around his neck. "Oh, thank you, Gregory."

He let her hang there a moment. In fact, he closed his eyes and luxuriated in the feel of her. "I decided tonight when I saw you on the stairs with those two brutish footmen . . ."

"They were awful louts."

". . . That anyone who tries this hard to escape their lot must have a very good reason for doing so."

She squeezed him even harder, then pulled back to look at him. "It's true that belowstairs I was very worried about being a valet here. I even wondered if it were worth it. But it is." She gripped his shoulders and gave him a little shake. "It *is*."

He marveled at her devotion to her dream. "Tell me," he said, "what is it about making sugar sculptures that makes you so . . . excited?"

She laughed. "They make people happy, that's why. Including me."

"It's as simple as that, then?"

"Of course. It's the same way I can't give up tea. Or sleep. Or—"

"Or what? What else can't you give up?"

Her eyes were large and dark, her skin glowing in the firelight from the bedchamber. "Nothing." She stepped back and looked away from him again, her arms crossed over her chest. "I think you should go now. Tomorrow is another long day. At least we'll start it and end it in the same place." She looked back at him and gave him an awkward smile. "That will be nice."

He took a step toward her, and she stumbled back onto her pallet. "What are you doing?"

He stood still. "Nothing."

"Then—then why are you still here?"

He scratched his temple. "You just seem a bit angry at me. And it disappoints me. I was looking forward to seeing you."

"You were?"

"Of course. Why do you sound so surprised?"

She shrugged again.

He wasn't sure that he should ask, but he did: "Are you jealous of Lady Damara, by any chance?"

She reacted as he suspected she would. "Why would you think that? I want you to marry someone, Gregory. The sooner, the better."

"Right," he said.

There was that silence again.

Slowly, she rubbed her eyes with her index finger and thumb. "All right." With an abrupt change in her demeanor, she looked him square in the eye. "I might have been a little jealous. The few times I've seen you in London, you're always with these beautiful women, and then the papers speak of how all the debutantes want to waltz with you—"

"Yes?" He came up to her, put his hands on her waist. "What of it?"

She bit her lip and looked away again.

"Pippa?"

"Blast it all, I hate you sometimes."

"I know." He felt his mouth tip up at the corner and wondered why it was that no matter what she said, he still adored her. He always had. From the time they were small.

But what did it mean, to adore someone?

He adored his sisters, didn't he? And Mama. He adored Alice, too, their housekeeper. He'd also adored his grandmothers and Mother—when they were alive.

Obviously, adoration was a feeling he reserved for women—he'd never adored sweets. He'd longed for them and gobbled them down when he got them. And he'd never adored Tiger, their old dog. In his younger years, Gregory simply loved him and wanted to roughhouse with him on the grass. He'd definitely never adored his father or his brothers, mathematics (his favorite subject), or boats (which he was also mad for).

No, there was something about that word *adore* that he reserved for women who were special to him.

And he adored Pippa.

Maybe it was because her profile was stunning. He hadn't noticed that before. He longed to run his finger down it, from her forehead to her chin, and then her neck . . .

Had he adored Eliza?

No.

And he was ashamed that he'd taken it as far with her as he had, and hadn't adored her as every woman deserved to be.

Pippa released a little laugh, then looked back at him. "It's just that I sometimes wish . . ."

"What?"

"That I intrigued you the way those women do," she confessed. "But of course, you already know that. You saw my notebook in Eliza's garden, and I'm over you, I promise. But I still want to know what it is—and how to get it—the ability to attract the notice of a man like you, not just on a dare—"

He stopped her with a kiss.

And what a kiss it was.

What a kiss it could be, he thought, when Pippa kissed him back with her whole heart.

For that was what she was offering him, he knew, even if she didn't realize it herself.

Her whole heart.

She was never one to disguise anything.

Chapter Thirteen

"No." Pippa's lips felt plump and warm, ready to be kissed by Gregory again. But she couldn't. She mustn't.

"You're especially beautiful tonight," he whispered in a husky tone. His dark eyes held her in place the way the moon held the tides.

"We can't *do* this." She pushed against his chest and walked around him into the bedchamber to stand before the fire, her arms wrapped around her middle.

Oh, dear, her legs were bare.

She looked up and saw him staring at her, at her legs, and then back at her face. A little shiver ran through her. "Sorry. I didn't have a night rail. I took one of your spare shirts. You packed more than I was able to manage."

"It's all right. I've seen you like this before." Pippa's cheeks burned. He went to a corner and pulled a banyan off a hook. "Here. Use this." He came to her then like a gallant knight and held out an arm of the silky robe. She slid it on, enjoying the slippery feel of it. He did the same for the other arm, and then came to stand in front of her, where he took the two ends of the belt and smartly tied them at her waist. "There."

She smiled. "*You're* the valet. Not me. You've been so all day long."

"I have, haven't I?" He walked to the far side of the bed and poured a glass of wine.

She listened with satisfaction to the sound of the liquid gurgling from the bottle and into the glass.

"Would you like some?" He held the glass toward her.

Slowly, she nodded.

He poured another for himself, and then he walked over to her, the sound of the floorboards squeaking a reminder that the rest of the house was falling asleep—or perhaps staying up to play, depending upon the guest and his or her carnal intentions.

When she took the glass, he raised his toward her. "Cheers."

A little reluctantly—well, if she were honest, *very* reluctantly—she clinked hers with his and said what was truly on her mind: "As much as I might like it to be, this can't be another seduction scene, Gregory. I'm not one of your many female admirers willing to be bedded at your whim, like Lady Damara."

"I agree. You're not in the least like her or any other female I know."

"Thank you. I'll decide when seduction is to occur, if ever. It might be years from now—"

"Years? That would be an awfully long time."

She shrugged and took another sip of wine, and together they watched the flames in peaceful silence. "People can live on memories, you know."

"I'd hate to do that. The real thing's so much better."

She huffed. "I know we've spent some very intimate moments together, and it was truly lovely, but I intend to follow through on my plan to go to Paris." She allowed her mouth to tip up. "I'll admit, you've hit upon quite an effective way to keep me here in England. But it's a diversion only, and as I told you at the inn, I comprehend your strategy—if that's what it is."

"I'm flattered you think I'm that clever, but that's not it at all." His gaze was serious when he lifted a hand to pull a long strand of hair off her face. "It happened. And when it shouldn't have, I'm the first to admit it. But it's almost inevitable when a man and woman are thrown together as we've been—not to mention all the expectations Bertie has voiced about us." He lifted a shoulder and let it drop. "I understand your point, in other words. Fun is fun, but plans are plans. And ne'er the twain shall meet."

"I—I'm glad you understand." She shifted a few inches to the right, away from him.

"And you're breathtaking, even in a man's shirt. Especially in a man's shirt." He took her free hand and squeezed it. "You talk as if other women have some secret that you don't—and they do, I admit. But you're so much more interesting, just being you. You don't need any secrets."

"I must admit I'm averse to them." She pulled her hand back carefully and wrapped it around her goblet. "How long have you been able to wrap women around your little finger?"

"It's not something I work at," he said. "But it's true that somehow I'm never wanting for female companionship."

"And you're not speaking of your stepmother and sisters, are you?"

"No," he admitted wryly. "Although when you throw them in the mix, I have more female companionship than a fellow knows what to do with." He tossed off a wry grin. "Even in America, where I concealed my identity as a wealthy earl much of the time, I was plagued with female companionship."

"Poor you." She'd imbibed half her glass now. Her arms and legs were beginning to warm up very well.

"I'm not complaining," he said. "I enjoy the company of women."

"Obviously." Her tone was dry.

"Excuse me," he said, "but no one teases me without retribution." He put his glass down near the single candle and threw himself back on the bed, where he lay on his right side, one leg tucked up to his knee. "I dare you to join me." He patted the coverlet. "Your punishment will be my complete indifference to your feminine charms while we discuss what we're to do with you after the house party. What with your being valet not only to me but to Mr. Dawson, we won't have much time to plan, otherwise."

"That's a grand idea," she said, warming up to him again. "I can't believe this is happening, that we're not going back to Plumtree."

She put her wine down next to his and crawled onto the bed, feeling as if they were two ill-behaved children preparing to break into the pantry and steal a cake. She stretched out full length next to him, her head resting on the heel of her open palm. "I'll start," she said.

"Go right ahead. Just remember, this is conjecture at this point. Don't get too excited."

Excited?

His eyes were hooded, their deep blue depths unfathomable. His broad chest and muscular arms reminded Pippa that she was smaller, weaker.

A shiver went through her. Gregory was all man.

"After the house party," she began, "you'll take me to Plymouth and drop me off so I can sail to France, where I'll immediately take up my post as companion to the lovely old lady who's actually expecting me."

"That's convenient."

"Fated," she corrected him. "She hadn't spoken to Uncle Bertie in forty years when she wrote him about needing a companion."

"Very well. How would you get to France safely?"

"I'll maintain my disguise, which I admit I can't stand—the wig is itchy, and when I wear my binding"— she saw his pupils dilate when she said *binding*—"I have difficulty drawing a deep breath. But the disguise serves its purposes."

"That's not nearly enough," he said. "You'd need to carry a pistol."

"You can teach me to shoot while I'm here, then." She grinned. "I'm going to be the first English lady of the leisure class to be trained by an international expert in the art of confectionery. *Ever*."

"If this were to happen, you'd be beginning a small revolution, in other words," Gregory murmured.

"Exactly. Who knows? Maybe another young lady in a similar position will look to my example and throw over expectations and do something completely marvelous and unexpected, too."

"And if it involves marzipan, all the better," he said.

"Don't talk down to me, Gregory." Her banyan slipped off her shoulder.

"I'm not. I meant metaphorical marzipan." He pulled her sleeve back up and patted it. "Something sweet, decadent, frivolous yet somehow completely necessary for happiness."

His voice was getting husky again.

"I know you're jesting, but you're actually describing perfectly why I like sugar sculptures." She reached behind her and picked up her glass of wine, took a sip, then set it down. "Do you want your wine?" she said over her shoulder.

He shook his head. "I don't think so." But he sounded distracted, as if he weren't really listening to her anymore.

"Gregory? Are you all right?"

"I think I'm failing at my objective. Your feminine charms are definitely attracting me."

She threw herself down to face him again. "Good." She winked at him. "You deserve it. I refuse to go anywhere. Be tempted."

"Fine," he said. "But I'll outlast you."

"I doubt it."

"I know I will. Because in about two seconds you're going to go storming out of here into your little dressing room."

"What do you mean?"

He shook his head. "I can't take you to Plymouth."

"What?" Her stomach dropped to her feet. "You said—"

"I said I wouldn't return you home. But I never said I'd expedite your journey alone to Paris. Even after all you say—even if you were to learn to use a pistol—I still don't believe it's safe. You'll be found out, Pippa."

"Have I yet?" she snapped.

"No."

"But these two weeks will be stellar practice," she insisted, anger building in her like steam trapped in a teapot.

"It's not enough," he said. "You'd be an unprotected woman in a foreign city, and it goes against my conscience to dump you at a seaport—"

She leaped off the bed. "You're right. I *am* leaving."

"I told you not to get too excited. That this was all conjecture."

"All I heard was the word *excited*. And then I thought about your chest and the muscles in your arms!"

"That's not *my* fault." He leaped up after her. "I propose instead that you live in London with my family, and we hire a confectioner to tutor you. Plus—"

"You've already mentioned that, and I said *no*."

"That's not the extent of my proposal. A trip to Paris can be arranged. You'd go with me and the women of the family. We could stay for several weeks. Perhaps a whole month."

She hesitated. "That's a generous offer. But I'll need more than several weeks or a month. You know if I go with your family, it will be difficult to meet with Monsieur at all, especially as I'll need to dress as a man. Your mother wouldn't approve."

"No, she wouldn't," Gregory said, "but dressing as a man wouldn't be necessary. I'd pay him such an incredible amount of money, he wouldn't dare turn you away, even as a woman."

"That would be a great relief." Slowly, she began to unwrap the ties of her banyan. "But I must say no. I can't have you paying my way. It isn't right. And I want to stay half a year at least."

"You need to learn how to compromise, young lady."

She raked a hand through her hair. "If I asked you to compromise on pursuing *your* dream, would you?"

He hesitated. "No, but—"

"Never mind," she said. "I'm not sure you *do* understand because I'm not sure you have a dream!" She let the banyan drop to the floor. "I'll get to Plymouth without you."

"Oh, no you won't." He picked up the silky garment and threw it in the corner.

She turned her back on him and began to unlace the tie at her neck.

"What are you doing?" His tone was low, threatening.

She paused. "Nothing that would interest a man immune to my charms." She braced herself, and then she lifted the edge of her shirt, pulled it over her head, and dropped it to the floor.

Why not?

She was never going to marry. She had nothing to lose. And she'd already bared herself to him anyway.

Nakedness was nothing to be ashamed of, either. She was a girl who'd walked her whole life on the moors, had felt a kinship with the earth and all of nature. She wasn't ashamed of her body. And she knew that Gregory, of all people, would be the one person she'd be tempted to share it with.

She already had.

Not that she really intended to do so again tonight—but she would entice him with her form. Oh, yes, she would. Call her a tease—she didn't care. She was frustrated with this man who was controlling her life, and if it meant she had to strip naked to shake his smug confidence, then she would.

"It's not going to work," he said, already guessing her plan. "If you think that this display is going to make me forget my duty, you're wrong, madam."

She walked over to him, reached up on her tiptoes, and

kissed him. "I *want* you to think worse of me," she whispered. "I want you to be tortured by the sight of me. Maybe then you'll let me go." She ran a finger down his neck. "But first, you'll teach me to shoot. And loan me a pistol."

"No," he said softly, and took her shoulders. "You're not going. At least not alone."

She couldn't help the little tears that welled in her eyes. "I can't ask you to make this into a Sherwood family holiday. You're not my husband, Gregory. Nor will you ever be."

"You'll take no man to be your husband," he said. "So what am I to do with you?"

"Resist me," she whispered, and ran a finger down his shirt.

"Stop it." He grabbed her hand. "We can figure out a way—"

"Resist me, Gregory," she said again, and nuzzled his neck with her mouth.

"You're being ridiculous," he said. "I won't think the worse of you and give up the role I told Bertie I'd play. I won't let you go, no matter how many times you try to seduce me. I can't believe I'm even saying those words— *you* trying to seduce *me*. It's outrageous, preposterous—"

"Resist me," she said for the third time, then looked straight into his eyes and cupped him between the legs. He surged to hardness—and despite every ounce of will that flared in his eyes, she knew she had him where she wanted him.

"Damn you," he said, and lifted her in his arms.

Heady with victory, she wrapped her hands around his neck and kissed him with lush abandon. *So there, Gregory Sherwood, Earl of Westdale!*

He pulled back. "Where did this she-devil come from?"

She smiled. "I've been here all along. You told me yourself at the Old Oak Inn you knew I was this way. But you still did your best to ignore me all these years." She kissed him lightly on the lips.

He released a sigh. "I suppose I did."

"Certainly you did. Just as you also know you're a gifted architect and are ignoring *that*."

"I'm not ignoring it."

"Yes you are. You're brilliant at it. You have a chance to design a dog cottage that John Nash himself will look over."

"To hell with John Nash," he snapped. "It's a damned dog cottage. I should be building museums, theaters, grand mansions—"

"Exactly!" Her eyes sparkled with triumph. "So what's holding you back?"

"I'm a busy man," he muttered.

"Yes, you're a future marquess." She tried to put as much stuffiness into the title as she could.

"Hah," he said.

She knew she'd made him angry because his pupils narrowed.

"I know you're letting your own dreams go to the dogs," she blithely went on, "but what are you going to do about mine? Force me to let them go, too? I suppose misery loves company. Well, here I am. Company. What do you intend to do about it?"

"You're diabolical."

"Not nearly as diabolical as you."

"What is it with you tonight?"

"It might be the wine," she said. "Or it might be that—" Oh, bother. She didn't know how to explain that around him she felt alive, not afraid of anyone or anything—including him. So she kissed him again, and when she pulled back said, "Please drop me on the bed. I want to *bounce* into decadence."

So he did. And she *did* bounce. After which she stood on her knees and kissed him while he stood guard of her virtue at the side of the bed.

"That's enough of your seducing me," he said when she'd finished unwrapping his cravat. "It was a lovely game—you proved your point that I can't resist you and, in fact, lose my head seeing you naked—but now it's done."

But she ignored him—she could tell he wanted her to, anyway—and unlaced his shirt, her mouth as prim as a schoolteacher's. "If we're going to ruin our long acquaintance—I wouldn't dare call it a friendship—we might as well do it in as pleasant a manner as possible."

"I told you, Pippa, this is enough—"

No it wasn't. Not yet. He was still too controlled. He was on to her game, and so far, all the risks she'd taken hadn't paid off.

So she kissed him again, and somehow she managed to get his shirt off. It involved her rubbing her naked breasts against his chest until he capitulated, but her strategy worked.

And when he refused to lower his pantaloons, she knew instinctively to turn her back to him, lift his hands to her breasts, and grind her bottom into his belly. If that didn't work at getting him to disrobe, then she was out of ideas.

Or perhaps she wasn't . . .

Surely, there were many ways to seduce Gregory, and she intended to find out what they were. She wouldn't stop until she found one that worked.

With her hand cupped over his as he massaged her

breasts, and with every gyration of her hips, she felt him surrender a little more, until she turned to face him again and had no problem unbuttoning his placket and sliding his pantaloons down. She merely distracted him with more kisses, this time to his ridged belly.

It was such a pleasurable way to bring him down a notch.

"God, you slay me," he muttered as his erection sprang free. "You beautiful, beautiful girl."

And with those words, her heart softened—but only a tad—because in his voice she heard such—

Such feeling.

What was happening to the aloof Gregory that she knew?

She was afraid she was getting in over her head. But before she could think another thought or kiss another part of him, he jerked her up by the elbow. Not hard, but firmly.

He kissed *her* now—not the other way around. His kisses were controlled, taunting—and when she reached down to touch him, he swiped her hand away.

"I've let you think you had the advantage," he whispered. "Get ready to learn a lesson."

"I don't think so," she said, but she was afraid. The place between her legs was moist and wanting. Her breasts ached for his touch. And her mouth longed for the invasion of his tongue.

Naked as the day he was born—which was the most attractive way she'd ever seen him—Gregory crawled onto the bed next to her and pulled her down beside him. She landed on his chest, and he pinned her by wrapping one leg around the backs of her knees. An instant later, he'd rolled over—and she was beneath him.

She pushed against him, but he held her fast. "No," she said. "It's not going to work."

"Oh, really." His tone was skeptical.

"Yes."

"Don't move," he said.

Not that she could. He had her legs good and trapped. He reached to his left and took a goblet of wine, a tiny dollop of which he then poured into her belly button.

"I said it's not going to work." But she secretly thrilled at the action.

He ran his tongue around the tiny pool of burgundy-colored elixir while caressing her rear. She arched her belly toward him, wanting more. It was torture—exquisite torture—what he was doing to her. Finally, he licked and kissed the wine away.

It made the kiss he bestowed on her mouth next extra sweet. His hard, manly chest covered her breasts, his legs mastered her own, and he hooked her left knee with his elbow and brought it high. Her sex was exposed like never before, and she felt an intense thrill that turned to deep, erotic pleasure when he played with her softest flesh with his fingers, skimming it with a featherlight touch that drove her mad.

When he managed to suckle one of her breasts at the same time, she moaned with the pleasure of it, so intense, so unexpected, yet so right—

A bit of heaven.

Who else? she thought. *Who else but Gregory?*

She needed him to do more.

"I'll be furious if you stop," she said. "You really won't want to see me in that state."

But he did stop. He stopped everything, sat up on his

haunches, and picked up his cravat from the bottom of the
bed.

Her heart was racing, the place between her legs was
wet, and her breasts tingled in the open air. "What are
you doing with that?"

"I want to put it around your eyes," he said. "You'll
feel me. Not see me."

"Can't we simply blow out the candles?"

He chuckled. "But then I won't get to see *you*."

"That's not fair. Why do you get to see me—and not
the other way around?"

"Because it's enjoyable." He leaned over her and kissed
her deeply. "You said you liked simple things, frivolous
things. Things that make you happy. This is one of those.
It will make us both happy. I promise."

"Your version of marzipan," she whispered.

"Yes."

So she allowed him to tie the cravat around her eyes,
which he did with many kisses to her mouth, her ears,
and her jaw.

And then he laid her gently down and licked delicious
circles around her nipples. When he took one in his
mouth and teased it with his teeth, she jerked with the
sheer delight of it and cradled his head with her hands.

"Gregory," she murmured, while he suckled and nipped
at her breasts. "I didn't know it could be like this between
a woman and a man until this afternoon. And now—there
are more wonders, aren't there?"

"Yes." He laughed against her skin. "This is only the
beginning," he whispered, and chose that moment to
tease the pearl between her legs, making her moan against
her will in the darkness behind his cravat, which smelled

of him, all soap and linen and something indefinable that meant Gregory.

What would he do next? She couldn't even guess and shivered at the excitement of entering a new world which she'd never imagined could entrance her so.

He spread her legs wide, and she winced at the knowledge that he was seeing her completely vulnerable in the candlelight. A bit of fear crept into her head—fear that he'd find her lacking somehow.

"Gregory," she cried softly.

"You're stunning." He laid a hand on each of her knees. "I could look at you all night."

"Really?"

"Yes." He kissed her right knee. "Don't be afraid."

Even so, she couldn't help giving a little whimper, but it turned into a cry of pleasure when she felt the trickle of something saturate the sensitive folds between her legs. Not wine, this time—something slightly more viscous.

But what?

Whatever it was that Gregory was stroking against her feminine core—up and down, over the nubbin that guarded her womanly harbor—was exquisite torture.

And then she knew. He brought something small, round, and smashed to her mouth—something pulpy, and she realized he'd taken a grape from the table and used it to tease her.

He rubbed it against her lips then licked off the juice. Then she felt a plump, broken grape around her nipples. She moaned at the indescribably pleasurable feeling—everything was so much more intense when she couldn't see. Gregory sucked and licked her nipples bare again, murmuring how delicious she tasted while he did it.

And there was yet another spurt of juice against the place that most ached for him.

"No," she protested.

"Oh, yes," he replied.

And before she could answer, the heat of his mouth covered her vulnerability. She was lost for words. Gregory teased her with his tongue and his mouth—her chest rose and fell as she tried to catch her breath. But she couldn't.

She couldn't.

He put his finger inside her—then two—and she arched high, but he wouldn't let her go. He was relentless in his pursuit, making her wrap her ankles behind his neck, his mouth merciless against her flesh until she gave a loud cry into wave after wave of pleasure. Her release was so intense, she cupped her breasts, still sticky and wet from the juice, for respite against the onslaught, kneading them as she slowly descended, her head tossing from side to side, helpless little sobs rending the silence.

Weak and wrung out, she felt him lay kisses up her belly—he was chuckling, damn him!—until he reached her mouth, where his kiss was musky and exotic with the scent of her. And then he unwrapped the cravat covering her eyes. When she looked into his eyes and saw a flicker of triumph there, she realized he'd won.

He'd seduced *her*.

Damn Gregory Sherwood!

She tried to slap him, but he caught her wrist.

"I hate you," she said. "I wasn't going to lie with you and do these things—"

"I know," he said softly back. "It takes two to compete in these sorts of games, Lady Pippa, and tonight, you were outplayed. If it makes you feel any better, I've been in your position. You'll get over it."

And with that, he picked himself off the bed, blew out all the candles, and walked naked into the dressing room. The door closed behind him, and in the darkness, her body limp with exhaustion and sated with furious pleasure, Pippa fell instantly asleep.

Chapter Fourteen

Gregory woke the next morning ornery but also with more energy than he'd had in ages, which surprised him as the pallet was comfortable enough but not nearly as pleasant as a plump mattress. But sharing a bed with Pippa hadn't been an option. He'd wanted her to get some real rest, so he'd headed to the dressing room after their completely unexpected but highly memorable romp.

Guilt shot through him. Last night he saw so clearly how frustrated she was, how she'd wanted to rattle him. He'd let her go through with her ploy—then turned the tables on her.

Yes, she'd said some harsh things that still infuriated him to recall this morning, but had it been the work of a gentleman to seduce her into submission?

No. It hadn't.

Now, with the early morning sun streaming through the tiny windows above the dressing table, he wondered how well she'd slept.

Raw carnal memories shot through his brain, and his body reacted as he knew it would. He craved her body, was enchanted by the way she'd responded so passionately to him. Even now, it made him happy to think of how spent she'd been when he'd left her on the bed, one arm folded under her head, her legs limp and tangled, her boyishly slim hip facing the ceiling, and her eyelids heavy with satisfaction.

Groaning, he rolled out of bed, ignoring the rod of steel between his legs that reminded him of how blasted attractive he found his country friend. It was inconvenient, this new fascination he had with her, but it existed. He'd have to deal with it by leaving her alone. He didn't think she'd make any further overt sexual attempts to break his will and get him to do her bidding, but now that he'd had a few tastes of her earthy nature, he was hooked.

It would be a rough, rough road staying away, but he must.

Entirely naked, he cracked open the door to the bedchamber to see that she was gone and the bed neatly made. He couldn't help feeling disappointed that he wouldn't see her hair spread over the pillow the way it had been last night and maybe catch a glimpse of a strawberry-tipped breast.

But how had she got her clothes? Her wig? Her spectacles? They were all in the dressing room. He couldn't have slept with her creeping about the pallet, could he have? Was he that pathetic—sleeping so deeply he hadn't heard her?

He walked back into the dressing room and saw that, sure enough, her things were gone. "God," he croaked aloud, rubbing his jaw in the looking glass, "how embarrassing."

The childhood warrior in him—the one who'd have ridden that imaginary piebald stallion and saved the world from dreaded enemies—didn't like knowing he could be taken by surprise.

"There's no need to be embarrassed," he heard from the door, and nearly jumped out of his skin. "You're dealing with someone who excels at being invisible, as all good servants should."

It was Pippa dressed as his valet—and it was entirely expected that such a servant might see his employer naked. "Good morning, my lord." She looked boldly at him, her spectacles glinting in the sunlight, her wig giving her an elfin look. "You were sleeping like a baby when I sneaked in here this morning."

"Was I? How did *you* sleep?"

"I don't remember," she said firmly. "I've laid out your clothes on the bed. But I called for a bath. Yesterday's travel dirt must be gotten rid of first."

He put his hands on his hips. "Do you really think this is a good idea—your acting as my valet?"

She shrugged. "It's too late to go back. I'm already quite used to seeing you naked. Feel comfortable flaunting your body about the room as much as you care to. Don't mind me."

She took a hard look at the part of him that was still at full attention and shut the door behind her.

"Don't mind me," he muttered.

The door opened again, and she tossed him the silk banyan she'd donned last night. "On second thought, two footmen are bringing up the hot water. So you might want to put that on."

"Oh, really? I might need some help, *Harrow.*" He threw the garment back at her.

"Very well." She pointedly ignored his irritated gaze when she held out an arm of the robe in proper subservient fashion. In silence, he slipped one arm in, then turned to put in the other. Finally, when he pivoted back around to face her, he lifted his arms to shoulder height. Without a word, she tied the silk belt into a proper manly knot and left it dangling at his side.

"There," she said, sounding satisfied with her handiwork.

"Hmmph," he responded.

She lowered her spectacles a fraction of an inch. "May I be so bold as to say, my lord, that your exercise at Gentleman Jackson's—or wherever you go to stay fit—is reaping its rewards? Keep it up. We don't want that waistline to be anything but trim."

He narrowed his eyes at her, but she lifted her chin—like a girl—and stalked out without shutting the door.

So this kind of behavior was his payment for bringing her to utter ecstasy last night?

She popped her head in once more. "Oh, and I'm recommending the blue striped silk waistcoat and the navy blue coat. Buff breeches as you might be traipsing about outdoors today. Your boots are freshly polished. And you've got one stocking with a hole in it. I'll have it mended by this evening."

The door shut again.

"Fine," he called through it. "Mend that stocking, why don't you!"

"I look forward to it," she called back primly.

He was in a foul mood now. Was he nothing but a doll for her to dress? Did his physical form move her so little? She'd admired his body the way someone might a fine racehorse. There wasn't a bit of reticence in her when she put the banyan on him, either, even though he made sure she saw every inch of him as he turned before her.

What did she really hope to accomplish with this "competent valet" act of hers?

He wouldn't think on it at the moment. He had something else to do, and that was to tweak his plans for the dog cottage—after he got ready for the day, of course. He stalked into the bedchamber, where Pippa was opening the door to the same footmen who'd escorted her last night to his bedchamber. Between them, they carried four buckets of steaming water. A copper tub already sat before the fire.

"We'll be back with more in a trice," said one, after they'd dumped the buckets into the tub.

"Don't bother," he said. "This is plenty of water to bathe in."

"Very well, my lord," they said in unison, and backed out of the room, shutting the door behind them.

Pippa grabbed the doorknob. "I'm leaving, too, to assist Mr. Dawson. When I come back, you'll be done with your bath, and if you need help with your coat and cravat, I can do that." Her cheeks were pink.

But something in him couldn't resist goading her after the treatment she'd given him.

"Mr. Dawson can wait," he said. "You can help me with the bath." He threw off his banyan and swung his leg over the tub to stand inside it.

She froze for a second then moved toward the dressing room. "All right," she said coolly. "I'll get you a cloth and some soap."

He watched her bustle away. The girl had mettle. When she came back with the equipment, he said, "Soap it for me, will you?"

Her eyes grew large. "You're teasing me, and you know it, Gregory Sherwood." She thrust the soap and towel at him and hastened to the door.

"Teasing you?" he called after her. "You said yourself that you're my valet!"

Her back was to him. "You always did this when I was your lieutenant. You knew I was mad for you, and you'd try to make me do frightening things like race across the yard of the mean old crone in the village. You'd dare me with a perfectly straight face. Well, I'm not accepting this dare. I don't want to be your valet anymore."

"I can go along with that," he said, soaping his belly. "The truth is, I don't need one."

Still she wouldn't look at him, and it made him realize how difficult it must have been for her this morning, playing the role of the indifferent yet capable valet.

His pride took flight. "Oh, all right. I'm sorry if I offended you last night. I understand why you're treating me so coldly, and I don't blame you. If it's any consolation, your humiliation at being bested can't be nearly as agonizing as my own frustration at being—"

"At being what?"

"Unable to touch you again. I won't go against your wishes."

Her shoulders sank. "I don't think I should see you naked anymore—I mean, after this bath of yours."

After? Did that mean that she wasn't quite ready to give up the sight of him in the buff just yet?

"Fine," he said, suppressing a smile. "So we've called a truce?"

"Yes," she said quietly.

He squeezed the wet cloth over his belly, the sound of the trickling water loud in the room. When he looked up, she had turned around to face him.

His ears filled with a drumbeat that was beginning to echo in his veins. "Pippa—"

"I'm scared." She had the same fearful look in her eyes that she'd had in bed with him the night before. "What's happening? I can't stop thinking about you—and me—and what occurred last night. You *are* more than a tease. I believe you now, what you said in your carriage—you're dangerous. I shouldn't be here. I need to leave this house, the sooner the better."

With one sure movement, he wrapped a towel around his middle. "Come here," he said.

The tension in the room was thick.

"Come *here,* Pippa," he said. "I'm not going to frighten you."

Slowly, she walked over to him and allowed him to pull her into a one-armed embrace.

He squeezed her hard, as if they were mates. Boys on the battlefield who'd come through the wars. And then he kissed her cheek. "We're all right," he murmured against her ear.

She looked down at the floor, her eyelids translucent, her face too pale and soft to be a man's. "Oh, bother," she said in a strangled tone. She looked away from him, then back, her eyes registering confusion and something else—something that pained her.

He felt some alarm. What was wrong?

And then much to his astonishment, she reached out a tentative hand, undid his towel, and let it drop to the floor.

"My God, Pippa, you just said—"

"I'm not doing what I did last night," she insisted in a rapid-fire voice, her cheeks bright red. "I'm not trying to coerce you. Honestly. I—I just want to see . . . before I go to Paris."

He held his breath as she touched him, and of course, the expected happened. He became rock-hard.

She sucked in a breath.

"This isn't a good idea," he said, suppressing a groan.

"It's too late for that," she said, sounding distracted. "Much too late." She bent down and retrieved the soap from the floor of the tub and played with it in her hands. "Once I get something in my head—" She sent him an apologetic look. "Consider my interest in you this way—and my lack of pride in revealing it—a parting gift to a man who enjoys being in charge."

"Not always," he said, his eyes flickering with heat.

She flushed in response.

"You know I won't stop you." His tone was utterly serious. "You might regret this later. I know I probably will. But—"

"Enough talking," she said with a smile. "I've taken over, and you must be patient. Everything will be fine. You'll see."

He gave a light laugh. "Your concern for me is most appreciated, but I promise you, unnecessary."

And then she grabbed hold of him, gently but firmly, and began to stroke his sleek member. It felt good—more than good. It felt divine. And it endeared her to him even further, seeing her so curious and unwavering in her determination to do whatever she wanted to do.

"I'm not finished," she said.

"I'm not objecting," he returned.

She began to wash between his legs and cupped him in her soapy hand. He dipped his head and closed his eyes. Total hedonism wasn't something he'd expected to indulge in this morning.

"I love seeing you this way, feeling you this way," she murmured.

He opened his eyes. "I'm at your mercy at the moment," he said in a ragged whisper, and leaned the flat of his hands on top of the bureau behind him.

She went back to his sex, caressing it so perfectly that he swiped her hand away. "You don't know what you're doing—where you're going with this."

"I don't care," she said. "We're going there. No more talking."

And she returned to her ministrations.

Fine, then. Gregory spread his legs, threw his head back, and let pleasure take him where it would. He'd no idea how an unversed sprite like Pippa could have brought him to one of the most gratifying releases of his life. But she did. And afterward, she stood stunned, her hands completely frozen upon him while he allowed his chin to drop and his eyes to close once more. "God," he said on a sigh. "How is the rest of the day going to compete with that?"

Her chuckle was nervous. "I'm glad you liked it."

He looked up and arched a brow. "*Liked* it? That's an understatement. I won't be able to think of anything else, all day. Who would ever guess that I'd be craving my cheeky valet?"

She blushed. "I didn't say we'd do it again."

He gave a soft laugh. "I never said we would, either." She couldn't seem to keep her eyes off him when he grabbed the dry towel off the floor and wrapped it around himself once more. It was quite flattering. And arousing. "Now your curiosity is satisfied—that's what this was all about, wasn't it?"

"Yes. Last night was an eye-opener, and I'm afraid . . . I'm afraid it got me extremely curious."

"Understandable," he said, unable to keep the heat out of his voice.

She backed away and tilted her head. "Now, my lord, I really must go."

He hesitated a moment. "Are you sure?" he dared to ask. "You don't have to quite yet . . . if you don't want to." He let her wonder what he meant, that he was perfectly willing to do to her again what he'd done last night.

If she asked, he would grant her anything, he realized.

Her eyes flared wide, so she must have guessed what he meant. "Good heavens, no. I really must go."

"Very well." He'd be all business if that would help. "By the way, I won't need your assistance dressing. I'll be busy most of the day, too. When you're done with Mr. Dawson, don't feel you have to do anything else. That is, don't let anyone engage you in the chores of the house. Retreat here—and tell them if you're hungry that you plan to eat in here, too. When you get bored, go browse through the library, walk in the garden, or even borrow a mount and go riding. You're the valet of a future marquess. So act like it if you wish."

"Thank you," she said. "I think I'll explore the grounds after I visit with Mr. Dawson."

"Right." Gregory walked naked to the dressing room and turned around. "And *Harrow*?"

"Yes?"

"The valet act—it's only for outside of this room. I'll wear the banyan from now on, and you'll be Pippa henceforth when you're in here. I'll tie my own cravats and put on my own jackets. I'll also shave myself."

"I'm afraid you'd better." She had a twinkle in her eye.

"Is that a threat, or an admission that in your hands, a razor is an instrument of torture?"

"Certainly not the second. I excel at shaving Uncle Bertie. Nor is it the first, much as you'd enjoy the idea of fending off a potential murderess. It's actually that I'll be holding your face in my hands—upside down. I don't know that I could do it without laughing." And to prove her point, she giggled. "Don't you remember?"

"What?"

"When I made you lie that way on the ground—we faced each other and saw each other upside down. We'd draw two little dots on our chins for eyes, and when you look at the person's mouth and chin that way, they become little people with upside-down smiles."

"Oh, right. I do remember. Let's do it again."

"Later," she said, and then blurted out, "Although I don't know . . . I might not be able to see your mouth the same way ever again."

"Really?"

She nodded, her face turning bright red.

And suddenly, he knew what she was talking about.

He allowed himself a slow smile. "That's not such a bad thing, is it?"

"It is when you can't *do* that again." She sounded wistful.

"Do what?" he asked, striving to look the picture of innocence.

"Gregory!" She stomped her foot. "You know exactly what I mean."

"Kissing and cavorting between the sheets? Against taproom doors? Or in tubs? Is that what we may never do again? Because you're a sugar sculptor destined for greatness, I'm an architect designing dog cottages, and we'll both be on opposite sides of the Channel very shortly, achieving our unparallel destinies?"

"Yes." She looked away, clearly in a huff. "You're impossible."

He laughed. "I'm only teasing you. But I must agree.

Our kissing days are numbered." And he pulled the dressing room door shut behind him.

"They're *over*," Pippa called to him, always wanting the last word.

"Have a good day," he called back.

"No, *you* have a good day," she insisted before bustling out the door.

He waited until he heard her leave the bedchamber and then he allowed himself to fall onto the pallet, his face turned to the side.

She'd been the perfect sexual companion. To hell with the upside-down smiley faces. She was right—he'd never be able to see her mouth that way again without wanting to kiss it, and the rest of her.

He was rapidly becoming much too interested in her that way. He hadn't been lying—the rest of the day would rot in comparison to the morning.

He allowed himself ten seconds to close his eyes and think about what had happened in the tub. After those seconds were over, he vowed to open his eyes and focus on his rather puny purpose at the house party: to work on that dog cottage design.

He'd already met the pack of Irish wolfhounds last night in the drawing room. There were five of them, yet he'd not been inspired, as much as he enjoyed their scruffy, sweet faces and thumping tails. Perhaps if he went to the site of the dog cottage and saw where it would actually be, fresh ideas would come to him.

Attention from John Nash was a worthwhile goal for a man who wanted a career as an architect. And Gregory did. He wanted it as much as he wanted anything, which wasn't saying much, actually. Because there was nothing that truly stirred his soul these days.

Nothing.

Except Pippa.

And that was only a recent development. He'd nip it in the bud. His conscience reminded him that he couldn't do it soon enough. But then he saw one of her hairpins on the dressing room vanity and he remembered her last night and today.

He gazed at himself in the looking glass, saw the hunger in his eyes.

He'd told her he was dangerous. He'd *told* her. Could he really be held responsible if they happened to fall together again that night? And every night thereafter at the house party?

He refused to answer the question. He ignored his own misgivings—ignored logic—tucked the pin in his pocket as a good-luck token of sorts, and left the room.

Chapter Fifteen

Pippa adjusted her wig one more time in the looking glass in the upstairs corridor. She wished she could giggle as she used to when she thought about looking at Gregory's chin and mouth upside down. But instead she sighed . . . he had a perfect, supple mouth.

Very well. All she had to do was get through the day without thinking anymore about him at all. She could *do* that.

She'd think about Paris. Would Madame DuPont be kind? Where did Monsieur Perot work? But then all the Gallic imagery—the Left Bank of which she'd heard so much, Nôtre-Dame, that glorious edifice, and the gorgeous French fashions—all of it was replaced with an image of Gregory standing naked in that copper tub. He should've looked embarrassed or shy, but he hadn't. He'd looked like a living, breathing Greek god used to being admired, but not in a conceited way. He merely appeared comfortable in his own skin.

She remembered also that casually posed question he'd asked her near the end of the morning's exhilarating encounter, something along the lines of . . . did she really want to go just then?

She knew what he'd been suggesting.

And she'd been sorely tempted.

But, no. She was off to help Mr. Dawson because she needed to act like a valet—and she would not be dissuaded by a dangerous charmer who also happened to be her friend.

She might not want to be a valet, particularly, but at least she wasn't at home with Mr. Trickle breathing heavily through his mouth a few feet away from her at the table. And she had to be thankful she wasn't now married to Mr. Hawthorne and sharing his bed.

Oh, no. Now that she knew what went on there . . .

She felt a pleasurable, warm weight in her lower belly—it was that wanton named Desire, moving at a languorous pace lower and lower, finally settling between her thighs and refusing to move unless given some attention, some *proper* attention.

Doing her best to ignore her own entirely inappropriate impulse to turn around and visit Gregory again, Pippa sped around the corner and knocked rather hard on Mr. Dawson's door.

"Come in," Mr. Dawson said in that friendly, sweet way of his.

A burst of affection for him filled her at the sound of his voice. That—and her commitment to being the most excellent valet on earth—served as a lovely distraction. When she opened the door, he was already in his shirt and breeches, thank God. She spent the next half hour shaving him—which she heartily enjoyed, as she spoke about the people she loved at home, not mentioning any names, and of her never-ending fondness for walking the moors, especially when a wild wind moaned over the gorse and low, gray clouds scudded across the sky. Afterward, she picked out his waistcoat and coat. She also tied his cravat and shined up his boots. It was an entire hour before she was finished, but it had flown by.

"You look very dashing, if I do say so myself," she said.

"But these are the clothes I always wear," he answered.

"Yes, but it's how you put them on that matters. Today, you had me to help you, and with every tweak of your cravat and buttoning of your waistcoat, I was beaming sincere admiration of you. In fact, if you were forty years younger—" she said flirtatiously, and then suddenly remembered she was a man, not a girl.

His eyes widened, and he tilted his head as if he found her most curious. "Yes?"

"If you were forty years younger," she continued without missing a beat, "why, you'd be snapped up in an instant by a discerning young woman. As it is now, don't be surprised if some of the elderly matrons at the house party find an excuse to sit by you when you dine." She winked at him.

He gave a blustery sigh. "The last thing I need or want is an elderly matron speaking to me of her servants, her pickles and jams of which she's so proud, her bonnets— all of which look alike to me—and her grandchildren, especially the infants. I believe if you've seen one you've seen them all."

"Mr. Dawson."

He gave a little chuckle. "I'm an old curmudgeon and proud of it. Fortunately, Lord and Lady Thurston put up with me, anyway. What can they do? I'm Lady Thurston's cousin. I was thirty when she was born. I lived next door and remember everything—the tantrums, the sulks, the wretched *tendres* when she got older . . . Of course, she's the apple of my eye. But I don't tell her so."

"You should!"

"Why?" He raised both graying brows. "Then she'll stop making me my favorite jam tarts."

"You just said it annoys you when elderly matrons speak to you of jams—"

"You're a cheeky valet," he said.

"Indeed, I am." She smiled.

"We're rather alike." He sent her a sly grin. "In fact, I'm taking you in with me to breakfast. Things seem to happen around you, Harrow."

She gasped. "I can't sit at the table. Not with the other guests."

"No, I suppose you can't. But you can wait in the corner, and I'll bring you a plate of eggs."

"Sounds lovely."

"I hope Marbury will be there," he said, all innocence.

"Why?" she asked.

He shrugged. "No reason." But he had a twinkle in his eye.

She stood still. "Why, Mr. Dawson, I think you're hoping Marbury and I will get into some sort of row!"

"I don't know what you mean," he said, but he was chuckling as they descended the stairs.

The breakfast room was empty except for one man— Lord Marbury. Pippa and Mr. Dawson exchanged a knowing look.

"I'm going to disappoint you," Pippa whispered to him. "I vow to be on my best behavior."

"We'll see about that," he whispered back.

When they walked into the room, Mr. Dawson said,

"Good morning, Marbury," as if he were a sweet old man and not a mischief-maker.

Of course, now Pippa knew better.

"I wanted to say good morning first, Mr. Dawson," said the earl, "but I was busy scratching the back of one of the wolfhounds under the table with my boot. I love them like family already. And now that I've identified their temperaments, which range from moody to panting, I plan to make a nuanced adjustment to my design for the doggy cottage."

"Oh?" Mr. Dawson asked in a pleasant manner, his eyes roaming over the plentiful dishes on the sideboard.

"But please," Marbury said, "don't tell Lady Thurston that I'm going to such supreme effort. I want her to be utterly shocked when she lays eyes on the sketches." He rubbed his chin. "On the other hand . . . she might need her smelling salts, so if you'd like to prepare her in advance for my genius, you have my blessing."

"You've put me in quite the dilemma," Mr. Dawson said, and held a cup out to the footman to fill it with steaming tea. "To tell my cousin—or not to tell?"

Pippa sidled past Marbury and obediently sat in a chair in the corner. She laced her hands in her lap, but then she decided that looked too feminine, so she cupped them over her kneecaps and tried her best to glower.

Marbury turned his round shoulders to stare at her. "What the devil are *you* doing here?"

"He's with me," Mr. Dawson said in his placid manner, and filled a plate with eggs.

Marbury tucked an entire piece of bacon into his mouth. "You do what you like, Mr. Dawson," he said with his mouth full. "I just find it odd to see a valet lounging in the same room as his betters. But you know how it goes.

Someone like me—a person with tremendous design vision who also love dogs—has bigger things to think about than Harrow and where he sits. I think it's bloody marvelous he's here, actually. It's a bit of comfort seeing him there in the corner, the same way it's a solace having these slavering beasts under the table."

Mr. Dawson's brow puckered, but he said nothing. When he brought Pippa a plate filled with eggs and a fork, he winked. She thanked him, winked back, and began to eat. The footman, pouring Marbury's tea, cast her a secret envious look, and she knew that she'd best avoid the kitchens today.

Just as the fellow put the teapot on the tray near his station in the opposing corner, a few sharp woofs and growls and then a thump came from beneath the dining table—dogs in the midst of a brief argument over territory. There was a clattering sound from where Lord Marbury sat, followed by a yowl emitted by that same gentleman. He pushed back his chair.

"Harrow?" he yelled.

Pippa jumped up with her plate. Good God, what had happened? And then she saw the overturned cup and the small milk pitcher on the carpet—and his wet lap. He sat stiff as a statue, his face in an awful grimace. Poor thing—he must have been preparing his tea and been jostled by the dogs.

The footman moved swiftly to his side. "Let me help you, sir," he said in a low voice.

"Hot and cold hit me at the same time," Marbury whimpered. He waved off the servant. "Harrow? Get over here. These are my best pantaloons. Save them."

She held her plate to the side and approached. "Why don't you go to your room and change them first?"

He opened his mouth to answer, but a dog the size of a small pony clambered out from under the table and knocked into Pippa and her plate, causing the eggs to slide right into Marbury's lap.

His eyes blazed. "You didn't," he said in a menacing whisper without looking down.

She gulped and allowed her glance to flick at the new mess in his lap. "I—I'm sorry."

The wolfhound turned right around and tried to gobble up the feast, pushing his long snout into the crevice between Marbury's rounded belly and his thighs. He swatted hopelessly at the hairy head. "Footman!" he barked. "Come get this mongrel!"

The footman struggled with the hound but only managed to bump the table and cause a dish of sausages to hit the floor. This led to a stampede from beneath the table as the other hungry beasts dashed for the savory prizes. Marbury, surrounded by great quantities of wiry fur and slobbery tongues, was frozen in his panic.

"Do something, Harrow. Help me!" He held out his arms.

Mr. Dawson kept eating his porridge, watching with great interest but with only a mild expression on his face.

Pippa fought her way between two hounds and grabbed a square ivory linen serviette from the table. She dunked it into a goblet of water and began dabbing at Marbury's soaked lap. The sodden pantaloons gaped at the front panel where a hound had obviously devoured a button in his zest to find some more egg, and Pippa shuddered at the notion of retrieving food remnants from beneath the flap.

Between Marbury's howls of protest and the canine snorting and snuffling, Pippa hardly noticed when a loud cough escaped from Mr. Dawson, but she glanced up to see him shaking with silent mirth, his lips compressed but his eyes sparkling with unshed tears. He gave her a quick wink, one that she knew said, *I told you so. Things happen when you're around.*

Before she could even return a smile, Marbury yelped when one of the hounds snatched the edge of a tea-soaked serviette from his lap and took off for the dining room door.

"Come back, you hairy beast!" Marbury snapped. He managed finally to get to his feet, waving his arms wildly to dispel the remaining animals.

But the serviette thief wouldn't stop. It kept going—and so did the serviette. *Why, it's unraveling*, Pippa realized.

Standing next to the distraught earl, she gaped in amazement. The serviette wasn't a serviette, after all. It was long and narrow, and it was . . . it was—

Her eyes got wider—

So did Marbury's.

So did Mr. Dawson's.

And even the footman's.

The hound flopped down in the doorway with the fabric hanging out of its mouth and trailing across the floor.

It was a *cravat*. Before Pippa could even begin to wonder what had happened, she rushed over and tugged upon the cloth until the dog let it go.

"Thank you," she mumbled to the pilferer. She balled up the sodden rag, terribly embarrassed by the turn of events. Apparently it had been rolled tightly and placed—

Inside Marbury's trousers.

That gentleman, for once in his life, was silent. Mr. Dawson blinked. Pippa knew—

Pippa knew she had to say *something*. She inhaled a

deep breath. "Good for you, Lord Marbury," she said doggedly, "for wearing the latest trend—er, the er, the *cravotch*. It's all the rage in Europe."

"Cravotch?" Mr. Dawson asked, his eyebrows almost to his hairline.

"Yes, the cravotch," Pippa said. "Cravat . . . crotch. It's a word recently invented by a stylish French wit." She gave a weak smile. "Er, only the best valets know it. Yours must be very good, Lord Marbury. Very knowledgeable."

"He is," the fellow said smugly, "and I can't wait for him to arrive. I think I'll bring him to breakfast, too." He swiped at the remaining food particles on his pantaloons. "Now if you don't mind, Mr. Dawson, I believe I've been through enough this morning with the dogs, all in the name of authentic research, which is crucial if one wants to design a doggy cottage *par excellence*. And now, I must go repair my person. Harrow?" He held out his palm for the offending—or was it glorious?—garment.

She offered the cravat with great relief, and he snatched it up, stalking toward the door with his pride somewhat intact—she hoped.

A commotion in the entryway at the front of the house caught her ear—some laughing and talking between a man and a woman. Beneath the strips of cloth binding her breasts, Pippa felt her entire upper body tighten. It sounded like Gregory—and Lady Damara.

At the breakfast room door, Marbury nearly barreled into the cozy pair. Lady Damara had her arm possessively through Gregory's, and Pippa's heart nearly stopped. They looked beautiful together—she with rosy cheeks and a few tendrils about her ears, and he, his usual vigorous and very male self.

"Westdale," Marbury said between gritted teeth.

"Marbury," Gregory replied with no venom, only mild amusement. "What's that in your hand?"

Marbury arched one brow high. "You mean . . . you don't know?"

"No," Gregory said patiently. "It merely appears to be a sodden lump of linen."

A delicate furrow appeared on Lady Damara's pretty white forehead.

Marbury gave a short laugh. "Oh, Westdale, I pity you." He looked back at Pippa. "Harrow, what kind of valet are you? Not sharing the latest in modish fashion with your own employer?" He looked at Gregory's breeches—which left little to the imagination—and his eyes widened. "Well, excuse *me* if he had good reason for his silence," he muttered.

And he rushed past the pair, jostling Lady Damara so that she nearly lost her footing and gave a small cry. Gregory caught her other arm to steady her, and Pippa inwardly gasped as she watched Lady Damara manage to pull him closer, close enough that there was not a bit of space between her bountiful breasts and his strong biceps.

Her heart blazed with jealousy. Were they a pair? They certainly acted like it. Why else did it take them a few seconds to separate, as if they were longtime lovers who couldn't bear to be apart? And when they finally did—Damara giggling and cooing silly things about how she couldn't wait to show Gregory the amusing portrait of Lord Thurston's great-grandfather in the upstairs gallery—Gregory made a gallant sweeping motion with his hand to encourage the lady to walk in front of him to the sideboard.

Pippa was furious with Gregory—although she didn't know why. He was merely being a gentleman. Small acts of chivalry didn't mean that he was smitten with Damara. And, of course, it followed that neither did any cordial behavior he showed Pippa mean he had a *tendre* for her.

But something in her didn't like that logic, as soothing as it was supposed to be. *That's because you* want *Gregory to have a* tendre *for you!* a tiny voice in her head said.

"Good morning, Mr. Dawson." Gregory spoke in a pleasant manner to Pippa's new friend, who returned the greeting. "And good morning, Harrow. May I assume you accompanied Mr. Dawson to breakfast this morning?"

"Indeed, he did," said Mr. Dawson before Pippa could speak—which was a good thing. Because her throat was choked with all sorts of emotions, and she wasn't sure her valet's voice would be steady.

"Good thing, too," went on Mr. Dawson. "He saved Marbury's pantaloons *and* his pride. Ask him to tell you more about it. He's too modest, otherwise."

"No," said Pippa, before she realized she was speaking out of turn. "I refuse to speak about the Cravotch Incident."

"Cravotch Incident?" Lady Damara asked. "What's a cravotch?"

Pippa simply stared at the wall behind Lady Damara's head.

Gregory chuckled. "Harrow's not your usual obedient servant," he said to his female companion. "If he doesn't want to cooperate, he won't."

"He *is* very odd," she said, staring at Pippa as if she were a fascinating painting in a museum. Then she looked up at Gregory, her eyes as wide and exotic as a Siren's. "You surprise me all the time, Lord Westdale, with your unorthodox choices. Hiring cheeky servants must be the least of them." She lowered her lashes and gave him a coy look. "I love a man who dares to venture into risky territory. I wonder how far you're willing to go in other areas of your life?"

Her voice became breathy on the last few words, which she spoke so lightly that most people would merely nod their heads at the remark. But the subtle arch look Lady Damara threw Gregory wasn't missed by Pippa. She didn't excel at flirting herself, but she remembered Eliza and her strategies to capture a man, and at the moment, Lady Damara was doing her best to ensnare Gregory.

"Well, I *did* go to the American frontier," Gregory said.

Surely, Pippa thought, he knew what Lady Damara had been hinting at—and it wasn't a plea for him to tell her about his time in America! Her eyes narrowed but she continued to look completely absorbed in the chair rail that marched along the wall.

"That was an adventure," he went on. "I could tell you about it sometime. Especially the part about killing the rattlesnake that entered my tent while I was sleeping."

Pippa's eyes nearly popped out of her head. She wanted to hear about that!

But Lady Damara's smile faded. "Yes, I suppose you could."

"Later, perhaps," he said. "Shall we dine?"

"But wait," Pippa blurted out. "You forgot to mention that you're incredibly inventive in your design work, my lord. That's the territory where you excel at breaking boundaries." She knew she was in dangerous territory but couldn't stop herself. "Too bad the mediocre commissions you've accepted don't reflect that vision."

Gregory's face froze.

Lady Damara's wide eyes grew even wider. "How *dare* he!"

"Yes, well, sometimes Harrow pushes his own boundaries too far for my taste." Gregory's jaw was tight, and his mouth a thin line.

But as a valet, she could conveniently look over his head, which she did. One part of her hated that she'd upset him, but the other knew she needed to wake him up, somehow. She didn't have much more time in his company.

"As I was saying, Lady Damara"—Gregory's tone was muted but polite—"shall we dine?"

"La, I never eat," Lady Damara said with a pretty sigh.

Pippa hated her.

"Especially sweets," Lady Damara added.

Pippa hated her all the more.

But like a good servant, she kept her eyes averted when the couple glided by her. It was maddening, truly, for she longed to toss Gregory a scornful glance to let him know that she didn't care: He could fall in love with the wily, undernourished Lady Damara. He could have a wicked liaison with her, too.

Pippa had more important concerns to worry about than what Gregory did with his time—her own future was at stake. Every second that passed made her long more and more to leave this blasted house party, where she'd be forced to watch Lady Damara work her charms on the Earl of Westdale.

She walked to her designated corner and did her best to sit meekly down, succumbing only briefly to the temptation to cast a highly disapproving glance at Gregory's back at the sideboard. Lady Damara's shoulder was touching his upper arm.

The woman was such a hussy!

Or perhaps it was that there was no room to spread out. Yes, that must be it. A footman had come in with another hot dish and was busy situating it on the sideboard, and when he'd finished, he withdrew.

Pippa breathed a sigh of relief when, instantly, Gregory moved over to increase the space between him and Lady Damara, who picked up a grape from a bowl of fruit and popped it in her mouth.

"How rude of me," she said. *Yes, it was,* Pippa agreed. "But I simply couldn't resist. They're at the peak of ripeness. Do try one, Westdale."

And she held up a plump, juicy grape.

Pippa found herself riveted to the scene, her own mouth hanging open in horror. But she slammed it shut when Lady Damara actually pushed the grape into Gregory's mouth, allowing her fingertips to caress his lips while she held it there. And she wouldn't let go—not until he bit the grape in half.

No, thought Pippa. *No, no,* no*!*

Lady Damara's lilting queen of the fairies laugh rang out. "We're like Zeus and Hera. I could feed you all day long and never tire of it."

Gregory mumbled something unintelligible in return, and when he turned around to carry his plate to his seat, Pippa couldn't help herself.

She sent him her best death stare.

She'd only done it once before, and that was when she was fourteen and he'd been nineteen. On the night of Uncle Bertie's birthday dinner, he'd brought her a book of poems by Shelley and said, "No doubt your young girl's heart must be pining away for the man. My stepsisters are constantly sighing over his poetry. You have that treacly look about you right now."

And everyone at the table had laughed.

Well, she'd been practicing for weeks how to look at him at the table to tell him with her eyes that she loved him! It had nothing to do with Shelley, that look—it had been about him. And then he'd made fun of her!

Treacly, indeed.

And now that same look came back to her, but tenfold, because she was furious at herself in a way she hadn't been when she was fourteen. He'd told her he was to be avoided. Why did she keep ignoring her head? And as for her heart, it was firmly committed to following her dreams. Mother's sad face flashed before her eyes. In the space of two husbands, she'd changed completely, from a fabulous actress to a shy rabbit.

No man would keep Pippa from *her* dreams.

Gregory's expression, when he caught her gaze, was inscrutable.

Damn him.

She'd like to put his Irish self into that doggy cottage with the Irish wolfhounds. And she'd dearly love to drop a plate of eggs all over him and let those dogs clean up after her.

Chapter Sixteen

Dawson rose from his chair. "Harrow and I were about to go on a walk. Any recommendations?" He looked between Gregory and Lady Damara. "I'm torn between the lake and the woods."

Lady Damara's cheeks turned shell pink when she looked at Gregory. "I highly recommend the folly myself."

"Do you?" Mr. Dawson looked mildly intrigued. "So the lake, then."

She nodded. "There's something about that pile of stones that sets my heart racing. It's difficult to believe it's been there only four years and not four hundred."

But she looked at Gregory as if *he* were the one who set her heart racing. Had he kissed her at the folly? Pippa seethed just thinking about it. She knew how Gregory kissed. He'd send any girl's heart racing.

"The folly's an attractive piece," the womanizer in question remarked. "I wonder who designed it?"

Mr. Dawson hesitated. "A nobody, I imagine."

"It stopped a little short of being ironic, in my opinion." Gregory shrugged. "A folly should represent more than an homage to the past if it's to be noteworthy."

"Are you suggesting this folly falls short of the designer's intention?" Mr. Dawson asked.

Pippa was listening intently.

"Perhaps not," said Gregory. "Perhaps he purposely made it nothing more than a pile of stones and thought no one else would notice. After all, that's about all that most people expect from a folly. I get the feeling the past isn't a subject that excited the designer's interest terribly much."

More houseguests entered the room along with their host and hostess, whose eyes were agog at seeing the valet among the diners. Pippa gave them a low bow and made her escape while Mr. Dawson fielded the usual polite inquiries after his health and other guests remarked on the lovely sunshine and cool temperatures.

She hurried to the entryway, where the butler and two footmen stood guard not only of the house but the upper-crust British way of life. The far side of the front door is where she waited for Mr. Dawson. The butler and two footmen glared at her, and she did her best to look humble.

"Who the deuce do you think you are?" the butler hissed. "Eating with the proper folk. Lady Thurston is very upset, I've no doubt."

"It's not my fault." Pippa shrugged. "Mr. Dawson asked me to enter the breakfast room with him."

"But he's only a poor cousin." The butler drew in his ponderous chin. "He has no status in this house. You can expect a proper set-down in the kitchen tonight."

"I won't be taking my meals there," Pippa told him. "I'll eat in Lord Westdale's chamber."

"Right," scoffed the butler. "The future marquess." He pointed at Pippa. "You'd best watch your back. There's nothing worse than a hoity-toity servant coming here and ignoring our house rules."

"If I'm not the first, then what are you so upset about?" Pippa asked him, kicking her boot on the marble floor.

"*Stop* doing that with your boot," the butler said. "You'll leave a mark, and one of the maids will have to clean it."

"Sorry," she said, abashed.

"And you are the first," the butler said. "Not even the Prince Regent's servants took their meals anywhere but the kitchen."

"*Prinny* was here?" She was vastly impressed.

The butler nodded. "Four years ago. The folly was built in his honor."

"My goodness," she said. "I can't wait to see it!"

"We're very proud of our grounds," said the butler. "You make sure you show them the proper respect."

"I promise." Pippa meant it, too. She'd never intentionally be ill-mannered toward anyone or anything. "Look," she said apologetically, "I'm very sorry I've got everyone's back up in the servants' hall. I—I'll eat my meal there tonight. I'll do my best to fit in better. I won't venture into the breakfast room." She straightened up and lifted her chin. "You'll see a new man in me, starting here and now."

The butler's glare softened, and he offered a ghost of a smile. "That's better, lad."

"As soon as I finish with Mr. Dawson." Pippa gestured with her thumb over her shoulder. "He asked me to go on a walk with him. I can't go back on that promise."

"Very well." Once more, the butler glowered. "But if you plan to be here two weeks, you'd better change quickly. Right, boys?" He looked at the two footmen, who nodded their heads in unison.

"See?" the butler said. "The household is behind me. So watch your step."

But before Pippa could say, "Yes, sir," Mr. Dawson bounded out of the breakfast room, his face lit with a huge smile. "A walk," he said with spirit. "It's just the thing we both need, Harrow. It's been a memorable morning, and a walk will only improve it, I think."

"Yes, sir, we've had enough excitement." She ignored the fact that the butler was looking at her through slitted eyes. "A peaceful walk will do us good."

Until Gregory had gone to America, cultivating tonnish manners had felt as natural to him as breathing air. His drawing room conversation was generally scintillating; his waltz, superb; his company at White's, Tattersall's, and Gentleman Jackson's was much sought after. In short, he was the supreme London gentleman, and his Irish roots, fascinating family, and future prospects only made him a more compelling figure to his peers in society. Invitations of all sorts were boundless: to routs, soirees, balls, Venetian breakfasts, and to the beds of genteel widows and actresses alike.

He'd been invited to join the elite world of architects, too, by both his father and Uncle Bertie. Everyone had been welcoming to him. He had the family background and the proper education, after all, and he was beginning to get a few commissions. Nothing big, but a man had to start somewhere, didn't he?

But more and more lately, Gregory had begun to feel a fraud. London and the knowledge that the Season had been under way for a month didn't excite him as it once had. He actually dreaded going back to confront the silver salver that he knew would be overflowing with invitations on his desk. His secretary would be chomping at the bit to catch him up on all the goings-on in Town, as well

as getting his approval for the new furniture that he'd ordered on Gregory's behalf. The town home Father had
just bought for him as his own residence was in dire need
of being filled up, and Mama and the girls would be going
in and out of the building over the next month with drap-
ery makers and painters.

And now, sitting next to Lady Damara, who'd dragged
him out of the house to the folly, Gregory felt especially a
fraud. He'd tried to tell her the evening previous that he
wasn't interested in an affair, but she hadn't understood
him or was ignoring the hint. At the folly, she'd angled
for a kiss several times. She *was* extremely attractive, he
must admit.

At one point, she'd pretended that her bodice had slipped
on its own, and he'd caught a glimpse of rosy nipple. He
could have done anything or nearly nothing with her at
that point, and she would have been satisfied—even with
a chaste stolen kiss.

The old Gregory would have taken advantage of his
position and her infatuation or her ambition and indulged
in a pleasurable dalliance with her. But he'd looked away
when her bodice slipped, giving her a chance to fix it.
And after she had, he'd taken her straight back to breakfast, claiming extreme hunger.

When he saw Pippa dressed as a valet and parading
about the breakfast room ten minutes later, he'd nearly
laughed out loud with relief. He felt more alive around her
than he did around a thousand Lady Damaras. If he'd had
her at the folly, she probably would no longer be a virgin
by the end of the excursion—at least in his fantasies.

"So I think you should consider a spa area," Lady
Damara was saying to Lady Thurston.

The only reason Gregory noticed was because as she spoke, her hand glided lightly over his thigh.

Lady Thurston looked at her husband with a grave face. "Do you think so, too, Kelso? A spa is in order?"

"But of course they need a spa," said Lady Damara before Lord Thurston could speak. "How else does one stay healthy? A cool bathing area must be had, well ventilated with an opportunity to bask in the sunlight or shadow, depending on one's whim." She lifted her teacup and sipped, quickly replacing it in the saucer as her eyes opened wide. "Oh, yes, and if possible, refreshing mineral waters. Have you thought of that, Lady Thurston? It might extend their lives. You could order a crate from Bath, and the caretaker can offer them a daily dose."

Gregory had ignored Damara's first sensual attack, but when she rested her hand upon his thigh once again and then began dancing her fingertips toward a target he could not possibly misconstrue, he cleared his throat, threw one leg over the other, and crossed his arms over his chest, all in an effort to appear a little antsy in his chair because he was a red-blooded male who'd rather be outside shooting or hunting. He tossed Damara a blasé smile to avert an emotional scene later and tried to resume his attention upon the table conversation.

Here he was, surrounded by the powerful and elite of society, cultured people who could speak with ease on the theater and music scenes, the political climate, and the quality of modern literature as opposed to classical—and he was bored to tears.

He was never bored at home with the family or at Uncle Bertie's. At either place, they could converse on the same subjects, but there was a layer of warmth and liveliness to the dialogue that was missing in most of his social interactions.

Lord Thurston, good man that he was, was also the same man who consistently voted to adjourn parliamentary sessions early so he could resume his sporting life as soon as possible, no matter what crisis lay before the country.

"I don't know, my dear," he said to Lady Thurston. "A spa? I'd have to think on the pros and cons. But perhaps you should ask an architect. We've got one right here. Is it tomorrow you'll be turning in your sketches for our perusal, Westdale?"

"Yes." Lady Thurston smiled at Gregory. "They'll all give them to me tomorrow night. I assume you found it amusing to discover that you weren't the only architect from whom we requested sketches?"

"It was a surprise, yes," Gregory said. "But I welcome the competition."

"You should," said Lord Thurston. "Nash himself shall look them over. He's a good friend of ours."

"This might be quite an opportunity for you," added Lady Thurston.

"I agree." Gregory took a sip of tea and wondered where Pippa was at the moment.

"Do tell, Lord Westdale." Lady Thurston giggled hopefully. "Have you designed a spa for the dogs? And if the answer is no, would you consider amending your plans?"

"A commission might lie in the balance," Lord Thurston reminded him.

Lady Damara laid her fingers on Gregory's arm. "Please say you did design a spa, or that you will. The Thurston wolfhounds are a delightful throng of hairy beasts, but Lady Thurston is right—they need their own space, and it should be special."

"They can visit here as guests," Lady Thurston said, "but their cottage shall be their new home."

"You did tell me that," said Gregory, "so I designed an area specifically for the caretaker's comfort."

"Because you must have someone in good health tend to them," said Lady Damara.

"Of course," said Lady Thurston. "Lord Westdale, about that spa?"

She was certainly persistent.

Gregory exhaled. "I assumed the dogs would bathe in the lake, as they always have, according to your letter."

"Yes, I did mention that, didn't I?" Lady Thurston sounded impatient. "But I like Lady Damara's idea of the spa better. It's more—"

"Civilized," provided Lady Damara.

"Exactly." Lady Thurston beamed at her friend.

"And it will be a charming sight when guests come to visit," said Lord Thurston. "Perhaps a more popular destination than our folly."

Lady Damara clapped her hands. "The early bird gets the worm, Lord Westdale," she said. "Had you not come to breakfast, you'd never have known of Lady Thurston's secret wish."

Gregory didn't mention that the secret wish hadn't been wished at all before Lady Damara had mentioned it.

A footman came by and began pouring everyone a fresh cup of tea.

"None for me, thanks," said Gregory, and pushed himself out of his seat. "I think I'd like to ride out to see the far reaches of the property." He strode to the window and flicked back the curtain.

"Want company, Westdale?" Lord Thurston asked.

Gregory looked over his shoulder. "Don't bother,

Thurston, although I thank you for the offer. I'll be riding hard, and I know you complained of your back last night. I wouldn't want to put it out."

"You're such a thoughtful guest," Lady Thurston murmured, and shared a not-so-secret smile with Lady Damara.

Gregory knew then that if Lady Thurston had a vote with the dog cottage designs, he'd already won it. And judging from the pleased look on Lord Thurston's face, Gregory had won his vote, too.

If he came up with a design for a spa, that is. That seemed to be the crucial requirement.

He spun around again. "Are you sure a drawing room won't be enough for the dogs? One with a cozy fire and five large beds strewn about? Leaving enough room for their own private sofa to climb upon and sleep above the fray if they so choose?"

Lord Thurston chuckled. "I like the sound of that."

"But we need more," Lady Thurston insisted. "We need a spa."

"Very well," he said, and returned his gaze to the window while the three at the table went back to discussing London life and the latest scandals.

Gregory had a brief pang of guilt about Marbury. Even though the fellow had worked hard in his own way to sidle his way into his host's good graces by courting Mr. Dawson's favor, he didn't stand a chance at winning the commission if Lord and Lady Thurston had anything to say about it.

But there was still hope for the eccentric lord. It was possible that Nash could easily overrule the Thurstons—he should, as the expert—and choose Marbury's plans, whatever they were. Gregory had seen Marbury's work before—he was competent and true to form, even bold.

Or it was entirely possible that Nash would prefer the sketches of the other competitors, Brian Forrest or Lord Rochelle. But as the Thurstons were the great architect's good friends, he'd probably take their wishes into consideration—or at least pay them lip service before making his decree. He was a politic fellow, John Nash. He could open doors for Gregory should they establish this small connection—and if Gregory could find a way to expand upon it.

His heartbeat increased when, out the window, he saw Pippa and Dawson in the distance. Pippa was brushing at the back of Mr. Dawson's coat, which had hay clinging to it. Immediately, Gregory's curiosity was sparked. What had they been doing in the stables?

Mr. Dawson was swiping Pippa away, rather like a cat does a mouse, but Pippa kept returning until his coat was impeccable again. They were both laughing, and when Pippa was finished, Mr. Dawson pulled some hay off her coat, too.

Then she pointed at the sky, and Mr. Dawson raised a hand to shield his eyes, and they watched a distant point, turning their heads to follow it. Pippa stood with her hands loose and open at her sides, her whole expression enrapt. Gregory couldn't see what they were looking at, but he longed to.

The girl, he realized, was brazen, yes. There she stood, pretending to be a man, all so she could follow her dream. She was outrageous. Ridiculous.

But she was also brave.

You're not, the thought came to him. *You're also not*

good enough for her. And here you've been trying to escape marrying her.

He was filled with a great dark cloud of self-loathing. "Right," he said. "Off to the stables."

The crowd at the table had grown now. The other two architects had arrived, as had several couples who were friends of the Thurstons. One husband and wife had arrived only an hour previous, and another couple, he overheard Lord Thurston say, was due in the afternoon.

The house party was in full swing.

No one observed his leaving, not even Lady Damara, who was too busy chatting with Lady Thurston to notice when he slipped out of the room, wretched, alone, and wanting it that way.

Chapter Seventeen

Being with the amiable Mr. Dawson made everything more bearable for Pippa. And taking a walk was already clearing her head. It was a nippy morning, so the first thing they did was meander to the stables. It would be warm and cozy, and they hadn't met any of the Thurstons' horses yet. Pippa was a real horsewoman, so she was anxious to ride. Mr. Dawson wanted to climb into the hayloft because it was his practice to climb into every hayloft he could. It reminded him of being a boy. The hayloft had been his favorite place to hide and read books.

He'd climbed in haylofts all over the world, he said, as far away as the Orient and Mexico. So once they were done with that required bit of travel up a sturdy oak ladder and back down again, they wandered to the lake, where Pippa enjoyed exploring the folly.

"It's lovely," she said, stretching out on one wall on her back, her hands folded under her head.

Mr. Dawson didn't linger there. He went down to the lake where he picked up some smooth skipping stones.

Pippa basked in the warm sunshine, finding herself on the precipice of a lovely nap. As she was falling into that comforting state—she was still truly exhausted from both the daytime and nighttime adventures of the previous day—she heard her companion call to her. Sitting up, she shook herself back to alertness, clambered to her feet, and followed him to the water's edge.

"So," he said, flinging a rock across the water's smooth surface, "what's going on with you and Lord Westdale, Harrow?"

Pippa's heart nearly burst from her chest. "What do you mean?"

Mr. Dawson turned to look at her full on. "Come, now. The faces you made at him in the breakfast room made it very clear to me that something peculiar is brewing."

"Faces?" she said weakly.

"Yes. Awful faces."

Pippa sighed. "Sometimes I hate him."

"And?" Mr. Dawson threw another rock.

"Sometimes . . . oh, Mr. Dawson, may I speak truthfully? Will you reveal my secret if I share it with you?"

He chuckled and went to sit on a log. "Come here." He patted it.

She sat down and wanted to cry. But she wouldn't. She thought of how if she could only get to Paris, Monsieur would help her find true happiness.

True happiness was not relying on anyone else but only on her own skill with almond paste and nougat, marzipan and spun sugar.

"The only secret of yours I'd ever tell is if you were plotting to kill someone," Mr. Dawson said. "And even then, there are a few people I'd allow you to murder quite ruthlessly."

"Mr. Dawson."

"It's true," he said. "The Thurstons' butler, for one. He sets a nasty tone in the house. But somehow, I don't think you're an assassin." He shot her a wry look. "Although this morning, you appeared as if you wanted to kill Lord Westdale."

She laughed. "I did, didn't I?" Her laugh trailed off, and there was an awkward silence. At least it felt awkward to her. Mr. Dawson looked perfectly at ease.

"Why?" he asked.

She bit her lip. The question was framed so simply, and it was such a complex answer! Where to begin? She scratched her nose. Then turned sideways on the log to look directly at him. "Mr. Dawson, I'm a woman," she said in her normal voice.

"I know," he replied.

She gasped. "Are you serious?"

He nodded complacently. "Everyone will guess by week's end, I'm sure. Twice now you've spoken in a woman's voice. The first time was in the carriage when Marbury was asleep and I was drifting off." He inclined his head toward her. "You spoke to Lord Westdale as you normally would, then remembered your disguise and stopped yourself. You had a refined accent, I noticed."

"Oh, dear." She gazed out over the glassy water. "My name is Lady Pippa Harrington. My late father was the fifth Earl of Claxton."

"Ah. I believe your mother's an actress? She used to be a fairly well-known one."

Pippa blushed fiercely. "Yes."

He smiled fondly at her. "And the other time you gave yourself away was when we were looking at the geese." She loved that he didn't seem to care about her parentage on either side. "You were obviously excited, and—"

"I forgot. I forgot my disguise for a moment because I love geese."

"And the way you climbed into the hayloft? My dear, you were so dainty, it was almost laughable."

Pippa frowned. "You mean you really haven't been in haylofts all over the world? We climbed that ladder so you could test me?"

"No." Mr. Dawson laughed. "It's still true that I'm the Hayloft King. And I wasn't testing you at that point. I already knew." He patted her hand.

"I take great comfort in knowing that we're still friends," she said.

"Of course."

"Do you think—do you think anyone else knows?"

"I doubt it. No one has spent as much time with you as I have. Except Marbury. He's come close."

"Oh, God, I'd hate for him to find out."

Mr. Dawson stood and pulled her up. "I think he will, my dear. Your days here as a valet are numbered. Any moment now, one of the footmen is going to pummel you for being so cheeky. Boldness in a valet isn't approved of belowstairs."

She swallowed hard. "I don't know what to do. I was already thinking I'd like to leave." And she told him everything, all about her history with Gregory and Uncle Bertie's birthday, and of that horrible day in the garden at Eliza's house. And she told him how she hated Lady Damara, even though she had no right to and would probably go to hell for it. She also explained exactly why she'd refused to go home to Plumtree and how sugar sculpting was everything to her, apart from the moor and home.

"You're not going to hell," Mr. Dawson said. "And you *will* get to Paris. By hook or by crook."

"Did you really just say that?" she whispered. "It's one of my favorite phrases."

"Yes," he said, "I did. *I'll* go with you to Paris—and I'll stay long enough to establish you there—"

"Even six months?"

"Yes, I have a sister who makes her home there—"

"You *do*?"

"She married a French shopkeeper, and they live in a lovely home in a charming part of Paris." He reached over and turned her chin toward him, gazing at her with a serious expression. "But we can't have you dressed as a valet. You're going to meet Monsieur as a woman. And if he's a true artist, then he'll recognize the artistry in your own soul and want to help."

"Do you think so?" Her heart was nearly bursting with hope.

"Yes. We'll even hire a maid to take with us so you're properly chaperoned."

She hugged him. "Oh, thank you, you dear man."

"No need to thank me," he said, pulling her arms off.

"Oh, yes there is," she insisted.

"Remember that beneath my mild exterior, I'm drawn to trouble. But I'm an even bigger admirer of honesty. So there are two caveats," he told her.

"Oh?"

"You'll have to tell your family what you're doing. We'll see them before we go."

Gregory had said much the same thing. She felt a twinge of regret that she wouldn't be pleasing him with her plan, but going with Mr. Dawson and a chaperone— well, she couldn't ask for more than that.

"I'd like to go to Plumtree first." Her heart felt instantly lighter. "They think I've run off to marry Gregory . . . and it's going to be a very sticky situation when they find out I didn't."

"If you go with me, you'll avoid that angst entirely. I would assure them of your safety."

She smiled. "That relieves my mind. What's the other caveat?"

"You have to tell Lord Westdale you love him before we go."

"What?" A cold pit formed in Pippa's stomach. "Confess that I love Gregory?" She was shaken to the core at Mr. Dawson's challenge.

"It's obvious to me that you do," he said.

"Certainly, I do." She sank onto the log, her hands trembling. "And I always have." It was a fact, like the changing of the seasons. "But I'm not a glutton for punishment. I told you what happened in the garden at Eliza's when he deduced that I cared for him. He stormed off."

"And he might do it again," Mr. Dawson replied kindly. "But I won't be party to your scheme unless he's heard the words from your own mouth. If you want to go so badly to Paris—with me to ease the way—you'll tell him."

Pippa stared at her friend. "You drive a hard bargain."

"You can always go on your own."

She could, and she'd planned to. She'd been prepared to dress as a man every day and spend much of her time as a companion to Uncle Bertie's friend. But to be able to go with Mr. Dawson would make getting to Paris and staying there easier, less intimidating, and without a doubt much more fun.

Tell Gregory the painful truth—which could be over in thirty seconds—and have an ally in Paris for as long as half a year?

Or keep her pride intact and go it alone in the City of Love?

"I'll have to think about it," Pippa confessed. "I appreciate the offer, but you're asking for something I'm not sure I can deliver."

"I'm aware of that," Mr. Dawson said.

She kissed his cheek before reverting to her valet self—which meant she kept a respectful distance from him for appearances' sake—and they walked back to the house in companionable silence.

Gregory marched to the stables, said hello to Oscar, who was enjoying some rest and solitude, and asked Lord Thurston's stable hand for the most difficult stallion. His name was Prince, and he was a piebald.

"He's gorgeous," Gregory said, and fell in love with him on the spot when the great animal nudged Gregory's shoulder with its nose—hard, as if he were testing his mettle.

"The master seldom rides him," said the stable hand, who was a brawny lad about Peter's age. "I keep him exercised."

"You do an excellent job of it," Gregory said, and felt a twinge of homesickness for Peter, who loved loitering at Tattersall's.

Prince's skin rippled with muscles, and his coat had a healthy shine to it. His eyes were clear and alert.

When Gregory mounted the stallion and cantered up the long, winding drive, his spirits lifted. Nothing was as bad as all that when you were on the back of a fine horse. It was easier to remember his purpose: to keep Pippa safe and get her situated happily. That was the great challenge. All the rest—winning the commission for the dog cottage, avoiding Lady Damara, and returning to his busy social life in London—were secondary concerns.

He galloped Prince over several fields and across a stream and past a lone farmhouse, where the overseer lived. At a small road, Gregory turned left and found himself passing a row of cottages, all of them neat and clean.

He slowed Prince to let a gaggle of young girls cross in front of them, five in all. Each of them carried a bunch of weeds mixed with flowers.

"Look!" cried the tallest of them. "It's Lord Thurston's finest steed, Prince!"

The girls gathered about with toothy grins and excited chatter. Gregory gave them permission to pat Prince's nose and stroke his mane. The stallion was well under his control and obviously enjoyed the extra attention, judging from the way he nudged the girls' shoulders if they stopped petting him for even an instant.

At a nearby doorway, a mother with a baby on her hip waved in greeting. "Come in and visit," she called to him. "Have a cup of tea and a slice of my new bread and jam with my husband. He's on his break at the moment."

So Gregory turned Prince around and tied him to a tree. Two boys ran over and begged to look after him. Their exuberant hoots when he tossed them each a copper coin made him chuckle.

Happy children. They were a tonic. Someday, in the far distant future, he'd like to have his own.

For the next thirty minutes, he enjoyed the company of the farming couple, who were all that was good and generous. Their home was spotless and cheery, although he noticed that the chimney smoked, and the front door hung by its hinges. He'd have to mention those very real problems to Lord Thurston.

The overseer should be more closely looking after

these people, he thought as he shook the farmer's hand and tickled the baby's pudgy toes.

"Send our best to Lord and Lady Thurston," the wife said, and placed a small pot of gooseberry jam wrapped in muslin and tied with twine in his hands. Still on his mother's hip, the baby reached out to grab it, and Gregory let the infant slap his tiny fingers on the muslin top. "This is for their breakfast," the mother added proudly, "and yours. I hope you enjoy it."

"I already know how delicious it is." He raised her roughened knuckles to his lips. "Thank you."

His heart was touched by the pure and simple pleasures he'd experienced during the unplanned visit. Outside, he said good-bye to the children, put the jam in a satchel behind the saddle, and swung himself onto the piebald's back.

When he reached the overseer's house, he'd already made his decision: He was withdrawing his sketches for the dog cottage from the competition. Certainly, the Irish wolfhounds were a grand pack of animals, but it was too frivolous a commission. He wouldn't be proud of it. There were people on Lord Thurston's estate living in far less luxury than those dogs would be, and he just couldn't see himself signing his name to the project.

John Nash would have to be introduced to him another way—which was like asking for the moon. Because for that to happen, Gregory would have to produce an astounding design.

And he didn't know that he had it in him.

But for now it was enough that he was saying no to the dog cottage. Let someone else design the canine spa.

He couldn't wait to tell Pippa.

When he dismounted at Lord Thurston's stables, he

saw that another carriage had arrived, and two new horses were being seen to by the stable hand—a pair of matched grays. He conversed with ever-loyal Oscar and the young man who'd helped him earlier. Each of them remarked on the grays' spirit and beauty.

Gregory then told Oscar and Lord Thurston's man that he'd enjoy watering and brushing Prince down himself, that neither of them needed to take on the job. He felt at ease in the stable, and for the first time, was truly glad to be at the house party.

In less than twenty-four hours, so much had happened. So much had changed.

Running the curry brush in small but vigorous circles over Prince's coat, he was admiring the magnificent musculature and sheer strength of the animal when a thought sprang to mind: *You want Pippa to be proud of you.*

Well, so what if he did? He craved his parents' approval, too, and he enjoyed the admiration of his brothers and sisters and Bertie. Was it such a crime that he'd want Pippa to be proud of him, as well? She was Bertie's great-niece. It made sense.

Now that he was withdrawing his sketches, he could leave Thurston Manor. He'd no reason to stay. He'd promised Pippa he wouldn't take her home, but he *would* take her to London. He was going to miss their togetherness in his bedchamber exceedingly much, but she'd be much better off with his mothers and sisters—

And he'd be much better off having the temptation of bedding her out of the way. His parents' house was sacrosanct. She'd be safe as a nun there from his lustful impulses. And he could concentrate on improving his design skills.

He walked Prince to his stall and saw him into it.

Closing the half-door behind him, he saluted the stable hand, who pulled on his forelock and thanked him for his help.

He strode purposefully toward the house, feeling different . . .

Better.

He inhaled a deep breath and let it out, then scanned the tops of the trees the way Pippa had with Dawson. It didn't matter that he didn't see anything yet.

He was looking.

Chapter Eighteen

Pippa cast a sideways glance at Mr. Dawson. He had a kind, distracted smile on his face as they hiked back to Thurston Manor after their revelatory conversation. She could tell he was a man at peace. Perhaps that's why she was attracted to him in the first place. He'd confessed to her that he liked excitement—but he liked honesty more.

So should she tell Gregory she loved him? Or shouldn't she? What would it hurt to get it off her chest once and for all? Perhaps it would free her to focus better on her sugar sculpture—because as of this moment, she couldn't stop thinking of Gregory kissing her, laughing with her, and making her feel beautiful when she was naked and vulnerable.

Honesty. It compelled her to admit that Gregory mattered so much to her that she was running away to Paris partly because she couldn't bear not being with him when she wasn't his love.

His love.

It was like a fresh bruise on her heart every time she faced the truth: She loved him with everything, and he—

Well, he put up with her out of loyalty to Bertie.

She looked toward the house and saw him walking up

from the stables. Her pulse instantly quickened, and she lifted her hand in a wave. He waved back, and a hot flush spread through her limbs, making her feel that weak, almost dizzy wonder that she knew now was more than infatuation.

It was love.

Love-of-a-lifetime sort of love.

The kind she would never, ever get over.

Perhaps that was why she'd been so glad to stumble upon this passion of hers for sugar sculpting. She loved it on its own merits, but it also served as an escape from burdensome, sad feelings about Gregory and the role she would never play in his life as lover, best friend, and soul mate.

And why was she so sure about that?

Because she felt certain he'd already had his love-of-a-lifetime, too, with Eliza.

Pippa would never forget that look on his face when he'd discovered Eliza with Lord Morgan in the garden.

"There he is," said Mr. Dawson, "the object of your affection." He threw her a mischievous glance. "Pardon me. He's *one* of your loves. I fully sympathize that there's the sugar sculptor in you wanting to get out, too."

"And sugar sculpting is far more reliable a love than a fickle man who told me himself to avoid him because he's dangerous."

"I have no doubt he is," Mr. Dawson agreed. "But perhaps he is in ways he's not even aware of yet. I get the feeling Lord Westdale is doing his best to avoid finding out."

"Do you? Why?"

"There's a leashed power I sense in him."

"Oh, yes." She herself sensed it when he'd loved her

body so well the night previous. The frustration, the tortured anticipation she felt in knowing he wasn't giving her everything—

Not yet.

"It's what makes him so compelling a figure to the *ton*," Mr. Dawson said, "why cartoons are drawn of him and gossips mull over his every action. I suspect they're waiting for him to . . . let go. Expectations are high—for failure or success. Whatever he does, it won't be ordinary, and he and everyone else know it."

"Yes," said Pippa, quickening her pace. "In a way, it makes me pity him. It makes me long to shield him from their prying eyes, from those uncaring fools who merely want to be entertained at his expense."

"Pity is the last thing he needs," said Mr. Dawson. "He needs someone to believe in him. But, Pippa"—she liked hearing her new friend speak her real name—"he must believe in himself first. Otherwise, all the support in the world won't matter." His brow furrowed as he studied her intently. "You do know that, don't you?"

"Yes, I do. It's hard to accept—but I do. What I've said about his talent fell on deaf ears."

"It's a shame," Mr. Dawson said. "Because until he does believe in himself . . ."

"What?"

"I think you're best off in Paris. It's the main reason I'm willing to take you there."

It was a sad, sad reason. But the way she felt—joyless and despairing—hearing Mr. Dawson express his thoughts out loud was confirmation enough for her that she was, indeed, in over her head with Gregory.

Even from this distance, Pippa could see that his gait

was lighter than it had been yesterday. He must have taken out a horse. She craved doing the same thing, and she'd love to ride with him, especially if they could find a secret place to dismount and—

There she went again. Daydreaming of kissing him. Fantasizing about opportunities to show him she adored him. She imagined him kissing her against a tree trunk, running his hand over her breast, taking her down onto the grass, both of them stripping naked, and him loving her completely.

My Gregory, she thought. *No one else's.* She held her chin resolute. *Least of all Lady Damara's.* It was silly of Pippa to think that way—tragic, actually—but the message of her heart refused to be silenced by logic.

But it must. And it was up to her to do it.

"I'm glad we had this talk," she told Mr. Dawson.

"I am, as well." He looked straight ahead and not at her, because they were getting so close to the house. "I don't often wax poetic—I abhor maudlin emotion, to tell you the truth—but sometimes we meet people in life we're meant to meet, and for me, you're one of those people."

"You're one for me, too," she replied. "I felt an instant bond with you at the inn."

He chuckled. "For me, it started when you came running over, insisting that you would shine my boots."

"For me, it was when you told Marbury you wouldn't eat in the private dining room. I liked how firm you were, yet kind. You reminded me of Uncle Bertie."

Mr. Dawson stopped beneath a tree not far from the front door of the house. "The ancient philosopher Heraclitus spoke very wise words that are always apropos."

"And they are?"

"'Character is destiny.' I believe fate dangles opportunities before us—but it is up to us to seize them or ignore them."

"I'm glad you didn't ignore *me*," Pippa whispered because now Gregory was fast approaching.

"My dear, ignoring you is rather difficult," Mr. Dawson replied, his usual placid expression in place. She recognized it now as his social mask.

"I'm glad you found me so." She angled an amused glance at him, but her body was already thrumming with awareness of Gregory.

"Mr. Dawson, Harrow," he greeted them. "Lovely day, is it not?"

Pippa soaked up the view. He held a pot of something in his hand—jam? pickles?—and his hair was a bit flyaway at the moment. He must have had a good gallop. His cheeks were flushed, and his cravat slightly askew. Even so, he seemed more . . .

Solid.

Confident.

And not just outwardly. He'd always been able to convey an impression of self-assurance. But there was something else in his gaze, something playful—something open to adventure. It reminded her of how he used to be when they'd played Captain and Lieutenant. She hadn't seen that look in years.

It was interesting—and exhilarating—to observe.

In fact, the change was so obvious that she and Mr. Dawson exchanged a brief and inquiring look.

"I'm off," Mr. Dawson said. "Good to see you, West-dale. At the moment, I'm gasping for tea. Feel free to join me." He pulled his handkerchief out and swiped at his forehead. "Pity Harrow can't. Your valet's made me an excellent walking companion."

"I'm glad to hear that." Gregory grinned. "I'll see you in a moment. I've got a job for Harrow first."

"Right," said Mr. Dawson vaguely, and smiled his farewell, conveying nothing to signify that he knew Pippa's entire story.

Pippa almost blushed. How would Gregory feel if *he* knew Mr. Dawson was in on the charade?

And should she—or shouldn't she—tell Gregory she loved him? That he was the captain of her heart? That she would enter any fight with him, stay by his side through thick and thin, bask in their spoils, grieve their losses, loyal to her last breath—and loving him forever?

It was time to decide.

Now.

But how to know whether to keep silent—or risk it all?

"I've got something important to tell you," he began with a simple earnestness that she'd not heard in the sophisticated city gentleman in a decade, at least.

She recalled a lovely, warm memory: one time when he'd handed her a sack of crab apples. "Throw these," he'd said in that same heartfelt voice, "at the enemy. Today it's Robbie, Billy, and Patrick. Not me. I'm on *your* side."

And then she knew what to do. She knew simply because at this moment, she saw that old Gregory before her—the one who was on her side.

"I've got something very important to tell *you*," she interrupted him. "Sorry, but I'd appreciate it if you let me go first—Captain."

Their eyes locked, and her love bloomed even more. Their almost lifelong bond was the only sun and rain it needed to grow.

"Go ahead, Lieutenant," he said softly.

"Right." She swallowed hard, girding herself, because she'd made her decision. She'd tell him she loved him. And it wasn't simply because doing so would make it easier for her to get to Paris and stay there. She was doing it because—

Character *was* destiny.

If she wasn't brave enough to live authentically—owning her love for Gregory, no matter the consequences—going to Paris was merely running away.

And she was better than that.

She was *so* much better than that.

"Gregory . . ."

"Yes?"

The front door of the house opened wide, and a cluster of people spilled out, all laughing and talking.

Blast. A horrible distraction. Perhaps telling someone you loved him outside under a tree a mere twenty feet from the front door of someone else's house—especially when a house party was going on—wasn't a good idea.

Pippa couldn't help turning to see what the commotion was about as it was only a few feet away. Neither could Gregory.

Situational awareness. It was key in a good soldier.

There were Lord and Lady Thurston, both looking jolly; Lady Damara, sulking a bit, although she was surrounded by several women talking at once; as well as several men Pippa hadn't seen yet. She suspected one or two of them might be the other architects.

Lord Marbury came outside next, cackling with glee about something, and then—

Pippa sucked in a breath.

Good God, there was—

Eliza.

Lord Morgan.

And their baby, the very picture of Gregory, with black curls and vivid blue eyes.

"Surprise!" trilled Lady Thurston at Gregory. "Your old friends are here!"

"And with the new baby!" Lord Thurston echoed his wife's enthusiasm.

Gregory had known of their propensity to have an amusing mix of guests at their house parties, but this wasn't amusing—

It was diabolical.

But he didn't have time to be angry about that. His heart was going so fast, he could barely breathe—for that baby in Eliza's arms looked so much like him, he had to wonder, was it his?

Could their one brief coupling have produced a child?

Of course it could have. And if it were so, he had a son.

A son!

The natural wonder he felt was immediately supplanted by a sorrow so sharp, it nearly doubled him over. If it were true, this would be a far worse loss than losing Eliza or Dougal.

Losing a son.

A *son.*

His parents would grieve forever.

He would grieve forever.

He had to remind himself to stand straight, tall, and with all the gravity a future marquess would model in the face of what was to others utter social embarrassment but to him was possibly the worst tragedy of his life—seeing a babe who was possibly his own son before him and not being able to acknowledge him as such if it were so.

He had to remind himself to breathe, all the while pretending he was perfectly at ease.

A son . . .

"Hello, Westdale," Lord Morgan called from the throng, a happy grin on his face.

The coward. He was safe on those stairs, wasn't he, surrounded by all those people? Gregory hated him more than ever. Dougal would be father to *his* boy? If he'd had a pistol in his hands, he'd have gladly shot him.

Eliza's smile was more brittle. "Westdale, so nice to see you again."

He was struck by the sight of her. She was more beautiful than ever—perhaps because she looked weary. Her face—despite the new lines that had appeared around her eyes—had been softened by motherhood.

By love.

Because it was clear she loved the babe in her arms.

She didn't even wait for Gregory's reply before she beamed at the infant, not half a year yet, reclining safe and content in her arms.

"Hello," Gregory called back to them. It was all he could manage, and he wasn't even polite. He was cold. Stiff.

The company on the stairs, almost as one, quieted, all except the baby, who cooed and waved his arms about.

Out of the corner of Gregory's eye, he saw Pippa, her back taut, her eyes wide. For a split second, he caught her gaze and saw utter desolation there.

It had happened. It was the thing he'd dreaded more than anything else, he realized now. He'd lost the respect of a woman he adored.

The woman he *loved*.

Yet again, he had a flash of wonder—of joy—followed swiftly by grief.

It was another tragedy of monumental proportions, as blunt and hard a blow to his spirit as the first, when his old lieutenant put her head down and walked away, down the path alongside the house, to the servants' entrance.

His life as he knew it—at least the essential part he never wanted to change—was over. What was left?

Nothing but duty: duty to the title and to his family.

Duty to the House of Brady.

But Father had trained him well. So had Mother, and then Mama. He swallowed and came forward a few steps. "My turn to hold him," he said with good cheer, and held out his arms.

He felt like an old man. An old, foolish man.

The crowd, as one, came down to meet him.

Eliza brought him the baby. He could smell her old scent, which did nothing for him anymore, mixed with the newer scents of baby skin, powder, and fresh linen. "Here you are," she said quietly. "His name is Walter, after Dougal's father."

"Don't drop him," Marbury called to him.

When Gregory felt the wriggling weight of Walter in his arms, the crushing heaviness in his chest lifted slightly. Walter, even if he were his son, would come to no harm as the child of this couple. They both had large, stable families—conventional and wealthy—and there was no doubt that this baby boy would be loved completely and forever.

Walter giggled from somewhere deep in his belly as he batted his tiny hand at Gregory's face. Gregory was certain his nose must be the object of such amusement. He'd broken it in a boxing match five years earlier, and the slight bump on it now made him look like a clown, according to Peter and Robert, and sometimes Cynthia, when she was particularly perturbed at him for bossing her about.

After a suitable thirty seconds of admiration, he passed the baby back to his mother. Gregory's forearm accidentally brushed against the side of Eliza's breast when he lifted Walter high to avoid just that, but the sensation provoked no romantic feelings. In fact, when he watched her go back into the fold of spectators and kiss her husband on the lips, Gregory couldn't believe that he'd ever been hell-bent to marry her, that he hadn't seen the real woman he'd made love to . . . the woman in love with another man—his best friend, Dougal.

And where had he been not to see that Dougal loved Eliza?

He thought over that circumstance as they all walked to the lake to see the folly. He joined in the lively conversation, even making a joke or two that made Dougal laugh. Both times Gregory saw the hope in Dougal's eyes, and both times he intentionally turned away from him. No, he wasn't ready to be his friend. Dougal hadn't been honest with him.

For the umpteenth time, he went back to the fact that neither had Peter, for that matter.

Why?

What was it about Gregory at that point in his life that his very best friend and his beloved brother weren't *honest* with him?

He walked to the edge of the lake alone and wondered.

"Don't," said Eliza, who'd appeared at his shoulder. "Please don't torture yourself."

"What do you mean?" he asked, his voice hoarse.

"Walter isn't yours," she said. "I swear."

Gregory let out a loud breath that was part moan. The short-lived courtship story—his and Eliza's—had been fraught with high drama, the kind that could rip one's soul in half.

Thank God it hadn't quite happened to him. It had been such a near miss—such a near, near miss.

Relief flooded through him. But he was still so sorely rattled, he held on to the view of the geese flying overhead, following them until they disappeared beyond the trees, as if they were a lifeline to calmness . . . to peace.

But they couldn't be. Not as long as Pippa was upset. He knew very well she thought that baby was his. He couldn't wait to get back to tell her otherwise, and to speak another truth—that he loved her.

But first, he must be the gentleman and give Eliza her say.

"It was very close," his former lover said quietly. "Walter's age and size—and of course, his hair coloring and those curls—fueled the rumors. But he's the image of his grandfather. His likeness in his baby portrait is uncanny. And if anyone really wanted to—but of course, they don't—it's easy enough to do the math." She heaved a great sigh. "He was conceived almost four weeks after you left for America. Ironically, it happened the first time Dougal and I were . . . together. When he learned I'd been with you, too, we parted ways. A week later, we were together again. He said he loved me so much, he knew that if I were with child, he would love the baby as his own—even if it were yours. I believed him, and not only that, I loved him all the more for that declaration. We were married by special license a few days later."

Gregory didn't say a word. He was overcome. They were together, and they had no secrets. What was it like—to be able to trust someone else that much?

"Dougal hated you for a long time," Eliza went on somberly. "But I told him not to. I told him it was entirely my fault. Not yours. I was adrift . . . My choices were my own. I knew exactly what I was doing. My parents wanted us together. I was miserable, but I surrendered to them. To you. The very next morning, I couldn't stop thinking I was throwing away my life, and I told Dougal I loved him in my back garden. The truth is, Gregory, I ruined you, and not the other way around."

He looked down at her. "No, Eliza. I wasn't marrying you for the right reasons, either. You deserve a man who loves you. If it makes you feel any better, the truth is, I'm fine now. More than fine. I'm in love."

"Oh, Gregory." She wiped away a quick tear. "I'm so happy that's true."

"Don't cry," he said. "It's all right. I still wish Dougal had been honest with me. But it's in the past, and I'm ready to move on—to move past this. All's forgiven. If you'll forgive me, too."

"Of course I do." She reached for and caught his hand, holding it to her heart. "I don't care that everyone is staring at us right now. Why do you think they brought us here, encouraged us to bring the baby? To see drama unfold. The idiots."

Gregory allowed himself a small chuckle at that. This spirited Eliza was so different from the quiet debutante he'd known.

"I'm only too happy to give them what they're looking for," she went on. "But what they don't know—or don't care about—is that real human hearts are involved, and they still need healing."

That was true. Seeing baby Walter had actually brought home to him how vulnerable he was. He'd been reacting to life, almost shutting down. He hadn't been operating from the center of his being where the piebald stallion pawed the air, where all his hopes and dreams shone brightly, lighting the way to a destiny he could create if only he were brave enough.

Eliza released his hand. "Dougal and I had no idea you were coming here, and even though at first it felt like a giant catastrophe—a dirty trick—right now I'm glad. *So* glad. I didn't realize what a burden this has been, how many nights I've lain awake wondering how you're doing. How many times I've looked at my men—Dougal and Walter—and felt sorry for them for the loss of you in their lives. And *I'd* caused it."

The others had scattered now. Perhaps the presence of a smiling baby in the arms of Lady Thurston made them ashamed that the two-penny drama they'd hoped to see unfurl before them was actually more the culmination—or the remaking—of a genuine tragedy, enough so that they made an attempt to respectfully look away.

Everyone but Dougal, who stood frozen at the folly, watching them on high alert.

This time when Gregory caught a glimpse of Eliza's husband over his shoulder, he didn't look away from him.

Like a broom, a bundle of scraggly emotions that came from the hundreds of wonderful times he and Dougal had shared—as well as the occasional crisis—brushed through him and swept him clean, leaving only one thought:

Best friends.

Did that not mean something? The same way *brother* meant something?

And it came to him then why Dougal and Peter hadn't been honest with him—even why Eliza hadn't been. He hadn't let them in. Not really. He hadn't let anyone know him. Not since he was thirteen.

The memories slashed him hard.

"Swear you won't tell, darling. It would only hurt Daddy's feelings."

"I swear, Mother. I'll never tell. Never."

"What's wrong, Gregory?" Eliza asked worriedly.

"Nothing." But that was a lie. Everything was wrong. His façade was cracking in the worst way. But he mustn't let it. He mustn't.

"Dougal!" Eliza gripped Gregory's arm hard so he couldn't escape, the way a mother would. "Get over here *right now.*"

In the mirrored surface of the lake, Gregory saw a peaceful world reflected there, a world he wished existed. Now that he was trying to breathe again, he realized that here on shore, he'd been walking underwater since the day his mother died . . . and slowly drowning.

The next thing he knew, Dougal was at his side.

"Everything all right?" He looked hard at Gregory, his eyes lit with concern.

Dougal was a good man. He'd taken on Eliza's baby willingly. He didn't care that Walter might have been Gregory's son.

What if—

What if Father didn't care that Gregory had been fathered by someone else?

But of course he would! Otherwise, Mother wouldn't

have acted so fearful that Gregory would tell the secret. She wouldn't have sounded so ashamed . . .

But there was Dougal, stepping up. He couldn't be the only man in the world to have done so with a willing heart.

A tiny ember of hope lit Gregory's heart.

"I'm all right," he said. "Really. And I want to apologize to you, Dougal. You've always tried to be a good friend to me. And I—I didn't quite let you. If I had, we never would have gotten to the point we did."

Dougal laughed. "We made a mess of it, didn't we? I'm sorry, too. I should have told you I had feelings for Eliza. I had no idea she did for me, not until that day in her garden, and then"—the couple looked at each other—"and then there was no turning back."

"We won't leave you ever again." Eliza wrapped her hand through the crook of Gregory's right arm.

"No, we won't," said Dougal. "But it means you must be Walter's godfather."

"Yes," said Eliza. "That entails a great many duties. He likes being carried around like a great sack of potatoes at the moment. And I suspect he'll demand to build a fort with you when he's older. Since you're an architect, of course."

"I'd consider it a great honor," Gregory replied with a grin. "I accept on all counts."

"Remember our first fort?" Dougal asked him.

And together they walked back to the house, talking about how spectacular that stronghold had been.

Chapter Nineteen

Pippa couldn't believe how closely she'd come to giving up her last vestige of pride and telling Gregory she loved him. What a big mistake that would have been!

Yes, the confession would have been over in thirty seconds. But she knew now that those thirty seconds would have haunted her the entire half-year she planned to stay in Paris. They'd have haunted her *the rest of her life*.

Her hat in her hand, she walked through the kitchens in a stupor, not believing what she'd seen with her own eyes: Gregory's child.

He'd slept with Eliza.

The rumors were true. All it took was one look at his face as he looked at that baby to know that he and Eliza had been together, that his body had been intimately joined with hers.

No wonder he'd been so desperately angry that day in Lord and Lady Baird's garden.

Pippa liked to think she wasn't judgmental—after all, the night before, she'd come to pleasure under the skilled manipulation of Gregory, master lover. He was very tempting. No wonder Eliza had succumbed.

But was he over his feelings for her?

Or not?

His face had registered shock when he'd seen the baby. And then when he'd looked at Eliza, all Pippa could see was his utter despair—despair that he'd lost his child, no doubt. But perhaps there was also despair that he'd lost the child's mother.

He'd tried so hard to hide his devastation beneath a veneer of politeness, but he was broken. She'd sensed it, even if no one else had.

How could she not wonder if he still loved Eliza? Especially now that she realized how powerful love was: Mix it with the compelling force that was sexual intimacy, and one could hardly be expected to easily recover—if ever—from the captivating combination that had the entire world in its thrall.

It was why there was Shakespeare. And Shelley. And every other poet, writer, playwright, painter, and composer who'd ever experienced both the victory and surrender that came with opening one's self to another.

She felt like knocking her head against the wall. How many times would it take for her to learn that Gregory wasn't hers and never would be?

But instead of useless self-pity, she decided to work on the mission—most likely, with no allies. First, she'd tell Mr. Dawson she hadn't kept up her end of the bargain, and he was free to withdraw his offer. Next, assuming he would, she'd leave the house party on her own in the morning, and she already knew how. She'd ride on the back of the milk wagon that came by before dawn. She'd heard the house cook talking about it. She'd go as far as she could and then sell her earrings. After that, she'd purchase a ticket for the coast. She'd travel to an unlikely port— which would mean Plymouth was out of the question, being the closest major one. She'd go east as far as South-ampton and get lost among the hordes of travelers queuing up for berths aboard packets heading to France.

And then she'd work as a companion and pray that Monsieur Perot would take her on. She'd go back to her original plan and approach him as a man. It was too dangerous, otherwise.

She found Mr. Dawson in the drawing room, standing at the tea tray and gulping down a cup of tea.

"Come in, Harrow," he urged her, then poured himself another cup.

She walked briskly past a disapproving footman into the room. She didn't care anymore about following house rules. She wasn't hurting anyone talking to Mr. Dawson anyway.

It turned out he wouldn't let her go alone to Paris, after all.

"I heard about the baby," he said in a low voice. "We don't know if it's Westdale's or not, but it's an ugly environment to be in right now here at Thurston Manor. I need to get you out of here. I blame my cousin for this debacle. Shame on her. And shame on her husband."

Pippa rather thought Lord and Lady Thurston were wicked, too, to purposely create an awkward situation. "Are you sure you'll still come with me?"

"Of course." His voice was so reassuring, Pippa nearly choked up. "In fact, I've already sent a footman to the stables. They're readying us a carriage now." His brow furrowed. "I refuse to ask my cousin for permission or tell her where we're going. She's brought this on herself."

"I'm so grateful for your help, Mr. Dawson. Where are we going first?"

"Let's talk in the carriage," he said. "Swallow a cup of tea as fast as you can, and then pack swiftly. We must leave before the others come back."

"I'll skip the tea." She moved to the door, then came back and took a biscuit off a china plate. "But I'll take one of these, thanks."

"Snitch them all, why don't you?" He chuckled. "We might need them."

"Very well." She poured them into her hat and trotted to the door again. Her heart felt lighter, now that she was taking action and she had a friend to share her adventure. And blast it all, she was hungry. They had at least several hours' travel ahead of them.

The first leg of Pippa's journey to Paris was uneventful. She and Mr. Dawson left ten minutes after their conversation, long before the majority of the guests had come home from the excursion to the folly.

"I designed the thing," Mr. Dawson said as the carriage rocked back and forth over the bumpy road. They'd long left behind the smooth gravel drive of Thurston Manor.

"The folly?"

"Yes." He smiled.

Pippa was astonished. "I had no idea you were an architect."

"Very few people do. I'm the architect who never makes the papers. I labor in a dreary office and lend my expertise and intuition to important men like John Nash."

"You know John Nash?"

"Very well—Lord and Lady Thurston are acquainted with him through me."

"But they tried to act as if he's one of *their* dear friends and that you're their country cousin of no real consequence—but much beloved, of course."

"Typical of them. Lady Thurston has always enjoyed being in the limelight. I let her. I couldn't care less if I am."

"Were you at Thurston Manor, then, on Nash's behalf, to evaluate the dog cottage designs?" Pippa asked. "Lady Thurston said he's planning on helping them choose the winning one."

"I was." Mr. Dawson spoke without a great deal of enthusiasm. "I was to send over my recommendation to him. He'll ultimately choose the winner, but I was to play a small part."

"That's hardly a small part," said Pippa, and then she remembered their conversation about the folly they'd had earlier that day. "Why did you pretend you didn't know who designed the folly?"

"I quibbled. I *am* a nobody. But I must say I was most impressed with Lord Westdale's evaluation of the design."

"Were you?"

"Yes. He was uncannily accurate—he thought that perhaps the designer wasn't fond of the past. Which is true. I don't like it."

"Why is that?" Pippa asked.

He smiled gently. "I was married for thirty years, and my wife died, five years ago, right before I was asked to design the folly."

"I'm so sorry."

"Thank you. So I was in no mood to elevate the past. I'm still not fond of rehashing it. But my cousin insisted I design the folly for Prinny's visit to Thurston Manor. As much as he is a purveyor of arts and culture, I have very little respect for the Prince Regent. So that mawkishly sentimental pile of stones is actually a testament to my dislike for him—and my dislike of the past. Now, however . . ."

"What?"

"Now I wish I'd reached beyond my own trifling feelings and built a true monument worthy of the ages. The best artists forget themselves in their work. Whatever they create is for everyone, not to satisfy a petty impulse. Now every time I look at that folly, I'm reminded of my own meanness."

"You're not mean," Pippa insisted. "You're human."

"I suppose I am." Mr. Dawson chuckled.

"What will Lord and Lady Thurston do if you're not there to help them with the dog cottage sketches?"

Mr. Dawson shrugged. "They'll have to figure it out for themselves. I know for a fact John Nash won't be interested in helping them if I'm not involved."

Pippa's shoulders sank. "I feel sorry now for the designers."

Mr. Dawson sighed. "I knew you'd say something like that."

She bit her lip. "I can't help thinking of Lord Marbury, of how hard he tried to ingratiate himself with you. He thought you were only a cousin—can you imagine how much more eagerly he'd have worked to win your favor had he known you were John Nash's colleague?"

"Thank God he didn't know. I could hardly take another second of his company."

"But if you thought his design was best, you would have recommended it, correct?"

"Of course. I can separate personal feelings from my business dealings. However, a good architect knows how to get along well with others. He consults with the customer and the contractors." The carriage gave a hefty bounce then—an unexpected pothole, perhaps—and Dawson paused to reposition himself on the seat. "He stays abreast of trends. A good architect certainly doesn't work in a vacuum."

"I wanted Gregory to win that contest, silly as it was," Pippa confessed. "Perhaps it would have boosted his career to make contact with John Nash. And now . . . now I've ruined his chances and everyone else's—just so I could pursue *my* dream."

"If talent is there, it will out, I promise you," Mr. Dawson assured her. "One lost opportunity doesn't stop the ambitious. Nor does it stop the creative soul with a passion for his work from continuing to create. What's the other option? Quitting? Not for the truly dedicated." He gave a wry smile and fixed her with a direct look. "Missed opportunities weed out the pretenders."

"You're certainly blunt," she said, feeling a bit intimidated.

"I'm merely speaking the truth. Take it, or leave it." He crossed his arms over his chest and looked out the window, looking every inch the influential architect and not merely the sweet little man she'd thought him.

Funny how there were different sides to people, how they could change right before your eyes. For now he leaned toward her, his palms on his knees. "Let's consider your Gregory, for instance," he said in a low, menacing tone.

"Mr. Dawson." She shrank back in her seat. "You sound so . . . *angry.*"

He frowned. "I'm not angry. I'm merely observant. Your precious lover—"

"What?"

He made a wry face. "Let's be honest, Lady Pippa. The man is a renowned rake. I don't hold it against you if he had his way with you, but I certainly hold it against *him*. Here he's gotten a babe on Lady Morgan—"

Pippa caught her breath. What mortifying talk!

"We can't be sure of that yet," she said hastily. And it was true. She'd been so willing to believe that he was Walter's father—as had Gregory, obviously, from that stark look on his face when he first saw the baby—but Eliza had been married for almost a year, and it was perfectly possible that little Walter had been a product of her union with Dougal.

"You're naïve," Mr. Dawson said when she explained that reasoning to him. "Westdale has thrown away so many chances. I've seen his work in London. He has great potential. And he shows up at my cousin's to design a dog cottage? It's a waste of his talent."

"He had misgivings," said Pippa. "He only designed the dog cottage because Lady Thurston asked him to— and he wasn't excited at the prospect. But when he heard John Nash was involved, of course, he grew more interested."

"As if John Nash would respect the designer of a dog cottage. He wouldn't, I assure you." Mr. Dawson's cheeks were bright red.

"I—I had no idea you disliked Lord Westdale so." Pippa's heart was pounding so hard, she was afraid she'd faint. Suddenly, going to Paris with Mr. Dawson was a terrible idea.

"He doesn't deserve you," Mr. Dawson said with fervent disgust. "He's a lucky man to have your heart. He's a lucky man to have his talent. And what do either you or his talent mean to him? Nothing."

It hurt Pippa to hear him say that. But what if he were right?

"I know you must be tremendously fatigued," she said in a soothing voice. "You mean well, but you're frightening me with how savage you're being toward Lord Westdale. Perhaps you should sleep."

"No." A stubborn, closed look came over Mr. Dawson's face. "There's no time to sleep. And by the by, if I had a chance to do it all over again, I'd not let John Nash take the leading role in the projects we worked on together—it would be I. Every time I see that folly, I lament that that's how the world will remember me."

"The world will remember you as a nice man, Mr. Dawson, who lost his wife and suffered a broken heart. It will remember you as a loyal consultant to John Nash, a position of great honor." She laid a gentle hand on his knee. "Please, let's stop at the next inn and get you a draught. You're not your usual self."

"I'm fine," he said, and rubbed his eyes. "I do miss my wife. I miss her dreadfully." He pulled out a handkerchief and ran his thumb over the worn embroidered initials on its corner. "And to think Lord Westdale would waste his chance for love. The man doesn't appreciate what he has."

"You've already said that," she said. "And he appreciates me very much. I'm the one who's been pushing *him* away."

"You have? Whatever for? He's a fine man. Don't you recognize that?" He looked up from the handkerchief, studying her as if she were very odd, and her nervousness ratcheted up a notch.

He was clearly ill, not malevolent. She could barely keep up anymore with his contradictory statements.

"What did you mean when you said there's no time to sleep?" she asked him.

He gave a short laugh. "Just what I said. There are sketches to be done. If young Lord Westdale won't believe in his own talent, I'll do it for him. I'll keep you with me until he produces a decent design. I'd be the first to recommend him to Nash if he'd focus on the work and stop dithering."

"Keep me with you? Aren't we going to Paris?"

He shook his head. "No. I've decided to take you to a place no one will know us. What would you rather do, Lady Pippa, cultivate your own dream—or get Westdale going on his? Don't be selfish." Suddenly the fanatical light in his eyes dimmed to a sorrowful one. "I sympathize with the lad. I was there one time myself—a genius who lacked confidence. I never evolved." His eyes blazed once again. "But *he* could. He simply needs help."

"But you just said if he really wanted to succeed, he'd follow through of his own volition." Pippa sat ramrod straight, fear gripping at her every fiber. "And now you're going to force the issue by kidnapping me?"

Mr. Dawson waved a hand. "That's just talk. You know I'm not absconding with you. You wanted to leave Thurston Manor anyway. I'm only borrowing you to light a fire under Lord Westdale—and I'm also protecting you from him."

"You're doing a lot of things." Her voice shook. "And none of them are in the least bit your business."

But he didn't look concerned one iota.

She prayed someone would notice they were gone. What about the driver? He couldn't have been aware of Mr. Dawson's state of mind when they'd left Thurston Manor.

If she could only get to him.

She intentionally yawned. "Are we stopping soon?"

"No." Mr. Dawson shoved her hat at her. "Eat these biscuits if you're hungry. I told you to drink tea but you wouldn't." He pulled out a flask. "Here's some water if you need it. We won't be stopping all night. I paid the coachman to keep driving. The carriage has lanterns."

"Where are we going?"

"I can't tell you that. But the farther we are from Thurston Manor, the better."

Pippa felt the blood drain from her face.

"But you needn't worry," he continued. "It's a cozy space—a folly I designed with an underground room. We'll be safe there." She was amazed at his totally unconcerned air, his ability to speak of their situation as though he were discussing plans for a picnic.

Her jaw clenched. "Please don't make me go into an underground room."

"There will be a candle. And a few blankets. I won't leave you there long," he said. "I'll write Lord Westdale and tell him he can have you back when he draws something spectacular." He slapped the knuckles of one hand into the palm of the other, squeezing tightly. "And I do mean spectacular. I won't accept anything but the best."

"You're not staying?"

"Of course not. How am I to mail my note to Westdale if I'm locked in a room with you?"

Pippa stifled a cry. *"Locked?"*

Mr. Dawson shook his head. "I thought you loved him. You shouldn't be complaining so much."

"Surely you don't want to hurt me, do you?" she asked in a shaky voice.

"Of course not." For a second, the Mr. Dawson she knew and loved gazed back at her.

"Then, please," she said, "let's find another way." Tears stung her lids.

"There is no other way," he replied gently. "Today's fiasco proved that. Lord Westdale needs a good comeuppance. *That* will shake him out of his lethargy, Lady Pippa. Take heart."

Chapter Twenty

Gregory could breathe again. Eliza and Dougal had stayed with him at the lake until he felt on solid ground, and together they'd walked back to the house talking about the fort, and then they'd moved on to life and its odd turnings, how it always seemed to manage to bring things full circle, no matter how hard one tried to avoid just that. They remarked, each in their own way, on how if people would stop running from whatever bothers them, they would see that the pain they feared would suffocate them was nothing compared to the agony of avoidance.

Gregory had been running ever since his mother died. The truth was, he was afraid his father wouldn't love him if he knew what Gregory knew.

A boy needed his father's love.

And so, it seemed, did a man.

Somehow, the three friends also managed to talk of the weather, their parents, the state of the economy, and how important it was for babies to get enough sleep. Grown-ups, too. At which point, Gregory realized he'd like nothing better than to crawl into bed and get a good rest. He already knew his sleep would contain no dreams, and that he'd wake restored, ready to start again—

For the first time since he was thirteen.

The irony was, everything seemed bleak right now between him and Pippa, and he was no closer to being a hugely successful architect than he was before. And he was still running from the fact of his origins.

But something had happened that morning with Dougal and Eliza. Learning their story had brought him a little hope that maybe Father wouldn't hate him or resent him—or want to send him away—if he found out that he wasn't Gregory's natural parent.

It was only a small hope. He'd spent over a decade fearing the worst. He couldn't simply let that deep-seated dread go.

And it didn't matter anyway. Gregory couldn't tell Father anything. He'd sworn to his mother he never would. And yes, he'd been very young when he'd made that promise, but it had been his *mother*. Even now, a lump rose in his throat at the memory of her.

He'd loved her desperately.

It had been her last wish.

He was *still* her protector.

What kind of son would ever betray his mother, especially one who wasn't here to defend herself?

Nevertheless, that little hope was there, a quiet, glowing ember in his heart.

He took Dougal and Eliza to see Prince, the piebald stallion, in his stable and told them how freely he'd galloped across the Thurston properties. They belonged together, Gregory thought, as he described Prince's virtues—he and the horse of his dreams. Right then and there, he decided that in the morning, before his departure, he'd offer Lord Thurston a ridiculous sum to make Prince his own.

It was a small, first step, a direct flouting of his rule that he didn't deserve to indulge his childhood dream.

Maybe he didn't. But he would dare to, anyway.

Baby steps. Baby steps to facing the truth. If he only gained enough courage, he'd stare that enormous truth down.

But not yet.

Perhaps not ever.

Even as hope and doubt warred within him, he showed a little courage with his friends. Before he entered the house, he told Dougal and Eliza in confidence everything that had occurred the last couple of days, including the fact that he loved Pippa and was desperate to marry her—but that he worried he'd made a hash of things.

Eliza was, of course, teary-eyed with concern that her old friend Pippa was hurting and promised Gregory she'd talk to her about Walter and assure her on that account. She also sheepishly said she'd ask Pippa's forgiveness for using her that day in her garden as a decoy while she and Dougal sneaked off to kiss. And finally, she laughed thinking of Pippa dressed as Harrow and was surprised she hadn't recognized her.

Glad for his friends' support, Gregory left them and looked for Pippa inside the house, but no one knew where Harrow-the-valet was. He wasn't worried—yet—because he knew that she was the type of person who would need to walk or ride off her troubles. So he headed to the stables to find her, but she wasn't there. It frustrated him that he couldn't locate Oscar or one of Lord Thurston's stable hands, either, but a quick walk past the stalls showed him that all the horses were present, at least the ones he re-membered. But it was a vast stable, and several stalls on the far right were empty. Had they always been so? He wasn't sure. A quick check of the equipment showed no sidesaddle missing, however. He distinctly recalled there being three of them.

He made a quick jog back to the folly. But no Pippa. His heart started racing and his breath sped up, but it was still far too early to panic, he told himself. He dashed through the woods calling her name, but only birdsong greeted him.

Jogging back to the house, he felt he'd missed something, and then realized what it was. The gray carriage was gone from the motley collection in the stableyard. He remembered noticing it because it was drab. He'd made an offhand remark that it was a shame someone didn't paint it a pretty, glossy black, and a stable hand had told him that the servants took it to church, that it was the master's spare, rarely if ever used by members of the family.

Gregory went straight to the kitchen entrance. "Does anyone know where the gray carriage went?" he asked Cook, her assistant, the kitchen boy, and the two footmen who were seated at a table, succulent slabs of meat pie before them.

Shock registered on all four faces. He knew houseguests never set foot in the kitchen. For a moment, no one spoke.

"I only want to find Harrow," he said. "Please do feel comfortable speaking."

"I thought he was your valet," the kitchen boy piped up. "I liked him, I did, even if several of the footmen didn't."

"That's enough, Richard," Cook admonished the boy, then looked at Gregory. "Harrow stole all the biscuits off the plate in the drawing room—put them in his hat, he did. But he was helped by none other than Mr. Dawson." She huffed. "I don't go making biscuits for people to snitch them all, Lord Westdale. If you'll pardon my saying."

"I don't mind your saying that at all." He placed a hand on the kitchen boy's shoulder. "And Richard, what do you mean, you *liked* Harrow? Is he gone?"

Richard nodded his head. "He and Mr. Dawson left."

"Where did they go?" he asked.

The kitchen boy gazed round the assembled company with his brows lofted, and as one, the four of them shrugged.

"They left so fast, no one knows," said Cook. "I just heard Lady Thurston calling for Mr. Dawson, and Mr. Jones—our esteemed butler—had to tell her he was gone, that he'd taken a carriage while all the stable crew and our guest drivers are helping the overseer clean out the woods on his property. He's offering in return a hearty meal, some ale, and fiddle playing."

"Isn't that nice?" said her assistant, sighing.

"Yes, indeed," said Cook. "And Lady Thurston was furious Mr. Dawson recruited her favorite footman to drive him and vowed he'd have to explain himself when he came back." She pursed her lips and gave a knowing nod, enjoying her role as informant of such goings-on. "Until he does, Mr. Jones is in the doghouse for not alerting Lord and Lady Thurston right away, but how could he? They were at the folly with their guests, you included."

"Right, thanks." Gregory swept past them to the stairs leading up to the first floor.

"I don't begrudge Harrow the biscuits, my lord," the kitchen boy called after him. "He was a right 'un. And I'm proud to say that this house can provide a traveler with sustenance when—"

But Gregory didn't hear the rest. He was already taking

the steps three at a time. He'd no time to look for Dougal, but he told Mr. Jones to find him immediately.

"Is something wrong, my lord?"

"Yes, Harrow is missing. Along with Mr. Dawson. Do you know why they left?"

Mr. Jones's eyes widened. "No, but I hope you find them soon. Mr. Dawson was acting a bit odd."

Gregory's hands turned to ice. *"Odd?"*

"I didn't think anything of it. Harrow's just a valet, but I got the impression Mr. Dawson was upset at him. Or at *something*. Harrow was a bit agitated himself, so I don't even know that he was aware of Mr. Dawson's pique. I didn't give it another thought after they left."

"I wish you had. Harrow was *my* valet."

"Right, sir. I should have checked with you." He scratched his head. "The truth is, I was glad to be rid of him. He was too—"

"Don't tell me he was too cheeky."

"That's exactly what—"

"When you find Lord Morgan," Gregory interrupted him in steely tones, "tell him to gather the men immediately and send out parties looking for the gray carriage carrying Mr. Dawson and Harrow. They'll have to saddle their own horses as the stable is empty of help."

"Very good, my lord. I'll get on that right away."

And then Gregory ran to the stables himself and saddled Prince, lamenting every second he wasted fumbling with the straps and buckles but talking to Prince the entire time, telling him that he knew he'd lead him to Pippa.

Pippa couldn't hurt Mr. Dawson, no. He'd obviously snapped. Somewhere in between the wise, sweet companion she'd instantly liked and this agitated stranger sitting before her now, grief and regret had broken his spirit, stolen his good health, and sent him to this dark place. He was ill and needed a doctor.

But she could stop the carriage.

She guessed they'd been on the road almost two hours, and she was praying the whole while that Gregory would find her.

Please, she said over and over in her head. *Please come.*

But there were several directions a carriage could take from Thurston Manor. How would he know which one to choose?

She couldn't simply stand by and wait for Gregory. This desperate adventure had to end as soon as possible, and it wasn't all Mr. Dawson's fault that she was embroiled in it. He'd given her excellent advice: She should have told Gregory she loved him before she left.

She'd been foolish. Impetuous. She should have spoken to him honestly from her heart and been willing to listen to what he had to say. And now she only hoped she'd get the chance to do so again. He might want nothing to do with her at all. She'd made a big mess of things, from the beginning. When Hawthorne had attacked her, she should have gone straight to Uncle Bertie.

What had stopped her from asking her beloved uncle for help? Why didn't she make him understand that *nothing* and *no one* could stop her from going to Paris?

Of course, it was expectations that had driven her every move. Pippa hated not to please people—was afraid to push back at her family's and society's notions of what was best for her. And look where her own dithering had gotten her—into a carriage with an ill old man who wanted to put her in an underground chamber, of all places.

She could no longer afford not to assert herself and would start now. "I have to get out of this carriage immediately," she told Mr. Dawson. "Nature calls, and I can't wait."

He drew in his chin. "We can't stop."

Pippa stomped her foot. "We must. Do you hear me, Mr. Dawson? *We must*."

He glared at her and shifted in his seat. "Don't cause any trouble."

"You're the one causing trouble," she said. "Either you stop this carriage now, or I'll jump out."

"You wouldn't dare."

"Oh, yes I would."

He glowered. "Very well. I'll get the driver to stop. But only for a minute, and don't think to run. I handed him two loaded pistols and told him to use them if you tried to escape."

"How dare you?" A great fury rose in Pippa's chest. "What kind of man are you? And what kind of footman would go along with you?"

But she remembered the sly faces of Cockney and Square-jaw and was sure the driver was one of them.

Mr. Dawson was more agitated than ever. "Shut up, Harrow." He wrung his hands together. "Forget what I said. We're not stopping."

Pippa ripped off her wig. "Look at me, Mr. Dawson."

He did, and his eyes widened—but then he averted them.

"I'm not Harrow." She took off her spectacles, threw them on the seat, and began ripping the pins out of her hair. "I'm Pippa. You remember. I told you. I'm Lady Pippa Harrington."

He shook his head and continued staring at the carriage door. "You must stop talking."

"I won't." She tossed her head, and all her Titian curls fell around her shoulders. "You must look at me. And listen to my voice. I'm a woman. " She was alarmed by how clenched his fists were on his lap. "Harrow was an invention. I'm not a valet. I was playing a game, and you are, too. But this is a very dangerous game. People could get hurt."

Mr. Dawson grabbed her hat and turned it over, letting the biscuits fall to the floor. "Put this on your head," he said, and tried to hand her the hat without meeting her gaze.

But she knocked it out of his hand. "*No.* And since you refuse to cooperate, I'm going to have to open the door and jump out."

He snatched the hat from the floor and glared at her. "Where's Harrow? Bring him back." Then, as though the air had been let out of him, he slumped in his seat, his eyes defeated. "*He's* a fine fellow. Things happened around him. I wanted to be that way, too."

"I can't bring Harrow back," Pippa told him. "Harrow is gone forever . . . like your wife."

Mr. Dawson flinched.

"But you have the memories of her, don't you?" Pippa asked immediately, hating to hurt him in his addled state, but she had to try to get through. "Just as you remember Harrow running up to you to ask to shine your boots, you have memories of your wife to comfort you."

He said nothing, but his head dropped.

"The best part about memories is that the good ones last forever," she said softly. "They can comfort you when you're lonely. And then you can also share them with friends." She paused, giving him time to absorb her words. "I want to be your friend—*me,* Pippa. We can laugh about Harrow and how he always got into trouble, and we can talk about your wife."

Mr. Dawson still looked at the floor, but he released a sigh that gave Pippa hope. The slump of his shoulders, the vulnerable top of his head, where his gray hair had thinned, and the loosening of his fists on his knees made her reach out and take one of his hands and squeeze it hard.

"I'm so sorry, Mr. Dawson. I'm sorry for the loss of your wife. And I'm sorry you didn't properly use your opportunity to build that folly at Thurston Manor the way you knew you could. I propose we go back there now, to your cousin's house—where you are loved dearly—and tell Lord and Lady Thurston we'd like to knock down that folly and build another."

Slowly, he looked up. "But it's too late."

"No it's not." She smiled at him.

"I don't have it in me," he said. "I'm a nobody."

"Well, a nobody isn't such a bad thing to be." She didn't have to be the next Monsieur Perot. Being Pippa was good enough for her. "We're all nobodies, Mr. Dawson. Even the somebodies feel that way sometimes."

"Do they?"

"Yes," she said, "I'm sure of it. And the nice thing about being a nobody is that you can be yourself. How many somebodies can make that claim?"

He gave a little laugh. "Not many."

"I'll bet they'd give anything to have the freedom to be a nobody again—to be able to walk on the moor and be a speck on the landscape, to read uninterrupted, or think for hours without anyone making demands on their genius." How many people like her, she wondered, did the great Monsieur Perot have to fend off? "How about if we ask Gregory to help you? You can build the folly together."

The more she thought about it, the more she liked the idea. Gregory could be a sort of mentor for Mr. Dawson. And yet—he could also learn from the older man's experience with having too many regrets.

Gregory still had time on his side; Mr. Dawson didn't.

Her confused friend's eyes softened with interest and perhaps a bit of excitement, but he said nothing, just wrung his hands.

"It's all right, what's happened," she told him. "When they find us, I'll tell them you simply need some rest. And attention. You won't get into trouble. And I promise you, Mr. Dawson, that Gregory will act as your assistant with the new folly. I'll be there, too, as Pippa, because that's who I really am, and we'll celebrate your great triumph together. This folly, I believe, should have a plaque on it dedicating it to your beloved wife."

His shoulders began to shake, and Pippa went to his seat to hold him. She let him cry against her, and she held him close, murmuring sweet, comforting words. And when she felt enough time had passed, she pulled back and said, "I'm going to ask the driver to take us back to Thurston Manor. Are you ready to go?"

He nodded, and she took off her coat and made a pillow for his head. Then she lifted his feet up onto the seat and made sure he was properly situated to take a nap. He drifted off after a few moments. She opened the door to the carriage and called to the driver—Square-jaw—to turn around.

"Good God, who are you?" he cried.

Oh, dear. She'd forgotten she'd taken her hair down!

Well, the charade was going to be over anyway, when she got to Thurston Manor.

She chuckled. "I'm Lady Pippa Harrington, and Harrow is gone forever. Watch your manners, young man, and if you get us back to Thurston Manor safe and sound, I'll ask Lady Thurston to give you a second chance. But you'd better never, *ever* be a cruel, selfish lout again. I'll write Cook every three months for three years to check on you, and if you disappoint me in the least, I'll send Lord Westdale after you."

He was so dumbfounded, he couldn't speak.

"You could hang for kidnapping, too, you know." She was enjoying her speech. "If you're not shot first by Lord Westdale, who's surely approaching now."

"Please don't let either of those things happen, my lady." His voice trembled.

"Well, you'd best agree to my terms, then. Tell your Cockney friend the same thing, or I'll see to it he's out on his ear, too. Or worse."

"Yes, my lady." Square-jaw's face was paler than usual. "Of course, my lady."

She pulled the door shut, and the carriage was on its way back to where it belonged.

When she fell back against her seat, she was trembling all over. But after a few minutes, she felt all right. She knew if she waited long enough, she'd hear the sound of Gregory's voice.

That knowledge is what kept her from crying over Mr. Dawson, from lamenting her lost opportunity to go to Paris—there'd always be others, she told herself—and from worrying about what the future held.

Because now she was going back to Plumtree, to see

Uncle Bertie again, and to call Mr. Trickle and Mr. Hawthorne out for their despicable behavior. The Toad probably tried to sell her away to Hawthorne behind Mother's and Uncle Bertie's backs.

She'd tell Uncle Bertie and Mother that she wasn't going to give up and would make it to Paris—not London—by hook or by crook and take Mother with her. And while there, she would somehow find a way to work with the greatest pastry chef the world had ever known.

She tried to tuck away her sorrow about Gregory, that he might still love Eliza. But it was difficult not to contemplate that entire situation. Apart from her own stake in it, it was possibly very tragic. She felt sorry for Gregory—if Walter were his son, how sad he would be not being his father!

It was only then that she allowed the sobs she'd held within to escape, and she cried silently into the cravat she'd pulled from her neck. Her tears weren't for herself, though—they were for the man she loved. They were for Gregory.

Chapter Twenty-one

Pippa's nose was swollen, but she didn't care. Her head throbbed, as well, but none of it mattered. All that mattered was getting back to Thurston Manor.

But the carriage slowed and then came to a stop. Mr. Dawson stirred and opened his eyes. He looked groggy but harmless, lying there on the coach seat.

Nevertheless, Pippa's terror returned, and she took off her shoe, the only weapon she could find if Square-jaw was up to no good. She opened the door to the carriage and peered up at the box. "What's going on?"

"The horses need water," he called back to her. "There's a small inn up ahead. You look in need of a strong drink yourself, just a swallow or two. And perhaps you're hungry. I think we should stop, my lady."

She liked how he'd tacked on a *my lady* so meekly at the end of his brief but thoughtful speech. Relief coursed through her veins. "Of course," she said, putting on her best lady-of-the-manor accent. "Mr. Dawson's not feeling well. I'm not sure he can get out, but we'll not tarry long. You must be hungry and thirsty yourself."

"Don't worry about me," Square-jaw said. "But, my

lady, shouldn't you put on your spectacles and cravat again and put up your hair? They won't understand why"—he cleared his throat—"you're dressed as a man."

She restrained a smile. "Good idea. I was prepared to jump out just like this for a bit of a stretch."

She pulled the door shut, glad to see Mr. Dawson dozing again, and went to work gathering her pins and her wig and restoring her appearance as Harrow. Her fingers trembled as she curled and pinned, over and over. She wasn't managing the job nearly as well as usual. But it was only one short stop, and afterward, she'd never have to go through the arduous routine again. The cravat, too, she hastily tied. It must look a mess, but again, who cared?

When she finished, she hoped Mr. Dawson wouldn't be confused in a bad way if he woke up and saw her looking a semblance of the proper valet again.

But he slept on. Thankfully.

At the inn yard, he didn't stir when the carriage stopped. Pippa put on her somewhat flattened hat and got out. No one was about, which immediately made her wary—no telling what Square-jaw might do—but she did hear a great deal of noise to the side of the inn from the stables. Much to her relief, a pair of horses came around the corner, pulling a discreet black carriage. The driver was dressed smartly and looked vaguely familiar somehow, but she couldn't figure out why. She'd never seen the man in her life.

Square-jaw leaped down from the box and took off his cap. "I'll take care of the horses," he said low, "and while I'm at it, I'll keep an eye on Mr. Dawson, my lady."

"Very good," she said, then added sternly, "I'm trusting you'll get up to no funny business. No driving off without me. And do watch Mr. Dawson closely. We can't afford to have him run off in the state he's in. Remember who's got a tremendous interest in my welfare and the health and well-being of anyone I care about: Lord West-dale himself." She only hoped that were true. "And *he's* backed by the entire House of Brady, which is headed by a powerful marquess and his equally influential wife. Did you know that Lord Brady—"

"I'm aware of that," Square-jaw blurted out, his voice suddenly tight. He was crushing his cap between his fingers in the worst way. "I wouldn't dream of disappointing you—*Mr. Harrow.*"

Oh, good heavens. She'd forgotten to speak in her valet's voice. But there was no one about . . . just that driver pulling round, but surely he hadn't heard. The horses were making a bit of a commotion, and—

She wore a carelessly wrapped cravat, but she felt a prickly sensation on the back of her neck that compelled her to turn around.

A couple stood there: a man in the prime of his life, handsome and assured, and a woman about his age, stunning and dressed in the height of fashion. They both stared at her.

"Do we know you?" the man asked politely in a charming Irish brogue.

"I recognize you, but I'm not sure how," the woman murmured in a kind voice filled with curiosity.

"Greetings, Lord and Lady Brady," Pippa choked out in her valet's voice.

Now she knew why she recognized the driver. He was wearing the same smart coat with large gold buttons that Gregory's driver wore.

There was a tickle at her temple, then a fleeting tap against the back of her hand. She looked down and saw a hairpin in the dirt. A long tendril of hair unfurled like a silky copper-colored ribbon and brushed her cheek.

Heaven help me, she thought, and slowly raised her head.

Lady Brady's mouth hung open. "It's Lady Pippa Harrington, dressed as a man!"

"Hello, Lady Brady," she said again, but in her regular voice—albeit quieter than usual.

"Faith and begorra, 'tis true." Lord Brady never took his eyes off her as he reached into his coattail pocket, pulled out a flask identical to the one Gregory had in his carriage, and took a slug.

Suddenly, Pippa's throat felt parched and her knees wobbled. "C-could I have some of that, please?" she whispered. She knew exactly what a remedy for a host of ills it was.

The Brady carriage began to acquire spots all over it . . .

"Help her, Michael!" Lady Brady called out sharply.

Lord Brady took Pippa's elbow, and Square-jaw took the other.

"Steady, lass," the marquess murmured, and held the flask to her mouth.

All it took was two—nay, *three*—quick sips to restore her. Pippa blinked, the fire in her throat spreading slowly out to her shaky limbs. "Your family's blend truly *is* from the leprechauns." She shot Lord Brady a quavery smile.

Lord Brady chuckled. "It's saved many a woman—and man—from fainting spells."

She turned and smiled at Square-jaw. "I'm fine, thank you."

He backed up quietly. "I'll get on with the horses, then."

Lady Brady approached and took her hand. "Are you

better, dear? I'm so worried about you. What's going on? Why are you away from home? Does your mother know where you are? And what about Lord Carson?"

Horrible guilt overwhelmed Pippa. "No. They have no idea where I am or what I'm doing. They think—"

How was she to explain?

"You must tell us," Lord Brady said in a firm manner. "You're a young lady out and about, unchaperoned—"

"Oh, I do have Mr. Dawson in the carriage," she said quickly, then bowed her head. "Not that he's a good chaperone. He intended to get me one—he promised. Before we crossed the Channel. But we had to make a hasty exit, you see, from the house party . . ."

Lord and Lady Brady were staring at her again as if she were mad.

She scratched a temple and realized she was making no sense. "It's a long story, and—" A huge sigh escaped her. She'd made a royal mess of everything. "And Gregory, I'm afraid, is involved." There was a stunned silence. "But it's not his fault!" she added quickly.

Lord Brady ran a hand over his face and looked up at the sky.

"Oh, Pippa," said Lady Brady. "What on earth—"

Pippa nodded. "I know. It sounds awful. You'll have to come back with me to hear the rest. We should probably go, as a matter of fact. They'll all be out looking for us. And Mr. Dawson is ill—he's in the carriage. I'm worried about him." She was mortified to feel a lump form in her throat, but she pushed it down. "The truth is, it's been a *very* long day."

She only squeaked out the last words, but that was better than saying nothing at all.

"Oh, you poor girl," said Lady Brady, and wrapped

Pippa in a hug. It felt *so good*. "I don't understand what's going on at this point, but it will all be better soon."

"I hope so," Pippa mumbled into her shoulder, and squeezed back tears.

She stood up straight again.

Lord Brady, his arms crossed, observed her with a furrowed brow, his serious expression only making him appear more handsome and imposing than ever. "Yes, it's clear we need to accompany you to this house party, young lady. I'm assuming since Gregory is involved, it's Thurston Manor we're talking about?"

Pippa nodded and felt her cheeks burning. She had hoped they couldn't guess! She busied herself with straightening her cravat.

"You don't have to do that anymore," Lady Brady said gently.

"Oh. Right." Pippa smiled awkwardly and dropped her hands. "Thank you for reminding me."

Lady Brady's gaze was steady on her, and there was a knowing glimmer in her eye . . .

She knew. She *knew* something was going on between her and Gregory!

"Well, Lady Pippa." Lord Brady's tone was brisk. "You'll ride with Lady Brady in the Brady carriage, and I'll sit with Mr. Dawson."

"Oh, dear!" Pippa exclaimed before she could help herself. "I'm so grateful for your willingness to trade places with me, my lord, but I think I should be with Mr. Dawson when he awakens. He's already discombobulated, and it might frighten him to see anyone else . . ."

She trailed off, knowing she might sound ungrateful.

"That's all right, dear," said Lady Brady. "You ride with Mr. Dawson. We won't tell anyone you're unchaperoned, and we'll be right behind you in case you're in need of assistance. Merely open the door and wave."

"I will. Thank you." Pippa smiled at her, and felt that she and Lady Brady shared a sort of bond already. The lady might not know exactly what was going on, but surely she sensed that Pippa cared for her stepson.

"You've just arrived," said Lord Brady, sounding a little softer now, "and we're about to depart. Why don't you freshen up while I send my tiger inside to procure you a cup of lemonade? And we'll arrange for a simple meal to take in the carriage with you." He reached again for his flask and handed it to her. "Perhaps Mr. Dawson could use a sip of this when he wakes up."

"I'm entirely grateful to you both." Pippa was overwhelmed, in fact, by their kindness in such an awkward situation. "And if you don't mind, my driver will need a tankard of ale and something to eat, as well, please."

"Of course." Lady Brady's eyes were still filled with concern. "Now, once we get back on the road, we won't worry about a thing until we get to Thurston Manor."

"Then we'll have questions," said Lord Brady. "Quite a few, in fact. I can't wait to talk to Gregory." He chuckled, but there was nothing lighthearted about it.

"Don't scare her," said Lady Brady, and swatted his arm playfully.

His face took on a stubborn quality. "It's not Lady Pippa who should be frightened," he said, "but *my son*. The House of Brady had best be in good order. If it's not, I'll see to it that it will be set aright. Immediately." Pippa felt herself shaking—just a tad—in her buckled men's shoes. "Now if you'll excuse me, please."

He made a light bow to both of them and stalked off to the rear of his carriage, where he spoke to the tiger.

Lady Brady put a delicate hand on Pippa's arm. "Please don't worry about Lord Brady. He's Irish, and he's got a temper. It rarely comes out, but when it does, it's best to stay out of his way."

"I understand," Pippa said. "I—I'll be back in a few minutes." She began to walk away, but Lady Brady caught up with her.

"You're not going anywhere alone," she said. "And definitely not round the inn to the back. We'll find a place to freshen up inside. You're a lady, however you're dressed, and you're still in a mild state of shock. From what, I don't know. But it must be *very* interesting if it involves your dressing as a man."

From the sideways glance the lady sent Pippa, she could tell that there was only one thing to do. "Would you like to ride with me and Mr. Dawson to Thurston Manor?" Lady Brady's face brightened. "I can tell you everything, from top to bottom."

Almost everything.

Well, maybe half *would do.*

"Oh, yes," said Lady Brady. "I'd love that. And Lord Brady won't mind a bit. He's got a fine book to read, and he might even take a nap. He'll want to be at his best when we arrive."

"Lovely," said Pippa, and felt a wave of nerves assail her. But there was really no turning back. She'd caught herself in this net all on her own.

On their way into the inn, Pippa was oblivious to the fact that she had that long lock of hair dangling near her face—that is, until two farmers who strode past her and Lady Brady stopped dead in their tracks.

"What the devil?" said one.

"She's a woman!" cried the other. "Dressed as a man!"

"It was a dare," she called over her shoulder, remembering how often Gregory used to make her accept his.

"Ohhhh," one of the farmers said, his face lit with understanding.

"And it's none of your business, gentlemen," Lady Brady said airily. "Move on, please."

Which they both did, with alacrity.

After her lemonade and back in the carriage, where Mr. Dawson snored lightly on his seat, Pippa removed her hat, hairpins, wig, cravat, and spectacles. Then she had a bit of bread and cheese. When she felt more herself, she determined to tell Gregory's mother as much as she could—without embarrassing her to the point that she'd need smelling salts.

But that point never came. Lady Brady kept nodding, and listening, and never once did a judgmental expression cross her face.

So Pippa found herself having divulged all of her story.

Well, *almost* all.

Certainly far more than half.

"Poor Mr. Dawson." Lady Brady stole a glance at the sleeping figure then returned her concerned gaze to Pippa. "And I'm so very sorry for you, for undergoing such a trauma."

"I'm fine." Pippa tucked a strand of hair behind her ear. *"Now."*

"Everything else pales in comparison to the fact that you're safe, thank heaven." Lady Brady squeezed her hand. "But we still have other issues to address."

"Of course," said Pippa.

"If you don't feel up to discussing them now, I understand. Perhaps you'd like to rest?"

"No, thank you." Pippa swallowed. "It would relieve

my mind to talk with you about the last few days. I think I could use an advisor as I don't have my own mother here. But even if I did, I'm not sure Mother would know what to say. She has so many concerns of her own."

"I understand," Lady Brady said kindly. "I'll be happy to help." She took a cleansing breath, and Pippa did, too. "So," Lady Brady said quietly, "you slept in Gregory's bedchamber."

Pippa nodded, and although she was frightened, she kept her gaze on Lady Brady's.

"Is there any chance you're with child?" The marchioness tilted her head just so and waited.

It was a delicate moment, indeed.

Pippa's cheeks heated. "I can assure you on that point. Absolutely not."

Lady Brady gave her a tender smile. "I know how it is, dear, to fall in love. I know the perils. There are many."

"You do?"

"Oh, yes. Pleasures, too." Lady Brady gave a light chuckle and looked out the window, lost in some memory— perhaps a recent one. Judging from the way the marquess and marchioness clung so cozily to each other in public, they were very much in love.

Pippa found herself with her own dreamy smile on her lips, too, thinking of Gregory. But she quickly erased it. It wouldn't do. This was Gregory's second mother she was talking to, after all.

"The road to true love isn't easy." Lady Brady was still watching the scenery go by out the window. The sun was past its zenith—and shining brightly on the passing field. "And not all of us find it. But if you do, your life doesn't suddenly become a pretty cake with pink icing." She looked back at Pippa and arched a brow. "Does it?"

"Most definitely not," Pippa agreed.

"But having someone to share in your joy and your grief, when it comes—as it will to all of us—is a great blessing." Lady Brady patted her hand. "So my advice to you, dear, is to pursue true love if you think you've found it. I can't imagine Gregory going through what he has with you and not caring for you very deeply."

"Really?"

"He could have turned around and taken you back to Plumtree. But something in him didn't want to."

"I was putting pressure on him. I feel guilty about that now."

"Don't. You have a right to your feelings." She took Pippa's hand in her own. "I have no doubt you swayed him, but not simply because you know your mind. I suspect that beneath all his bluster, Gregory wanted to make you happy."

Pippa's eyes boggled.

"And"—Lady Brady raised an index finger—"he wanted to stay in your company. If he dropped you off in Plumtree, he'd have to leave you there."

Pippa blushed. Again. "Do you really think so?"

Lady Brady laughed and nodded. "Of course. This is a man whom other men make way for when he walks into a room. He's not someone to be pushed about. He has his own reasons for everything he does. And my dear, I believe *you've* become his priority." She squeezed her hand. "Do you love him?"

"He's everything to me," Pippa said. *"Everything."*

"Oh." Lady Brady's eyes pooled with tears. "How lovely to hear you say that about our Gregory."

Pippa took a quick swipe at her own eyes. "I hope he loves me, too."

"Darling, I suspect he *must*." Lady Brady gave a hearty laugh.

Pippa felt a surge of hope. The very idea that Gregory might love her sent butterflies ricocheting through her stomach. "I don't know, Lady Brady. I wish you could have seen the way he looked at Eliza today. I'm afraid he still loves her."

Lady Brady sighed. "He never loved her."

"He didn't?"

"No. After he left for America, Peter told us what had happened in the garden. Gregory was about to propose to Eliza."

"He was?" Pippa's heart sank.

"Yes," said Lady Brady, "but it was for the wrong reason. Let me explain from the beginning, if I can."

"Please do." Pippa would hang on every word.

Lady Brady got that happy, distant expression on her face again. "I've known Gregory since he was very young. I was working as a seamstress, running my own small shop, in London."

"You *were*?"

"Yes. That's a story to save for later"—she waved a hand—"but suffice to say, the boys used to come in to be measured for their clothes. The ten-year-old Gregory was always quite rambunctious—your typical boy who hated to stand still to be measured—but he was also very solicitous of his mother. I was always very impressed by this quality in him. After she died, he was still all boy, but he was also very hard on Peter and Robert, ensuring they behave when they came to see me to be measured. I could see that he felt a sense of obligation to be the big, responsible brother. But he began to be inflexible, and I sensed sadness—a heaviness—beneath his cheerful countenance."

"That's exactly what happened to him at Uncle Bertie's." Pippa sent her a wry smile. "He used to be an amusing companion. He enjoyed being with me even though he was five years older. But after his mother died, he never showed me affection again. He spent all his time in Uncle Bertie's library."

"What a shame," said Lady Brady, looking deeply pained.

"Just a few nights ago," Pippa went on, "he took responsibility for me from Uncle Bertie's shoulders, and I didn't like it one bit. I can admit to you now that not only was he interfering with my plans to go to Paris—it upset me that he was willing to marry me off to another man. Although I understand he was also trying to relieve Bertie of the stress of seeing me well placed."

Lady Brady gave a short laugh. "Yet again, I suspect Gregory had his own motive there. He might not have wanted to admit it to anyone—especially himself—but I'm sure his interest in your welfare goes beyond his obligation to assist Bertie."

"Do you?" Pippa would love it if that hypothesis were true.

Lady Brady pulled back and observed her shrewdly. "Tell me, Pippa, did you leave the house party more to get to Paris—or to escape Gregory?" She wore a mischievous smile.

"To escape him." She spoke quietly, astounded at the knowledge that Gregory had become her focus now, even more than her dream.

Lady Brady shook her head sadly. "I've heard the rumors,

too, of course, about Walter's parentage. I'm good friends with Eliza's mother, as you well know. It was a trifle awkward, but she came to me as soon as those rumors started and assured me that Walter is *not* Gregory's son. He looks exactly like Dougal's grandfather, and we're women—we both counted back, and the lad was conceived not long after Gregory went to America. The idea made for a good scandal. But it simply wasn't true."

"I'm so glad." Pippa's heart felt a great deal lighter. "For Gregory's sake. The way he looked at Walter . . . it was heartbreaking, really. The pain I saw on his face was almost too difficult to witness. I'm sure he wondered if Walter were his! And then he did what he usually does—he put on a brave face."

Lady Brady sighed. "I wish I had known he wasn't sure himself. I would have told him what Eliza's mother said. I assumed he and Eliza hadn't—"

She hesitated, and Pippa knew very well why.

"Oh, it was probably silly of me to presume there wasn't a chance." Lady Brady's cheeks turned slightly pink. "Especially as Peter informed us that Gregory was about to offer for Eliza. It could be why he took it so hard when he discovered Dougal was involved—not because Gregory loved Eliza but because his best friend, of all people, stood between him and his duty."

There was a brief silence, more sad than awkward. Neither one of them liked to think about that day.

Pippa decided she must be completely honest. "Even if Gregory does care for me"—she simply couldn't be bold enough to assume he *loved* her—"I have *plans*, Lady Brady. I—I'm afraid to marry. I've seen what happened to my mother. You know the story. She was a thriving actress with a great deal of *joie de vivre*—but no longer. I can't believe that Gregory is like either of Mother's husbands, but I'm frightened of becoming something I don't want to be. For example, I have no particular desire to be a London hostess—I hope you don't mind my saying so."

"Not a bit," said Lady Brady with vigor. "From the time I was ten years old, one of my greatest passions was—and is—sewing. I haven't stopped just because I'm a marchioness. Yes, I'm very active in the social whirl in London, with all the busyness that entails. But I've found I do enjoy it. And it's because I'm with Michael." Her eyes softened, and Pippa was flattered she used his baptismal name with her, as if they were bosom friends.

"He never once asked me to give up my sewing," Lady Brady went on. "I'm proud that I can stitch a frock that any queen in the world could wear proudly. I made the one I'm wearing now."

It was a light blue muslin with a row of matching darker-hued blue ribbons running down the center of the skirt, from right below the bodice to the sophisticated flounced hem.

"Did you?" Pippa was so impressed. "It's beautiful. And very French."

Lady Brady grinned. "Thank you. And I'll have you know I still work on commission occasionally. For a while, when Janice was at boarding school in Switzerland, I made gowns for her European schoolmates, some of whom were princesses. They adored her clothes and couldn't believe her mother made them." She chuckled. "Once a lady makes money, Pippa, it's difficult to give it up."

"You're such an inspiration to me, my lady."

"I don't mean to be." She smiled. "All I'm suggesting to you is that if you have a passion, it's wonderful to be able to share it with the man you love. In marriage, two people should honor and respect—my goodness, they should *celebrate*—the talents the other person brings to the relationship. Those gifts are part of who we are. In my case, it wasn't just sewing that I loved. All women are encouraged to sew. I also loved designing clothes for other women and girls and running my own shop. Not many gentlemen of the *ton* would approve of that, much less marry a woman in that position."

"Exactly," said Pippa. "But Lady Brady—"

She didn't know how to say it.

"What, my dear?"

"Gregory doesn't want me to go to Paris to study sugar sculpture. Not really. He did offer to take me with you and your daughters for several weeks, which was generous of him. But he's very disapproving of the idea in general. He says I have a duty to marry. He insists I should be in London."

Lady Brady drew back. "Did you say Gregory offered to take you to Paris?"

"Well, yes."

The marchioness laughed loudly enough that Mr. Dawson stirred in his sleep. "Pippa"—she laid her hand over hers again—"Gregory adores his sisters and me, but he can't stand traveling with us unless we're outnumbered by the men in the party. Since he left Oxford, he's turned down every opportunity to do so, claiming that the women of the house bring too many trunks and in general create such a fuss that he has a headache for days on end. He's quite adamant about it. So the fact that he said he'd take you to Paris with us in tow"—she laughed again—"I can't wait to tell Marcia, Janice, and Cynthia."

"You can't?" Pippa let a little chuckle escape.

"This is proof enough for me," Lady Brady said, her

chuckles subsiding. "I'll bet my very best gown—the one I wore to Janice's presentation at Court—that Gregory's in love. I probably shouldn't say so, but a mother knows—it's the little things."

"That's very kind of you to bet your best gown." Pippa felt like laughing one second and crying the next, she was so stressed—and euphoric—from being in love and not knowing what to do about it. "But I think I'll have to hear the words from Gregory himself."

"Of course. Ask him why he wants you in London. I *dare* you." The marchioness grinned.

"I will, then," Pippa said, and grinned back.

Chapter Twenty-two

It was three o'clock when Gregory saw the gray carriage in the distance, coming toward him at a spanking pace, another carriage following behind. His relief was so great, he didn't even think what the presence of the other carriage could mean. He pulled Prince up short so he could catch his breath. The piebald gave a whinny of frustration, but Gregory soothed him with some comforting words: "She's back. We have another chance, Prince, to win her."

He hoped. He'd spent the past few hours on the wrong roads, searching in the wrong direction. What if the carriage were empty—or contained only Mr. Dawson?

He must have properly conveyed his concern to the horse because Prince stood alert—his ears pricked, his neck long—and waited, too. Well in advance of the two carriages' approach, Gregory put his palm in the air to alert the one in front—the one he hoped carried Pippa—to his presence. The driver began to slow almost immediately, and some twenty seconds later, came to a full stop in front of Gregory. The next one did the same.

And Gregory's heart nearly stopped. The black carriage's driver wore the signature Brady coat, the one with the large, flat gold buttons.

What the devil?

"Horace! Is that you?" he yelled at the top of his lungs.

"Yes, Master Gregory!" the driver of the black carriage called from the box. "I mean, Lord Westdale!"

He heard a door flung open from that second carriage. A second later, a well-dressed gentleman leaped down to the road. "Gregory?" It was Father. "Your mother and I are here to pay a visit."

Good God. Father came striding down the road, stood beside the gray carriage's door, and crossed his arms. He looked none too happy. What did he know?

And what the *hell* was going on?

But Gregory couldn't take time to wonder. Seeing Pippa was all.

"Hello, Father," he said somberly, then looked at the driver of the gray carriage. "Where is she?" he yelled from Prince's back, and didn't care who heard the agony, the desperation, in his voice.

"It was a mistake," the driver said in a low, frightened tone. "That old man made me do it. I just want to go home. Lady Pippa is inside, and she promised if I behaved—"

"*Is* she inside?" Gregory held his breath. The driver nodded, and Gregory released it silently.

Pippa was back. Thank God.

"Here's our chance, Prince," he said in a low voice, and slid off the saddle. His legs were sore from the bruising ride, but he walked straight and tall to Father.

"We need to talk. Back at the house." Not just about Pippa, either.

But now wasn't the time.

"Ye're right," said Father, in his thickest Irish brogue.

Ah. That meant he was extremely angry. But at the moment, Gregory didn't care.

His hands curled into fists at his sides.

He wanted to get to his woman!

"Allow me." Father opened the door, and Mama's beautiful face appeared, a soft smile on her lips.

Gregory's heartbeat became a smidgen less erratic. Always, Mama brought ease to a situation.

"It's good to see you, son," she said, and let Father take her by the waist and swing her down.

Together, they walked past Gregory toward Prince. A few moments later, he heard his horse-mad father talking low to Prince, admiration in his tone. He was, no doubt, holding on to the prized stallion's reins for Gregory.

But Gregory didn't bother to look.

His eyes were on Pippa, who stood inside the door frame of the carriage looking down at him with her hair cascading around the shoulders of her voluminous shirt, which had come loose from her breeches.

Only two yards—but an entire world of hurt—separated them.

"Lord Westdale," she said from her perch, "please tell me something."

"Anything," he replied.

She jumped down to the ground. "*Why* do you want me in London?"

His answer came as naturally as breathing. "Because I can't live without you. Because I *love* you, Pippa. My darling, if only you knew how—"

But before he could go on, she leaped into his arms.

"*Gregory.*" She wrapped her legs around his middle,

her arms about his back, and kissed him as hard as she could on his mouth. And then she buried her face in his neck and held on tight. "Don't let me go," she whispered.

"I won't," he whispered back, and kissed the top of her head. He looked up to see he was facing his parents, with Prince. Several horsemen appeared in the distance, including a woman on sidesaddle. "Never again."

Pippa pulled back a fraction of an inch. "Mr. Dawson is sleeping, but he's ill. He'll need help. But don't let anyone hurt him. Please. He's grieving his wife—and he has big regrets about his life. He broke down, but I think with the proper care, he can be restored."

"I won't let anyone hurt him," Gregory vowed.

She slid down his body, and reluctantly, he released her.

"I'm going to be with him now," she said. "I'll ride back with him to the house. If you don't mind being in charge of explanations about Harrow to everyone but your mother, who already knows all—"

"All?"

Her cheeks bloomed red. "Almost all," she said with a giggle, and then her eyes grew round. "My goodness, there's quite an audience here."

A gaggle of riders came up wearing sober miens, their horses at slow walks. The riders drew up their own horses near Prince and Gregory's parents. All of them appeared surprised to see them, as well as the second carriage. But they said nothing and sat expectantly, their eyes riveted on Pippa—in her man's clothes.

She sent them a little wave.

"Don't worry," Gregory murmured. "They're far enough away we can say what we need to. Even though they can't hear, they're getting a thrill just watching us, especially you, the valet who's really a woman in disguise."

Pippa smiled. "The gossip's going to be delicious. But back to Mr. Dawson: I'd like to take him directly upstairs to bed. I'm going to be his valet one last time."

Gregory kissed her brow. "That's a fine idea. Would you like some company? Your old friend Eliza would love to see you. She's heading this way now."

For a split second, Pippa looked ill at ease.

He squeezed her shoulders. "Don't worry, all's well now." *Almost all.* He pulled her tight beneath his chin, inhaling the now-familiar scent of lavender in her hair. "Let me explain—"

"Shhhh." She pulled back and put a finger to his lips. "You don't have to explain anything to me. Your mother and I talked. I know how difficult this situation was for you, and you'll be glad to know—"

She leaned close to his ear and whispered, "Walter is definitely Dougal's son."

"I know," he said.

"You do?"

He grinned. "Yes. I spoke with Eliza. My love, I'm sorry we were ever together the way we were. I hate to cause you pain. And Eliza's brokenhearted that she's hurt you. Neither of us ever loved the other. It was a mistake."

"It's all right. Even if the baby had been yours, I never would have stopped loving you. Ever. I simply thought you still loved Eliza. That look on your face—"

"That look wasn't about her at all. It was about Walter, yes, but there's more. It was about me, too."

"What do you mean?"

He took her by the waist and stared deep into her eyes.

"I need to know you'll stand by me. Because I have something rather shocking to tell you. But first, I have to confide in my father. It's about our family, about something that happened long ago, but it has public implications. It will be difficult to hear, love, and if you do decide it's too much to bear, I'll understand."

"Nothing will be too much to bear," she insisted. "I love you. I'll stand by you, no matter what."

He pulled a lock of hair off her face. "One thing more about Eliza and that day in the garden. I went there to give her my mother's ring and ask her to marry me."

"I know," Pippa said. "Your mother told me."

"She did?"

Pippa laughed. "We're women, darling. We *talk*."

"I suppose you do, especially in confined spaces when you're together for hours—"

"And we have someone we love in common." Pippa chided him with a glance.

"Right, then." He chuckled. "My point is that I had entirely practical, heartless reasons to want Eliza as my wife. And I'm so glad that fate intervened in the form of a certain stubborn young lady with a sketch pad, who was present to witness the luckiest moment of my life—until now—and that was when I saw Eliza and Dougal kissing and appearing madly in love, which they clearly were. Thank God I stumbled upon that scene. Or I'd never have discovered *real* love—with you."

"Oh, Gregory." Pippa's voice was soft, sure. "It's always been you. And I still have that drawing I made in the garden. I wouldn't throw it away, as much as it caused me pain to look at it. It represented my deepest longing—to be with you."

They shared an intoxicating kiss.

"There's no doubt in my mind that my firstborn will have a mother with fiery hair and a temper to match." His voice was gruff with desire for her.

She laughed and they kissed again, their bodies fused from mouth to knee. But it was no longer enough. He had to make her his—and soon.

He was still lost in the heady sensation of being wrapped around his beloved, still marveling that everything was right between them, when a loud cough interrupted them. "My lord, should I take the carriage and Mr. Dawson back to Thurston Manor?"

The driver, whom Gregory recognized as one of the surly footmen at the manor, kept his eyes on a distant object as though he were doing his best to maintain their privacy, but his red face gave away his discomfort.

"Lady Pippa will ride with him, along with her friend Lady Morgan. Lady Morgan?" He beckoned to Eliza with a hand.

She leaped down from her saddle and came running over to give Pippa a huge hug. "Hello, old friend!" The two women clasped each other close with no sign of release. "Count on you to wear the unusual thing. Only you could carry off breeches so beautifully."

They both laughed and finally pulled back, flustered yet happy, Gregory was pleased to see.

Eliza looked searchingly at Pippa's face. "Please tell me you're all right. Let me ride back with you to Thurston Manor."

"I'd like that." Sincerity infused Pippa's words. "We have so much to catch up on. Walter is an absolute *love*." She winced happily on the word *love,* as if she couldn't contain her delight in the chubby baby.

"Isn't he?" Eliza mirrored Pippa's over-the-top expression. It was something Gregory had often seen women do when discussing babies. And then she flung grateful arms around Pippa again.

Relief made him squint up at Dougal and grin, and Dougal rolled his eyes and grinned back. Gregory didn't realize how much he'd wanted Pippa to embrace his old friends—even if he hadn't, for so long. And the main reason was because he was proud of her. He was proud of *them*. And he wanted to show everyone he'd ever known how lucky he was and how different his life would be, now that he'd found the love of his life.

Over her friend's shoulder, Pippa looked at Gregory one more time. It was torture being separated from her, as lovely as the reunion with Eliza was. Gregory winked to assure Pippa he was going nowhere she wasn't—and that soon, *soon,* he'd have her to himself again.

She sent him a saucy wink back, which made him even more desperate to get her in his bed—any bed, for that matter. A carriage would do, too. Or a hayloft and a blanket. He didn't care—although, he reminded himself, he wanted their first time together to be special.

He'd have to think about where he'd take her, and he'd have to plan the wedding that was going to come sooner rather than later, too.

Eliza took her old schoolmate by the hand, and together, they entered the carriage, Pippa going last. He enjoyed the view of her bottom in those breeches and was tempted to slap it, had an audience of gawking men and his mother not been watching.

He didn't show it, but Gregory hated to shut the door behind Pippa . . . hated to be parted from her even for a second.

"The marchioness and I will meet everyone at the

house," Father announced, and looked up at Lord Thurston, one of the riders. "Sorry to spring a visit on you with no notice, Thurston."

Their host waved a careless hand. "I'm always honored to host the Marquess and Marchioness of Brady at Thurston Manor," was his gracious reply.

As they approached him, Father and Mother wore perfectly neutral expressions on their faces, but Gregory knew—

He knew they couldn't wait to get him alone to talk to him.

"See you at the house," he told them as they walked by.

Father allowed his brow to furrow. Mama blew him a kiss.

It was odd how Gregory wasn't frightened anymore about what was to come.

Once they'd entered the Brady carriage, he went to Prince, mounted him, and led him out of the way. "Make room," he told the riders, who obeyed without a word. He noticed they'd chosen to stay rather than lead the carriages home.

Oh, well. The reckoning had to come at some point.

"You can go now," he called to the footman-driver.

As the vehicles rolled away, he saw Pippa's and Eliza's heads bent together inside the first one. They were probably overseeing the care of Mr. Dawson. Mama and Father looked straight ahead in the second, and when they, too, were past, Gregory looked to the cluster of men on horseback. "Thank you for coming out. All's well that ends well."

"Wait a minute," said Marbury. "You've got a lot of explaining to do, *Westdale*."

"Not to you," he said bluntly, then looked at Lord

Thurston. "But I certainly owe you and Lady Thurston an apology."

"Right." Lord Thurston cleared his throat. "I'm all ears, young man."

"Under the guise of a valet named Harrow," Gregory said smoothly, "Lady Pippa Harrington has been hopelessly compromised by her presence in my bedchamber at Thurston Manor, and the right thing will be done. She and I will elope to the island of Guernsey, where no special license is required to marry immediately. It's obviously much closer than Gretna Greene. We'll depart in the morning and sail in a private yacht from Torquay." He looked confidently around at them all. "You'll each receive an invitation to the postnuptial celebration at my father's estate in Ireland, although the date, of course, has yet to be set."

"So the cheeky valet is really a lady." Lord Thurston scratched his ear. "You know, Westdale, my wife's going to love this story. I'm not so sure about Lady Damara."

"Whether they love it or hate it, I'm assuming it will be all over London in the next few days," Gregory said dryly.

"You're probably right," Lord Thurston agreed.

"By the way, I withdraw from the dog cottage competition," Gregory told him quietly. "Thank you for the opportunity, but I must decline. I've other, more pressing projects that will demand my time."

Lord Marbury gave a yelp of delight.

Gregory sent him a wry look. "I'm delighted you're delighted, Marbury."

"Indeed I am," he said with a grin.

"It's a shame," said Lord Thurston, "but I understand."

The other riders nodded their heads sympathetically.

"Those other projects you mentioned," the architect

Mr. Forrest said, "the ones that will demand your time . . . we commiserate with you, old chap. Parson's mousetrap isn't an easy thing to enter."

"It'll *squeeze* you," said Marbury.

"Good luck," said another rider. "You'll need it."

There was a chorus of weakly offered *good lucks* from some of the others.

"He doesn't need luck, you idiots," said Dougal. "He's got love. Excuse my poor manners, Lord Thurston."

"No offense taken," Lord Thurston said mildly.

"Yes, thank you, Lord Morgan." Gregory shifted in his saddle. "Actually, I wasn't choosing an amusing way to say my future wife's demands will take all my time. I really do have other design projects to work on. And I can't wait to get to them. It might have to happen in Paris, but it will happen."

"Paris?" Marbury scoffed. "What kind of place is *that* for design inspiration?"

Nobody said a word.

"Oh, right." Marbury had the grace to look down at the ground. "Paris."

Everyone burst into laughter, even Marbury.

"I'm such a dunderhead," he said.

No one disagreed. And then they raced each other back to the stable, hollering like banshees, pretending that nothing could rein them in—not even love. They knew it was a lie, and they were *glad* it was a lie.

But while the horses streaked down the road, they were knights-in-arms together, upholding the old code that—given a chance—boys will *always* be boys.

Chapter Twenty-three

It was time. Well past time. Gregory knocked on his parents' bedchamber door at Thurston Manor.

"Come in," trilled Mama.

Pippa, Gregory thought, his hands loosely curled at his sides.

Just *Pippa.*

He walked over the threshold.

Father stood with his arms out while his valet brushed down his coat. "Done yet, Patrick?"

"Yes, my lord. You're looking very well, too."

Gregory met Patrick's gaze and nodded pleasantly. He'd never think of valets in the same way ever again.

Mama sat in a rocking chair, sewing. She looked up with a bright smile. "You'll never guess what I'm stitching," she said, as if nothing untoward had happened that day.

"What?" Gregory peered over her shoulder.

"It's your father's old wedding coat. The one he wore to marry your mother. It's in need of repair, and I took it on a whim to Dawlish."

Gregory was dumbstruck. "Why would you repair it? Especially when . . . he wore it to marry my mother?"

Mama sighed. "Because it's an important part of the family history, my dear." Her tone was puckish. "I've mended your mother's wedding gown already. And mine. A mouse got to it and nibbled a hole in the corner. And then there's the family baptismal gown. It's getting so fragile, it's almost frightening to attempt any fixes, but I believe it's imperative to preserve important clothes. They take us back to certain moments in our lives. Don't you think?"

He thought of Pippa's yellow velvet spencer with the oversized buttons. And her brown striped cravat, and a smile curved his lips. "Yes, I see what you mean."

Mama held up the coat. "One of you boys might wear this someday," she said in breezy fashion. "Maybe even you. If it will fit."

"It'll fit all right," said Father. "We're the same size." He nodded at Patrick, who left the room and shut the door quietly behind him.

Gregory waited for the change he knew was to come.

And it did. Father's face was icy when he turned to face him. "It's whether you'll have a wedding that worries me," he said in an ominous voice. "I'm thinking we're in need of one. *Without delay.* The integrity of the House of Brady is at stake." He threw out his hands. "Good God, Gregory, my boy, what kind of *shenanigans* have you been up to? A young lady dressed as a man? In the middle of an inn yard telling her driver she's under your protection and that of the entire House of Brady?"

Gregory gave a short laugh. "She said that?"

Mama nodded gravely. "I'm so glad she did."

Gregory blew out a breath. "Mama, Father, I understand your anger, and I'm sorry for it." He was amazed how steady his voice was. "And I agree, Father. There will be a wedding without delay. We leave tomorrow morning." He told his parents his plans to take Pippa to Guernsey via Torquay.

"All right, then." The news mollified his father somewhat. "But tell me how it came to this, that my son is running off with his bride to Guernsey." He crossed his arms and frowned at Gregory.

Mama let out an exasperated breath. "The usual way. He fell in love." She glared at Father. "Now don't you be forgetting how it is, Michael Sherwood, when you meet your soul mate."

Father shifted his feet, a stubborn cast to his mouth. Mama's taking on his Irish accent whenever she was riled with him never failed to amuse Gregory, although he'd be a fool to show a trace of amusement now.

"I've already talked to Pippa," Mama told Father in a more indulgent tone. "I'll tell you everything you want to know tonight. In *bed*." She angled an arch smile at him. "Meanwhile, let's give the two young people credit for doing the right thing."

Lord Brady drew himself up as if he hated to be chastised by his slip of a wife, but there was a gleam in his eye, too. Of respect for her, that was clear. And no doubt there was also the other usual reason a man's eye gleams when his wife talks about bed.

"Gregory needs a good dinner that will sit well in his stomach," Mama continued peaceably, and went back to sewing. "And he'll require a good night's rest before he leaves in the morning. Carping parents will only give him a headache."

"Whatever you say, Lady Brady," Father said, a mild scowl still in place, but his voice was soft and full of love.

Gregory restrained a smile. Mama had Father wrapped around her little finger, she did.

"Thank you, both of you," he said, "for being so generous with your patience and your love." The lump in his throat he hoped wouldn't appear did. "I can't tell you how much I appreciate you and love you in return."

"That's enough, lad," Father said gruffly, but Gregory saw a sheen of tears in his eyes.

What could he do but walk to his father and hug him? Who knew if it would be the last time, considering the news he was about to share?

And then he did the same for Mama, reaching down to lay a kiss on the top of her head.

"We adore you," murmured Mama, reaching up and placing her hand on his cheek, "and we're so happy for you. I love Pippa already. She's to be my fourth daughter, and I couldn't be more pleased with your choice."

"Thank you, Mama. I'm glad." Gregory moved a few steps away. He put his hands behind his back and spread his legs. His palms were sweating, and his heart was going a mile a minute. He was back to being thirteen.

They both looked at him expectantly.

"Is there something else?" Mama asked.

"Swear you won't tell, Gregory."

"I swear, Mother. I'll never tell. Never."

Gregory took a deep breath. His knees began to tremble.

Pippa, he thought.

Just *Pippa.*

"Lad?" Father squinted at him. "What's wrong?"

Mama had her hand to her heart. "Gregory, darling, tell us. Please."

"Mama?" he said calmly. "Father?"

"Yessss?" they said in unison. By now, Mama, still seated, was gripping Father's hand.

Gregory looked straight at the father of his heart. "I need you to reconsider the question of the coat. It may fit me well, but I'm not meant to wear it. I'm not your son," he said, his voice cracking. "Mother told me the day she died."

"Gregory—" Mama gasped.

"Son—" Father said.

"I'm so sorry, Father." Gregory clenched his hands tighter behind his back. "I hate to disappoint you and to be the person who besmirches the memory of my beloved mother. But I can't go on like this. I know I was born within the confines of the marriage and am your legal heir, but I'd much rather be your bastard son and get nothing. *You* are my true father. No one else. And I can only pray that you'll forgive Mother."

There was a palpable silence in the room, and in it, Gregory felt them both struggling to come to grips with his words—with the truth.

He looked at Mama and hoped she'd understand. "My mother never meant to hurt anyone. But she wasn't like you. She was careless. Like a child, in a way." He dropped his head. "She didn't mean to hurt you, Father. Or me. And I'm sorry"—he looked back up and saw both his parents quietly wiping their eyes—"I'm extremely sorry that I'm hurting you now."

The pain contorting their faces was like a body blow, and he found it difficult to breathe.

"But it's time for me to release this secret," he choked out. "I want to be able to love Pippa and you and my siblings freely, without shame, without any darkness weighing me down. I hope you'll forgive me. And I hope—I pray—you'll still love me."

"Oh, Gregory," Mama whispered, tears streaming down her face. She stood and held out her arms. "Come here. Of course, we still love you."

"Thank you, Mama," he said softly, and entered her embrace.

But Father had turned away. He was at the fireplace, and his shoulders were shaking. One soft sob punctuated the silence.

"He'll be all right," Mama whispered in Gregory's ear. "Give him a minute."

Oh, God, it was the worst pain on earth to see his father cry!

"I shouldn't have said—"

"Yes you should have," Mama assured him. "Long ago. But I understand you wanted to respect your mother's wishes. I wish she hadn't put such a burden on you, but she's your mother, and I don't want to speak ill of her in any way. She did what she thought was right, I'm sure."

Gregory was only half listening. "Now Father will hate her. He'll hate me. I've brought him such grief and disappointment."

"No," said Mama. "None of this is your fault. Give him a moment. And don't despair. He has something to say to *you* now."

"All right." Gregory wiped a tear from her eye with his thumb. And then he stepped away from Mama and advanced a few steps toward Father.

"Don't!" Father held up a palm, his eyes on the fire in the grate. "Don't take another step, boyo." His brogue was so thick, Gregory could barely understand him.

But he froze, as ordered.

It was his worst fear come true.

Mother's plea for silence came back to him full force: *"It would only hurt your father's feelings and embarrass the family."*

Father hated him.

So did the marquess—for what he'd done to the House of Brady.

"I'm going to tell you the true story of your birth," Father said suddenly, and looked up at him.

"Wait a minute." Gregory's mind raced. "You *knew*?"

"Yes." Father's face was sad yet also loving. "I've always known."

The world as Gregory knew it dissolved at that moment, the way an etching in the sand is carried away by the sea.

Father came to him and laid a hand on his shoulder. "I asked you to stay away a minute ago because I needed to come to *you*—and not the other way around. You're my son. And I will fight for you and run after you, and *I will be your father*. If I'd known you'd been bearing this burden all these years—alone—I'd have told you myself the story of your birth. Because it doesn't matter. It doesn't matter at all. Never in a million years would I not love you—my own boy. My firstborn. The son of my heart."

The son of my heart.

New words for Gregory to brand upon his soul.

"Father." For that's what Michael Sherwood truly was . . . his father. And it felt so good to say the word, to beckon the man he'd needed to know loved him for who he truly was.

Father pulled him toward him, and they held on to each other for a good, long minute, basking in the truth of their love for each other, a truth unfettered by secrets.

And then Father released him, and in a voice that was soft and informative, without a trace of rancor or disappointment, told Gregory the story of his birth.

"I met your mother through one of my best friends, Daniel Jeffers, at Trinity," Father said. "He was madly in love with Nora. She was exciting and amusing. She was also very pretty."

Gregory sent Mama a questioning look. With a soft smile and a nod, she confirmed that she was familiar with this story—which was another shock to Gregory: *Mama knew, too!*—and that he could safely assume Daniel Jeffers was his natural father.

The knowledge filled a gap in Gregory's understanding of his personal history, but other than his feeling a keen interest in his origins, no emotions accompanied the revelation.

"Nora came over to Dublin every chance she could get," Father went on. "I got to know her quite well. They were a special couple, those two." He chuckled then was silent for a moment, lost, it seemed, in good memories.

When he came back to the present, his eyes grew sad. "It was three days after we graduated that Daniel came to me and told me he was off to get a special license to marry Nora. He confessed he'd slept with her, and he loved her desperately. But on his way back from seeing the bishop, Daniel's curricle overturned, and he was killed."

"I'm sorry you lost a good friend," Gregory said, and felt a pang of loss himself.

How tenuous was his own existence! Were it not for Daniel, whose life had been cut tragically short, Gregory wouldn't be here in this room, now, with the parents he loved.

"Aye." Father grimaced. "It was a sad day. It still hurts to recall it. I had to tell Nora, of course, and in her grief, she came to rely on me for comfort, as I relied on her. We'd been friends for several years by then. I truly cared for her, and she for me. She'd no idea I knew she'd slept with Daniel, and I never said that I knew. I didn't want to embarrass her. But it seemed like the right thing to do, a mere five days after Daniel's death, to ask her to marry *me* by special license. I was a romantic lad. I knew Daniel would appreciate my looking after Nora, especially as she might be pregnant. And I believed I could come to love her."

"Did you?" Gregory asked.

Father looked at him, and Gregory saw immediately that the source of his pain had to do with Mother.

"We did our very best to love each other," Father said gently. "We had three boys together, and you brought us great joy. But it was more a friendship than love between your mother and me. We respected each other and had great affection for each other. I wish I could tell you we had more."

"I understand," Gregory said, feeling sorry for Father and Mother, both. "It's sad." He scratched his head. "Now that I know myself how close I came to marrying Eliza, the wrong girl entirely, I understand. Don't feel guilt, Father. You did the best that you could."

"Thank you, son." Father heaved a sigh. "Your mother obviously never realized I knew she'd slept with Daniel. I thought it was the right thing to do, to protect her sensibilities. She relied a great deal on the good opinion of other people, although she pretended not to care. But now I regret my choice. We never spoke of why she had our first child a month before you were due. Babies do come early, after all. But perhaps if we'd shared everything, she never would have felt the need to burden you with her confession."

"Father, you can't regret your choice," Gregory said. "You were thinking of Mother. Mistakes don't change the big things. You and I—and Mama and the other children—we're a family. A strong, loving family. And every day, it's getting bigger. And better."

Father and Mama exchanged a tender, private look.

"Gregory, son," Father said, "it's glad I am that you're the spitting image of Daniel. It was clear from the day you were born that he fathered you. And the fact that I took an entire month before I dared consummate my own marriage to Nora is further proof of your origins. The size of you, your robust health—you were a full-term baby, lad, and you were the product of love between two wonderful people. But you're also our son—mine and my lovely bride's"—he grabbed Mama's hand—"and what you just said confirms beyond our wildest hopes how ready you are to lead the House of Brady someday. You make us extremely proud."

"Yes, dear," said Mama. "You do."

Gregory didn't know what to say. He was overcome with gratitude. Love. Excitement about the future—

And then he remembered he had one more thing to say. "I haven't been good to Peter. I've let misguided jealousy and guilt—guilt that I might be usurping his place as your heir, Father—come between us."

"You don't need to feel that way anymore, darling," said Mama. "You're exactly where you should be. The law says so, and our hearts do, as well."

"Thank you, Mama. But I want Peter to know the whole truth. I need to explain why I made it impossible for him to confide in me. And I want his blessing as next in line to the marquessate."

"He won't be second in line to the marquessate for long," Father said with a chuckle. "You're bound to have a passel of sons."

"I'd like nothing more." Gregory grinned. "Meanwhile, I want his unwavering, honest support, and I can't get that unless he knows me completely. I think once I explain the circumstances, he'll see that Mother is not to be judged ill. And you said so yourself, Father—my beginnings don't matter."

Mama and Father exchanged glances, then looked back at him.

"I think it's a fine idea," said Father.

"I agree," said Mama.

"If Peter gives you any grief—" Father began.

"We'll come to grips with it," Gregory said. "Nothing's worse than secrets." He paced back and forth a moment. "In fact, I don't see why I shouldn't tell all my brothers and sisters the story of my birth. It's no more exciting or interesting than Mama's. It will become another family legend."

"He's right!" Mama stood. "Why not?" She turned to Lord Brady.

There was a moment's stunned silence, and then Father said, "Yes, why not?"

The three of them laughed at the same time. Gregory couldn't remember the last time he'd felt so free, so ready to take a step forward and claim his real life as his own.

"This calls for a celebration with some fine Irish whiskey." Father's excitement was palpable as he took out his flask, hurriedly poured three drams into glasses Lady Thurston had provided them in their dressing room, and passed them around. "To new beginnings," he said. "*Sláinte*."

"*Sláinte*," Gregory and Mama said in return.

They clinked glasses and downed the whiskey in a gulp.

It was a Brady tradition *par excellence*.

Gregory grinned.

Father waved a hand at him. "Go on with you now. Don't say another word. You've been through enough as it is today—and the past dozen years. Go see your ladylove with a light heart. And if we don't get another private moment with you before you leave, your mother and I wish you Godspeed on your journey tomorrow."

"Thank you," he finally managed, and with a quick kiss to Mama's cheek, and a slap on the back from Father, he departed their bedchamber, a new man.

Chapter Twenty-four

The next morning, dressed in Lady Eliza's second-best sprigged muslin in honor of the special traveling day, Pippa sat next to Gregory in the carriage, her head leaning on his shoulder. She loved that they'd been able to depart Thurston Manor without a chaperone. She was already ruined, they were as good as married, and the entire household as well as all the guests were bursting with pride that such a scandalous affair had taken place while they were in residence.

The fact that the Marquess and Marchioness of Brady were there, as well, to witness the unfolding of the drama added yet another layer of excitement. And when Lady Brady presented Gregory with his own father's marriage coat from long ago—properly mended under the left arm, of course—to wear on his wedding day, every woman in the household cried.

How serendipitous that she'd brought it to Dawlish! Who cared that she always carried her mending?

"It was the Irish in her," said the marquess, even though his wife hadn't a drop of Irish blood in her veins. "She's fey as they come."

And then he'd kissed her on the nose, as if she were his

own little leprechaun, which disgusted Marbury. He told
everyone so behind Lord Brady's back, including Pippa.
In his haste to spread his mean quip, he'd forgotten she
was to be the marquess's new daughter-in-law.

But Pippa merely pointedly stared at his crotch as punishment, and walked away.

"It's the height of fashion, my cravotch!" he'd called
after her.

She'd taken special delight in ignoring him.

Of course, everyone said they'd known from the beginning that Harrow was a woman disguised as a man,
except for Lady Thurston, who upon first seeing Pippa
descend from the carriage in breeches and with her hair
in an aureole about her face, fainted on the spot.

Or so she pretended.

Because she revived instantly and then fainted again
when her husband—along with the Marquess and Marchioness of Brady, of all people—walked into the house
with Gregory and Pippa. After Lady Thurston recovered
the second time, Lady Damara made sure to tell her
hostess—and Gregory's parents—that she'd always known
about Harrow's identity but was too proper to say anything.

Whereupon the marquess and marchioness, apparently
unfazed, left the room for tea. Meanwhile, Lady Thurston
objected to Lady Damara's silence—how could she not
have told her dear friend the great secret?—and pained at
being left out, even questioned how proper Lady Damara
truly was.

Whereupon *that* lady packed her bags and departed in
a snit the next morning.

But no one noticed her leaving. Everyone had eyes only
for Pippa and Gregory, the two lovers whom Lady Thurston made sure to separate properly their last night as her

guests. She placed Pippa with Lady Eliza for safekeeping, and Gregory and Dougal slept above the stables—Gregory in Oscar's bed and Dougal on the floor. The two friends were up drinking half the night with Oscar, who retired at three o'clock in the morning to Gregory's bedchamber.

It was a story that Oscar would share with his children and their children for the rest of his life, how he'd slept in an earl's bed and woke up to a servant laying him a fire, bringing him a cup of chocolate to sip before he'd even set his feet on the floor, and greeting him with, "Good morning, my lord."

But what Lady Thurston didn't know is that right before dawn, Gregory stole into Eliza's room, winked at her when she woke, and kidnapped Pippa right from beneath her friend's nose.

Only for a few minutes, he assured Eliza, who yawned and went back to sleep.

He rushed Pippa out of the house and down to the folly. And there, sitting side by side on the stone wall, they ate pears and drank wine—"It's not Italy but close," Pippa said—and watched the sun rise together while Gregory told her the story he'd held secret for so long.

When it was done, Pippa wiped away tears. "I wish you'd told me," she said. "All those years, I thought you didn't like me—"

"I *didn't*," he admitted with a laugh, and hugged her close. "But that was only because I was angry. And confused. And desperately afraid. Out of everyone in the world, you were the closest to learning the truth. No one else even guessed, except you. Because you knew me better than anyone."

"I did, didn't I?" She sniffled, but she couldn't help feeling a bit proud.

He nodded. "Even at age three, you'd poke and prod and demand that I take you out on the moor to find a grass snake because you knew I'd like it. And when we eventually saw one, I did, because of course, we don't have snakes in Ireland."

"No." Pippa giggled. "I really did that?"

"Oh, yes," he murmured back, and they shared a long, delectable kiss.

If Marbury hadn't shown up, demanding to know why Pippa was in a night rail and why he hadn't been invited to drink with Gregory, Dougal, and Oscar above the stables, it would have become far more than a mere kiss.

Now, in the carriage a few hours later, Eliza's favorite gown was in Pippa's bag—a lovely blue silk trimmed with tiny ivory flowers at the bodice and sleeves. Pippa would wear it at her wedding. Her new mother had offered to lend her one of her own Parisian-inspired creations, but Lady Brady was far too petite. Eliza's gown would do very well, and when Pippa returned from Guernsey, Gregory's mother would make her a whole new wardrobe.

She couldn't wait!

"We'll get to Torquay this afternoon," Gregory said, his arm wrapped tightly around her, his hand caressing her shoulder. "And tomorrow morning, we're off to Guernsey."

"I wish we didn't have to wait," Pippa said.

"For what?" Gregory looked out the window at the passing countryside.

On the fringes of Dartmoor, the landscape was wild and barren, and as much as Pippa loved it, it was comforting to be inside the cozy space with a strong, virile man by her side.

Gregory's carriage was luxurious, the walls lined in

blue velvet, the leather seats soft and buttery to the touch. Pippa hadn't been able to note any of those details the first time she'd landed in the space, bedraggled, exhausted, and soaked through. But now she did notice, and she had something on her mind.

She glanced sideways at her soon-to-be husband. "I wish we didn't have to wait for—"

But she didn't know how to say it.

Gregory's eyes widened, and his hips lifted off the seat a fraction of an inch. "Are you saying—"

She bit her lip. "I *think* I'm saying what you're thinking."

He turned and tugged at the tie at her bodice. "Are you saying something like this?"

She nodded.

"How about this?"

He shrugged down her shoulders, exposing the top half of her breasts, two little half-moons of rosy nipple showing.

"Yes," she said, "I'm saying that."

His eyes darkened with desire, and he removed his coat, tossing it on the seat opposite. "Are you certain?"

She smiled. "*So* certain. This is where we began, in a way—this very carriage—even though we've known each other forever."

"Yes," he said, and pulled his shirt over his head. Tossing it atop his coat, he grinned. "Remember that blanket?"

"How could I ever forget the blanket?" She grinned back.

He made a face. "It happened *how* many days ago?"

She unlaced her ties all the way. "Only two."

"I can't believe it," he said.

"Neither can I. Look at us now."

"It was a long time coming." He folded her in his arms and kissed her like a dying man in the desert who'd come upon an oasis.

And she kissed him back as if the world were about to end.

They pulled back, breathing hard.

"What took us so long?" he asked her.

She winced. "So many things. Including your warning me away from you. It only made me want you more, you know."

"Of course I knew that," he said. "Which is why I really am as dangerous as the papers say."

"I'm more dangerous."

"Are you?" His eyes glinted with something dark and delicious.

She nodded. "Are you ready?"

And in a matter of three minutes, they were stark naked and Pippa was in his lap, thrilled at the evidence of his arousal below her.

"What if Oscar hears us?" she whispered.

"He won't," said Gregory.

"How do you know?"

He pulled his cravat off the floor and dangled it in front of her. "I can use *this* again, but on your luscious mouth instead of your taunting eyes," he said in overly dramatic fashion.

She giggled. "The cravat certainly has many uses I'd never dreamed of."

"Do you trust me?" Gregory asked her, and she nodded. "This could be fun, Lieutenant. You've been captured. I'm an enemy captain, and I have to win you over to the bad side."

"It will never happen," she said. "I'm not so weak, but very well. You can try."

He was about to put the cravat around her mouth, but she pushed his hand away. "One more thing."

"What?"

"In this scenario, *I'm* the captain from the good side. And you're the lowly lieutenant from the bad side. You've kidnapped me and can't believe your luck."

He seemed to really contemplate the idea. "All right," he eventually said.

"And one more thing," she added.

"Yes?"

"I get a promotion if Oscar doesn't hear me. I want to be a major now. Or perhaps a general. Yes, I like the sound of that." She kissed his nose.

"We'll see," said Gregory, grabbing her wrists, putting them above her head, and kissing her neck. "You're my prisoner," he murmured, and she shivered.

A few seconds later, her mouth was tied shut and her hands were slung through the blue velvet loops on the side wall of the carriage. Her legs were spread, and Gregory was between them, kissing her breasts, teasing her lush feminine flesh with his fingers, and finally, grabbing her hips in his hands and pulling her to his mouth. He probed with his tongue, nuzzled with his mouth, and brought her to an explosion of pleasure that she felt she couldn't contain—but the handy cravat did its work.

While her hands were finally able to release their vise-like grip on the straps and she hung limp from them, Gregory approached her once more. "General."

"Hmmm?" she murmured drowsily from behind her enemy lover's cravat.

"I've defected. I'm going over to your side now."

She shook her head.

He kissed her belly. "This isn't the way I want to have you. Not the first time."

She raised her brows and nodded vigorously.

"No," he said firmly. "I have a plan. You're going to have to wait." And then he untied the cravat.

"But—"

"No buts," he said.

"I'll never be able to ride in this carriage again without—"

He wouldn't let her finish. He devoured her mouth, and she sensed the need in him. "Are you sure?" She felt wistful on his behalf. How she longed to make him as needy for her as she'd been for him!

"Very sure," he said.

"How much longer?" Pippa asked much later that day.

They were in Torquay, and they'd just finished a delicious dinner of roasted trout, small new potatoes, and a light glazed-carrot dish.

Gregory stood and stretched. "I'm tired," he said.

"I hope not too tired," she said back.

He put his hands on his hips. "Lady Pippa Harrington, are you going to be this way when we're married?"

"Of course." She stood, too, and looked at him.

"You'd better be." He grabbed her around the waist and slung her against him. "You're a demanding wench."

"Are you a pirate now? That would be most amusing. And compelling."

He chuckled. "I agree. But no, tonight I'm simply Gregory, the man who loves you."

"Oh, that's very sweet," she said softly. "I didn't know you were so romantic."

"Close your eyes," he whispered.

She put her hands over her eyes.

"I'll tell you when you can open them," he said from farther away.

She laughed. "I'm nervous." And she was. She felt a tingling sensation all over her body.

"Not much longer," he said.

"Hurry!" She stretched up on tippy-toe.

"All right," he said, "open your eyes."

She opened them and saw crab-apple blossoms all over the bed.

He came to her and held her hands. "I used to hand you bags of crab apples to throw at the enemy. But tonight, we're moving to the next step, crab-apple *blossoms,* and they're used only to celebrate two people together . . . two people in love."

Tears blurred her vision and she gave a happy little hiccup.

"Are you all right?" he asked her.

She nodded and sniffed. "I love them. I love *you.*"

He gave a low laugh. "I love you, too, and I'm glad you're happy."

He undressed her before the fire, and then he lifted her in his arms, carried her to the bed, and lowered her to the fresh-smelling sheets that had been dried in sea breezes.

He took a handful of blossoms and gently showered them over her breasts. And then he stood back and undressed himself, shimmying out of his breeches last. Not once did he take his eyes off hers, but when he was naked, he raked her entire body with a bold, appreciative gaze that was also humble—which made her love him all the more.

"Are you glad you have me this way?" she whispered.

He only nodded, but she saw his throat work.

Seeing him emotional made her throat tighten, too, and her eyes sting.

She held out her arms, and slowly he crawled onto the bed and lay beside her. For the next few blissful moments, they whispered words of love to each other, caressing each other's bodies, almost reverently.

But Pippa didn't want to wait too long. She knew her man was ready, and that he needed her, so after a few more minutes, she rolled on top of him and lay where she knew their bodies would meet. He taught her to spread her legs over him, but he wouldn't let her sink down on top of him. He tantalized her, even teased her—but then he rolled on top of her and took control.

She wanted him desperately and begged him to make her his. And after suckling both her breasts and driving her mad with longing, he spread her legs with his own and, with a few quiet, comforting words and a long, passionate kiss, sank deep into her while she rose to meet him.

"Oh," she said, the pain sharp but the word full of wonder. There was ecstasy in her brief agony, and soon the pleasure outweighed the discomfort, and she was lifting her hips and arching into him, wanting completion—

Wanting *him*.

"Forever," Gregory said against her ear. And when she was lifted high, buoyed by love, he came with her, and they were fused as a single being, all boundaries gone.

The world below them was good. And it was wide. And it was waiting for them to explore it together.

Epilogue

The Paris sun labored to find its way through the thick clouds swollen with rain that threatened the celebration taking place in the courtyard behind Lord and Lady Westdale's town house on the Rue de Jarente. No measure of gray in the sky could darken the spirits of the family and friends gathered there, though. Excited chatter and laughter bounced off the cobbled pavement, curled around the black wrought-iron railing that stood sentry about the new Lady Westdale's prized roses, and floated out onto the street, where two gentlemen stood listening.

Lord Marbury took Mr. Dawson's arm and ushered him up the steps. "Careful now, Roger." His voice was gentle, but he could do that because no one else was listening. "We're here for quite an important occasion, you know."

They'd arrived just that morning to attend the christening of tiny Albert Michael Sherwood, Lord Sherwood. The little honorary baron was second in line to become the Marquess of Brady. Standing before the massive oak door bearing the Brady crest, Marbury watched Dawson run a finger over the elaborate etching.

"Why, this looks just like the wax seals on Pippa's letters to me," he marveled.

"That's right," Marbury said. "We're at Gregory and Pippa's home now."

Not that he called them that—but Mr. Dawson did. He was family, of sorts.

Marbury felt a twinge of envy—all right, he felt a *cartload* of envy. He also felt guilty about it because he was envying such a nice old man, one who'd gone just a little bit mad and come back from the edge better than ever.

Because now Mr. Dawson was *interesting*. Occasionally, when his mind wandered, he'd curse and drink too much—just like Marbury. Before his mental lapse, he'd been rather bland. But the folly he'd designed with Gregory and Marbury was the most ironic masterpiece of a folly England had ever seen, and Lord and Lady Thurston couldn't keep people away from it.

Nobody cared about their dog cottage. It was a shame, as Marbury had won that commission.

But a canine spa couldn't compare to a folly that brought visitors from all over the world to see the stairs that went nowhere—Westdale's contribution—and the heart-shaped window that faced the setting sun—Mr. Dawson's idea. Marbury had provided a lot of harping criticism, but only to Gregory, not to Mr. Dawson, of course.

The front door of the house opened, and a butler stood with a lithe girl with blond curls and huge blue eyes peering around from behind him.

"Oh, I just knew it would be you!" She beamed at them. "Pippa asked me to wait in the front hall after the note came with your arrival time."

Marbury returned her grin. "Why, Lady Cynthia, how did you become even more lovely and delightful since I saw you last at your brother's post–wedding feast?" He bowed over her outstretched hand.

"Gregory told me you'd speak that way again." She giggled.

"What way?"

She giggled again. "Like a charmer, the kind you can't trust—but that in your case, you can't help yourself. He said you're *very* trustworthy."

"I am that," he said with pride, and pulled Mr. Dawson over the threshold.

Cynthia ushered them into the hall, where their hats and coats were taken, all the while chattering away. "Isn't this so exciting? I've never been to Paris. And everyone's here. Baby Albert is adorable! Pippa doesn't want you to miss a thing, so I'm to take you right out to the garden." She paused, waiting for a response, it seemed. But before Marbury could open his mouth to give one, she sped ahead. "So sorry you had to miss the christening. It was delightful. And now we're on to the party. Pippa has made the most wonderful sugar sculpture, a landscape of the moor that has sugar-spun grasses and shrubs and mosses and even a marzipan mother goose with her babies." She took Mr. Dawson's arm and squeezed it. "She says you love geese, too!"

The girl's a natural monopolizer of conversation, Marbury thought, admiring her, *almost as good as I am.* He felt a great compulsion to go buy her a giant platter of French pastries as a kind gesture, or even put her in his will, and was appalled at the avuncular turn his thoughts were taking.

They were on the steps leading to the courtyard. The garden beds were in full bloom, and heady scents from lavender to rosemary captivated Marbury's senses. He didn't like to admit his fondness for flowers, so he maintained his prevailing new expression, which he'd softened from jaded to mildly interested. Tables and chairs draped in white linen trimmed with lace were scattered beneath sweet chestnut trees. Their branches would provide shelter from the midday sun, should this corner of Paris be fortunate enough to get some. Otherwise, they were merely hazardous to anyone wearing false hair, such as himself.

As Lady Cynthia had promised, everyone was indeed here.

At one table sat Lord and Lady Brady, heads close together and hands clasped. They were deep in conversation and seemingly oblivious to the proceedings.

Why, they still appear to be lovers with eyes for no one else, Marbury thought, and saw Dawson notice, too, his lips curved in the sweet smile that their friend Pippa so loved. Perhaps the old man was thinking back to romantic moments with his own missus. Marbury hoped he was—and felt not a single twinge of longing to marry himself.

"Gregory, Pippa, do come see Lord Marbury and Mr. Dawson," called Cynthia, pulling Mr. Dawson by the hand toward the largest group gathered in a corner. A Titian-haired young woman—Pippa herself—broke away and hurried toward them, a small bundle swathed in white cotton embroidered with tiny blue ducklings in her arms. Several other members of the group followed, laughing and chatting, behind her.

"Mr. Dawson and Marbury, how wonderful to see you!" Pippa was even lovelier now that motherhood had worked its magic, a soft light shining from her eyes. "Gregory, my love, come quickly! Our most important guests have arrived!"

Marbury's chest swelled. He was important?

She held the bundle out, pulling a corner open to more fully expose the face of her little son. "Isn't he handsome?"

Her smile was one of pure joy, and Dawson's eyes shone with unshed tears. Marbury's did, too, as a matter of fact, but he cursed them silently and urged their instant remission. When that didn't happen, he pretended to sneeze and made quick work of the silly things with his handkerchief.

He was still stuck on being important. Enough with babies and their utter gorgeousness.

"Pippa, my dear." Mr. Dawson leaned in and kissed both her cheeks. "He's beautiful." He then turned to Gregory. "Fine work, lad. I'm proud of you both."

Westdale put his arm around his shoulders and squeezed. "We're exceedingly glad you're here to share this special day with us." He leaned toward his wife and ran a gentle thumb over their son's wee, dimpled chin.

Marbury did *not* want a one-armed embrace from Westdale, so he backed up a step. But the newly married earl managed to reach out and slap his shoulder—hard— and grinned at his former nemesis turned design partner, because admittedly, that's what Marbury now was, and their business was thriving.

"Thanks for getting our mentor here safely today," Westdale told him. "I trust your travel went well, that Mr. Dawson didn't have you scaring up valets to shine his shoes for him, did he?"

Marbury chuckled. "Must you remind me of that marvelously pompous ass you stumbled upon in that inn? He was a memorable fellow, wasn't he? But let's move on." He snapped his fingers. "I've learned the secret to shiny boots, one that Beau Brummel claims does the trick every time. A good soft cloth . . . and the finest champagne!"

They all laughed.

"It's not funny." Marbury glowered round at them all. "It's costing me a fortune."

"You know, my dear friend," Pippa began brightly—

Marbury looked behind him, then saw that she was talking to him. "Yes?" he asked in an imperious tone, for old times' sake.

"If you hadn't asked me to become Mr. Dawson's valet," Pippa started again with a sincerity that twisted his cold and puny heart, "and if Mr. Dawson hadn't accepted my services, I might not be married to the man of my dreams right now nor borne our precious son."

"Ah now, let's give credit where credit's due," broke in Mr. Dawson. "From what I know of your history, your uncle Bertie is the one who fought long and hard for this day to arrive."

Pippa's face clouded but only for a moment. She smiled gently into the baby's face, then looked up at her husband. "It's hard to believe he's been gone these eight months now, isn't it?" Her eyes grew misty, and she spoke to the bundle this time. "Young man, you have some quite large shoes to fill, don't you? Albert Michael Sherwood, your great-uncle Bertie would be thrilled to know you carry his name. Just wait until you hear the stories we have to tell you!"

Any gloom the family felt was apparently soothed away by the balm of happy memories, Marbury was pleased to see. He was becoming softhearted around this bunch, and it scared him. What would he do when they stopped inviting him to their festive gatherings?

He didn't want to contemplate the notion, so he glowered at the chestnut tree branches and silently cursed them for being so twiggy beneath those fresh spring leaves of theirs.

"My turn to hold my godson," came a cheery voice.

Marbury turned toward the new arrival. *Ah, the middle sister.* Quite possibly his favorite of the ladies in the House of Brady.

"Hello, Lady Janice. How glad I am to see you again." He bowed to her, annoyed with his plain sincerity, but she brought it out in him.

"And I'm so glad to see *you,* of course." Lady Janice smiled, her blue eyes bright, then turned to Dawson. "And Mr. Dawson, how lovely to have you here." She kissed his cheek.

Mr. Dawson had developed a soft spot for Janice during the week the family celebrated Pippa and Westdale's elopement. The festivities were held at Ballybrook, the Bradys' sumptuous estate in Ireland. Both Janice and Mr. Dawson shared a fondness for books—she tended to lose herself in their pages just as Dawson did. Marbury watched the two of them now and was glad to see the old man so happy.

But he wondered if Janice truly was. He recognized her intelligence and charm, but he also sensed a sadness behind her cheerful smile. Looking at her now, laughing with her family and that obnoxiously happy couple, Lord and Lady Morgan, he had to wonder if there might be an insecure and frightened girl hiding behind the pages of Janice's books.

He'd grown quite fond of the entire family, and in his own daydreams, she'd become the little sister he'd always wished for.

God forbid anyone find out how sensitive he'd become. "Is there whiskey available?" he croaked just as cries of "Toast!, toast!" filled the garden.

Thank God. A distraction from his own mawkish

thoughts. And drink to assuage the flicker of loneliness that flared up at moments like this, an emotion he'd deny with every breath in his pleasingly round, perfect body until the day he died.

Lord Brady gestured to everyone to gather near a beech tree with a bench resting beneath it. And then the patriarch leaped nimbly upon the bench to create a make-shift stage. He bowed to the ensuing applause.

"As ever, his lordship can't be passing up the opportunity for an audience," the droll voice of that crazy Irish housekeeper named Alice rang out. "Could it be that bit o' blarney in him, I'm wonderin'?"

The crowd erupted in hearty laughter.

Alice gave Lord Brady a good-natured wave and then turned her attention to the newest Brady man in her life, holding Albert over her shoulder and patting his tiny bottom.

Marbury noted that today she wore her usual cobalt-blue gown—a watered silk, no doubt in honor of the occasion—her hair in a tight chignon, and a frilly, lace-trimmed apron. The apron was completely inappropriate for a party, he mused critically, but she'd worn the same thing at Ballybrook. She probably *slept* in an apron.

He'd never forget that at Ballybrook one afternoon, he'd tried to insult the strident Alice in a jovial fashion by comparing her to Wellington, which was actually a compliment. But she hadn't taken kindly to his light remark and had given him a tongue-lashing like he'd never received before or since, telling him that if he intended to consort with the members of the House of Brady, then he'd best drop the false pride and wretched manners and become a decent human being.

She was a harsh taskmaster, that Alice, but Marbury couldn't help liking her, just a little.

Heaven help him. She was on her way to see him now.

She put her nose up to his. "Lord Marbury," she said in low tones, "I'll have you know you've earned the right to tease me now. You're an honorary member of the family, having taken excellent care of Mr. Dawson and alleviating the worries of my darling Gregory and his beautiful bride, Pippa. So fire away."

She crossed her arms over her bodice and waited for an insult.

But for the first time in his entire life, Lord Marbury was unable to speak. The lump in his throat wouldn't permit it, nor could he see very well. Alice had become a big, cobalt-blue blob.

"Come now, my lord. Let's hear it," she urged him.

"You rot, Alice," he finally choked out. "That apron is ridiculous."

"And you're an English heathen," she said back. "But I can put up with you, I suppose." She held out her arms.

He fell right into them and blubbered like a baby. He was pathetic, he knew, but it was worth it. He'd never been happier in his life.

Before the toasts began, Pippa sat in a chair at the party next to Marcia, her sister-in-law and dear friend, both of them cradling infants in their laps. Just three months before, Marcia had had a second beautiful baby, another daughter. The first was named Caroline, after Marcia's mother, which was appropriate as they had the same white-blond hair. She was two now and had a special fondness for her uncle Robert, who was carrying her this very moment on his shoulders. The new baby was Suzanne, after Duncan's late mother. Little Suzy had her father's dark hair but the piercing blue eyes of her mother.

Though the ladies had met a few times during their childhood years, it wasn't until Pippa joined the Brady family that their bond became close. And now that they both shared the experience of young motherhood, they'd become inseparable whenever they met at family gatherings.

Marcia called to her husband, Duncan, who was pushing their son Joe on a swing, the squealing boy's toes touching the leaves on the chestnut's branches on each forward push. "Darling, not too high now! Remember that Joe got an early start on the shortbread Alice brought from Ballybrook . . . we certainly want it to remain in his tummy!" She turned to Pippa and whispered, "Honestly, I think that fatherhood was invented so that our men could revert to boyhood again."

Their mutual laughter bubbled upward, into a sky which showed patches of blue through the thinning gray clouds.

But it was merriment well earned, not without struggle. Pippa and Gregory had come to Paris to seek out Monsieur Perot, Mother in tow to get her away from the Toad and remind her that she was still capable of adventure. Monsieur Perot had immediately offered his tutelage to Pippa, much to her grateful surprise. Mother had remained for several months exploring Paris and gaining back much of her old self, but then she'd returned to Plumtree, to her comfortable and familiar existence. It wasn't long after when the news of Uncle Bertie's death came, casting a gloomy shadow over their sunny Parisian life.

Pippa and Gregory traveled to Plumtree for Uncle Bertie's funeral and to help settle his estate. In his will, he'd left his theaters to Pippa as promised, but she made arrangements for those to be signed over to Mother—to Lady Graham and Lady Graham alone, Pippa adamantly insisted. The Toad would have not a single say in the running of the theaters, and Gregory delivered that injunction with a promise of quick and brutal action should Trickle try to circumvent it.

Trickle whined and carried on a bit, but Mother somehow dug deep into herself, pulled out a bit of the plucky actress from yesteryear, and told her husband that he'd have to find another residence. She planned on running a high-class enterprise, and his presence certainly didn't lend itself to anything remotely connected with gentility.

Pippa smiled, remembering her mother's stony expression and ramrod posture. She'd flung her arm out, as regal and beautiful as Lady Macbeth. "Out, damned Toad," she'd cried.

Pippa had never been more proud of her.

Mr. Trickle had swelled like the amphibian he resembled and made the rude croaking noises they'd come to expect from him. An hour later, he'd packed his bags, and the last Pippa heard, was acting as personal assistant to Lord Hawthorne.

Good riddance.

She gazed with fresh pride at Mother now, who instead of wearing Uncle Bertie's old cast-off costumes that she used to alter, was outfitted in Parisian style—thanks to Lady Brady, who sent Mother new gowns she'd custommade for her every quarter.

Mr. Dawson would never be the same man he once was, but he was family now. He adored Mother and was slightly stagestruck by her, which Mother found gratifying. Never had a man held her in such esteem, although Gregory and Lord Brady competed every day with Mr. Dawson to be the most chivalrous, sincerely admiring man of Lady Graham's acquaintance.

Yes, Pippa was well pleased that her mother had found her own calling . . . and her voice.

The call for a toast continued as footmen wandered among the family and guests with brimming flutes of champagne. Once again, Pippa's father-in-law's hearty voice called for order.

She leaned forward, intent on hearing every word.

"Today is special," Lord Brady began. Lady Brady stepped closer to him and took his hand. "My darling wife and I couldn't be filled with a greater joy on this day when we have our beloved family and friends gathered to celebrate." He gazed at Lady Brady—Pippa's new second mother who'd welcomed her into the family with open arms—then swept the crowd with fond eyes and began to toast every member of the cozy gathering. "I see my boyos, Peter and Robert, fine young men that they are . . ."

At the mention of Peter's name, Pippa looked at Gregory. He raised his glass at his next youngest brother, who raised his glass back and grinned. The exchange gave her deep satisfaction. The brothers had repaired their breach, thank heaven. All was well between them.

As Pippa listened to the toasts, she wondered how this perfect day had come to them. It hadn't been an easy road to finding true love. Years and years it took her and Gregory to discover what Uncle Bertie had known all along . . . that they were soul mates.

And though there were rocky moments here and

there—two strong-willed people, both of them creative, could never agree on *everything,* could they?—their lives were incredibly rich.

Love changes everything, Pippa thought, remembering her sugar castle with the broken turret. Marcia held up her infant daughter and kissed her sweet, fat cheek. Pippa looked up at Gregory, who'd come to put his hand on her shoulder.

"You were right, Uncle Bertie," she whispered just as the sun peeked from behind a cloud and shone upon the chestnut tree, causing little golden dapples of light to fall over the baby sleeping in her lap.

Read on for an excerpt from Kieran Kramer's next book

Say Yes to the Duke

Coming soon from St. Martin's Paperbacks

Chapter One

Lady Janice Sherwood had literally waltzed through two London Seasons, and she still hadn't found a husband. Everyone knew what a proper young lady did when she wasn't in demand. She rusticated in the English countryside in the hopes she'd be missed.

Which was why Janice found herself at the beginning of the autumn social whirl leaving Town in an unmarked Brady carriage on a day that promised an early snow. Sure enough, after several hours, the passing fields began to look like the tops of sugar cakes. The low *hish-hish* of crystal formations hitting and sliding across the window panes lulled her maid Isobel into a light doze. The girl woke only when they passed over a small bridge.

"We're here," Janice told her. *Not jail, exactly, but close.*

"I hope the country's as peaceful as you say, my lady."

"It's *very* peaceful, Izzy."

The horses' hooves sounded hollow on the short wooden span beyond which the Duke of Halsey's castle loomed, its flat, mullioned windows like staring, rectangular eyes. Off to the right of the stone edifice was the stable block—massive, with three arched double doors. And lending beauty and dignity to the entire impressive scene was an elegant lake nestled in expansive grounds punctuated by low stone walls, manicured hedges, and the occasional copse of trees as far as the eye could see.

With a light jolt to the springs, the carriage returned to the snow-covered road, and they passed a lacy tree fronting the hedge on the left. The tree's delicate limbs were like outstretched hands holding millions of diamonds. But in the midst of Janice's admiring the stunning tableau came a sharp dip, a *snap*, and a strong lurch to the right, followed by a bounce and the awful sound of shattered glass. The carriage came to an abrupt stop, and Janice found herself in Isobel's lap.

"Bloody hell!" The sound of Oscar's aggrieved voice came through the broken window now facing the ditch, where large shards of glass lay scattered in the snow. "Are you two all right in there, my lady? Please tell me you are."

The other window, still intact, faced the sky. Snow rapidly covered its surface.

"We're fine, Oscar!" Janice yelled. "No worries. But you must have taken a tumble off the box. Are you all right? And what of the horses? Please see to yourself and them before you come near us."

"I'm fine," he shouted back, "and thank goodness, the horses are unharmed. But Victor's jumpy. I'll get him settled, and then I'll come for you."

She ignored the rapid beating of her heart and tried her

best to get off of Isobel. After a few awkward seconds, she wound up in a crouch looking down at her traveling companion. "Are *you* all right?"

"I'm fine." Isobel's forehead puckered. She looked a bit like a pudding that had caved in. "So far I don't *like* the country, my lady."

"Oscar will get us out," Janice said evenly. "And we're almost to the castle anyway."

"You!" A man's nasally voice—clearly not Oscar's—rang out in the distance. "Where's my bottle of wine, you idiot?"

Janice recognized the cultured, posturing accent of someone from the London set.

"Wine?" another man could be heard asking. His voice was rich and strong, like a hot brew. "But Your Grace, you didn't ask for wine."

Your Grace? Janice stiffened. The rude man must be the Duke of Halsey.

"Don't question me!" the duke roared. "You were supposed to put two bottles in my saddle bag. Do you have no brains in your head, oaf?"

"I brought your flask of whiskey, Your Grace, but I'll return to the castle to get your wine if you so desire."

Janice felt a stab of sympathy. She recognized that tone. Beneath the servant's stalwart replies, he was weary, accustomed to curbing his frustration with an unreasonable employer. She remembered hearing the same sound in her mother's voice in those long-ago days when Mama had had to deal with imperious customers at her sewing shop in London.

"Yes, you'll return for the wine," the duke howled. "And no groom in my stables talks back to his betters. Ride back this instant and get it, damn you, if you want to keep your post. Then meet us in the western woods. Robertson, Gilroy! Wait up!"

A horse whinnied and galloped off. The duke's, no doubt.

Janice felt a strong stab of annoyance. Did no one see past the occasional tree and hedge that there was a broken carriage in the road?

"Hello, you there! Groom!" Oscar called out a moment later. "We could use some assistance!"

There was the sound of a horse approaching, and then a brief, muted conversation ensued between Oscar and the hailed servant.

Good. Janice's posture relaxed slightly. Surely the duke's wine could wait, once their untenable circumstances were known. If His Grace decided to fire the man anyway, Janice would certainly go to the groom's defense.

She could hear Oscar working with the horses.

"My lady, could you help me?" Isobel asked, still trying to sort herself out.

"Oh, right. Sorry." Janice attempted to pull the girl to her feet just as a loud thump on the carriage wall sounded, inciting a shriek from Isobel.

And then a face appeared at the unbroken window.

But it wasn't Oscar. It was a swarthy younger man— late twenties, possibly, his tanned brow wide and imposing beneath unruly saddle-brown hair. There was a grim set to his mouth, an almost cruel hardness suggested by his chiseled cheekbones, and a ruthless expression in his piercing light brown eyes. He opened the door, and a tiny bank of snow landed like a mantle around Janice's shoulders. Isobel gave a little sputtering cry.

"You're obviously unhurt, so I'll dispense with the niceties." The groom's voice was as rich and strong as before, but now it was also openly dark and bitter. "What's your business here? Decent folk don't come down this drive."

Janice was so taken aback, she merely stared at him while snow fell like a curtain into the carriage interior.

"Speak up, madam, why don't you?" he taunted her. "Or are you and your so-called maid in your cups already? Good God, it could be the reason neither of you is injured. You're so full of drink, you probably bounced about the carriage like rubber balls in a bucket when it went off the road."

"How dare you speak so rudely?" Janice's voice trembled with rage. "Where's Oscar, my driver?"

Isobel gave a little hiccup of anxiety.

"See?" He ignored Janice's question and looked accusingly between her and Isobel, who blushed. "Drink may keep you warm on a frigid day, but you won't be indulging here. I'll spare two minutes to pull you out. I'll not risk my job for the likes of you."

"We don't want your kind of help," said Janice. "*Where is Oscar?*"

"Seeing to the horses. *He's* a decent sort, at least. After I remove you, you'll wait in the stables a half hour—under guard, mind you—until I get back. When I do return, I'm going to throw you both on the back of my horse and take you to the village before the snow gets too deep. You'll stay at the Pig and Whistle until the mail coach comes through. I can promise you this"—he intruded further into the space above Janice's head—"you won't ever set foot inside Halsey House." His voice was low and menacing, his formidable shoulders blocking her way out entirely.

Isobel began to cry.

"See what you've done?" Janice scooped some snow off her neck, flung it into his face, and was happy to see him scowl. "Be gone. We don't need assistance from the likes of you." For good measure she pushed her gloved hands against those granite-like shoulders and gave a mighty shove.

He didn't budge. "You'll get it whether you like it or not."

Well, then.

"*Oscar!*" she yelled at the top of her lungs, directly into the stranger's face.

He winced mightily at that.

And then she snatched up her reticule and gave him a good wallop with it. The soft velvet pouch contained only a few small items, sadly.

But it was the principle of the matter.

"You're a regular shrew, I see." He eyed her coldly. "I sent the beleaguered Oscar to the stables to look after the team. A few minutes apart from you will do him the world of good."

"You"—Janice said, gulping in deep breaths—"are *despicable*."

"That's what every charlatan and thief says when they're kept from their dirty business. Now *you*"—he pointed at Isobel—"will come out first. You need to get your head straight quickly, or you'll fall off my horse."

"I don't think I can stand," whimpered Isobel. "I'm a bit wobbly."

"Whose fault is that?" he said with smug scorn.

"Oh, shut up," Janice told him. "She's wobbly because you're frightening her to death, not because she's been drinking spirits." She turned to Isobel. "Of course you can stand up and get out," she said, and finally managed to pull the maid to her feet.

While Oscar lifted from above, Janice assisted by

pushing from below. The entire time, Isobel shrieked, "Oh, oh, oh," over and over and wiggled her legs until Janice said, "No more talking and wiggling. *Help* us, Izzy."

Whereupon Isobel found the wherewithal to focus on the task at hand and discovered herself outside.

"Go stand by my horse," the groom told her sternly.

"But I'm afraid of horses."

"You've more to fear from *me*, young lady, than Argo," he said in an intimidating voice.

Isobel let out a whimper.

"Ignore him, Izzy!" Janice shouted at the same time as a black-and-white shaggy thing scurried below the window facing the ditch.

What was that?

A dog, of course. For the briefest moment, it paused and looked up at her, its dark eyes glinting with fear and something else—could it be pain? It ran on.

Was it hurt?

"Let's go," he ordered Janice.

The snow came steadily on, drifting down lazily wherever it could find space to descend into the vehicle.

The scornful curve to his lip incensed her further, but she held her temper in check. "There's a small dog out there. Is it yours? Or the duke's?"

"I don't see a dog," he said testily. "And the duke only keeps hounds."

"Did *you* see a dog, Izzy?" she shouted around him through the open door.

"No, my lady!"

"Look for it, will you?" Janice called to her. "There's something wrong with it. We must help the poor thing."

"Right, Lady Janice." Isobel perked up. "I'll look."

Janice heard the timid movement of the maid's feet through snow and was glad to have distracted her.

The groom lifted his head, exposing taut, tanned skin over corded muscle in his neck. "Don't go far," he warned the maid, then looked back down at Janice. "Give me your hand."

How dare he order her about so!

"I'm perfectly able to get out myself." And she was. She could climb trees as well as her three stepbrothers, Gregory, Peter, and Robert, and she was leagues ahead of her sisters Marcia and Cynthia when it came to athletic prowess. "And I wouldn't accept help from you if you were the last person on earth."

Besides, something was wrong with that dog. What was it doing in a ditch in this weather? Why did it slink past the window? It was afraid. She knew it. And she hoped Isobel would find it any second and report back to her.

"I'll give you thirty seconds to haul yourself out, and then I'm coming after you." He slid back down the side of the carriage, and then his boots made their own decisive crunch through the snow. She could hear him murmur something affectionate to his horse.

"You're a bully!" she shouted to him, more incensed than ever. "I'm the daughter of the Marquess and Marchioness of Brady, and you're going to regret ever treating me so vilely!"

"Do you know how many desperate titled ladies have appeared at the duke's door with haughty attitudes, no money in their pockets, and a burning ambition to become the next Lady Halsey? I haven't even mentioned how many pretenders and outright lightskirts have wreaked their own sort of havoc here. I care nothing for your pompous speech. All I care about is seeing you gone."

"Who made you the keeper of the castle? The duke and the dowager will be incensed when I tell them—"

"You'll never see either one. Now hurry up."

Much to her chagrin, it took her three tries to hoist herself out. The snow made the edge of the door slippery, and her wearing gloves didn't help. Her fingers felt clumsy and thick. But her main impediment to progress were her limbs, which were trembling with fury.

Finally. She found herself perched a bit crazily on the side of the vehicle, her right palm supporting her on the roof. She peered over it to the far side and saw the broken rear right wheel, but couldn't care about that right now. She had to find the dog. She slid down the side wall, behind the intact left front wheel, and her booted feet landed firmly on the ground.

The groom was lighting a cheroot and leaning on his saddle.

"I thought you didn't have time to lounge about," she protested.

"I don't. It's not difficult to remove a stubborn woman from a carriage with a cheroot hanging from my mouth. You're lucky you got out when you did. Let's go."

"Do you not have a heart? We need to find that dog. I overheard the duke asking you for wine—"

His face went colder than ever. "You did?"

She nodded. "I'll tell him it was my fault you're delayed—"

He showed no expression as he watched her rant, merely took another drag on his cheroot and pushed himself off the horse's side. "That's one I've never heard before. A dog story. Clever."

"It's not a *story*."

"Right. I'll go look for the dog, and you'll disappear into the castle, where you'll promptly turn into a helpless female, claiming that your driver lost his way to another destination, all in the hopes that the duke will give you shelter and fall in love with you. I'm sure you thought it divine providence that your carriage lost a wheel nearly at his doorstep. But it has nothing to do with Fate. Halsey's simply too selfish to fill the holes in the road."

Janice forced herself to look away. She had a dog to locate. It needed help. She'd seen desperation in its eyes.

It was no wonder she craved canine company. Dogs were reliable. They didn't compare her to other women and find her wanting. They didn't care about her dowry. And she'd never met a dog with whom she wouldn't mind sleeping, while the prospect of inviting any gentleman of her acquaintance into her bed—and they ranged from the boorish, the sporty, the bookish, to the politely bland— made her break out in a sweat.

"Come back, Isobel! It's time to go!" the groom called without looking over his shoulder. Instead, he lowered his cheroot and allowed his eyes to travel up and down Janice's body.

She couldn't believe a servant would be so brazen. She lifted her chin in the air and stared daggers at him. *Men*. If it weren't for parental expectations she must satisfy, she'd consider swearing off the two-legged beasts entirely.